P9-BYH-370

Praise For
WHITE HORSES . . .

"POWERFUL." —*Charleston Post* (SC)

"HYPNOTIC." —*Richmond Times-Dispatch*

"*WHITE HORSES* WILL REVERBERATE IN READ-ERS' IMAGINATIONS FOR A LONG TIME."
—*San Francisco Chronicle*

"UNFORGETTABLE CHARACTERS . . . A haunting, gripping story about women and love."
—*Virginia Pilot*

"FULL OF WONDERFUL MOMENTS." —*People*

"PASSIONATE, SPELLBINDING."
—*South Bend Tribune*

Continued on next page . . .

MORE PRAISE FOR *WHITE HORSES*...

"VIVID ... TAUT ... GRIPPING."   —*Best Sellers*

"MEMORABLE ... striking in its emotional implications."   —*ALA Booklist*

"MASTERFUL AND BRILLIANT."   —Michael Malone

"HOFFMAN WRITES BEAUTIFULLY."
—*Houston Chronicle*

"AS POWERFUL AS ANYTHING I'VE READ IN A LONG, LONG TIME."
—Tim O'Brien, author of *The Things They Carried*

"HOFFMAN CAPTURES—WITH JEWELED PRECISION AND DAZZLING INTENSITY RARE OUTSIDE OF POETRY—THE BEAUTY OF THE PHYSICAL WORLD."
—*Newsday*

"HOFFMAN'S WRITING HAS NEVER BEEN SO LYRICAL."
—*Philadelphia Inquirer*

AND ALICE HOFFMAN . . .

"ALICE HOFFMAN TAKES SEEMINGLY ORDINARY LIVES AND LETS US SEE AND FEEL EXTRAORDINARY THINGS."
—Amy Tan

"HOFFMAN SEEMS CERTAIN to join such writers as Anne Tyler and Mary Gordon . . . a major novelist."
—*Newsweek*

"HOFFMAN IS ONE OF THE BRIGHTEST AND MOST IMAGINATIVE OF CONTEMPORARY WRITERS."
—*Sacramento Bee*

"HER NOVELS ARE AS FLUID AND GRACEFUL AS DREAMS."
—*San Diego Union-Tribune*

"A READER IS IN GOOD HANDS WITH ALICE HOFFMAN, able to count on many pleasures. She is one of our quirkiest and most interesting novelists . . ."
—Jane Smiley, *USA Today*

"SHOWING THE MAGIC THAT LIES BELOW THE SURFACE OF EVERYDAY LIFE IS JUST WHAT WE HOPE FOR IN A SATISFYING NOVEL, and that's what Ms. Hoffman gives us every time."
—*Baltimore Sun*

White Horses

ALICE
HOFFMAN

BERKLEY BOOKS, NEW YORK

If you purchased this book without a cover, you should be aware that this book is stolen property. It was reported as "unsold and destroyed" to the publisher, and neither the author nor the publisher has received any payment for this "stripped book."

WHITE HORSES

A Berkley Book / published by arrangement with
G. P. Putnam's Sons

PRINTING HISTORY
Putnam edition published 1982
Berkley edition / November 1993

All rights reserved.
Copyright © 1982 by Alice Hoffman.
This book may not be reproduced in whole or in part,
by mimeograph or any other means, without permission.
For information address: G. P. Putnam's Sons,
200 Madison Avenue, New York, New York 10016.

ISBN: 0-425-13980-8

BERKLEY ®
Berkley Books are published by
The Berkley Publishing Group, 200 Madison Avenue,
New York, New York 10016.
BERKLEY and the "B" design are trademarks of
Berkley Publishing Corporation.

PRINTED IN THE UNITED STATES OF AMERICA

10 9 8 7 6 5 4 3 2 1

To Elaine Markson,
to Ron Bernstein,
to Faith Sale

CHAPTER
ONE

✝

THEY LIVED IN A HOUSE IN SANTA ROSA THAT WAS always darkest in summertime. Bedspreads were draped over the windows in the living room, venetian blinds were drawn, the screen door in the kitchen was lined with old newspapers that filtered the sunlight through faded print. The refrigerator always held a pitcher of lemonade— made with fresh, sour lemons and tap water; mosquitoes and long-winged dragonflies circled on the back porch waiting for the opportunity to dart inside. By early July most people in town went into their front yards, drawn by the scent of water. Although the river ran nearly ten miles outside of town, its odor seemed to cover the distance in between, rising up from the asphalt, the dirt driveways, the yards, touching sunflowers, roses, and chard with a film of brown water and fish.

On particularly hot days, when the temperature reached ninety long before noon, the smell of the river called children out of their houses and summoned them to the tall, yellow fields just outside town; and even Teresa, who never strayed far from home, went to the window and breathed in the cool air. There were times when Teresa thought briefly of running away, following that river scent right through town, past the highway and the fields, not stopping until she reached one of the small towns where houses were built on high wooden stilts, their doors well above the water in times of summer drought, only inches away from the currents after the October rains. But Teresa had only passed through these river towns on occasional fishing trips with her father; she had been to river beaches only twice, on class outings at the end of the school term; she didn't even know if the river ran north to south or east to west. So she stayed at home; if Teresa might get lost on the paths and dirt roads which crisscrossed the river, she could never lose her way on the cracked cement sidewalks of her neighborhood, in the empty lots behind the shopping center, or the dark corners of her own cellar, where jars of canned vegetables and fruit lined the wooden shelves—there the blackberry jam shimmered like rubies, apricot preserves were the color of honey, a wonderful pale gold. During the summer when she was eleven, Teresa believed that the crickets who lived in the weeds that sprang through the sidewalk were trying to speak to her. At night, while the rest of the family slept, she sat in her bedroom on the second floor, close to the window, listening for the words she was certain those insects were forming, waiting for a clear green song.

There were times when Teresa fell asleep still listening for the crickets' message, her feet curled beneath her as she sat in a wooden chair, her long braids still neat and tight. There were other times when she stayed awake nearly till morning, convinced that if she were quiet enough, if she waited long enough, the night would reveal itself to her in a slow stream of syllables shaped by wings; a song only she could understand.

After these all-night vigils, Teresa could easily have slept until afternoon if her mother, Dina, had not had definite plans for her. As far as Dina was concerned, six a.m. was the best time to work in the garden; the higher the sun rose, the more dangerous the day became. Dina was certain that every jump in temperature could force arguments to rise from the dust, ghosts could appear in the midday haze. Although she let her husband and two sons sleep, Dina needed an assistant to carry the shovel and spade, she needed her daughter to chase away the black squirrels and hungry birds, and so, when the sky was milky and gray, she went to wake Teresa.

Whether she found her sleeping daughter in bed or in the chair by the window made no difference to Dina. "Hurry up," she would whisper, pulling the sheet out of Teresa's fingers, or tapping on the back of the wooden chair. "We have to get out there before it's too hot. The sun won't wait for us," she would warn.

No matter how tired she was, Teresa dressed quickly; and while her older brothers, Reuben and Silver, dreamed in the room right next door, Teresa combed her hair into new braids, and then followed her mother downstairs. There was always a pot of thick, hot coffee in the kitchen, and Teresa and Dina would stand side by side drinking from blue and white porcelain cups. This was a treat—no other girl Teresa knew, at school or in the neighborhood, was allowed coffee, not even when it was mixed with hot milk and sugar. If it stunted her growth, Teresa didn't care; the coffee was wonderfully dark, it was hotter than the breath of the men upstairs when they turned in their sleep. Teresa stirred sugar into her cup and watched through the window as hummingbirds drank from the sage at the edge of the vegetable patch.

Soon, the men upstairs would leave; but when Dina and Teresa first went out to the garden Teresa's father was just putting on his workboots. Reuben, the oldest son, would not walk down to the Safeway where he crated vegetables until eight-thirty, and it would be hours before Silver even woke up. When they weeded and hoed, Dina wore a chiffon scarf covering her long hair, Teresa a cotton kerchief which rubbed against her ears. Both wore canvas gloves, which allowed them to tear out dandelion roots and ragweed from the south end of the garden without any scratches or scars. By seven-thirty, when Teresa's father had slammed the front door shut behind him and walked out to the dirt driveway, Teresa and Dina had already weeded the first row of tomatoes. Harry Connors, known to his friends as King, didn't even glance over toward the garden. He walked down the driveway and got into his pickup truck. All summer long he had been working construction in Santa Rosa; it was rare for him to have a job so close to home, and spending so much time with his wife set King's nerves on edge. He found himself wishing for jobs which would take him farther and farther away from home—to Arizona, or Oregon, or southern California. Because here at home, nothing he did ever seemed to be right.

"Other people have cars. Look what we have," Dina said when she saw King in the pickup. "Other people have cars," she called to her husband.

In the driveway King Connors stepped on the gas; the engine jumped and then died. King Connors got out, waving a wrench. "Let's see you get us something better," he said to Dina as he threw open the hood.

"Me!" Dina laughed. "I don't even have a job. What would I pay for the car with—turnips? Blueberries?"

Teresa left her spade on the ground and walked to the driveway; she watched as her father checked the carburetor, her eyes were as large and as guarded as lanterns.

"What the hell are you looking at?" King Connors asked when he noticed her hanging on the fender. "You got some complaints, too?"

Teresa traced her finger over the chipped paint on the hood. King Connors's sister had the car Teresa had always wanted; a two seater, light enough to take the curves in any road at top speed, whiter than pearls. When King Connors closed the hood and climbed back into the truck, Teresa followed him and stood by the open window.

"How about a Corvette?" she asked.

King Connors was already late for work; he had two teen-age sons still asleep in their beds, and a wife who spoke more to the plants in her garden than she did to him. "What the hell do you know about Corvettes?" he said to his daughter.

"That's what Renée drives," Teresa told him.

"Renée." King Connors turned the key in the ignition, started the motor, put the truck in reverse, then leaned out the window and looked at Teresa, eye to eye. "You want a fancy car?" he said as he edged the truck down the driveway. "Then you go on and move up to Portland. Move in with my goddamned sister."

Teresa watched the truck disappear down Divisadero Street before she returned to the garden; one of the pickup's taillights was cracked all the way through, the metal bumper hung on by a welder's thread.

"He told me to move in with Renée if I wanted a fancy car," Teresa told her mother.

"That's a good one," Dina said. She handed Teresa a spade. "The last thing in the world that woman wants is children. If she had any she couldn't afford to keep that sports car of hers."

Later in the morning, when Reuben had left for his job at the supermarket, and the sun was stronger, Teresa worked alone on the third row of tomatoes. Dina stood in the shade of the house, one hand over her eyes; she looked at the heat waves that shimmered in front of the eucalyptus trees with the same distrust she had felt when she had stared at the rose-colored mesas on the outskirts of Santa Fe years before.

When she was growing up, Dina rarely ventured any farther than her own house. Inside the family's walled garden there were always roses in July, gardenias in August. Even when on the other side of the wall the earth was nothing more than dust, fine enough to run right through a woman's fingers, the garden bloomed. Dina went only to the market, or to friends' houses, or on walks with her father in the evenings when the mesas seemed as blue as water. It was not until she was eighteen and met King Connors that Dina went beyond the New Mexico state line; it was then she first saw the asphalt of the interstate heading west toward Arizona.

King Connors had come to New Mexico temporarily; he poured concrete at a power plant in Los Alamos, and on his days off he drove to Santa Fe. He sat near white adobe walls and drank beer; he thought about women, and about going home to California, where a tree did not have to be carefully watered and pruned in order to grow. He met Dina accidentally, at a dinner party given by a family he barely knew. They ate barbecued chicken and rice; Dina wore a white cotton dress, and she was thankful that her father was the only one who accompanied her and that her mother hadn't come along to keep her under her watchful eye. When King Connors left New Mexico three weeks later, Dina was with him, her eyes shining when she saw the sign welcoming her to California, her hand in his, fingers entwined.

Although nearly twenty years had passed since Dina had left New Mexico, she could still remember each rosebush that grew in her father's garden; she could still hear her mother's voice telling her to stay in the shade, warning that heat and harsh light could produce evil spirits, wrinkles, despair. After a girlhood of cautious flowers and garden walls, Dina had never been able to trust the outdoors. So she stood by the southwest corner of the house, watching her daughter water the vegetable garden, stepping into the sun only to chase away jays when they landed between the rows of tomatoes.

"Fix your scarf," she called when Teresa's kerchief slipped, exposing her head to the sun.

Teresa didn't hear her mother's warning over the spray of the hose. She aimed the water at the plants and through the drops she could see a car pull up on Divisadero Street. The man behind the wheel wore a sports jacket even though it was a record-breaking day filled with dry, yellow heat—the sort of day when no man Teresa knew would ever wear more than jeans and a T-shirt.

"You're drowning them," Dina said, coming from the shadows to grab the hose from Teresa. Puddles had formed around the tomato plants, leaves drooped.

"They can't even breathe, how can they drown?" Teresa said.

Dina looked at the sky and shook her head. Her eyelashes were so long that whenever she cried each tear caught and her vision grew blurry.

"Well, how can they drown?" Teresa demanded.

"I can never teach you anything," Dina said. "You're too much like me. I would never listen either; I thought I knew everything."

Teresa was silent now; she had no idea what it meant to be like Dina. It had always seemed that Dina had no past, certainly not one that was talked about. Teresa knew that Dina had come from New Mexico, but she had no idea when or why, she did not even know her mother's maiden name. To Teresa, Dina might just as well have always been in Santa Rosa, she had probably never been a child, never listened for crickets or put lightning bugs in a Mason jar, she had never watched the slow white orbit of evening clouds or looked for ghosts in the clothes closet.

"You're like me, and Reuben's like your father," Dina told Teresa as she put away the hose. It was clear to everyone that Reuben was Dina's least favorite child—she barely paid attention to him, it didn't matter to her if he stayed out all night long, she never wondered where he was or when he was coming home. It was Silver she worried about, Silver who reminded her of a man she had never met, a man her father had told her about years before: an Aria, an outlaw, the man Dina was sure Silver would one day become. "It's Silver who's like no one we ever met before," Dina informed her daughter. "He's the one who's special."

When they had finished their work, they went inside to find Silver at the kitchen table, carefully polishing his new leather boots. Dina went to shower and wash the earth out from beneath her fingernails. Teresa took the nearly empty pitcher from the refrigerator; she reached for some lemons and the glass canister of sugar. As she was halving lemons on the drainboard next to the sink there was a knock at the door.

"Answer it," Silver told his sister.

"I'm busy," Teresa said as she carefully arranged lemon slices in the glass pitcher. Teresa stood on her toes; if whoever was at the door would back up only a few inches, she would be able to see him through the window above the sink.

There was another knock, but Teresa ignored it; Dina had told her never to trust strangers and she could not imagine anyone important enough to interrupt her lemonade.

"I told you to get the door," Silver said.

The knocking had stopped. "There's nobody out there," Teresa said, but could see the man in the sports coat as he backed away from the door to observe their house. "There's only some jays out there eating the vegetables,"

30% OFF NEW YORK TIMES BESTSELLERS • 10% OFF MOST OTHER HARDCOVERS

BORDERS®

BORDERS®

BOOKS • MUSIC • CAFE

30% Discount on Current
NYT Cloth Bestsellers

■

10% Discount on Most Other
Hardcovers

■

Espresso Bar

■

Large Selection of Maps,
Art Posters and Sale Books

■

Music and Videos

■

Special Orders Welcome

Mon–Sat 9–11
Sunday 10–9

612 E. Liberty
Ann Arbor, Michigan 48104
Books 734/668-7652
Music 734/668-7100
Fax 734/668-2455
http://www.borders.com

she said matter-of-factly, for there was no way to protect the garden from every bird and snail that wandered through.

The man on the back porch who waited for Teresa to open the door had been hired to find Dina twenty years before. When Dina had run off with King Connors her father had followed them. He had taken the train from Santa Fe to Los Angeles, and then a Greyhound bus up to San Francisco. After a few weeks of searching for his daughter, the old man discovered that he hadn't the heart to look any farther. Everything about California upset him; the cold gray winter seemed to wrap itself around his bones. The fast cars on Market Street, the dark smell of seaweed and fish that ran through the gutters, the Pacific which threatened to swallow him—all made him homesick, heartsick, set him dreaming about Santa Fe. But before he returned home, taking the same bus and train he had come on, Dina's father had hired Bergen.

On the day when he stood at the back door, Bergen was no longer the young man he had been when Dina's father first came to him. His eyes were weak now; he had to wear sunglasses until dusk cut the glare of the day. He had given up his office across from the bus station in San Francisco—the rents were too expensive now, and he had had his fill of divorces and frauds. He had given up all of his cases but one—Dina.

Bergen had never really intended to find her; he had never even bothered to look. Twice a year he would receive a check from his client in Santa Fe; he cashed these checks believing that it was better for a father not to recover the sort of daughter who didn't want to be found. It was only recently, after receiving a note from the old man's wife insisting that he stop looking for Dina, that Bergen decided to find her. The old man, Dina's father, had died, too tired to prune his own roses, too old to chase away the lizards that ran across the top of the garden wall. Now that the old man was dead, Bergen had been stung by the blue tongue of remorse. He decided to find the woman he had never bothered to look for before.

This decision was rapidly turning dry; the longer Bergen stood on the back porch waiting for someone to answer his knock, the more he thought about getting back in his car, driving back to San Francisco on Highway 1, with the mild satisfaction of having tried. Stepping away from the door, Bergen could see a girl through the kitchen window, and he was certain that she could see him. Maybe because of his sports jacket, maybe because he looked so unsure of himself, Teresa sensed that opening the door to this stranger spelled trouble.

"I'm not going to tell you again," Silver said to her when Teresa insisted there was no one at the door.

"What will you give me if I open the door?" Teresa asked as she wiped her hands on a dish towel. But she knew, before Silver answered, that she would do whatever he asked—he was, always, her favorite. Lately it seemed he was everyone's favorite. Girls from high school called late at night, dialing Silver's number from single beds carefully made with pink and white sheets; they called so often that Dina took to leaving the phone receiver off the hook. King Connors, who had stopped taking anyone with him on fishing trips years before, had taken Silver with him twice this year. There were times at the dinner table when Teresa had seen Dina staring at her younger son, her lips parted, her gaze puzzled and admiring, as if she couldn't figure out, no matter how hard she tried, exactly where Silver had come from; he didn't seem to belong to anyone, he had never acted like anyone's child.

When Teresa teased him, Silver smiled. "If you answer the door I won't break your arm. How's that for a deal?" he asked as he spread a new coat of polish over his boots.

Bergen had removed his sunglasses to wipe his eyes; he blinked in the harsh light when Teresa opened the door. "Is your mother home?" he asked.

The old man's wife had written to him after the funeral in Santa Fe. "Don't bother anymore," she had written. "You won't get any more money out of me. Now that he's dead I'll tell you the truth; I just don't care. Don't send me any bills, don't go looking anymore, don't bother to find her."

But now here he was, in Santa Rosa, a few feet away from the tomato plants; his eyes were filled with late-morning glare when he came face to face with the old man's grandchild. The grandchild didn't open the screen door; but she took in every detail, from Bergen's black loafers to his button-down collar.

"Mama," she finally called, and Bergen was relieved. Soon he would be sitting in the dark, cool kitchen, sipping an icy drink and speaking with the old man's daughter; finally this last case of his could be put aside.

"Jesus Christ," Silver said to Teresa. "Why don't you invite the guy in? It's a hundred degrees out there."

Dina came into the room wearing a black cotton bathrobe dotted with a print of diamonds. Her wet hair was covered with a blue towel she had turned up like a turban. She ignored her children and went to the door as if she had been expecting a visitor; but she didn't open it, instead she studied Bergen through the screen.

The detective found himself searching for the young girl in the photograph the man from Santa Fe had given him so long ago. In that photograph every feature had been dark and sweet, the flesh of youth, a pose kept still and pure. The woman at the door seemed less alive than her own image; the eyes Bergen saw now were stony, the mouth a thin pale line of doubt. When Bergen didn't speak right away, Dina shifted the towel on her head. "What do you want?" she asked.

"Your father sent me," Bergen said.

Dina narrowed her eyes. "I don't believe you," she said through the mesh. "Why should I?"

Teresa stood by her mother; when Bergen wiped his forehead with a handkerchief, Teresa stared at his skin— it was flushed red, bumpy with heat. "Do you want some lemonade?" Teresa asked the detective with a sudden surge of pity.

Dina turned and glared at her daughter. "He's not interested in lemonade."

"Actually," Bergen said, "that sounds pretty good. Hot," he explained. "Hotter than San Francisco by fifteen degrees."

"We're very busy," Dina said to Bergen. "We don't have time to talk to you," she told him, as if he was a gypsy with a cart of medicine she had no use for.

Bergen lowered his voice; Teresa had to strain to hear him. "I've been looking for you for twenty years," he told Dina.

When he offered his business card, Dina opened the door just wide enough for the card to be slipped inside. She examined it closely. "It took you all these years to find me?" she asked. "I don't believe a word you're saying." She slipped the card back outside.

"Your father's dead," Bergen said softly. Dina didn't blink an eye, although for a moment she felt weak in the knees, as if she might faint from exhaustion or heat. "I just wanted you to know he had been looking for you all this time."

"Get away," Dina said, fighting against the memory of her father, but all the same still remembering the heavy black shoes he wore on Sundays, the clear, dark eyes that gazed at the mesa beyond the city, the silence that followed him whenever he walked into a room.

"Dina," Bergen said, tasting the name. "Do you mind if I call you Dina?"

At the kitchen table, Silver put down the polish and the boots. He noticed that his mother's back was straight as wire, that Teresa was leaning forward, hypnotized.

"Get away," Dina whispered as if Bergen were a ghost she could command, and wishing alone could force his flesh to dematerialize right there, on her own back porch.

"I was supposed to be looking for you," Bergen went on. "But I never looked." The family's two dogs, who had been wandering around the neighborhood all night, now returned to the yard. Reggie, the older one, went to lie in the shade of the eucalyptus, but Atlas, the young collie, climbed the porch steps. He sat by Bergen's feet and looked upward, as if he had known the detective forever, as if they were long-lost friends. Bergen put his hand on the collie's head. "It was easy to find you, when I finally tried. I looked through the payroll lists of a couple of construction companies in San Francisco and found your husband's name." Behind the screen door, Dina was swaying, she was knee-deep in memories. Bergen took the opportunity to open the door and press his card back into her hand. "If you ever need me," he told her.

Silver walked over and kicked the door shut with his bare foot. "You heard my mother," he said to Bergen. "She told you to get out of here."

The collie grew skittish when he heard Silver's raised voice; he carefully backed down the steps and hid under the porch. But Bergen didn't flinch—he had seen Silver's kind a thousand times before. Sometimes they were older, sometimes their faces were more lined by betrayals or scarred by knives, but they were the same sort: young men wanted by the wives they had deserted; boys who had stolen jewelry, or cars, or an older woman's heart; the kind who had cut right through somebody's last longing for innocence, which appeared deceivingly in the form of tight blue jeans and desire.

"I was talking to your mother," Bergen said easily.

"Are you deaf, or just stupid, old man?" Silver said, just as easily, but each word he spoke had the flare of violence at the edges.

"If your mother wants me to leave, then I'll go," Bergen said. As the detective spoke he didn't bother to look at Silver; he wouldn't have given two cents for that boy's fate. He kept his eyes on Dina, and the more he looked, the more she seemed like the girl in the photograph, a girl so beautiful she herself seemed surprised.

"I want you to go," Dina said slowly, though she was not at all certain of what she wanted at that moment— she had never expected such a moment to come, she had never imagined that her past would arrive in a Ford station wagon driven up from San Francisco on a hot afternoon.

"Now did you hear her?" Silver said, but the detective had already turned and was walking down the steps. Atlas came out from beneath the porch and walked with Bergen to the edge of the yard. "Just keep moving," Silver called through the door when Bergen stopped to look back.

But Dina knew Bergen was still looking at her when he got into his car. She went to the sink for a glass of cold water, and saw him behind the wheel, staring across the road, across the garden, staring right at her. When he started the ignition, Dina closed her eyes.

Teresa pressed her nose against the screen door and watched the detective drive away. Then she turned to her mother. "Who did he say died?" she asked.

"Nobody," Dina said, holding the glass of water to her forehead, remembering only then that she wore a towel wrapped around her damp hair, embarrassed that a stranger had seen her that way.

"The man in the jacket said somebody died," Teresa said.

"Don't be rude," Dina told her daughter. "No one likes a girl who asks too many questions."

When Dina went to comb out her hair and get dressed, Teresa sat at the table with her brother and examined Bergen's business card. "I don't care what she says," Teresa said to Silver, "someone died."

"Someone sure did," Silver said. He pulled on his boots and admired the soft leather. "Our grandfather."

"You're making it up," Teresa said. She knew there had been one grandfather—King and Renée's father, a logger who had lived his last years north of Spokane, in a town so cold butterflies didn't appear until the middle of June. But that grandfather had been dead a long time; he had lain in a bed with no sheets, struggling to push the breath out of his lungs. When Teresa was no more than a baby, the old grandfather in Spokane could no longer force the air in and out of his chest, and he had died before King Connors could drive up to pay his last respects.

"Didn't you think we had another grandfather?" Silver asked. "Didn't you think she had any parents?"

Dina had always seemed to walk without the faintest trace of New Mexico dust on her feet; she had never spoken of a mother, a father, a hometown, the heart that had captured her own and led her to California.

"This is just the beginning," Silver said. "Watch out. Pretty soon, we'll be orphans."

When Silver went out to meet his friends behind the Texaco station on South Street, Teresa sat alone, wondering how much more she didn't know about her family. She wished that Bergen would return with a briefcase full of charts, the facts of her mother's life. But the street was empty now; on the back porch, where the detective had stood, there was a jay with one bent wing curled under his body. The two dogs threw back their heads and howled, even though there was just the shadow of the rising moon, and the day was still as hot as it had ever been, the heat waves had become a row of metal daggers growing taller than the trees.

Two weeks after Dina heard of her father's death she still would not leave the house. Nothing King Connors could do would force her outside; she refused to hang the laundry on the line, instead she hung the wash in the kitchen, so that walking from the refrigerator to the stove meant navigating through rough white sheets. Dina also stopped working in the garden. Teresa did her best alone; she picked blueberries and watered the melons, but it was too big a job for one person, and soon she stopped weeding between the rows. Instead, she sat by the side of the house and watched the bees grow dizzy with pollen; she didn't even yell when squirrels filled their cheeks with tomatoes.

Now that she was left to herself in the mornings, Teresa thought more and more about her mother's family. But because Bergen didn't return and no one else would talk about the past, Teresa decided to look for it on her own. On a Sunday when King Connors was out in the driveway working on his truck and Dina was asleep in her room with all the shades pulled down tight, Teresa found what she had been looking for. In the bottom drawer of the living-room bureau, beneath a stack of lace tablecloths and napkins, she discovered a photograph album. Teresa went to sit on the couch; in her hands the leather album felt like flesh. She held on tight to the heart of her mother's past.

On every page were the faces of men and women who had lived years ago; there were adobe houses ringed with juniper trees, women dressed in cotton held up fans made of silk and mother-of-pearl. Teresa could see the smiles on those women's faces turn into laughter, she was certain she could hear their lapdogs bark. She didn't notice that Dina had walked into the room until it was too late. Dina grabbed Teresa and slapped her daughter's face. She reached for the album, then opened the drawer and threw the photographs inside. When she turned back to Teresa, Dina's face was hot.

"Don't you ever look in this drawer again," Dina said. She pulled Teresa up by her shoulders. King Connors came in from the driveway just as Dina was about to slap Teresa again. He held Dina's arm tightly.

"You fucking crazy woman," he said.

"Don't talk to me like that," Dina told her husband in the shrill quiet voice she used whenever violence circled over the living room like a cloud caught within the walls.

"She hit me," Teresa said.

"You hit her," King Connors said to his wife.

"Don't ever curse at me," Dina said. Her voice hissed like a ring of coiled snakes.

"Who did I marry?" King Connors said now. "Someone crazy. Someone who's a fucking lunatic."

"I was just looking at the photograph album," Teresa said, afraid of what she might have started between her parents. "I'll never do it again," she added.

"The album," King Connors said grimly. He went to the bureau and pulled out the bottom drawer.

"Don't touch it," Dina said, her words more like a curse than a warning.

King Connors smiled briefly before he threw the drawer. Slowly, the photographs Teresa had looked at slipped out; one by one they scattered across the floor.

"That's mine," Dina said, kneeling to retrieve the photographs.

"Yours?" King Connors said. "Nothing in this house is yours."

Once a fight had begun between Dina and King there was nothing that could stop it, it would go on until someone was black and blue, until someone was hurt or cried out loud. Afterwards, King Connors might go away for days, sometimes for weeks, not returning until whatever scars their fight had left seemed to have healed. Teresa sat as far back as she could on the couch; her spine felt as though the bones were held between long fingernails, twisted against the grain.

"Do you understand that nothing here is yours?" King Connors asked his wife.

"All right," Dina whispered. She looked up from the floor where she sat; the tortoise-shell comb had fallen from her hair and strands fell onto her neck in long, wild threads.

"Why did you marry me?" King said to Dina. "You've been making us both miserable ever since that day."

"I just wanted to know about the grandfather Bergen was talking about," Teresa said. Dina looked over at her quickly, and Teresa grew silent immediately.

"Bergen?" King Connors said. "Bergen?" he tapped Dina with the toe of his boot. "Who the hell is she talking about?"

Teresa knew now that she had made a mistake in mentioning Bergen. She watched her mother bow her head, she listened as Dina stuttered when she spoke.

"My father hired a detective," Dina told her husband. "He came here to tell me my father had died."

"After all these years he came here now?" King Connors said. "You're a liar," he whispered. "Who's Bergen?" he demanded.

"He's a detective," Teresa said.

"Did I ask you?" King Connors said to his daughter. "Who is he?" he asked Dina again.

"I already told you," Dina said. "He's just a detective. He was here for less than ten minutes, two weeks ago. I didn't even let him in the door."

"How can I believe you?" King Connors said. "Why didn't you tell me about him before? Maybe you've got another man on the side and you've been putting me through this torture for nothing."

Dina licked her dry lips with the tip of her tongue. "I didn't want you to get all upset," she said.

"Really?" King Connors said. "Since when have you ever thought about that?"

Anger poured out of King Connors in waves; he reached down and drew up a pile of photographs. "Your father," he said to Dina. "He's the one who made you think you were so much better than everyone else—the truth is— you're not." Smiling, King Connors tore the photographs in half. Dina looked at him, unbelieving, then she rose up, she gathered her skirts and ran to King Connors, she fell against him, her fingers at his throat.

"Oh no you don't," King Connors said. He loosened Dina's grip, but by the time he threw her onto the floor, she had left her mark: King Connors's skin was blue with the pressure of Dina's fingers, lines of blood ran down his neck.

Dina crouched down low to the floor; she gathered the torn photographs together. Teresa watched as her mother tried to piece together the women in white, the wicker furniture, the dog who jumped up into the soft desert air, the old man who sat beneath tall cottonwood trees. But it was no use, the photographs were beyond repair. No glue could hold those ladies in summer dresses together, no tape could fix the torn June days.

"I'm sick of all this," King Connors said. "Just sick."

Dina had begun to weep; her tears coated the wooden floor with salt. Teresa had never seen her mother cry, not even when King Connors came home from the construction crew tired and ready for a fight if anyone looked at him a little too long. Dina had not cried when Reuben fell out of the eucalyptus tree and broke both his arms, she had not wept when her old cat was run over as it slept in the middle of Divisadero Street. This fight was different than any Teresa had seen before—more final, sadder, without the slightest trace of hope. But now Dina was out of control; she held the torn photographs and seemed not to realize that her voice rose higher and higher. Each sob became a shriek. Teresa put her hands over her ears. She wished she had never opened the bureau drawer, she wished she was a million miles away.

"I can't stand it anymore," King Connors said. He looked down at his wife. "I'm warning you," he said hoarsely.

But Dina's wails rose higher still, her voice rattled the windowpanes and drove King Connors into the kitchen.

When he returned he carried a long carving knife in his left hand.

Teresa wished her brothers were home, especially Silver. Reuben might have calmed King down with a bottle of tequila and some lemons, but Silver would have protected them all, he would have dived for the carving knife. He would have been ready to rescue them from King, he would have even been willing to fight. But that afternoon both brothers were at a roadhouse where the bartender was easily talked into selling six-packs of beer to minors who didn't carry any false proof of age. Teresa was as good as alone because Dina was no help at all—when she saw King Connors holding the knife she threw back her head and laughed. She sat in the middle of the living room, torn photographs in her lap, staring King Connors right in the eye.

"Go ahead," she urged her husband. "Kill me. Kill us all."

Teresa believed that was exactly what King Connors planned to do. She closed her eyes. She prepared to die. But instead of seeking out flesh, King's knife tore into the bureau. Again and again, over and over, he stabbed the drawer that had held the photo album. White scars lined the wood, white scars were everywhere. When he was through, King Connors's breathing grew easier, he stared sadly at his wife. "What's the use?" he said. Then he went to sit in the easy chair next to the couch; he lit a Lucky Strike and when he tossed the match into a black marble ashtray he noticed that his daughter was staring at him.

"What are you looking at now?" King demanded. "Don't you look at me that way," he told her.

Teresa lowered her eyes—if she had tried to say one word she would have burst into tears.

"And don't you turn away from me when I'm talking to you either," her father told her.

Teresa didn't know where to look; she locked her gaze and stared at the wall just behind her father's head.

"Always look at me when I talk to you," King Connors went on. King noticed now that his daughter was so thin that her bones nearly showed. She was trying to keep her legs straight, but her feet didn't reach the floor, and just then his daughter reminded King of a small bird—a parakeet or a dove. King Connors backed down. "What the hell," he said, more softly. "You're okay. I didn't mean any of that. Come on over here," King Connors said. When Teresa didn't move he pointed his lit cigarette at her. "Come on, I won't hurt you."

Teresa got up and stood in front of her father; even sitting in the easy chair, he was taller than she was. His eyes were pale blue, like pieces of Canadian ice.

"Take my advice," King Connors said, "don't ever bother with the past. I mean it," he said as he drew in smoke and then exhaled. "It won't do you any good. It doesn't make your mother happy to look at those photographs—it only gets her all upset. Who wants to be reminded of everything you don't have anymore?"

Teresa tried to listen to King, but she could barely hear him, his words came from miles away. King Connors pulled the ottoman over, lifted up his workboots, and stretched out his long legs. "Don't even think about what used to be," he told his daughter.

Teresa felt her eyes closing, she was dizzy, she could no longer stand. When she collapsed and fell to the floor, Teresa knew what was happening, but her spirit was retreating into itself leaving behind only a thin brown shell.

"Get up," King Connors said after Teresa fell. "One hysterical female is enough."

Dina looked up from her torn photographs. "You heard your father," she said to Teresa. "Get up."

When Teresa didn't move, Dina went over to her; she shook the girl's shoulders, then put her ear to Teresa's heart. After a while, Dina turned to her husband. "Something's wrong," she said. "Something that could be evil."

"Evil?" King Connors said. "That's right. Talk like the ignorant woman you are."

Dina rocked back and forth on her heels. "This is all your fault," she told her husband.

King Connors got up and pushed Dina away. "There's nothing wrong with her," he told her. He bent down and listened to Teresa's slow breathing. He lifted her eyelids and saw the whites of her eyes. It was then he noticed that a bruise was already forming on the left side of his daughter's face, and the uneven flow of blood that oozed from a thin gash on her head.

"Put a blanket over her and clean up this mess," King told his wife. He backed away from Teresa; the sight of her blood on the floor made him queasy.

Dina went over to the telephone and picked up the receiver. "I'm calling a doctor," she said, but before she could dial, King took the phone out of her hand. "You know what they think when you bring a kid in with bruises?" King whispered. "They'll say we beat her. I could wind up in jail."

Dina looked over at Teresa, then turned back to King. "What do we do?" she whispered.

"Put a blanket over her," King said, and when Dina hesitated he took her arm roughly. "I'm telling you—she's going to be fine."

When Silver came home, late in the afternoon, the house was so dark that he stumbled in the hallway; there was a disturbing scent of roses, the fragrance was everywhere, in every corner, in every room. Two candles were lit in the living room, and the first thing he saw was Teresa, asleep on the floor, a blanket wrapped around her like a cocoon. As he knelt down, the odor of roses was overpowering, as if bushes and trees had taken root in the wooden floor. He touched her forehead; her skin was like ice. And as Silver's eyes adjusted to the candlelight he noticed Dina sitting on the couch.

"What's going on?" Silver asked his mother. "What's

wrong with her?"

Dina shook her head; she had been crying all afternoon
and her eyes were swollen and red. "We don't know
what's wrong," she admitted.

"Did you call a doctor?" Silver asked, and when Dina
shook her head no, Silver glared at her. He picked Teresa
up and carried her into the kitchen; the blanket trailed
behind them, catching on the floorboards and the furniture. King Connors was sitting at the kitchen table, and
when Silver walked into the room he was drinking a beer,
wishing that he was in any town but Santa Rosa—a town
where there were lemon trees, hot nights, women who
wanted to hold him tight, just as Dina had once done
before everything he did started to go wrong. When he
saw his sixteen-year-old son looking down at him with
so much heat, so much contempt, King Connors cringed.
If Silver had asked his father to explain his actions King
wouldn't have been able to answer: he was simply a man
who was afraid, someone who was certain he was meant
to be living another life. But the only thing Silver asked
for that day were the keys to the pickup.

"Don't be a fool," King said. "You don't have a license.
You can't drive a truck."

"Just give me the keys," Silver said softly, and for
the first time in his life he felt what he was doing was
absolutely right, he felt as though he had been made for
this moment. "I'm taking her to the hospital," he told his
father.

"There's nothing wrong with her," King insisted, but
he was backing down; the glare in his son's eyes burned
a hundred holes in his skin.

"I'm not going to ask you again," Silver said, and in
his heart he was an eagle, in his blood he was a renegade
who wouldn't take no for an answer.

King Connors reached into his pocket, he handed Silver
the keys to the pickup, then watched his son kick open the
screen door and carry Teresa outside. King went to the

window, and as Silver lifted Teresa into the pickup and then got in and started the engine, King felt as though he had just given up his last remaining rights in his own house, and at that instant he began to think about packing his suitcase and leaving Santa Rosa for good.

Out in the driveway Silver's heart was racing; he had only driven a car a few times before, borrowed cars which tore through the streets at top speed. But now Silver drove slowly. Beside him, Teresa slept deeply; her fists were clenched, her knees were drawn up, and her head rested on the seat so that her braids fell over Silver's right leg. The scent of roses still made him dizzy, but the closer Silver came to the hospital, the more sure of himself he became. He felt as if he were centuries old; he had finally managed to join that race of men Dina had always talked about: men who could stare down an enemy with one glance, whose nerves were like steel, men whose hearts always belonged to the girl they had saved. By the time they had reached the emergency ward, Silver looked at Teresa with a new sort of tenderness, and he carried her through the parking lot and into the ward with great care, and with the sense that he carried the most delicate thing on earth.

Although Silver was willing to wait, he had to leave Teresa in the hospital for testing. When she was examined there was no low blood sugar, no peculiar white blood count; Teresa's brain scan was normal, her heartbeat regular. Still, even the bruises she had received from her fall shouldn't have kept her from waking for eight hours while she was prodded by doctors and wheeled up and down corridors for more testing. When King went to pick up his daughter the following morning, he was sure that every nurse and aide could look right through him to see that he was the sort of father who hadn't the courage to drive his own child to the emergency ward. When the doctors informed him that they could tell him nothing about Teresa's illness he wondered if perhaps they just didn't want him to know.

They walked out to the pickup truck together. Teresa's cheek was covered with a white bandage, and King Connors kept his distance from her, as if he expected her to collapse at any moment. But once they were inside the truck, heading home, King could no longer avoid her, and when Teresa asked how she had gotten to the hospital, he told her the truth. As soon as she heard that Silver had been the one to take her to the emergency ward, Teresa looked out the window; she didn't want her father to see how thrilled she was that it had been Silver. What Teresa had always wanted, more than anything, was Silver's attention, and finally on a day in July when she was fast asleep and didn't even know it, he had noticed her, had even taken care of her, and all the way home Teresa thought more about her brother than she did about her mysterious disease.

After they had pulled into the driveway, King Connors went inside the house, but Teresa stayed out on the front porch and watched the sky grow dark.

"It might be psychological," King was telling his wife. "And it might be neurological, whatever the hell that is. That's all they told me."

"I know what's wrong with Teresa," Dina said, as she reached for a glass of iced coffee. "She's under a spell that brings a special kind of fever, and no doctor at that hospital will be able to help her."

Out on the porch, Teresa was waiting for Silver. When the lights in all of the houses on Divisadero Street were switched on he came home. Teresa shivered when she heard his boots on the cement, and when he sat down next to her on the porch she felt light-headed.

"So, how are you?" Silver said. He lit a cigarette and didn't even bother to cup it in the palm of his hand so that King wouldn't notice the smoke if he happened to look out the window or step outside for some air. Now that he had dared to talk back to his father, Silver could no longer allow himself any old fears of punishment.

Teresa shrugged and watched the smoke spiral from between Silver's fingers.

"Didn't they find out what was wrong with you?" he asked.

"I've got some sort of sleeping sickness," Teresa said.

"I know that," Silver drawled. "Tell me some new information for Christ's sake."

"You took me to the hospital," Teresa whispered.

"You keep telling me things I already know," Silver said.

"I'm scared," Teresa admitted. "No one knows what's wrong with me."

"Shit, don't be scared," Silver said. "I took care of you, didn't I?"

They sat together in the dark; through the open living-room window they could hear the TV that King had switched on, they could hear crickets in the garden, they could almost hear each other's heartbeat.

"Thank you," Teresa said finally.

"Just don't make it a habit," Silver told her. "Don't think I can watch out for you every other minute. I've got other things on my mind."

"All right," Teresa said.

"Do you understand me?" Silver asked.

"I said, all right." Teresa got up and went inside, slamming the front door shut behind her. But up in her room, she could still see Silver out on the front porch. She could see the outline of his white shirt, and the smoke from another cigarette. Later that night, Silver would open her door, but Teresa would already have fallen asleep. And so Silver never got the chance to tell her he didn't mean what he had said out on the porch—he would protect her—still Teresa dreamed of him that night, and in her dreams he rescued her a thousand times, and in return she thanked him a thousand times, she brought him gifts of chocolate, and rose-colored valentines on which his name was written over and over again.

Soon after Teresa came home from the hospital, Dina tried to explain all that a mysterious illness could be. They drank lemonade in the kitchen, and Dina examined her daughter's palm.

"It all looks normal to me," Dina said. "You've got a long life line and your love line is deeper than most. It could be brain fever." Dina nodded. "It could also be evil spirits, or a spell someone's put on you."

"Who would do that to me?" Teresa asked, wondering if she had committed some terrible wrongdoing.

"Let's just wait," Dina suggested. "If it's a fever it may come and go, but no fever lasts forever. Sooner or later we'll figure out what's wrong with you."

Teresa's illness did come again—infrequently, unpredictably, sometimes lasting hours, sometimes minutes. That September, during the first week of school, Teresa had the fever while reciting a poem in class. Her eyes closed while her mouth was still open, the lines of poetry lingering on her tongue. The teacher panicked; she left another girl to watch over Teresa and then rushed to the principal's office to call Teresa's house. Silver answered that call; he was rarely in school these days. He counted the hours until he could drop all his classes and look for a full-time job, one that paid enough so that he could buy himself a car, so that he didn't have to worry about money or continue to steal from his parents' savings, which Dina kept in a coffee tin beneath the kitchen sink.

When Teresa's teacher called, Silver was quick. Lying was not difficult for him, and protecting Teresa was easy. "My sister has a mild form of epilepsy," Silver said soothingly. "It's nothing but a slight brain fever that comes and goes," Silver went on. "It's nothing to worry about," Silver told the teacher. And sure enough when the teacher returned to the classroom Teresa was reciting the last stanza of the poem just as if she had never closed her eyes.

But there were longer spells too; bouts of fever which lasted too many hours to be so easily explained. Once or twice Teresa simply did not wake up in the morning; she continued to sleep through the day and into the following night, and there were times when Silver found himself drawn to her closed bedroom door, unable to ignore the odor of roses that seemed to surround Teresa whenever she slept.

During the longest spells, Dina lit candles around Teresa's bed. She closed all the windows, no matter how hot the second-floor bedroom was, so that she could protect Teresa from spirits and moths. Dina watched, waiting for whatever had happened to Teresa to unhappen. Soon enough the spell that brought on Teresa's sleeping sickness would evaporate into pools of evil that Dina could sweep under the bed. And Teresa was always relieved to find her mother watching over her whenever she woke up. She believed Dina when she promised that a fever could not last forever, that a spell could always be broken, and more than that—Teresa was certain that even though he sometimes acted like he didn't care, Silver was also watching over her, and it was he who would save her.

The first summer Teresa became ill was the last the family spent all together. The next year Silver began to smoke marijuana in his room; Reuben, with his earnings from the supermarket, bought an old Ford which he hadn't yet managed to get in running condition; and King Connors disappeared.

It had been a bad year for construction work, and all that spring King Connors was unemployed. He had sat around the house, sending Reuben or Silver down to the corner store for six-packs of beer. Sometimes he would go into the garden, which had become overgrown with early flowers and wild grass and leeks.

"What we need are lemon trees," he told Teresa, surprising her in the backyard when she went out to leave old loaves of white bread for the jays. "We could have lemon meringue pie," King said wistfully. "We would never have to go to the Safeway again."

But the climate in Santa Rosa was best for eucalyptus and pine, and lemon trees would have to be carefully watched, and King Connors must have known, even then, when he stood in the garden with his daughter, that he wouldn't be in Santa Rosa much longer.

Everyone thought King's presence would weigh down the house when he stopped working, but there were days when he was so quiet they all forgot that he was there, and when he finally left, it took some time before anyone noticed he was missing. One morning, before anyone was awake, King went out to the driveway. He got in the truck, clicked the emergency brake off, and slid out of the driveway. He didn't start the engine until he had silently rolled halfway down Divisadero Street. Later they discovered that the only things he took with him were a suitcase full of work clothes, a map of California, and the diamond ring he had given to Dina when they were first married.

When King had been gone for over a week, Teresa began to wonder if her sleeping spells were catching; she worried that her father had fallen asleep behind the wheel of the pickup, or that he had gone fishing and was dreaming in the bottom of a rented canoe. She longed to ask someone what had happened to King Connors, but nobody mentioned him, no one seemed to care. Dina cleaned the house with a new passion, singing to herself as she vacuumed and scrubbed. Silver and Reuben now brought home six-packs of beer for themselves instead of for King. A place was still set at the end of the table, just in case King Connors reappeared, just in case he swung his long legs over the back of a kitchen chair, and reached for potatoes or lamb. And then one night, with no warning, Dina told them they would all be going home. Her home—New Mexico. She told them all to pack, and before anyone had time to complain, they were on the bus to Oakland and then on the train to Los Angeles, where they would make their final connection.

Teresa looked out the window of the train, caught up in the motion and the open space. It was only when Reuben noisily crossed his legs that Teresa remembered there was an inside of the train as well as an outside. And the farther they traveled the noisier Reuben was. He was eighteen, he had plans which didn't include being on a train with his family, he ignored the dust that flew up from the train wheels and the stations they passed through without slowing down. But Teresa couldn't get enough of traveling; the sky was so bright, the fields so golden that Teresa had to blink and shade her eyes; still she didn't turn away from the window, she pressed her nose against the glass.

Dina had dressed in black for the trip, she refused to speak to the porters or to any other passengers. And Silver was bored, nothing more. He propped his boots up on the seat across from him; and after less than an hour on the train, he lit a cigarette. When he inhaled, Dina shook her head sadly; Silver stared back at her, amused, and he smiled when his mother whispered, urging him not to smoke.

"What are you going to do about it?" he said.

When he exhaled smoke, Silver fogged up the window. Teresa cleaned the glass with the cuff of her cotton dress; soot stuck to her sleeve. Although she felt as though she could ride the train forever, Teresa, like her brothers, didn't want to go to Santa Fe. She was afraid of the grandmother she had never met before. She wondered if she might be forced to visit her grandfather's grave, taken to the cemetery on a night when there was no moon, when there wasn't a star in the sky. Teresa felt better when she imagined that the train ride would last forever. She concentrated on the odor of oranges when they passed by long, green groves outside of Salinas, on the absolutely perfect color of the sky.

When Dina fell asleep, Silver took out a plastic bag filled with marijuana. He rolled a thin cigarette that he lit and passed to Reuben.

"This is bullshit," Silver said to his brother. "No way that I'm going to New Mexico."

"You're already on your way." Reuben smiled. Teresa looked at her eldest brother and watched him inhale; his eyes were the same as King Connors's; when he exhaled, his nostrils grew wide with sweet, heavy smoke.

"I might jump off the train the next time we stop," Silver said thoughtfully.

"Like hell you will," Reuben said. "You're looking forward to meeting every girl that lives in Santa Fe. You're going to try and convince them you're a movie star from California."

"If they want to think that"—Silver shrugged—"how can I stop them?"

Reuben leaned close to Silver and spoke in a whisper. "I don't plan to spend the rest of my life in Santa Fe, or in Santa Rosa either."

Teresa was certain they would not stay in Santa Fe; this was only a visit. After all, the house in Santa Rosa was waiting for them; the furniture was covered with clean sheets to catch the dust, dishes were still on the drainboard, the two dogs wandered around the yard, escaping every chance they had from the neighbor's where they had been left, howling at the moon on the porch of the empty house. And King Connors might have returned just as he had many times before; he might be watching TV, pulling the tab off a can of cold beer and wondering where everyone had gone off to.

"You talk big," Reuben now whispered to Silver, "but I'm really going to do something. I'm never going back." He nodded to Dina. "And believe me—she won't care."

They changed trains in Los Angeles. Silver bought more cigarettes at the station, Teresa stared at oil riggings, Reuben closed his eyes and smiled, occupied with secrets all his own. On the new train they traveled through Nevada and Arizona; they spent days on that train, eating the sandwiches Dina had made, watching the moonrise, getting on each other's nerves. Teresa bought Cokes at the canteen, and forced Silver into playing cards with her.

"You're gonna lose," Silver warned her before each game of gin, but in fact he let her win almost every time.

They finally crossed the New Mexico state line one morning, but they didn't reach Lamy, the closest station to Santa Fe, until dusk. When they got off the train, Silver and Reuben carried the suitcases and the boxes tied with blue string. Teresa followed, wishing she had more to carry, a heavy trunk to weigh her down so that she would not rise up and drift into the New Mexico sky. Because it was so late, the family had to share a crowded taxi. Teresa rested her head on Silver's shoulder and let the chatter of the other passengers cover her like someone else's hand-sewn quilt. The scent of a flower Teresa didn't recognize came through the open windows of the taxi, and above the road, in the highest branches of the trees, owls called to each other.

There were hundreds of red stars in the sky when they stopped in front of the house where Dina had grown up. There was the same adobe wall around the house Dina remembered, the same iron gate draped with dusty roses. Dina rang the bell, and the family waited, listening to the wheels of the taxi as it drove over the pebbles and stones in the road. Before long a young woman, a maid, came to the gate and nodded for them to come inside. They were quiet as they followed her, as if they had all lost the power of speech. Dina's face was calm, she looked younger, anyone would have thought that with each step closer to the house a year dropped from her age. The moonlight made paths appear where there weren't any; the house shimmered and looked twice its size. Teresa was frightened; she had never been away from home before, and this place seemed more and more foreign all the time. Inside, Teresa's grandmother was waiting for them. Dina had sent a note days before on which she wrote only the time of their arrival and her name. The grandmother's white hair was pulled away from her face by combs made of shells, there were rings on all her fingers. Teresa looked over at Silver; she knew he was thinking that he could live for years on what those rings would bring in a pawn shop.

Teresa's grandmother left them standing; the two brothers held packages in their hands, the twine cut into their fingertips. There was dust on everyone's shoes, and the train still rolled in the back of Teresa's head. When Dina greeted her mother, whom she had not seen since the day she left home with King Connors, there were no kisses and no tears.

"I don't understand why you came back now," Teresa's grandmother said to Dina.

Dina shrugged; she herself didn't know. Teresa was tired; she leaned her elbows on a table that was nearly her own height, but she rested her arms too heavily, and the table tilted so that a pair of wooden candle holders fell on the floor. The grandmother looked over at Teresa and her brothers.

"His?" she said to Dina.

"Of course," Dina said. "How many husbands do you think I've had?"

Their grandmother pointed at Silver with her finger. Teresa heard Silver groan. He hesitated and the grandmother smiled. "Don't be afraid," she said.

Silver raised his eyebrows and smiled back. He acted as if fear was a word he knew nothing of. When he walked over to the grandmother, the old woman took his hand.

"This one is a beautiful boy," she told Dina.

When the grandmother took Silver's hand, the rest of the family knew they had been welcomed to her house. They stayed that whole summer, a season lost in heat and flowers. Teresa spent most of her time in the garden, she followed old paths, she climbed up and looked over the top of the wall so that she could see Santa Fe spread out below in a circle of lights. All that summer Teresa continued to feel like a foreigner. She never learned the names of any of the flowers that grew in the garden, she never found a name to call her grandmother. Silver and Reuben both spent all of their time in Santa Fe, coming home only after dark. For the first time in his life Silver felt rich, and he liked the feeling. Their grandmother had begun to give him money. No one else, just Silver, and he didn't even have to ask. He had enough for everything he needed, and some left over to bring Teresa presents— sugary candies in syrup, a gold-embroidered scarf, a small wooden puppet that danced on strings.

Teresa and Reuben were both happy to be ignored by their grandmother. Reuben left the house early, closing the iron gate softly behind him, and Teresa spent most days drawing pictures in the garden with pastels and a pad King Connors had given her for her twelfth birthday. Sometimes, when she was drawing, Teresa saw Dina walking in the garden; Dina didn't know anyone was watching her, her eyes were wet, her skirt trailed behind and caught on low branches, leaving scraps of material that clung like dark banners. One afternoon Teresa fell asleep in the middle of the day. She dreamed that she was older, old enough to dance with Silver at a party where all of the women wore summer dresses made of chiffon. When she woke up, Dina was kneeling next to her; Teresa wanted to cry, she could not believe she was still only twelve years old.

"How long did I sleep?" Teresa asked. Her spells had begun to frighten her less and less all the time; they were mysterious still, but comfortable, like a recurring dream.

Dina shrugged. "Not so long. A couple of hours. Maybe the air here is getting rid of the spells."

"I don't think so," Teresa said. She didn't want to give her mother any reason for staying in New Mexico. "It's just something I'll grow out of." Teresa had heard this many times from King Connors.

Insects flew through the air; Dina waved away the bugs and sat next to Teresa beneath a cottonwood tree. "This was one of my father's favorites," she said of the tree.

"Did you meet my father when you still lived in his house?" Teresa asked.

"Your father? That big shot couldn't even stand a little hot weather. I wasted everything on him," Dina said, dragging a stick over the earth in neat lines. "I was stupid. I was so young I couldn't see straight."

Teresa wiped away the beads of sweat on her face and tried to imagine her mother as a young girl in this garden.

"I wanted someone to take me far away. Not necessarily to Santa Rosa." Dina laughed. "Just away."

"He wasn't the right one," Teresa sadly agreed. The right one would never have owned a pickup truck, the right one would never have had such cold blue eyes, so few words of kindness or praise.

"I guess I should have waited a little longer," Dina said.

When Teresa and Dina saw the young maid who had first let them into the house pass by on her way to shop at the market, they were both as quiet as conspirators. The maid's name was Annette; she had long blond hair and, although she was only eighteen, she had been working for Teresa's grandmother for three years. Annette probably would have been happy to sit under the cottonwood tree with Dina and Teresa, but they didn't want her to see where they were.

"She's not too smart," Dina said of the maid when the girl had gone out of the garden and closed the gate behind her, "but my mother could bribe her with one lump of sugar."

Teresa was now wondering how it might be possible to know the right one when he appeared. "What would have happened if you didn't run away?" she asked. "What would have happened if you waited long enough?"

"I still think someone would have come for me," Dina said. "Someone would have walked right through that gate. An Aria," Dina whispered.

Even now, so many years after she had heard about Arias from her father, Dina found herself listening for them late at night. After everyone else in the house had fallen asleep, she went to her bedroom window and unlocked the wooden shutters and looked toward the mesa, which was still the same blue color it had been on nights when she was not much older than Teresa. But Dina's belief that an Aria would find her in her parents' house grew dimmer with each day they spent in Santa Fe; the nights seemed shorter than they had when she was a girl, the time for an Aria to rescue her seemed past.

In the garden, under the tree which Dina's father had always watered so carefully, Teresa now wanted to know more than she had been told about Arias before. Dina always talked about them in words so tentative, so blurry, that Teresa had never truly been able to picture an Aria.

"What do they look like?" Teresa asked.

"What kind of question is that?" Dina said, annoyed. "I've told you—they still ride on horseback, they carry saddlebags that have buttons made out of turquoise. . . ."

"What color eyes do they have?" Teresa asked. "What color hair?"

Dina closed her eyes and pursed her lips; her hands shook as though she were in a trance. "Dark eyes," she said. Her eyes were still closed, her voice was soft and assured. "Dark hair—a little longer than most men wear it. Thin and tall." Dina opened her eyes. "But not too tall. And they have a certain fire in their eyes—and they're not afraid of thunder, and they're quiet—there are times when they just don't have to bother speaking."

It was nearly dinnertime when Dina and Teresa went back inside the house. Silver and Reuben would be home soon, they would all sit around the wooden table in the dining room and eat clear chicken broth, then pork cooked with cabbage and juniper berries. And all through dinner that night Teresa would find she wasn't able to eat, she would push the food over to the side of her plate. And she would stare across the table at Silver, and think about a man who wasn't afraid of thunder, a man with dark eyes who was so near to her she could have touched him if she had had the nerve to reach across the dinner table.

Later in the summer, Teresa decided that if Silver and Reuben could go off and explore Santa Fe, she could too. And so, one night, when fireflies lit the road into town, Teresa left her grandmother's house. But to reach the center of Santa Fe, Teresa had to pass the graveyard where her grandfather was buried. Dina had taken them all to the graveyard the day after they arrived in New Mexico. They had all worn black, they had bowed their heads; Teresa had been afraid that the bones would rise up through the soil and grab her by the ankle, they would pull her down into the earth, down to the place where worms devoured bright blue butterflies. All around the grandfather's grave had been the graves of Indians; seashells encircled the mounds of earth, all without headstones, all decades old. This time when Teresa passed the iron gates of the cemetery, she didn't go inside; she only stopped and peered over the gate, but the iron was so rusted that when she held her lips close to the gate, she breathed in iron. From there till she reached Santa Fe, Teresa ran. She ran down the road with her braids flying out behind her, and she didn't stop until she reached an open-air café. Even after she had climbed onto the raised platform of the café, she still wasn't certain that the bones in the graveyard hadn't followed her into the heart of the city.

Teresa smelled oranges and wine and bitter limes; she walked across the wooden planks that were painted pale blue, like robins' eggs, like some men's eyes. But now Teresa was shy. There were some families having late supper, but mostly the café was filled with men: men were on the outside platform ringed with small wooden tables, men were inside, where the bar and the dance floor were. And so Teresa sat on the wooden stairs; she breathed in the hot night wind that carried insects along in a steady living stream. She was not used to being out by herself this late at night and so Teresa edged closer to a family who sat at the nearest table, and she pretended she was theirs.

The woman of that family held a child on her lap; the man drank dark beer. As Teresa edged closer to their feet, they knew she was there, but they didn't ask her any questions, instead they passed her candies, pastel-green mints coated with sugar. Here at the café, the air didn't smell like iron: here no one wore black. There was music and someone's perfume, the odor of lilacs and musk.

The longer she was there, the less nervous Teresa was about being out alone at night, the more certain she was that if someone was looking for her, he would definitely be able to find her at the foot of the steps. Teresa munched the cool-tasting candies and nodded her head to the music playing inside. Each time a lizard crawled out from beneath the blue wooden planks of the café terrace, the family at Teresa's table called out and tossed pebbles, and the lizard would leap back under the floorboards; Teresa laughed as she heard it scurry away.

Teresa grew braver; she walked along the terrace of the café, looking through the windows into the bar. Inside, there were candles in glass globes burning on every table. Against the wall, couples sat, talking, taking a break from the dance floor to have a cigarette or to lean their heads against the white walls and kiss. They kissed on the lips, they kissed deeply, and sometimes a man leaned over and kissed a woman's neck, just the way Silver did when

Teresa saw him through the window.

Once she saw him, Teresa moved closer to the glass; she couldn't look away, though she wanted to. Silver's eyes were closed, his mouth moved as if he were drinking a glass of wine. The woman he sat with was Annette; she took her long hair in one hand and moved it away from her neck, then leaned her head back and smiled. Teresa stared as Silver and Annette eased onto the dance floor; they held each other so tightly it was difficult to tell where Silver ended and Annette began. Teresa wasn't the only one watching; nearly every woman in the café watched Silver, and it was clear each imagined herself in his arms.

Teresa sat down in an empty chair; Annette slipped her arm around Silver's waist. When Teresa looked at other men, in the bar or out on the terrace, their faces seemed to disappear; the café seemed suddenly awful: the music was too loud, the dancers barely moved, lizards ran in circles beneath the terrace. Teresa went back to her grandmother's house. She ran all the way home: she could swear she heard lizards running behind, right on her heels. She went through the garden and into the house; but once she got into bed, Teresa knew she wouldn't be able to sleep. And later, as she lay between cold sheets, Teresa listened to Silver slam the iron gate shut just before dawn and her eyes were open as Silver walked down the hallway to his bedroom, humming to himself, never imagining that anyone had seen him at the café— or that anyone felt betrayed.

In the days that followed, Teresa found herself wishing for a way to get back at Silver. One evening, as she walked in the garden, Teresa saw Reuben sitting in a wrought-iron chair, smoking a cigar and staring at the sky. She was still furious at Silver, and she thought that maybe Reuben could be her favorite brother.

"What do you want?" Reuben said when he saw her, and when he spoke his voice sounded just like King Connors's.

"When are we going home?" Teresa asked, thinking of the quick lizards at the café.

"Sooner or later," Reuben said. He exhaled, and smoke rings circled them both; he suddenly began to confide in Teresa more than ever before. Maybe he confided in his sister because it was dark or because no one else could hear, maybe he was not so much talking to Teresa as he was just talking. Reuben told Teresa that he had been working; in a local market he crated fruit, sticky with sun, covered with flies; he lifted wooden crates full of live chickens; he worked a cash register and drove a pickup full of groceries all over town. All of this so that he would not have to go back to Santa Rosa. Instead of going back home, he would go to Los Angeles. He was sick of how Dina treated him, tired of Silver always being the favorite. At least King Connors cared about him, he had phoned Reuben at his job, and Reuben now carried their father's address in Los Angeles in his shirt pocket.

"Let me go with you," Teresa whispered.

The moon was high, insects spun in the air, Teresa slapped mosquitoes back against the night.

"Now you just shut up about all of this," Reuben said. He had almost forgotten Teresa was there; he was wrapped up in his own plans. "If anyone asks you, you don't know where our father is, understand? And when I leave, you sure as hell don't tell anyone you know where I am."

She hadn't really wanted to go with Reuben, she had only wanted to go away and teach Silver a lesson. Teresa glared at her oldest brother; no matter how disappointed she was in Silver, she saw now that Reuben could never be her favorite. "Go ahead," she said to Reuben. "Go to Los Angeles. I don't care."

Reuben laughed nervously. "I was only teasing you," he said. "I know you won't tell anyone. I know you'll keep quiet."

But he wasn't teasing and Teresa knew it. He wouldn't go back to Santa Rosa, and he knew where King Connors was. Teresa thought how much easier it was for her brothers; they didn't have to wait for someone to come along and rescue them, they could go off and buy a train ticket to anywhere they wished.

At the end of summer, in the last week of August, Dina called her children to her room. The shutters over the window were closed and only a few rays of renegade light slipped through. For weeks now, Dina had stopped looking for traces of Arias. When the wind rose up in the evening and the vines on the trellis outside her window shuddered, Dina no longer imagined that a dark stranger was climbing up to the second-story bedroom, although not running over to the window to look out nearly broke her heart.

"We're leaving tonight," Dina said. "I made a mistake coming back here." Dina went to the window and opened the shutters; her children blinked in the sudden light. "We'll have dinner," Dina said, "and then we'll go. But don't say a word to your grandmother. When we pick up our suitcases and walk out the door, that's time enough for her to know."

That night they all dressed for dinner. The tension at the table made Teresa feel shaky; Dina, who rarely drank, had three glasses of wine and didn't touch her meal. Silver looked out the window and watched as Annette left the house to go home and wash her hair so that it would be dry in time for a date with Silver that wouldn't be kept. When the grandmother poured herself a cup of coffee, Dina cleared her throat. "I've decided to leave," she told her mother.

The grandmother stirred her coffee; the spoon hit against the edges of the cup. "You shouldn't have gone in the first place, and you shouldn't have come back. You do everything at the wrong time, Dina. You helped kill your father, then you came back. What do you expect me to say?"

Dina shrugged her shoulders. "You never cared about me," she said. "Only my father cared."

"Hah," the grandmother said, sipping her coffee.

"I know he did," Dina said. "He hired Bergen to find me."

"So he hired a second-rate detective?" the grandmother said. "So what?"

Dina got up and pushed her chair away with a sweep of her arm. "I don't have to listen to you."

"You should have listened to me," the grandmother said. "I told you not to go with that man of yours."

Dina went to the closet where they had hidden their already packed suitcases. She struggled to pick them up; her dress was already wrinkled, and they hadn't even started their trip.

"Well, don't expect me to come back again," Dina said.

"Who's asking you to come back?" the old woman said.

"Let's go," Dina said, signaling to her children.

"Not him," the grandmother said, pointing a finger at Silver.

"I said let's go," Dina repeated.

Teresa and Reuben got up from the table and went to the hallway where their mother stood. Silver sat in his chair, stone still.

"Did you hear me?" Dina said to Silver.

He was their grandmother's favorite, and, if he stayed, there would be nothing she wouldn't let him do; he could go out to the café every night, he could meet Annette and a dozen other women in a field near the graveyard where lovers went. If he stayed, he might inherit the old woman's jewelry, the house, everything she owned.

Teresa waited for Silver's decision. She could hear heavy breathing in the room, as if the dining-room walls had mouths, tongues, lungs filled with air.

"Silver stay here?" Dina laughed. "You've got to be kidding. In this house?" She looked at her son. "There's nothing here," she told him. "Believe me."

"Stay," the grandmother said to Silver, and Teresa nearly cried out loud; now she regretted having ever thought—however briefly—that Reuben might be her favorite brother. She couldn't imagine leaving Silver behind, and she wondered if she might be allowed to stay on, too, if Silver said yes to their grandmother. She could have a room at the rear of the house, she could wash all of her grandmother's laundry, on weekends she and Silver could go on long walks, in the opposite direction from the graveyard with the iron gates.

Their grandmother got up and walked over to Silver. He was still seated at the dinner table when the grandmother took her diamond earrings off and placed them in his hand. Silver kept his palm open; he stared at the diamonds, then he smiled. He clenched his hand into a fist and stood up. If he stayed in this house he was certain he would lose something, and not even diamonds could convince him to sit through a thousand polite dinners, afternoon teas, an old woman's adoration.

"I'm sorry," Silver said to his grandmother. He put the earrings into his shirt pocket, then kissed the old woman's cheek. As soon as he said no to their grandmother, Teresa forgave Silver for dancing with Annette. She watched as Silver walked toward the front door. When he stopped to pick up a suitcase, Dina went over to him.

"Give those earrings back to her," she said. "We don't need anything from her."

"Why should I?" Silver said. "I deserve them," he told his mother. "I was nice to the old lady and she paid me back. I earned them."

When Reuben and Silver carried the suitcases out to the road, Teresa stayed behind with Dina and studied her grandmother. The old woman stood beside the dining-room table. She looked older than anyone Teresa had ever seen before, and her eyes were damp.

"He's a beautiful boy," the grandmother explained.

"You can't have him," Dina said triumphantly.

"You," the grandmother said, shaking her head. "You were always stupid. You had to run off with the first man who looked at you."

"He wasn't the first to look at me," Dina said.

"You don't even know how to bring up children," the grandmother sighed. "You've taught that boy all the wrong things."

Dina and her mother kissed goodbye, but they kissed lightly, separated by bitterness and the knowledge that they would never see each other again. Dina walked toward the hallway and the front door, and as Teresa was about to follow her she felt a hand on her shoulder. It was the first time all summer that her grandmother had touched her, and the old woman's strength shocked Teresa.

"Don't think I haven't noticed you," the grandmother told Teresa. "I've noticed you—you're my granddaughter."

Teresa heard the taxi pull up outside; she was certain that their suitcases were already being lifted into the trunk, but it seemed she was unable to move, her grandmother was still holding on to her shoulder and she could smell the old woman's cologne, she could see the tears that had formed in her grandmother's eyes but had never fallen.

"I had my reasons for wanting Silver to stay here," the grandmother now said. "He's dangerous, and I know it, but what could he do to an old lady like me—break my heart?"

Outside, the taxi honked its horn, but Teresa was held by her grandmother's last words of advice.

"Remember to be careful," the grandmother told Teresa. "Be smart. And remember that I noticed you."

Teresa nodded and then ran toward the hallway and out the door. She stumbled in the garden, and when she reached the road Silver motioned to her to hurry.

"Look at these," Silver whispered, once Teresa was inside the taxi. He opened his palm and showed Teresa the diamond earrings. "These are going to buy me a car."

Silver put the earrings in Teresa's hand for a moment; they seemed to burn, they moved with a dry, hot life of their own. "I don't want these," Teresa said.

"Good," Silver said, taking the diamonds and returning them to his shirt pocket. "Because these sure aren't for you."

They drove away, down the gravel road, past the graveyard, past acres of flowers and dust. Then onto the train, and back to Los Angeles, where they would change trains. This trip seemed so much faster than the first that they were all surprised when they suddenly reached Los Angeles. Reuben inhaled deeply, as if he couldn't get enough air. Just after they had changed trains, Reuben decided to get off and buy a newspaper. He put his hand on Teresa's shoulder.

"So long," he said to her.

Teresa looked the other way; she knew that he wouldn't be back, knew he had King Connors's address in his pocket, that he had plans.

"Look at me," Reuben told her, and when she did, he shook his head. "Please understand," he whispered. "I have to try this. I just can't go back."

When the train wheels started turning, and the porters called out every destination, Silver leaned out the open window.

"What about Reuben?" he said. "Should I go out and look for him?"

"I'm not an idiot," Dina said. "I know where Reuben's going. He wants to be with his father—let him go."

"Maybe he didn't hear the train whistle," Silver said. "Maybe I should go look for him."

Dina shook her head and smiled. "I'm not going to take the chance of losing you, too," she told her favorite son. "It doesn't hurt so much to lose one child," she told them, but she didn't mention that it mattered very much which child it was.

So it was only the three of them who returned to Santa Rosa to be greeted by the familiar heavy curtains in the living room and the dogs who jumped over the neighbor's fence as soon as the taxi pulled up on Divisadero Street. Dina and Silver and Teresa were the only ones in the house when the windows were opened to let the cool air and the scent of the river into all the rooms, just the three of them who had coffee each morning, and they drank from the white and blue china cups as if they had never been anywhere else, as if they had never even been gone.

CHAPTER
TWO

✝

SILVER SOLD THE DIAMOND EARRINGS HIS GRANDMOTHER
gave him and then sank every cent into the old Ford
Reuben left behind. He got it running, then bought mag
wheels and new bucket seats. He had the body repainted—
black, like the darkest hour of night. Two weeks after he
had polished the car to perfection, he totaled it on the
River Road; he took a turn too quickly, he blinked for a
second too long. When it was over, Silver walked away
without a scratch, but the Ford had lasted less than a

month, and it now was out of commission forever, trapped in a ditch that would be filled with steamy rainwater by the first of November. And Silver couldn't help but wonder if his grandmother had put a hex on the diamonds she had given him, because suddenly—after a moment of fortune—he had nothing at all.

And so, in early autumn, Silver took a job at Leona's, a restaurant with a continental menu and enough dirty pots and pans for two dishwashers. That year Teresa never got the rides to school Silver had promised her, she never sat in the front seat of his fancy Ford, watched by admiring eyes as she was dropped off in front of the junior high. While Silver worked at the restaurant's sink, side by side with an old ex-con named Jim, both of them up to their elbows in slick water, Teresa drifted through a term of school. She sat in the last row of every classroom and was absent as often as she could find a good excuse. There were no longer black-and-blue arguments at home now that King Connors was gone—it was clear this time he wasn't returning, and since his departure Teresa's sleeping spells had eased up. But soon Teresa had a foolproof excuse for missing school—Dina was ill. Again, a nameless disease, but it wasn't sleeping that bothered Dina, it was every waking moment. Her hand shook, she couldn't sleep at night, she hadn't the heart to clean the house or go downtown to the welfare office and sign up for what was rightfully hers now that she had been deserted. The doctors at the Haven Street Clinic gave Dina Valium, which she flushed down the toilet. These same doctors suggested that Dina's insomnia, her rashes, and her fear that she might stop breathing in the middle of the night, all came from her mind.

"So fix it," Dina told them. "You're so smart—fix my mind."

When the doctors reminded Dina that only she could make herself well, she wondered if her family was cursed: no mind could have produced the red welts that covered her arms, no imagination could have filled her nights with desperate wheezing. Because Dina was sure that the doctors were wrong, because she was positive that her disease had a name and a cure, many of the days Teresa was absent from school were spent in the public library. There she looked through medical textbooks with her mother, and together they tried to find Dina's disease.

"Maybe it's this," Dina whispered as they leafed through a dermatology journal.

Teresa read the caption beneath a photograph of a red, scaly rash. "Only in India," she told her mother. "You only get this disease if you live in India and wash with contaminated water."

"Sure," Dina said, "that's what they tell you. Do you believe every word you read?" She rolled up her sleeve and showed Teresa her patchy skin. "They told me this was in my mind. You believe that, too?"

These days Dina was tired all the time, it was hard for her to believe she was not quite forty; she ignored the garden—the snails and the weeds quickly took over. With each month that passed since their return from New Mexico, Dina grew thinner; each evening she scraped nearly every bit of her dinner off her plate and gave it to the dogs. She never mentioned Reuben, she just packed all his clothes in a steamer trunk and had Silver carry it down to the cellar. She stopped drinking coffee, she never bothered to put seeds in the bird feeders that hung on the eucalyptus trees. After a while Teresa was so worried that she placed a collect long-distance call to her aunt in Portland. In less than a week's time, when the skies were gray and the roads were slick with flooding, Renée, King Connors's sister, drove down to Santa Rosa in her Corvette.

"What's going on here," Renée said when she saw the dishes in the sink and the cobwebs in the corners. She tossed her suitcase on the couch, smoothed down her hair, then kicked off her high-heeled shoes and changed her green silk blouse for a T-shirt. "First King and then Reuben." She sighed. "It's understandable, why shouldn't they take off? From the looks of this place, your mother seems to want to drive them all away."

While Dina was out, seeing a new doctor at the Haven Street Clinic who specialized in eczema, Renée enlisted Teresa to help clean the house. She filled buckets with soapy water, locked the dogs in the yard, and found the mop. "Don't you worry," she told Teresa, "I'll have this place back in shape before you know it."

When Dina returned from the clinic and found Renée's car in the driveway, she slammed through the screen door. "What are you doing here?" she demanded.

Renée hugged Dina's stiff body. "Darling," she said, "I'm so sorry about King." She backed up and took a good look at her sister-in-law. "What's happened to you?" she asked. "You look awful."

Dina glared at Teresa. "Did you invite your aunt here?" she asked.

Teresa felt like a traitor and she stuttered an excuse. "I called her," she admitted.

"It's a good thing she did call," Renée said to her sister-in-law. "I'm here to help you pick up the pieces of your life. It's the least I can do now that my brother's deserted you."

The entire time she visited, Renée let Silver drive her car. They left Dina at home and drove to the river, Silver behind the wheel, Teresa in back where Renée usually stowed suitcases and groceries.

"Whoa now. Slow down," Renée said when Silver drove too fast, but she didn't mean it; they could tell Renée liked speed because she rolled down her window and tied a chiffon scarf over her head and she switched on the radio full blast. And as they drove faster, even Silver, who hated anything to do with his father, had to admit that everything was better when Renée was around.

Teresa thought she would rather be like Renée than anyone else in the world; she began to confide in her aunt—finally she told Renée about the sleeping spells.

"It's a phase," Renée assured her niece. "I don't care what your mother's told you, there's no such thing as spells. When I was your age I used to faint now and then, but as soon as I had my first boyfriend I got over all that fainting. I had to. I couldn't trust my boyfriend long enough to faint, I had to keep my eyes open wide. You just wait." Renée nodded. "You'll see that it's just a phase."

When Renée discovered Dina in Teresa's room one night, it was easy for her to see that her sister-in-law didn't believe that Teresa was merely going through a phase. Teresa had fallen asleep in the late afternoon, and Dina was so accustomed to her daughter's spells that she immediately lit candles around the bed without even bothering to try to wake her.

"What the hell is this?" Renée asked when she saw the candles. "An exorcism?" She bent down and blew out the flames.

"You think you're so smart," Dina told her sister-in-law. "Do you know the doctors can't even figure out what's wrong with her?"

"That's because it's nothing," Renée said. She grabbed Teresa by her shoulders and shook her. "Wake up," she told her niece. "Open your goddamned eyes."

To Dina's amazement Teresa did exactly that.

"Was I having a spell?" Teresa asked when she woke.

"I don't know," Dina admitted. "Maybe you were just taking a nap."

"Maybe you found a cure," Teresa said to her aunt.

"There's no cure," Renée told her then. "Because there's no disease."

And although Dina disliked Renée, and could barely stand to look into the blue eyes which were exactly like King Connors's, Dina let her sister-in-law stay—what could she do—Teresa really did seem healthier, and there was nothing to accuse Renée of. Nothing until the night when Silver was brought home by the sheriff.

Dina opened the front door that night, she stared at the handcuffs around Silver's wrists and then turned to Renée. "This is because of you," she told her sister-in-law.

The sheriff stood with his hat in his hand. "He was doing eighty-seven miles an hour. I clocked him."

Renée lit a cigarette and smiled. She was wearing her jade-green silk blouse, and when she invited the sheriff into the living room, he smiled back. "My nephew was taking my car on a test run," she lied. "I just had new brakes installed, and I asked Silver to test them for me. So if my nephew was driving too fast, if he broke the law—you'll have to arrest me. It was my fault."

"You're just like King," Dina told Renée. "You walk right in and ruin everyone's life."

Silver had begun to breathe easier, he listened to Renée lie with admiration, he smiled at her like a co-conspirator when the sheriff uncuffed him, even though there were now dark marks around his wrists where the metal had bitten into his skin.

"My niece," Renée said, introducing Teresa to the sheriff. Teresa shook his hand and then backed away. "And my sister-in-law," Renée said, gesturing to Dina. "Bad times," she explained. "My brother left them."

"Sure," Dina said. "Tell everybody our business. I've had enough of this—I want you out of here. I married your brother—I didn't marry you."

"She's not herself," Renée said hopefully.

"Oh, no?" Dina said. She left the room, and when she returned she carried Renée's suitcase, scarves and satin caught between the locks. Dina opened the front door and threw the suitcase out.

"Really!" Renée said.

"You've got the picture," Dina told her. "I want you out."

Teresa looked over at Silver; she could tell that the white Corvette was riding right behind his eyes. She wondered if perhaps Renée might be thinking of taking them away with her when she left.

"You're not serious," Renée said to Dina. "Think of your children—they hardly have any family left. You don't even know where your oldest son is. At least think of these two."

"My oldest son is with his father," Dina said. "Why shouldn't he be? They have the same evil eyes, they belong together."

"She believes in spirits," Renée explained to the sheriff.

"Go ahead." Dina was furious now. "Tell this stranger the story of my life." She tapped her foot, faster and faster. She reached for a vase filled with straw flowers and then threw it against the wall. They all watched as the porcelain shattered and covered the floor with violet dust. Beneath the couch, Reggie, the old dog, whimpered and pawed at the floorboards. Renée tossed her hair and stubbed out her cigarette; she thought that if King Connors ever returned he deserved everything he got.

"Do you want to file a complaint?" the sheriff asked Renée.

Yes, Teresa thought. Oh, yes.

Since Dina had become ill with her strange series of ailments, the house on Divisadero Street seemed filled with nothing but sorrow, and Teresa believed they might all be happier if they left it behind.

"What about me?" Dina said. "Maybe I want to file a complaint. Maybe I'm tired. Maybe I'm sick and I don't want company I never invited in the first place."

Renée went to the closet and got her suede coat and her leather purse. "Teresa," she said, nodding. "Silver."

If there was anything Teresa wanted just then it was to ride up the coast to Oregon; Renée would be in the passenger seat, Silver behind the wheel, and Teresa would be safely cushioned in the back.

"I have to go now," Renée told them.

She's putting on an act, Teresa thought when her aunt bent down to kiss her goodbye. She doesn't want anyone to suspect that she's about to take us away, any second, any time at all now.

"Goodbye," Renée murmured as she walked away from Teresa and went to the door. Teresa ran to the window; she watched as Renée and the sheriff walked down the driveway, side by side. The act had gone too far; Renée wasn't looking back, she opened the door of the white Corvette.

"Good riddance," Dina said. "Take those goddamned blue eyes and go back to Oregon."

Renée talked to the sheriff through the open window of her car; then she turned the key, and a film of exhaust floated into the air. When she pulled out of the driveway, the patrol car followed, and in less than a minute both cars had disappeared down Divisadero Street. Later, when Teresa went to sit on the front porch she could still see a shadow of blue exhaust above her. And long after Dina had gone to sleep, resting more comfortably than she had in weeks, Teresa was still out on the porch. The temperature dropped, and the moon rose, and Teresa waited.

Silver let the dogs out of the house, then came out to the porch. He had planned to meet some friends who had managed to borrow a car, but when he saw Teresa sitting alone, he sat down next to her. He didn't ask her anything, but after a while Teresa turned to him as if she'd been questioned.

"I'm just waiting," she told him. "That's all."

"Oh, yeah?" Silver said. He leaned against the porch railing. "For who?"

Teresa was shocked, she had expected Silver to know. "For Renée."

"Ah," Silver said. "Renée." He took a pack of cigarettes from his pocket and lit one. "Listen to me—don't bother waiting for Renée."

"She'll be back," Teresa said. She didn't dare look at Silver. She couldn't risk taking her eyes off the street for a moment, just in case the Corvette silently drove by.

"She's not coming back here any more than King is," Silver said.

Teresa was stubborn. "You're wrong," she told him.

It was already too late for Silver to meet his friends and ride to the outskirts of town and drink beer till morning. So he stayed with Teresa until nearly midnight.

"You've got to grow up," he told Teresa when it was so late that Renée might already have reached the city limits of Portland, or she might just as easily have been turning to hold the sheriff in a dark room at the Lamplighter Motel on Sixteenth Street. "Forget about Renée."

"I can't," Teresa insisted.

"Will you cut it out?" Silver said gently. "Look, as long as you've got me you don't have to worry. All right?" he asked.

And Teresa nodded her head, but she did not go inside until there was no hope that Renée would return that night.

Up in her room she went to the window. Silver was out there alone, just he and the empty street. For weeks Teresa continued to watch that street from her window; she still listened for Renée's car horn to call to her. But after a while Teresa stopped waiting; she could no longer remember if the interior of the Corvette was black or brown. Soon, she couldn't even remember Renée's face, she couldn't imagine why she had wanted to drive up the California coast to Oregon to a place where the hills were even greener than the wings of the moths that gathered around those candles Dina continued to place at the foot of Teresa's bed to ward off evil spirits.

The one thing Teresa didn't forget was Renée's advice to find herself a boyfriend. In part she wanted to make Silver jealous—he was spending more and more time away from the house, there were nights when he didn't come home at all and neither Dina nor Teresa dared ask where he'd been. And so at the end of the winter, a month before her fourteenth birthday, Teresa began dating Cosmo. He was sixteen and considered himself to be a ladies' man.

"Everybody wants to be my girl," he reminded Teresa when she refused to have anything to do with him at first. "I'm the one for you," he whispered when they danced together one night in the high-school gym. But there was nothing about Cosmo that marked him as special, so she put him off, she didn't give him a second thought until she found him waiting for her one morning, parked in his Chevy right outside the house.

"Get out of here," Teresa told him. "Go away," she whispered, looking back to see if Dina was watching from the window.

"Give me a chance," Cosmo said. He followed her in his car and called out from the passenger window as he steered with one hand.

When they were a block away from the house, Teresa got in. "What do you want?" she asked. Instead of answering, Cosmo smiled slowly. When she saw his wide, even teeth, Teresa put her hand on the door. She was ready to jump from the moving car. "I'm only thirteen," she said. "I'm too young for you."

"No one's too young for me," Cosmo told her as he stepped on the gas.

Teresa wasn't certain if she liked his looks; she didn't even know his last name. All the same, she sat back in the passenger seat and clicked the lock shut on the door.

"Nice car, isn't it?" Cosmo said as they drove right past the junior high school. "It belongs to a cousin of mine. He doesn't care if I have my driver's license or not. He trusts me." Cosmo had put his hand on her leg. "I hope you're going to trust me, too."

And though she didn't, Teresa found herself agreeing to meet him every day after school. All through the month of February they parked in vacant lots; Cosmo taught her to keep her mouth open when they kissed. He told her he had first noticed her because of her long dark hair. He assured her that no one would know if she took off her shirt in the back seat of his cousin's car.

But soon after her fourteenth birthday, Teresa decided that she no longer wanted to date Cosmo, no matter how many girls he said were wild about him. One afternoon, when they had parked in a field near a peach orchard, Teresa told Cosmo the truth.

"I don't think we should see each other any more," she said.

"What are you talking about?" Cosmo said. "Of course we should see each other. Listen, Teresa, you don't know how lucky you are—girls fight over me with knives."

Still, Teresa couldn't be persuaded—Cosmo didn't even know her, he didn't look into her eyes and search for her soul, he didn't look any farther than the back seat of the borrowed car. And she didn't dare compare him to Silver—that would have been ridiculous, she would have found herself giggling each time they kissed.

"Okay, okay," Cosmo said when Teresa shook her head and insisted they weren't made for each other. "It's your loss. It's a shame, though," he sighed. "You could have wound up with a diamond ring one of these days."

"I'm sorry," Teresa said.

"You're sorry," Cosmo muttered, but then he turned to her and smiled. "Since this may be the last time we're together, let me really touch you."

Teresa frowned. He had touched her breasts every time they were together. "Where?" she asked.

"You know," Cosmo urged. "It's nothing," he promised. "It's not fucking."

Teresa unzipped her jeans and took them off. She closed her eyes when Cosmo put his hand inside the elastic waistband of her underpants. When Cosmo had finished Teresa got up and got dressed. She felt as though she had been watching a film in a dark theater, as if she hadn't been there at all.

"You're crazy about me," Cosmo told her as he dropped her off on the corner of Divisadero Street. Teresa got out and closed the car door. "Admit it," Cosmo called after her. "You can't give me up." Teresa didn't even bother to answer; half of her walked down the street, placing one foot in front of the other, but the other half floated above the sidewalk in a cloud of thick confusion. Her stomach felt stormy, everything inside her ached. When she reached home, Silver was out in the front yard. Teresa started to walk past him, but Silver grabbed her arm.

"Where the fuck have you been?" he asked her.

"I think I'm sick," Teresa said. She wanted to get to her own room, to the silent wallpaper—apple blossoms on thin branches which reached to the ceiling.

In spite of himself, Silver had been feeling more and more responsible for Teresa. "Don't give me that crap," he said. "I just saw you get out of a car. And I've seen you before. Who is that guy you're riding around with?"

Teresa was queasy, sailors and seas lurched in her blood. "I'm sick," she said. "I might throw up."

Silver wouldn't let go of her arm. "Who is he?" he demanded. "Tell me right now, or you're not going anywhere."

Teresa's head was filled with drums, the ground seemed farther and farther away. She wrenched her arm away from Silver and ran toward the house. Silver ran after her. Then he followed her through the living room and into the bathroom, where she leaned over the sink.

"You better tell me," Silver whispered.

Teresa held her stomach, her forehead was damp.

"All right," Silver said. "I'll just have to find him. I'll get the truth from him."

Teresa ran the cold water and splashed some on her face. As she reached for a towel, she looked down; there was a pool of blood on her shoe, a line all along the bathroom floor. "Oh, God," she said. She sat down on the toilet seat; there was blood everywhere. "I think I'm dying," she said.

Silver looked at Teresa and shook his head. He ran a washcloth under the faucet and handed it to her. "Here," he said. "Clean yourself up."

Teresa wiped her leg and then her shoe; she could feel blood pooling in her underpants.

"He put his fingers up me," she told Silver. Tears came to her eyes; she hung her head. "I'm dying," Teresa said. "I just know it."

Silver sat on the rim of the bathtub. "Don't you know anything?" he said. When Teresa didn't answer, Silver took a deep breath. "It's something that happens to women," he said. "Every goddamn month."

"It's my period," Teresa said, cheering up when she realized she wasn't about to die. "I saw a movie about it in school."

"Good," Silver said, "just go ahead and take care of it." He stood up to leave the bathroom, but his sister held him back. There were still tears in her eyes.

"I don't know what to do," Teresa whispered.

"I feel like I'm a goddamned nurse," Silver said as he reached into the cabinet under the sink. He brought out a box of Kotex and handed them to her.

Teresa examined the box. "What do I do with these?" she asked.

"Christ!" Silver said. "I don't know. Figure it out."

The churning in her stomach was still there, but Teresa felt calmer because Silver promised to wait for her outside the bathroom door. "Get me a pair of underpants," she called to him. She heard Silver mutter, but he went upstairs to her room. When he came back, he knocked on the door and threw the pants inside. Teresa put them on, positioned the Kotex, then washed her hands and walked outside to where Silver was waiting.

"Everything under control?" Silver asked.

Teresa looked at him scornfully. "Of course," she said. "Do you think I'm an idiot?"

"Just don't ask me any more questions," Silver said, glad to be done with the whole business. "And you just forget you heard all this shit from me."

"Where are you going?" Teresa asked when Silver walked into the living room.

Silver stopped at the front door. "Where the hell do you think I'm going?" he said before he went outside. "I'm going to find your boyfriend."

From then on, whenever Cosmo saw Teresa, he looked the other way. If he passed by her house he didn't even bother to honk the horn; if they happened to meet in town, he crossed over to the other side of the street. Teresa was so glad that Cosmo left her alone she never asked Silver what had happened, and although she wondered if he had given Cosmo a black eye or a chipped tooth, she certainly never got close enough to look. The fact that Silver had protected her made her dizzy with delight; he had done just what he promised to do that night Renée drove back to Oregon—he had taken care of her.

Teresa didn't have one sleeping spell in March or April, she didn't miss a day of school, and it was probably just chance that her good humor coincided with spring, and with Dina's recovery.

The detective, Arnie Bergen, had begun to telephone. He had not forgotten them, and in his mind the house was just as he last saw it, before their trip to New Mexico: the garden was in full bloom, artichoke plants crowded the rows, peppers and tomatoes were ready to pick, pumpkins had begun to grow on the vines. The first time he had telephoned he had been thinking about that garden; Teresa picked up the phone, then called to her mother. "It's the detective."

Dina waved her arms and shook her head no. "I'm not here," she whispered.

"All right," Bergen had said to Teresa after she told him Dina was out. "Tell her I'll call back next week."

The following week, on a Friday at the very same time, the telephone rang. Dina had been sitting on the couch watching the phone. All the same, when it rang she jumped. On the fifth ring she picked up the receiver.

"I'm not here," Dina said quickly. She tossed the receiver back into its cradle. Still, she didn't move, she stared at the phone and her skin felt alive, as if she'd been stung by electrodes. When the phone rang again, Dina picked it up, but this time she didn't say a word.

"Hello," Bergen said into the silence. "Dina?"

"What do you want?" Dina whispered.

"Is it all right if I call you Dina?" Bergen went on. "It's not rude, is it?"

"No." Dina considered. "It's not."

"I'm calling to see how you've been getting on," Bergen said uneasily.

"Just fine," Dina answered.

"Oh, good," Bergen said. "Very good," he said, and then he quickly hung up the phone.

That weekend Dina worked in the garden for the first time in months; she began to pull out the weeds that had all but taken over the vegetable patch. By Wednesday she was ready to plant the first row of tomatoes, and by Thursday she was already waiting for the phone call she knew would come the following day at exactly three-thirty.

"Hello," Dina said immediately.

"Just checking in," Bergen told her. "Just wanted to know if you needed anything."

"Needed anything?" Dina said, puzzled.

"Something for the garden?" Bergen asked.

"Compost," Dina said. "I could use some of that."

"Fine," Bergen said. "Just fine."

He appeared that weekend, the back seat of his car loaded with a hundred-pound sack of compost. He was wearing that same madras sports jacket he had worn the first time he came to the door—only now he wore a carnation tucked into the buttonhole. Dina and Teresa watched from the kitchen window as Bergen unloaded the compost.

"Some men bring bouquets," Dina said. "He brings a hundred bouquets."

"It's fertilizer!" Teresa said.

"Don't be rude," Dina said. "Open the door for him." She patted her hair into place, then gave Teresa a shove. Bergen had set the sack by the toolshed. He stood and surveyed the garden, but the way it looked now merged with the way he remembered it, and he saw begonias and healthy rows of corn where now there was nothing more than tall, unruly weeds. Dina had cooked today's lunch the night before; she had Bergen's plate on the table before he had walked through the door.

"You must be hungry," she told him, concerned, as though he'd traveled all the way from San Francisco on foot.

"I am," Bergen admitted. He took off his sports jacket and rolled up his sleeves before he sat down at the table.

"Hang his coat in the closet," Dina told Teresa.

When Teresa returned from the hallway closet, Bergen was quietly eating his lunch and Dina was at the kitchen sink, washing dishes. Teresa sat across from Bergen and watched him eat.

"So you're thirteen now," Bergen said to Teresa.

"Fourteen," Teresa corrected him. "Last month was my birthday."

"Pisces." Bergen nodded.

"Fourteen and one month," Teresa informed him.

"Ah," Bergen said. He cut his baked chicken carefully. "Nearly a grownup."

"Hah," Dina said from her place at the sink.

"Children grow up fast these days," Bergen said.

"You're telling me." Dina held a glass she had just rinsed up to the light. "And they never remember who walked the floor all night with them, they never remember who paid for all their shoes."

"No," Bergen agreed. "They never do."

"Did you ever catch a murderer?" Teresa asked.

"Can't say that I did," Bergen told her. "I mostly dealt with divorces, wills, that sort of thing." When Teresa looked disappointed he added, "I got a bank robber once." Teresa's eyes lit up. "He was wanted for back alimony, too—that's where I came in. He was holed up in Petaluma. A bad character."

"Did he try to shoot you?" Teresa asked.

"He had a gun," Bergen said. "I suppose he might have tried to shoot me."

When Teresa went to get Arnie Bergen some lemonade, the detective stared down at his clean plate. "I guess you think I have a lot of nerve, coming here like this."

"How can anyone get through this terrible life without some nerve?" Dina asked.

"I've thought about you a lot since the last time we met," Bergen said softly.

Dina checked the tortoise-shell comb in her hair. "How did you like your lunch?" she asked.

"Delicious," Bergen said. "Just wonderful."

They went out to work together in the garden; the smell of compost drifted over the neighborhood as Bergen followed Dina around the yard. Black and yellow butterflies moved from one tomato seedling to another, even though the ground was still so cold Dina had to wear heavy work gloves. When Silver came home from work at the restaurant, Bergen and Dina were still out in the yard. Teresa was at the kitchen table doing homework.

Silver went to the screen door and looked out. "What the fuck is this?" He said. "What's that old detective doing here?"

"Bergen," Teresa said. "His name is Arnie Bergen, and he brought fertilizer with him."

"That figures," Silver said as he went to the refrigerator for a beer. "He's a loser. It's written all over his face, big letters, *loser*." Silver sat at the table, pulled out his pay from Leona's, and then counted every penny. "Bet you he never solved a case in his life."

Bergen came up to Santa Rosa every weekend after that. On Friday nights Dina washed her hair and then she prepared the meal she would serve to Bergen on the following day. If he stayed in town on Saturday night and sometimes he did, Bergen checked in at the Lamplighter Motel on Sixteenth Street. There was a pool at the motel, and Bergen often invited the entire family over to swim. Silver, of course, refused; he wouldn't have given the detective the right time of day.

"Why the hell is she wasting her time on him?" he asked Teresa.

"I don't know," Teresa said. "I guess she likes him."

But when Teresa asked her mother if she was in love with Bergen, Dina laughed out loud. "That old man?" she said as she stroked cold cream onto her face. "I'm forty-one, he's close to sixty."

"Fifty-two," Teresa said. "I asked him."

"I could never be serious about him," Dina told her daughter. "You don't think I've sat around waiting my whole life for Bergen, do you?"

But as Dina spoke, even as she listed Arnie Bergen's faults, everything she did betrayed her. Every bit of cold cream, every dinner she had made for the detective, the look on her face each time he handed her one of the gifts he brought—loaves of bread, tablecloths, used books, a brown paper bag full of tulip bulbs, a bouquet of wildflowers, poppies and heather—showed just how delighted she was.

"You have to understand," Bergen explained to Teresa one day at the edge of the Lamplighter Motel pool, "your mother doesn't want to commit herself right now. After all, she's not a free woman. She's still legally married."

But every Saturday no one would have guessed Bergen and Dina were anything other than husband and wife. Dina cooked dinner and Bergen washed up afterward, wearing an apron tied around his waist. They would play cards or drink wine and listen to the radio. And then, after it was dark, they would sit out on the back porch in the moonlight and watch the yard as if they could hear the iris bulbs stirring beneath the earth, as if they could already smell the October cabbage.

At first Bergen assumed that someday he would move to Santa Rosa—if not into the house, at least nearby. He had a pension from his days in the service, and Social Security, and his belongings in his apartment in San Francisco could have easily fit into a few cardboard boxes. But Dina wouldn't hear of it; she liked things the way they were. Every weekend she was certain something would happen: a man would walk into her kitchen and her life would be wonderfully altered. She lived for Saturdays, she was wild about Sunday mornings, thrilled each time Bergen parked his car on the corner of Divisadero Street.

"For the last time—no," she said when Bergen once more suggested that he move up to Santa Rosa. "I'm a married woman."

"I can find King," Bergen told her. "I found him before. I found you."

Dina shook her head. "Nothing doing," she told the detective. "Why would I want him found?"

"To divorce him," Bergen answered.

"Hah," Dina said. "Do you think he'd give me a divorce? Do you think he'd give me anything I wanted?"

There were times when Bergen saw Dina through a haze of the past—her face was the face in the photograph he had carried in his pocket for so long; she was the girl who had run away, leaving behind a father who mourned her, running in the night toward desire without ever looking back, just running. But there were other times when Bergen saw Dina the way she really was—her fine hair streaked gray, the lines across her forehead and around her eyes where there was once the apricot flesh of youth, print dresses and hair combs made of tortoise-shell and silver. Whenever he saw her as she really was—when she walked across the kitchen to open the refrigerator and get a carton of milk or when she wrapped a sweater around herself and sat out on the back porch and breathed in the odor of the roses that grew at the edge of the yard, whenever he looked at her and saw a woman of forty-one, Bergen hated King Connors, he hated him more every day. Bergen had forgotten about the touch of time, he blamed King Connors for robbing the girl in the photograph of her youth, and he blamed King for robbing him of that girl.

"I could fix it," Bergen told Dina as they sat side by side on the porch. "I could make him give you a divorce."

"You don't know King. There's nothing you could say."

"Well, then," Bergen said after a time, speaking just loud enough to be heard above the crickets who sang in the vegetable patch, "I could kill him."

Dina didn't laugh the way some women would have, and she didn't doubt for a minute that Bergen meant what he said. She looked at the detective with a new sort of passion; she put her arm around him and felt his heat through both his clothes and her own. "My darling," she said.

She had never called him by anything other than his name, and now Bergen was trembling with courage and fear. "I could, you know," he said stubbornly.

"No," Dina said. "That's impossible. It would be a sin. We'll manage somehow."

"All right," Bergen agreed, though his hands were still sweating and his head was racing with murder plans. "All right," he said to Dina. "We'll manage."

Teresa was asleep upstairs in her room, Silver wouldn't be back until the night was through, and so, even though Bergen had already paid for his room at the Lamplighter Motel, they spent the night together in the bed Dina had shared with King Connors for so many years. Dina was shy, but Bergen was as careful as if he held a photograph instead of a woman. And they were sure to be quiet, quiet enough not to wake Teresa, quiet enough to hear their own breathing as they let their bodies travel backward in time, so that Dina still was a seventeen-year-old girl who had never left Santa Fe and Bergen was a young man with stars in his eyes. At five the next morning, only an hour after Silver got home from a night of fast cars and tequila, Bergen tiptoed down the stairs, got into his car, and drove back to the Lamplighter Motel. And when they next saw each other, five hours later, separated by the kitchen table and the Sunday *Chronicle*, Bergen and Dina acknowledged their night together with a brief smile exchanged so secretly no one would have noticed. And although they would be together from this weekend on, they never spoke about their lovemaking, they treated it like a dream or a slow-moving night film in which they were lovers both in the present and the nonexistent past.

It was not long after that first night Dina and Bergen spent together that King Connors came back to town. He was staying at the Lamplighter Motel, just down the hall from Bergen, although when Bergen left on Sunday afternoon to go back to San Francisco, King Connors stayed on. The two men never met; they wouldn't have recognized each other if they had passed the ice machine at the same time, though Bergen was convinced he would know King anywhere and would be able to spot Dina's husband as easily as he could sight a rattlesnake moving in the tall yellow grass. If Bergen was afraid that King might someday return to claim what was rightfully his—his wife, his house, the garden where Bergen had planted tulips and asparagus, the old detective had nothing to worry about. King Connors wouldn't have come back to stay for any money; a sack of gold coins couldn't make him spend another night with Dina or force him to go back and relive the crime of a sad, shared past.

King Connors wasn't back to stay, he was back only to ease his mind. He had come to make sure that there was still a roof on the house, that his children weren't dressed in rags, and that his wife hadn't wasted away to skin and bones. King had borrowed a car no one would recognize from a lady friend in Los Angeles. He wore a straw hat and a cotton scarf around his neck. If anyone had suddenly spotted him, he would have buried his face in the scarf and sped away in the other direction. He parked on Divisadero Street and studied the house by moonlight: the roof he had put on three years before was still as good as new, no screams came from the upstairs windows, buzzards didn't circle the chimney and cry through beaks of distress. King's guilt about leaving home had been eased once Reuben came to stay. But now Reuben was out on his own—he had an apartment in the Valley and a job rebuilding Volvos—and King wanted to be certain that his younger children were doing as well as his eldest. So when King saw Teresa leave the house to walk to school on a Monday morning, he followed her in the borrowed car; when Teresa stopped at the Texaco station to buy a Coke, King pulled up to the pumps, talked to the attendant, then walked to the soda machine. Teresa hadn't ever expected to see King again, but now when she saw him she wasn't surprised.

"How about going for a ride?" King Connors said, easy as pie, just as if he hadn't been gone for two years.

"All right," Teresa found herself saying. She got into the car and they headed down to the River Road.

"How can you drink a Coke so early in the day?" King Connors said.

"Easy." Teresa shrugged. "It's a matter of taste."

They drove out of town and west, crossed the river and then drove alongside it. Teresa stuck her head out the window and closed her eyes. The scent of the river took over, coating the interior of the car, leaving its damp imprint on Teresa's eyelids, interrupted only by the smell of sulfur when King Connors lit a cigarette and tossed the match out his window.

"That's how forest fires start," Teresa told him.

"Too early in the season," King Connors answered. Then he looked at her hard. "Since when do you tell me what to do?"

Teresa turned away from King, angry that he still felt free to scold her after all this time. She didn't turn to him until they had reached Guerneville, and King pulled over to park.

"Why are we stopping here?" she asked.

"I thought you might need something," King Connors said. "Some clothes for school?"

People from Santa Rosa didn't go shopping in Guerneville unless they had something to hide, unless they were deserters back for only a few hours. "My mother got me everything I need for school," Teresa said primly. "But I could use another Coke," she admitted.

King Connors gave her some money, and Teresa got out of the car.

"Do you know what's going to happen to you if you keep drinking so many sodas?" King Connors called through his open window as Teresa crossed the street to go to the drugstore. "You're going to be struck with stomach complications, that's what will happen."

Teresa kept walking, she opened the drugstore door and went inside; she didn't bother to listen to King Connors's advice, why should she? She pulled a bottle out of the cold case, paid the pharmacist, and went back to the car. They sat there, parked, and because King Connors didn't make a move to drive anywhere else, Teresa settled back and drank her soda. "You still sick?" King asked. "Still have that sleeping disease?"

"It's not too bad," Teresa said. "It's gotten better ever since we went to New Mexico." She looked at King, waiting for his reaction.

"Your goddamn mother," King said. "I know she dragged you all to New Mexico. Reuben told me. He was living with me for a while."

"I know it," Teresa said, annoyed. "He told me all about his plans. He told me everything, even before he did it."

"Oh, yeah?" King said. "And you told your mother?" he guessed. Teresa shot her father a look of disgust. "Of course you didn't," King amended. "I know you. You didn't say a word, kept it all to yourself."

"I was the only one he told," Teresa said proudly.

"He doesn't live with me now," King Connors said. "He's got his own place. Pretty nice, too. I've seen it."

"Silver's dropped out of school," Teresa informed her father.

"Doesn't surprise me," King said.

"And I might leave home." She hadn't the faintest idea what made her say such a thing, she hadn't thought of running away for some time.

"Oh?" King Connors said.

"That's right," Teresa said, caught up in it now. "I might be leaving town real soon."

"Just where do you think you'll be heading?" King asked, and Teresa considered. She thought she might try Oregon, or the East Coast, eventually Canada, the whitest part of Canada where the drifts were up to the rafters. "Because I'll tell you one thing," King said now, before Teresa had had a chance to answer him, "you sure as shit aren't moving in with me. I gave up twenty years, and what good did it do? It didn't make anybody happy. So just forget about it if that's what you had in mind."

Teresa jerked her head up; she closed her lips so tight that a gush of surprise escaped.

"I just don't have room," King Connors said. "It's not that I don't want you—but my place is small as a kennel. Even Reuben understood that."

"I never said I wanted to go with you," Teresa said quickly.

"All right," King said. "All right. So long as we both understand."

"What makes you think I wanted to go with you?" Teresa said. She turned her head and stared out the window, her eyes burned as if someone had held a match to her eyelids.

"Don't take it personally," King said.

Teresa turned and glared at him. "My mother's right—you're not the right one. She should have waited for somebody better to come along."

King Connors nodded and turned the key in the ignition, he made a U turn and headed back to Santa Rosa. Teresa was silent all the way back; as far as she was concerned, they had nothing more to say to each other. But King Connors wouldn't stop talking now, he went on endlessly about his work: he was a truckdriver, delivering lemons from the groves to huge warehouses, his truck always filled with new fruit. Teresa tried not to listen, but she could swear she smelled lemon flowers, she wondered if her father's skin would turn yellow, if bees would follow him wherever he went; she took a deep breath, and nearly sobbed when she exhaled.

Even later, when King stopped the car a block away from the house, he continued to talk about trees: the lemon trees where he worked, the orange trees that grew in the vacant lot behind his apartment building, sweet almond branches that brushed his head each time he walked out his front door. Teresa couldn't understand how a man could talk so much about a thing like trees, and she had never in her life heard her father say so many words all at one time. From that day on, each time she thought about King Connors, Teresa's head would be filled with the same scent of lemons there had been that day they drove to Guerneville; sometimes the fragrance would be so strong she would jump and turn around, certain that King was in the room.

It was late afternoon when King and Teresa sat in the parked car, talking to each other for the last time. King lit a cigarette, Teresa ran the empty Coke bottle beneath her lip and played a soft, shallow tune.

"You keep drinking that stuff and you're going to get poisoning of the stomach," King said, pointing at the soda bottle.

"I'm not afraid of poison." Teresa shrugged

Every time King inhaled on his cigarette, he coughed. They both stared straight ahead, watching dragonflies dart by the windshield.

"I was in love with her," King told his daughter. "It just turned out wrong," he said. "It turned out she thought I was somebody I'm not."

Teresa knew then that if she looked at him she would cry.

"I brought you something from southern California," King told her. He reached over and flipped open the glove compartment. He took out a brown paper bag and handed it to Teresa. Inside were a dozen apricots; they shone like trapped sunlight.

Teresa thanked him and closed up the bag—it seemed darker when she did, and she rattled the bag to make sure the fruit was still inside.

"As far as your mother and Silver are concerned, I wasn't here," King said.

"All right," Teresa agreed. "You weren't here."

"Maybe you'll forget me," King Connors said as he took a last drag on his cigarette. "I know you might. But I've got to save myself, understand? I've got a life, too, you know."

Teresa opened the car door and got out. She walked quickly, her eyes straight ahead; she didn't turn when she heard the car pull away, she didn't even wave. By the time she did look back, King Connors had already disappeared. So she walked on, and as she avoided the cracks in the cement, she took King Connors's name and respelled it a dozen times, until the letters added up to no name at all. By the time she reached home, Teresa was through with her father's name—it had been crossed out just like the name of any deserter. And before she went into the house, Teresa walked to the trashcan and lifted the cover, and when she threw the bag of apricots inside it fell so quickly that it might have been a bag of stones, rather than fruit the color of the sun.

That summer Teresa was sick even more than usual. She didn't want to walk out to the reservoir beyond Cannon's Field to go swimming, she dreaded supermarkets, parks, all public places; she was certain that she would fall into a deep sleep and a crowd would gather around her. And so, Teresa spent most of June and July alone. Dina was busy preparing for her weekends with Bergen, Silver had so many girlfriends he gave them appointments and grief one at a time, and hadn't the energy for anything else. Although Teresa had avoided nearly everyone at school, and didn't give anyone a chance to speak to her, she did have one friend, Maureen, the only daughter of the Raleighs, who lived right next door. On days when Teresa felt safe from her sleeping spells, the two girls sat in the yard; nearby Atlas and Reggie dug holes in the earth and panted with the heat. Teresa and Maureen counted hummingbirds and bees, and regretted being fourteen. At two o'clock, when the ice-cream truck drove along Divisadero Street, they bought raspberry Popsicles, which dripped onto the cement as they walked back home.

"What about sex?" Maureen asked one day.

"What about it?" Teresa asked. She had never mentioned Cosmo to Maureen, she had never confided in her friend, not once. In fact, Teresa had never trusted anyone with her private thoughts, not even Silver. They were stored inside her head, where they swirled about, rattling next to her brain, and those dark thoughts were what Teresa thought privacy was all about.

"Do you know anyone who's ever done it?" Maureen asked. Teresa shook her head; she refused to think of what she had done in the back seat of Cosmo's car as sex. "I bet Silver's done it," Maureen whispered. "I'll bet you anything he has."

"No," Teresa said, but she couldn't help but wonder about Annette in New Mexico, and the dozens of girls who telephoned.

"Ask him," Maureen said, "I'll bet you anything he has."

"Come on," Teresa said, erasing those thoughts of Silver with women who knew secrets about love, "let's go over to your house."

In return for allowing her to sidestep the topic of sex, Teresa let Maureen play the piano for her.

"First," Maureen said, as she sat on the piano bench in the Raleighs' living room, "the title song from the movie *Charade*, starring Cary Grant."

Teresa sat on a bone-colored loveseat and listened to Maureen play. Outside, on the Raleighs' front porch, Atlas whined and nosed the screen door.

"Now," Maureen said, turning to Teresa when she had finished her first number, "the title song from the memorable play, *Oklahoma*."

Atlas whined even louder, he was beginning to howl. Teresa tiptoed over to the door. "Go away," she told the collie. She and Atlas stared at each other. "Can't you be good like Reggie?" she asked him.

Atlas was quiet enough through the rest of the song, and Maureen finished with a flourish of chords. "Well, what do you think?" she asked when she was through.

Teresa walked over to the piano and ran one finger across the keys. She had not liked Maureen's performance—the heavy crashes, the jarring mistakes—but if she herself could play, Teresa imagined a much different sort of music: the sweetest octaves, the most musical chords, light but growing stronger with every note. "I wish I could play," Teresa admitted.

The other girl beamed. "I could teach you," she said. "I've had lessons for nearly five years."

Teresa considered. "I couldn't pay you," she said.

"You could give me your black velvet skirt," Maureen suggested.

As they were about to agree to a deal, Dina ran over from next door and banged on the screen door. "Teresa," she cried. "Get out here."

Teresa ran out to the porch; Dina's hair fell into her eyes, there was blood on her hands. "I've been looking everywhere for you," Dina said.

The piano in the living room no longer mattered, all thoughts of lessons disappeared immediately. Teresa forgot about the music she wanted to make; she stared at the blood on her mother's hands. She feared that Silver had been attacked by a gang of thieves, a knife had been twisted into his heart, or that Bergen had been shot by a convict he had helped send to jail years ago for nonpayment of alimony.

"It's Reggie," Dina said. "Something's wrong with Reggie."

Teresa and Dina ran next door, following a trail of blood, Atlas at their heels. They were out of breath by the time they reached the back porch.

"He's under there," Dina whispered as they both peered beneath the porch. "He won't come out."

"Reggie," Teresa called to the old dog. Atlas sat beside her as she crouched in the dirt; he whined, just as he had on Maureen's porch.

"He won't come out," Teresa told her mother.

Dina went into the house and returned with a clean white sheet. She folded the sheet in half and then signaled to Teresa. "We'll have to pull him out," she told her daughter. "Then we'll put him in this."

It was Teresa who reached under the porch and pulled Reggie out. Atlas shivered and pawed the ground. The other dog had hemorrhaged, and so much blood had poured out that he didn't even whimper when Dina and Teresa put him on top of the sheet. Dina was pale, she ground her teeth. "Old age," she told Teresa. "This is what happens."

Each of them carried an edge of the sheet, with Reggie inside the makeshift hammock. They walked the half mile to the animal hospital, leaving a thin trail of blood on the cement, as if a small bird had stepped in red paint and had then walked over every inch of Divisadero Street. Dina held the sheet with her arms behind her, she faced straight ahead. Once she turned and called to Teresa, "If he doesn't die, we'll have to have him killed."

"No," Teresa said.

"Put to sleep," Dina amended. They walked as quickly as Reggie's weight would allow. "They call it 'put to sleep,' and believe me they don't do it for free."

"We won't do it," Teresa insisted.

"It's all suffering anyway," Dina called over her shoulder. "That's what life is."

Atlas waited on the steps of the animal hospital when they went in. But here was no hope: Reggie was thirteen, almost as old as Teresa, and he had died while they were carrying him down the street. On the walk home, the collie stayed nearly half a block behind them; Dina walked in military fashion, her mouth set.

"That's life," she reminded Teresa.

It had been a summer of loss, a year of departures. And now Teresa stared at the cement as she walked home; she concentrated on not thinking about King Connors, and Renée, and the old dog they had just carried to the animal hospital. When they got home, Dina went inside to cook dinner, just as if she hadn't carried a sheet permanently stained with blood. But Teresa stayed outside in the yard. As Dina opened the refrigerator and reached for a package of chopped meat, Teresa slipped under the porch. She tried to get the collie to come and sit with her; she clicked her tongue and patted the ground, but Atlas turned away and stretched beneath the eucalyptus trees.

Under the porch it was damp and dark; the roots of the wisteria that hung above the doorway were woven through the earth. Teresa leaned her head against the cool dirt and closed her eyes. If she tried she could imagine that she was floating on the curls of music—she was better than any pianist, she was a musician in her mind, she moved with arpeggios, she flew higher with every chord.

When they found her, the following morning, Teresa's knees were pulled up and there were spider webs in her hair. Dina had searched the house the night before, Silver had borrowed a car and driven through the neighborhood calling her name.

"I'm going to kill her," Silver said as he and Dina bent down to watch Teresa sleep under the porch.

"Let her sleep," Dina whispered.

"I've been up all night looking for her," Silver said. "I'm going to break her neck."

Teresa shifted positions; her hair caught on a stem of wisteria root; she dreamed of moonlight and low octaves.

"Shit," Silver said. When he stood up, he noticed dried blood on his hand where he had leaned on the earth.

"Reggie," Dina nodded at the blood.

"Fucking dog," Silver said as he wiped the blood off on his pressed blue jeans.

They pulled Teresa out and Silver carried her upstairs to her own room. She didn't wake up, she had no sense of being carried, and when she woke she wouldn't remember being put in her own bed, between fresh sheets in a room where the shades were drawn and the darkness was nearly as thick as it had been beneath the back porch.

Lately there were times when Silver envied Teresa's

sleeping sickness, there were days when he wished he
didn't have to wake up. Every day was the same for
him; he walked over to Leona's Restaurant to clean last
night's dinner off white china plates, he stood over a sink
of steaming hot water and grease. Even the nights and the
weekends seemed pointless; getting drunk, getting laid,
driving in a friend's car at ninety miles an hour—all
of it seemed tame as toast, and so repetitive that Silver
could walk through every scene with his eyes closed. It
was the time in his life when Silver first realized that
everything he had always wished for just might not materi-
alize. A year earlier he had dreamed of freedom as he
walked out of the corridors of the high school for the last
time. He wanted a car, money in his pockets, his choice
of a dozen girls, all hot for him, all ready to open their legs
in the back seat of his fancy car. But as it turned out there
was no car, and no money, though he still had women—
blondes who had eyed him in school waited for him by
the kitchen door of Leona's, waitresses who were nearly
Dina's age slipped him their phone numbers. But none of
these women mattered, none could erase the fact that his
hands were scarred from burning dishwater, that he lived
with the cold humiliation of having lost something he had
never had.

Silver drank more than before; when he went out with
friends—many of them still in high school, concerned
with things Silver had long ago disregarded—Silver was
always the biggest drinker. He stuck to tequila, liquor
as mysterious as he imagined himself to be. He longed
for prairies; he would ride a wild horse like the ones
the men Dina called Arias rode; his hair would grow as
long and tangled as weeds. He wanted polished turquoise
and women in white and instead he got dishwater and
telephone numbers scrawled on the backs of matchbooks.
At the age of seventeen he was bitter—he wanted to make
a killing, to take some chances. He felt himself drawn to
something hotter than his own life, something that would

make the Santa Rosa sidewalks sizzle, something in the area of crime.

Slowly, Silver began to avoid his old friends. Some nights he went downtown alone, to the poolhall on Sixteenth Street, or a bar called the Dragon. He studied men older than himself—men with tattoos, with pasts in prison or on the road. He bought a knife with an ivory handle, and eavesdropped on the conversations of drug dealers. He was convinced that sooner or later he would hit a winning streak, it was all a question of timing, just a matter of time.

The first crime was nothing much—anyone with too little money and a little fire would have done the same. Silver enlisted two old friends, Eddie and Roland; together they managed to steal nearly two hundred dollars from the cash register at the Texaco station while the attendant wasn't looking.

"Kid stuff," Angel Gregory said to Silver at the bar of the Dragon when Silver boasted about the heist.

"Oh yeah?" Silver said to the older man. He reached into his pocket for a roll of bills and showed them to Gregory. "What do you call this?"

Gregory smiled and reached for his own billfold. Inside a diamond-studded money clip were fifties and hundreds; even Silver was impressed. "Let me know when you're ready for the big time," Gregory said. "Call me when you quit horsing around."

Silver knew that Gregory earned his money in drug deals—at least once a month Gregory traveled to San Francisco and brought back cocaine and marijuana.

"You mean you're looking for a partner?" Silver asked that night at the bar.

"Partner?" Gregory said. "Shit, I'm looking for a runner. Someone to make trips into the city for me."

Silver turned down the offer right then; he was no one's errand boy. And he wasn't too certain how he felt about dealing in drugs; if he worked out of the house the old detective, Bergen, would be nosing around. And anyway, Silver had plans of his own—with the profits from the first job he bought a gun from Jim, the old dishwasher at Leona's who had served time in Vacaville for armed robbery.

"You sure you know how to work it?" the dishwasher asked when they stood out in the alley behind the restaurant.

Silver was jumpy, but he stuck the gun in the waist of his jeans as if he had carried it all his life. "Sure," he said. "I know how to work it."

"Got the safety catch on?" Jim teased.

Silver quickly reached for the gun and checked it. "Of course I've got the catch on," he said.

"Takes practice," Jim said before they walked back into the kitchen. "A life of crime takes practice and hard work. But I think you've got what it takes," he said, patting Silver's shoulder. "All you've got to do is practice."

After Silver left the restaurant that night he strode home like an Apache, invincible and dark, he was an outlaw of seventeen who planned to knock over the Denny's Restaurant just outside town. That same week, late one night, when the horizon was pale blue and crimson, the three old friends pulled into Denny's parking lot in an Oldsmobile borrowed from Roland's brother-in-law. Roland stayed in the car, the gears set; he watched as Eddie and Silver got out and walked into the brightly lit restaurant. Inside, two truckdrivers on an all-night run to Eureka sat at the counter eating bacon and eggs. The waitress curled a strand of blond hair around her finger and leaned her elbows on the countertop. Silver and Eddie sat on the stools nearest the cash register; they ordered coffee, black, and didn't even bother to give the waitress a smile. They waited for the truckdrivers to finish their late-night breakfast, pay, and leave. When the truck pulled out of the parking lot, shivers ran down Silver's spine. But he was under control;

he finished his coffee and then told Eddie to pay.

Eddie stood next to the waitress as she rang up their bill; when the drawer of the register flew open, Eddie shot Silver a worried look and waited for Silver's okay. Silver nodded and stood up; he hid the register from the view of any passing car on the road. "Go ahead," he told Eddie.

"Give us everything you've got," Eddie told the waitress.

"Gladly," the waitress said, and she winked.

"The money," Silver said roughly. He took out the gun and pointed it at her. "All of it."

"Shit," the waitress said, and she loaded the paper bag Eddie handed her with bills. "I'm going to get fired," she told Silver.

"So what?" Silver shrugged. "What the hell do you care about a crappy job like this for?"

Eddie put the bag full of money into his pocket and edged toward the door.

"You just forget you ever saw us," Silver told the waitress. He waved the gun in the air and then returned it to the waistband of his jeans. "If you remember us well enough to describe us, I'll remember you. And I'll come back for you," Silver warned. He turned and walked out of Denny's; Eddie was waiting outside the front door.

"Come on," Silver said, walking on to the car. Silver sat in the passenger seat. Eddie got into the back; he waved the paper bag in the air.

"We did it!" Eddie cried as Roland stepped on the gas and the Oldsmobile tore out of the parking lot.

Even though he was silent as he leaned against the upholstery, in his mind Silver was disagreeing: he knew better than Eddie. He alone had done it, and victory ran through his blood and made him dizzy.

They stopped at a liquor store on Sixteenth Street and bought tequila, whiskey, and cigarettes. Then they drove out of town, having decided it was best to keep a low profile until the waitress had called the station house and notified the police. It was nearly six in the morning when they reached Cannon's Field. The grass was high, and they parked the borrowed car beneath the shadows of pines. Silver knew Cannon's Field as well as anyone; he and Reuben and Teresa had spent hours there when they were younger, they had swum in the reservoir nearly every day, they had explored every inch of dust and weeds.

"No one will look for us here," Silver told his friends. He got out of the car and opened the bottle of tequila and breathed so deeply he thought his lungs would burst. The river was less than five miles away from Cannon's Field, and a mist rose everywhere. Silver took off his shirt and laid it down before he sat on the earth.

"We're rich," Roland said as he came over. He flopped down and opened the whiskey.

"Rich?" Silver said as he divided the money into three piles. There was a hundred and twenty dollars apiece. "This is nothing compared to what we can do."

"What do you have in mind?" Roland asked.

"A Seven-Eleven store," Silver told him.

Roland shook his head. He had been nervous from the start; if he had had to do any more than sit in the car he would have backed down. "I don't know if I can get the car again," he said uneasily.

"You can get it," Silver assured him.

"I don't know," Roland said. "My brother-in-law's not an easy touch. And if we ever got caught and he found out what I used the car for, he'd kill me."

"We won't get caught," Silver said. He held up the tequila bottle to the rising sun and squinted.

"I don't know," Roland said. "People get caught all the time."

"He's right," Eddie said. He put his share of the cash in his pocket. "We should lie low for a while."

Silver took out the gun and ran his finger over the

barrel. "You're scared," he said to Eddie and Roland.

"Shit," Eddie said. "Scared?"

"You've got to have three guys for a stickup," Silver went on. "Maybe two, but it wouldn't be easy." Silver had learned all his secrets of crime in the dark in movie theaters and in bars. All his plans had been made a hundred times before, by small-time punks who stood around the bar of the Dragon, by Hollywood heroes and thugs. Silver's plans were those of imagined Indians, men who attacked in the night to round up the wagon trains before they collected diamonds and cash. "I'll tell you one thing," Silver said to his friends, "if you two are scared, there are plenty of ways for one man to get money. There are plenty of things I can do alone."

While Silver was drinking tequila with his friends in Cannon's Field, Teresa was getting dressed. She went downstairs, made a pot of coffee and drank one cup, leaving the rest behind for Dina. It was Saturday and there wasn't a cloud in the sky. When she left the house at eight the air was still cool with a breeze from the west. Soon, Bergen would arrive from San Francisco with a truckful of slate. He and Dina planned to build a border around the garden; if Teresa was home they would enlist her aid, if she was gone they wouldn't even miss her. So she made sure to leave early that day; she wore a bathing suit under her clothes; Atlas followed right behind her. Hawks had begun to circle over the foothills by the time Teresa closed the front door and began walking toward Cannon's Field.

Before long the day would be hot, at least a hundred degrees. After an hour of walking, Teresa felt limp; she would have taken off her shoes and walked barefoot if the asphalt hadn't already started to burn. And later, when she had reached the outskirts of town, she still kept her shoes on; the fields were dry and harsh, the burs that stuck in the collie's coat would have just as easily pierced the soles of Teresa's feet.

The river was too far to walk to, and on hot summer days it was crowded with swimmers and canoes. The reservoir in Cannon's Field was the best place to be alone, the perfect place to swim. Even when she reached the pine woods that separated the road from Cannon's Field, Teresa never thought anyone else might be there in the field. She walked where the grass was tall, where wildflowers whose scent reminded her of New Mexico grew. When she was fifty yards away, no farther than the hawks in the sky, Teresa noticed a car hidden in the woods. She looked at it, surprised, then squinted and turned to the open field as if searching for poachers.

She didn't even see the other two—at least not right away. All she saw was Silver, Silver sitting cross-legged beneath a California oak, raising a bottle of tequila to his lips, resting on the clean white shirt he had tossed on the ground.

For some reason Teresa didn't smile or call out; she didn't keep on walking, right past them and on to the reservoir. She knelt down, low to the ground, she hid in the tall grass and watched as heat waves began to rise in the field. She held on to Atlas's collar and made him lie down next to her. The two of them stayed there, not moving an inch, and a breeze so hot it did no good at all moved just above their head.

Out in the field Eddie, Silver, and Roland were drunk. The tequila and whiskey had mixed with last night's fear and this morning's courage to make their heads spin. Silver had nearly finished the bottle of tequila, Eddie rolled a joint.

"It's too bad," Silver was saying as Eddie passed him the joint, "that we didn't get enough money so I could get a car. With a car I could do anything."

"Can't have everything," Eddie shrugged.

"Oh, no?" Silver smiled. "I'm going to have everything. Every goddamned thing I want."

Fifty yards away, in the shade, Teresa wondered
where Silver had been all night. When he didn't come
home the house seemed much too empty, the floorboards
echoed, the crickets spun like sirens till morning. Watching him from this distance, Teresa could understand why
women always looked at Silver. Beside him, Roland and
Eddie were invisible. As she watched them drink whiskey and tequila, Teresa was suddenly thirsty. She ran
her tongue over her lips and wished for cold lemonade, gallons of ice water, cold raspberry sherbet. And
then suddenly they stopped drinking—all three of them
looked in the same direction, and Teresa could feel their
eyes over the field, through the heat. All three of them
jumped up, and then, for a moment, they stood where they
were. Nothing moved, even the sky seemed frozen, and,
beside Teresa, Atlas was perfectly still. The only thing that
moved was inside Teresa. Her breathing was raspy and it
hurt, everything hurt—the sun, the rough grass, her cotton
dress, the shoulder straps of her bathing suit.

And it seemed that before Teresa even saw them start
to run they were right in front of her. Maybe she had been
closer than fifty yards away, because before one breath
became another there they were. Atlas got out of her
grip and ran over to them, barking, curling his lip over
his teeth until he recognized Silver. Silver was standing
closest to Teresa—the gun was pointed at her head. He
had run to that spot knowing that someone was hiding,
someone had been watching them. And the tequila had
boiled over inside him. Before, during the robbery, he had
not known if he could really kill someone. Now he knew
that he could. With the right amount of alcohol, with the
right amount of fear, he could easily pull the trigger. Even
when he saw that it was only Teresa hidden in the grass,
Silver's pulse didn't calm down. He stood over Teresa,
certain that he had missed murder by seconds. In that
instant Silver discovered how easy it would be for him

to kill someone. Outwardly he looked no different, but inside his blood was wild.

"What the hell do you think you're doing?" Roland said to Teresa.

"She's eavesdropping," Eddie said. "Isn't that right?" he asked her.

Teresa wondered if she could run faster than any of them. Eddie and Roland staggered, and she had always been a fast runner. She could fly all the way home. But now her legs no longer felt like her own, and she wasn't certain she'd be able to stand.

"I know just what you came here for," Eddie said now. He sat down next to her. "I've seen you staring at me. I know you like me."

Eddie put his hand on her, and beneath his fingers Teresa's skin flushed with heat.

"I was going swimming," she explained. "I didn't even know you were here."

"Sure," Eddie said. He leaned even closer. "Come on." He nodded to the woods beyond the field. "After I get through with you, you're gonna mark this day down in your diary."

When Silver put his finger on the trigger to release the safety catch the sound was like thunder. That one click made them all turn to see that the gun was pointed straight at Eddie's heart.

"Don't move another inch," Silver said. "Don't touch my sister."

Eddie threw back his head and laughed. The collie stood close to Silver and whined softly, pawed the ground and shivered.

"Don't tell me what to do," Eddie said. "You're not the boss of this outfit. Who made you the fucking boss?"

"Face it," Silver said. "Last night would never have happened if I hadn't planned every move. You're a loser," he told Eddie. "What more can I say?"

"What do you mean by that?" Eddie demanded. "What

the hell do you mean I'm a loser?"

"Forget it," Roland said. "Why don't you two quit arguing?"

"What do you have against me?" Eddie asked Silver. "I'm not good enough for your sister, is that it?"

"That's right," Silver said. "You're not good enough."

"Maybe Teresa doesn't agree with you," Eddie said. He reached and ran one finger along her cheek. "You're pretty," he told her. "You really are."

Silver fired and the sound exploded above them. If Eddie hadn't moved to embrace Teresa the bullet would have gone right through his chest.

"Jesus Christ," Eddie whispered. The bullet had lodged in the pine tree directly behind him.

"What the hell is going on here?" Roland said. "We're all supposed to be friends."

Silver ignored Eddie and Roland. He reached out and helped Teresa to her feet. "Let's go," he told her. "You wanted to go swimming and that's exactly what you're going to do."

Teresa brushed off her dress, then waited for Silver to retrieve the bottle of tequila. She felt breathless, she wondered if her pulse would burst through her skin. Like an outlaw from the hills, Silver had rescued her; and now she followed him across the field, toward the woods and the reservoir. She would have followed him across the desert, she wouldn't have complained about lizards or dust.

"I'm not going to forget this," Eddie called after them.

"Leave him alone," Roland warned, putting his arm across Eddie's shoulders.

"I'm not going to fucking forget this," Eddie cried.

Silver turned and stopped in his tracks. "I'm finished with both of you," he said. "If I ever see either of you, if you ever bother my sister, I'll kill you. Understand?"

Eddie and Roland watched as Silver led his sister toward the reservoir. When they could no longer see Teresa's shadow, Eddie turned to Roland and whispered, low so that Silver wouldn't have a ghost's chance of hearing, "I think he really means it."

As they walked, Silver's boots left an imprint in the earth, tequila spilled from the bottle he held by the neck. They walked in a single line—first the dog, then Silver, then Teresa. Teresa watched Silver's bare back; he carried his shirt draped over his left shoulder like a cape, the revolver was tucked into the waist of his jeans.

"Where did you get the gun?" Teresa asked.

Silver stopped and turned around. "Did you ever smoke marijuana?" he asked. When Teresa shook her head no, Silver reached into his pocket for a joint, lit it, and passed it to Teresa. The smoke made Teresa dizzy, but she didn't complain. She inhaled, but then let all the smoke escape.

"Not like that," Silver said. "Keep all the smoke in," he advised. "Otherwise you waste it."

Teresa inhaled again and kept as much smoke as she could inside her lungs.

"Better," Silver said. "Much better."

They walked on; it was hotter and hotter, and Teresa's clothes itched, her head was light.

"Don't concern yourself with where I got the gun," Silver said now. "It's something I've got to have. Believe me, I don't like it this way, but I'm sure as hell not going to be poor forever. And let me tell you something, when I'm rich you won't find me in Santa Rosa."

"Are you going to Los Angeles?" Teresa asked, imagining a house without Silver, another deserter hidden in the orchards of southern California.

"Los Angeles?" Silver said. "Shit. You wouldn't catch me in Los Angeles. Do you think I'm a loser like Reuben? You think I'd waste my time looking for King?"

They finally reached a clearing close to the reservoir; near the green water, lilies grew like weeds, dragonflies buzzed. Silver sat with his back against a pine tree.

"Come over here," he said.

Teresa stood right where she was. Atlas had gone off to the banks of the reservoir and was chasing mosquitoes, his jaws snapping each time he caught a bug. Silver raised the bottle and finished the tequila, then let the bottle roll into a ditch.

"Come on," Silver said. He touched the ground next to him. "I'm not going to hurt you or anything."

When she went to sit beside Silver, Teresa was afraid, though she wasn't quite certain why. I could run, Teresa thought to herself. He's drunk and if I didn't want to be here I could run like lightning.

"Closer," Silver said now. His voice didn't sound familiar, his words were slurred and soft, and he looked as he had that night in New Mexico when Teresa saw him in the café. His arms had been around Annette's waist exactly the way they now encircled Teresa. When Silver put his mouth on hers he tasted like bitter liquor, like too sweet smoke. He kept his mouth pressed against hers for such a long time that soon Teresa felt she was smothering.

"You've done this before, haven't you?" Silver asked, but then he shook his head. "Don't tell me," he whispered. "I don't want to know what you've done before."

He kissed her again. Teresa felt as if she were losing herself, drowning by inches. Silver was drunk and seemed to be getting drunker with every kiss. His breathing was the same as she heard every night on the other side of the bedroom wall, his arms were the ones she had always wanted to hold her. Quite suddenly it was easy for Teresa, she listened to the sound of the mosquitoes moving just above the cool water, she closed her eyes.

"No one will know," Silver promised.

Teresa took off her dress; they were so close there was really no difference between her skin and his. Still, Teresa couldn't help but wonder if it was really Silver who held her, if it was really his face so close to her own. She stopped herself from thinking, she concentrated on the smell of the grass, on the turning of a hawk's wings overhead, miles above the reservoir.

"No one will know," Silver repeated, and Teresa shivered and watched him push down the shoulder straps of her bathing suit as if those straps belonged to someone else. They moved with the same rhythm, just as if they planned it, as if this hour had always been planned, right from the start. Every one of his kisses was thick, dizzying, crazy as a drug. Once, when he turned his head away from her, Teresa found Silver's mouth with her tongue, she held him as if she and not Silver had led the way to the reservoir, as if the whole thing had been her idea. And after that, how could she stop him? After kissing him how could she say no when he pulled down her bathing suit and unzipped his jeans? When his penis was first inside her Teresa put her hand in her mouth and bit down until she broke the skin; the pain was nothing more than following him into the desert, following him anywhere he wanted to go. And when he held her so tightly she thought all of her breath would be driven out, when he moved faster and faster, Teresa wouldn't have thought of telling him no, she knew it was too late for that when she first sat next to him, there were no excuses—she hadn't had one drink, and the marijuana had all escaped. She wanted to be there, and she didn't want to be there, and finally she just stopped thinking.

Once, when he was still inside her, Teresa opened her eyes—Silver's eyes were open, too, and they looked like Teresa's own, a dark mirror, the eyes of a twin. After Silver had kissed her one last time and had fallen asleep, the deep sleep of liquor and a night of robbery, Teresa still did not run. She didn't move until she was certain Silver wouldn't wake, then she slipped out of his arms, took her clothes, and walked down to the reservoir. She left her bathing suit and her dress on the bank and walked into the water. The line of blood on her thighs disappeared, the water surrounded her, tadpoles swam through her toes. The collie ran along the banks, following Teresa as she swam. She counted each stroke as she cut across the water, she counted until she was breathless and weak and her legs were shaking. When she had swum for such a long time that her arms hurt, Teresa looked over at the clearing and saw that Silver was sitting up. She got out of the water and dressed; she combed her hair with her fingers and quickly braided it. By the time Silver walked over to her, Teresa looked just as she had when he had first seen her hiding in the tall grass; only now her hair was wet, green beads dripped onto her shoulders and ran down her dress.

Silver shaded his eyes from the sun with his hand, he studied Teresa as if she were a stranger. He put on his shirt and buttoned it; he lit a cigarette and inhaled, but the smoke didn't disguise the scent of roses left behind on his skin. "Let's go," he told her. "Hurry up," he whispered. "Get that fucking dog and let's go."

They walked back the way they had come, and even though her skin was still filmy with reservoir water, Teresa felt burning hot. They cut through the tall grass and then stood by the side of the road to hitch a ride. Each time a car or truck passed by, Silver stuck out his thumb. To look at him, to stare straight into his eyes, no one would have guessed anything had happened, no one would have thought that these two standing by the road had moved like lovers just a little while before. They were two hitchhikers: a young man who wore a white shirt and scowled beneath the heat of the midday sun, a girl with dark hair who looked lost.

A half hour later no one had yet stopped for them. "Jesus Christ," Silver said. "Let's start walking."

They walked in single file by the edge of the road for nearly a mile, and finally, a station wagon stopped. Teresa and the collie got into the back, Silver sat in front.

The driver switched on the radio—loud—and, aside from the voice of the disc jockey, they were silent all the way into town. Teresa and Silver were let off on Divisadero Street, three blocks down from their own house. Silver held the door open for Teresa, Atlas jumped out and shook himself, then Silver slammed the door of the station wagon shut, and he started walking.

"I want you to understand something," Silver said when they were only a block away from home. They stood on a street corner. He twisted his knuckles, and they cracked, one at a time. "Nothing happened back there, understand?"

Teresa nodded her head yes.

"I was drunk," Silver told her.

That night there would be no stars, that night would be so hot everyone in town would sleep on rumpled sheets, wrinkled with sleeplessness. Through the bedroom wall, in the very next room, Silver would toss and turn, and Teresa would hear his every move, as she always did. But now, out in the sunlight, Teresa swallowed and turned to avoid Silver's eyes. She hadn't been drunk, she could have run, could have gotten away, moving faster than mosquitoes over the river, traveling on wings that were invisible with speed.

"When you go inside just act like nothing happened," Silver warned her.

"All right," Teresa agreed. "All right," she whispered.

"Good," Silver said. He breathed easier. He patted her head. "I knew I could trust you," he said. "I knew you'd keep your mouth shut. And anyway," Silver told her as they began to walk once more, "it's not as if anything really happened. Nothing did."

As they walked up the porch steps Teresa thought about the turning of the hawk's wings, she remembered the smell of dry grass and the depth of the jade-colored water that swallowed her up as she swam in circles. If she tried, she knew she'd be able to forget: everything could be erased, every memory wiped away by unmoving, unforgiving air. And by the time they had walked into the house, and the screen door had slammed behind them, what had really happened between them was already disappearing. Soon, Teresa wouldn't remember anything more than a brief kiss in the shadows on a day where everywhere else it was summer, and more than a hundred degrees.

CHAPTER
THREE

+

THAT SUMMER ENDED WITH A GOOD CROP OF TOMATOES
and yellow squash, it ended with a rash of fires up in the
hills where the grass was golden and parched. Teresa was
ill in late summer, she had one spell after another. If she
could have she would have slept forever, she wished for
a constant stretch of deep blue sleep, she wanted to avoid
the high temperatures, the August butterflies, the look on
Silver's face each time she passed him on the staircase
landing.

"What's wrong with you?" Dina asked her daughter. "You're always hiding in your room, you never talk to anyone. Are you antisocial? Are you sick?"

"It's nothing," Teresa insisted. "I just want to be by myself."

"Oh, of course," Dina teased. "You're such good company."

"Leave her alone," Bergen advised Dina. "Being fourteen years old is no picnic."

"I survived it," Dina shrugged. "Everyone does."

Up in her room, Teresa tried to clear her mind. She wanted desperately not to think—but it was no use. In spite of herself, she found she was going back into the past more and more every day. She sometimes found herself thinking about King Connors. If she strained she could almost hear him, out in the driveway at work on his truck before the sun had risen, then driving away while the morning was still bitter and dark. Up in her room Teresa found it wasn't so easy to forget. Late at night she heard Silver open his bedroom window and let the midnight air inside, she felt every step when he paced the floor. So when her sleeping spells came Teresa wasn't afraid—she wished for them, she wanted them, she couldn't think of any better escape route out of her room and into the night.

But she was lonely, there was no way around that, and so when Maureen from next door suggested that they start a babysitting service, Teresa quickly agreed. Anything was better than thinking about the past or listening for Silver to come home late at night. Teresa worked every weekend, every night she could. She sat in other people's houses, she kept the children up long past their bedtime, grateful for their company and the distraction of card games and bottles and tears. Maureen and Teresa pooled their earnings; in a month they had nearly a hundred dollars saved. It was just as well that Teresa had a job, because there was no longer any money left in King

Connors and Dina's savings account, and if Teresa wanted anything extra—a new blouse or a paperback book—she had to dip into the babysitting money, carefully noting her withdrawal in the blue notebook Maureen kept in her desk drawer.

It happened so quickly that Dina was taken by surprise one Monday in October—she had no money, not a cent. And when the payments could no longer be made on the house, and mortgage and tax bills filled a brown wicker basket, Arnie Bergen bought the house on Divisadero Street. The detective handed the deed to the house over to Dina the minute he had it, and to everyone's amazement Dina didn't put up a fight, she didn't tell Bergen to mind his own business, she didn't rip up the deed and throw herself on the mercy of the First National Bank. Instead, she kissed Bergen's cheek, folded the deed into a coffee can, and then hid the can in the back of the kitchen cupboard. There was no reason Bergen shouldn't buy the house, Dina explained to Teresa: he had money saved and few expenses, it was a good investment and he was a dear friend, a godsend. Teresa thanked Bergen by baking him a chocolate cake, which, in spite of his high blood sugar, he ate and proclaimed the best he had ever tasted. When he got into his car to drive back home to San Francisco at the end of the weekend, Bergen found a violet-colored envelope on his dashboard. Inside was a thank-you card with Dina's signature scrawled in pale ink, ink that rose off the paper and surrounded Bergen with gratitude.

Now that the house no longer belonged to him, everyone thought about King Connors. If he came back the house would look just the same to him. A mirage of plywood, a roof he had tarred only a few years ago, an oak banister he had restored with paint remover and steel wool, the stain of dark oil out in the driveway. But it was too late, and everyone knew it—King would never come back to Divisadero Street. How could he take off his workshirt and go to the refrigerator for a beer when

Bergen owned everything, even owned the yard where King Connors had always wanted to plant lemon trees, side by side, close to the house, so that the scent of early lemon flowers would wrap around the back porch. Bergen's name was on the deed now, even though Dina was the only one who knew where the deed was stored. Silver resented living in another man's house. If Silver was rarely home before, he was home even less now— on weekends, Teresa and Dina knew he wouldn't come back at all, he wouldn't set foot in the house until Arnie Bergen had driven back to San Francisco.

It was easy for Silver to escape on weekends; he had finally bought a car, a blue Chevy with white leather seats. He was no longer concerned with weekday schedules, with dirty dishes and back doors. He had quit his job at Leona's Restaurant; he possessed a new sense of time, one that had nothing to do with a time clock. On weekdays, when Teresa went to school, Silver didn't get home until dawn. He would sleep till afternoon, then at two or three he would wake and dress in one of the pairs of blue jeans he insisted Dina iron. After coffee and breakfast, Silver would leave the house and drive downtown to the Dragon. There he would meet Angel Gregory.

Silver had become a runner for Gregory; he drove all night to Oakland or south San Francisco to pick up packages wrapped in brown paper and tied with string, he sat on the last stool in Mission Street bars, one eye watching the door, just making certain that a midnight raid wouldn't keep him from driving back to Santa Rosa and delivering the merchandise to Gregory. When it came down to cutting and selling the dope, Silver was only a bystander, a mere messenger. Silver made the connections, but Gregory owned the connections, and the most important one was a man called Vallais. The big money belonged to Gregory, but Silver brought home two hundred dollars a week, enough to buy the Chevy, enough to satisfy him for the moment, but just for the moment—before long Silver was certain he'd be able to trade in his Chevy for something worthwhile, he'd drive to San Francisco in a brand new sports car, the metal would glow as he drove across the Golden Gate Bridge in the moonlight, every window open, every bit of starlight shining on his face.

True, at the beginning of the summer Silver had sworn he would never work for Gregory, but it was better than working at Leona's and far better than dealing with punks like Eddie and Roland. Besides, Silver didn't plan to be a runner forever, he planned to be the boss.

"Where do you go?" Dina asked one day when Silver came down to the kitchen for coffee. It was nearly four in the afternoon. "Where are you every night?" Dina said as she placed a cup and saucer in front of her son.

"I have another life," Silver smiled. "A secret life," he told Dina. "In the daytime I'm only a poor boy, ah but at night . . ."

"At night?" Dina asked.

Silver walked to his mother and stood very near. "A millionaire," he whispered.

Heat spiraled around Silver, as if something was burning under his skin. Dina pushed him away. "A millionaire? Then how about paying some of our bills?"

Silver went back to the table and picked up his coffee cup. "Why should I?" he said. "You've got Bergen for that."

"Arnie Bergen doesn't pay my bills," Dina said.

"All right," Silver shrugged. "If that's what you say."

"If you think something is going on between me and Arnie you're wrong."

"Don't give me any of that crap," Silver said. "Who do you think you're kidding? Not that I care. It's your life."

Dina went to the back door and kicked it open with her foot. She was embarrassed to admit that she was indeed involved with a man her son didn't approve of. "Get out," she told Silver.

"Oh come on," Silver said. "You don't want me to go."

"I mean it." Dina's mouth was tight, but as soon as she began to imagine a house without Silver, a house without that smell of fire, she regretted kicking open the door.

"You're not serious," Silver told his mother. He finished his coffee and left the cup on the drainboard near the sink. "What would you do without me?" he asked as he picked up his car keys from the counter. "After all," he told Dina as he walked out the door, "I'm your favorite."

It was true that he was her favorite. If it had been Silver and not Reuben who had jumped off the train in Los Angeles, Dina would have cried herself to sleep for months, she would have lit candles on the anniversary of that day every year for the rest of her life. It was not that Silver resembled anyone, though he had the same dark eyes as Dina's father and King Connors's long legs—it was because he was so much himself that Dina loved him more than her other children. She would have sacrificed the others to save Silver in a minute, and every time she looked at him she was sure he was the perfect stranger that she had known forever.

Dina had always heard about men like Silver, he was just like those outlaws her own father had called Arias— his name for the men who appeared out of nowhere, who rode white horses across the mesas with no particular destination other than red deserts, the cool waterholes, the streams that had cut their way through miles of black rocks. These Arias weren't lost men, Dina's father had made that very clear. They were riders who knew the way back to the cities they had come from; they knew the way home, to places as far away as Virginia and New York, as distant as Spain. But they never turned back, never went home, they were always traveling west, always moving toward the sun.

Dina's father was a settled man, he knew he would live to see each rosebush he planted flower and bloom. He owned a building-supply store that had been his father's before him. He never complained, never threatened to run off to another life. Still, he had an eye turned toward the hills, and when Dina was a child she and her father took nightly walks. They left Dina's mother at home and walked so far that they could no longer see any houses.

"Ghosts," Dina would whisper when they heard a noise from far away, a sound that might easily have been a branch breaking or the first hint of thunder.

"An Aria," Dina's father would tell her. "A man who travels at night."

In time, Dina discovered how her father knew about such men. When he was a boy, Dina's father had run away from home. He left in the middle of the night wearing heavy boots and carrying a leather pack filled with fruit and bread. He had gone off to the hills, to the place called the Black Mesa, where the rocks were moon-colored and cold. There had been an argument at home—the boy's father sometimes spoke more harshly than he felt and the argument had been petty, about something as stupid as clothes not hung in a closet, chickens not fed. All the same, Dina's father was a boy with a sense of honor; he headed toward the hills and stayed away without any thoughts of returning home. He wandered for three days, but on the fourth his food ran out, suddenly his boots didn't feel warm enough, he seemed much too far from home. And then one evening, soon after dusk, Dina's father met up with an Aria, a man who appeared on horseback, riding out of the east.

The rider carried thick saddlebags and wore a belt studded with turquoise. When he stepped off his horse he didn't have a shadow, and Dina's father found himself wishing that his own father was by his side.

"If you're lost, you don't belong out here," the Aria said, and Dina's father had to agree that he didn't. "As long as you know that," the Aria told the boy, "as long as you know you belong at home."

The Aria shared his dinner with the boy. The moon had risen and a great hawk circled the sky while the Aria wolfed down his food and then cleaned his pots with black sand. Dina's father noticed that his companion wore a silver gun, a pistol. Every star was brilliant, ten times its usual size.

That night the boy couldn't sleep. He imagined wolves and bears and untamed horses with diamonds set into their hoofs. At dawn the Aria lifted Dina's father onto his horse to take him back to Santa Fe. Every moment propelled the boy backward in time; he kept a watch for coyotes, he held on tight to a man who was so comfortable on horseback it seemed he had ridden across the mesa forever.

As they rode, sand flew into the boy's eyes; all the same, they got to Santa Fe much too quickly. The rider left him on the edge of the city, outside a bakery. They had barely spoken to each other, but when the Aria turned and rode off, leaving him on a street where cinnamon and cloves fell onto the sidewalk in dusty patches, Dina's father felt as though his heart was breaking. He would have given anything to be in the Aria's boots, or just to have followed behind, riding a pony who knew every command from a simple nod or the click of his tongue. But the Aria had guessed the truth right away—Dina's father didn't belong out there—he was a city boy who hadn't the nerve for black nights and even blacker desires.

No matter how hard he tried, Dina's father couldn't forget that rider, and on nights when there was thunder, when it seemed that wild horses ran across the mesas, Dina's father always looked toward the hills, and Dina could see his skin electrify with longing. Each time there was a rumor that someone had climbed over a garden gate to steal oranges or water, Dina's father was quiet; he looked down at the sand, searching for something timeless, something that couldn't be seen with the eye.

When her father had first begun to talk about the men in the hills, Dina was a girl of ten. She wondered if she might run away and join them. She imagined that there were women alongside the men, women who wore ruby earrings and were able to start a fire by rubbing sand between their fingers. When she told her father her thoughts, he laughed out loud. These women you're thinking of aren't in the hills, Dina's father told her, they live in houses at the edge of the city, their front doors are always unlocked, dinner is always cooking on the stove, ready to be served at a moment's notice. These women never know when their men will be home, or for how long. They never know if their men will bring home gold or just a bad case of lice. Some of them are married to Arias, and some of them aren't, but all of them wait in the doorway and sleep alone almost every night.

When the moon is full, that orange color it sometimes is, then the Arias may take these women with them. On these nights the women know why the Arias are gone from home so much, they know why their men don't really have a home, and never will. In the moonlight the women shiver, not because they're cold—it's the beauty of the night that chills them, it's knowing that until the next time they ride across the mesa they have to be content with windows and doors, with houses that are never warm enough and roofs that leak every time it rains.

Soon Dina stopped thinking about riding off into the night, but she had decided to ignore her father's advice. Don't ever look for one of these men, he had told her. These men are like wolves, they come out of the silence when you least expect them. They're partial to precious stones and cold blue loneliness, and sometimes they're evil and sometimes they're just proud, but they never act like we do. They don't think about right and wrong the way we do, they never care about yellow roses along a stone wall or dinner served on a china plate or someone to talk to. Any man who tells you he wouldn't give his skin to be one of them is a liar, Dina's father told her, although the smart ones know they'd have to give more than just their skin. But a woman who goes looking for them deserves every damn thing she gets, and what she'll get is loneliness, day and night.

Dina had been ready to take that chance long before she met King Connors. And so when she sat next to him in the garden she was already imagining dark night kisses, orange moons. Then and there, in the bright sunlight of a neighbor's garden, Dina decided that when he left town she would be with him.

"I'm leaving here as soon as I can," King told Dina that day. "Where I'm going there are blue herons and pelicans, a mist rises up from the river every morning, butterflies are yellow and as big as my hand."

"California," Dina said, she whispered the word like a chant.

"You can't go any farther," King Connors told her. "When you stand at Goat's Rock beach and look out, you might as well be at the edge of the earth."

As her neighbors served dinner, Dina shivered; she had always known this day would come, King Connors was the one for her, she was certain of it. Dina sat next to him on a wooden folding chair, too nervous to drink her lemonade. But Dina's father knew Connors for what he really was—a drifter who would've given anything for a home, even if that meant a trailer surrounded by fruit trees. When Dina's father squinted he could tell that his daughter was under some sort of spell—he could tell from her white cotton skirt pulled just above the knee, and her untouched lemonade. He called her aside; they stood under an apricot tree.

"You like him, don't you?" Dina's father asked, and when his daughter said yes, he ground his teeth. "Forget about him," he told her. "That man's nothing. There are a million more like him."

Dina's hair was pulled back and tied with a velvet ribbon; she leaned her head against the apricot tree and smiled.

She thinks she has a secret, the old man thought. She thinks she knows something.

"Will you just look at him," Dina's father said. "He's a nobody. Look at his boots, girl. Look at his hands."

After dinner, when the old man walked his daughter home from the neighbors' house, he knew he had lost her. "What do you see in him?" he asked.

"I thought you would know," Dina said. "He's an Aria."

"An Aria!" Dina's father said. He lowered his voice. "I don't even know if there is such a thing. I may have invented Arias."

Dina shook her head. "He's one of them," she told her father, and when she looked upward stars were falling out of the sky, horses were racing across the clouds.

On the other side of town, in a motel room that had blue walls and a small mirror above the bureau, King Connors packed up all his clothes. He paid his bill, then drove to a filling station where he gassed up his car. He cleaned the windshield and went inside the station to buy a pack of cigarettes and a map of New Mexico. Later, Dina went to meet him. When she climbed out her bedroom window at midnight, her father heard her fingers grab onto the ivy which grew up the chimney. After she had run across the yard and gone out the gate, the old man went upstairs to her bedroom. There, on the window ledge, he saw her dusty footprints. He pulled up a wooden chair and stared at the ledge until the marks had all but disappeared, and by that time Dina was already halfway across the Black Mesa, going west.

When Dina discovered that she was wrong about King, that he was as far from an Aria as a man can be, it was too late, she could never have admitted her error to her father. But these days, Dina felt it had not all been in vain; these days, she was certain her father had been describing someone not yet born. Dina wished that her father had lived long enough to find out that he had one of them for his very own grandson. His grandson moved across Santa Rosa like a night rider, his grandson didn't know the meaning of loneliness or fear. Dina knew that her father would have understood who Silver was, the boy was an Aria. Dina's father would have looked at Silver with admiration, he would have shrunk from him with fear, he would have blessed the boy twice.

"That boy," Mrs. Raleigh, Maureen's mother, said one afternoon. She and Dina both stood in their own yards, separated by a hedge of jasmine and weeds; they both watched as Silver got into his car and stepped on the gas, leaving tracks on the road behind him. "He should be in school," Mrs. Raleigh said. "He should be kept out of trouble."

"Impossible," Dina told her neighbor. "Silver lives for trouble. There's nothing he's afraid of."

"There are laws, you know," Mrs. Raleigh said. "There are jails. There's a lot to be afraid of for someone who acts as crazy as he does."

"I never worry about Silver," Dina said proudly from behind the hedge of jasmine. "Never."

Though he wouldn't have let anyone know, there were some things that did frighten Silver. The thought of working for Angel Gregory for the rest of his life, the prospect of being poor, the possibility that someday women would no longer want him. And Teresa. He was frightened of his sister, and he wasn't even quite sure why. When he avoided the dinner table he was avoiding Teresa's eyes, when he disappeared for weekends it wasn't Bergen's presence that drove him away, but Teresa's. The curve of her cheek sent shudders through him, one glance from her could fill him with sudden sorrow; there were times when he found himself wishing they were still children, that they would never grow up. Teresa didn't know how often Silver thought about her, she knew only what she saw, and she saw Silver avoiding her. Part of her was relieved, part of her wanted nothing to do with him. But in her heart she felt abandoned. The more distant she became from Silver, the lonelier she was, and she began to accept the offers she was getting from boys in school. She went to movie theaters and dances, she bought eyeliner and a pair of high heels, and soon after her fifteenth birthday she stopped braiding her hair and began to wear it loose. Silver pretended not to see the change in his sister, but he couldn't help but notice. Men stopped to stare when she walked down the streets, cars slowed down and offered her rides. The more she was asked out on dates, the less control Teresa felt she had over who she was; she came to believe that she was destined to be whatever was expected of her, and in time she went out with any boy who asked her.

After a while all the boys at school knew—if pushed, Teresa would bend; if talked into the back seat of a car or the bedroom of any stranger's house, Teresa would agree to almost anything. Sex was one step closer to forgetting; when boys whose names she barely knew wrapped their arms around her she almost forgot about Silver. Before long Teresa was a much surer lover than any of the boys— soon it was Teresa who led the way into bedrooms, but she remained a swimmer, drowning in the past, stuck in the jade-colored water of the reservoir. She became an actress: there were boys who were convinced she was wild about them, and by the following autumn Teresa had turned down three offers to go steady. Maureen, from next door, was impressed. She had had one boyfriend only, Larry, whose I.D. bracelet she wore until he asked for it back. One afternoon, the girls sat side by side on the Raleighs' front porch, watching the rain and sharing a cigarette Maureen had swiped from her mother's purse. Maureen talked about her break-up with Larry, there were tears in her eyes.

"When he kissed me," Maureen confided, "the earth moved."

"Oh, Maureen," Teresa said. She took a drag on the stolen cigarette. "If the earth moved it must have been an earthquake."

"We did it," Maureen said now.

"Did what?" Teresa asked, though she didn't really want to know any more.

"And now there's something wrong," Maureen said. The rain splashed over the porch railing just beyond their feet. Teresa buttoned her sweater and wished that Maureen would shut up. "I don't have my period any more," Maureen whispered. "I just don't have it."

Maureen and Teresa watched the rain; they didn't look at each other, their breath came out in cloudy streams.

"How long?" Teresa finally asked.

"Three months," Maureen answered. "Maybe I'm sick," she said hopefully. "Maybe I have a tumor."

"You're pregnant," Teresa said.

"I am not," Maureen cried. "I'm not. I only did it twice."

Teresa stared at the puddles on the porch. "What are you going to do?"

Maureen shrugged. "Nothing. What can I do?"

"What about Larry?" Teresa asked. "Aren't you going to tell him?"

"No," Maureen said, horrified.

With all of the boys she had been with in the past few months, Teresa had not thought once about getting pregnant—that was something that happened to other people, girls in other towns, never anyone she knew.

"Your parents," Teresa said.

"If you say anything to anyone, I'll kill you," Maureen said. "I'll never talk to you again."

Soon enough the Raleighs found out about Maureen without anyone's having ever said a word. By the end of the month, Maureen had withdrawn from school; two suitcases full of her clothes had been packed. On a rare sunny day in the last week in November, Mr. Raleigh washed his car and then threw the two suitcases into the trunk.

"I'm going away," Maureen whispered to Teresa across the hedge which separated their backyards.

"They can't just send you away," Teresa said. "They can't force you."

"It's all right," Maureen said. "It's not like I'm going to reform school or anything. It's just like boarding school; there's even a swimming pool. Indoors."

"I'm sorry," Teresa said.

"If you tell anyone at school, I'll never be your friend again," Maureen vowed.

"Never," Teresa promised.

"I'll just have the baby and then I'll come back," Maureen said. "Just make sure you don't get another best friend while I'm gone."

"Don't worry about that," Teresa said. "I would never do that."

When Teresa watched the Raleighs' car pull out of their driveway, she didn't for a minute regret not telling Maureen more of her own secrets. If she learned anything from Maureen's going away, it was to be more careful, to demand that her boyfriends protect her from pregnancy. She didn't care how, she didn't want to know how, she only wanted it done. And even though not one of her regular boyfriends protested, slowly Teresa dropped each one of them. The boys she knew were light years away from the perfection of an Aria, they seemed like children, and she wouldn't have imagined ever bringing any of them home—Silver would have sat in a corner and laughed at each and every one of the boys she had dated. If she went out with anyone, it had to be someone Silver would respect, or at least not laugh at. And that was why, one winter afternoon, Teresa found herself agreeing to go out with Silver's one-time friend Eddie.

Teresa was in a booth at Max's Café on Webster Street. She had stopped there after school to avoid a rainstorm and had ordered french fries and a large vanilla Coke. Now that Maureen was gone, Teresa was rich—she had inherited all of the babysitting, she worked nearly every night. On that afternoon, just after the french fries had been set on the table, Teresa was thinking about Maureen, wondering when her baby would be born. It was then she happened to look up—Eddie was at the counter, drinking a coffee, staring right at her.

Quickly, she looked away. Teresa hadn't seen Eddie since that day at the reservoir. She sipped her Coke, she was afraid to look up, afraid that Eddie might hold her responsible for the end of his friendship with Silver. Without looking, she knew that he had picked up his coffee cup and was walking down the aisle. When he stopped at her booth, Teresa felt as though her heart might escape through her mouth, so she kept her mouth shut. She looked up only when Eddie rapped on the Formica tabletop with his knuckles.

"Mind if I sit down?" Eddie asked. He had already placed his cup and saucer on the table.

Teresa shrugged. "Sure," she said, but she lowered her hands onto her lap, she didn't want him to see that she was shaking.

Eddie didn't fool around. "You look good," he said to Teresa. "Real good."

"Oh?" Teresa said. She reached for her soda and drank. "You think so?"

"Different," Eddie said. "Grown-up."

Teresa felt braver. "Aren't you going to ask about my brother?" she said.

"No," Eddie said, "I'm not."

"He's working for someone named Gregory now," Teresa volunteered. "He's almost never home any more."

"Yeah?" Eddie smiled. "Is that an invitation?"

"No," Teresa said quickly, then she met Eddie's gaze. He looked different, too, almost as good as Silver. And Teresa smiled when she imagined how angry Silver would be if she dated Eddie, how jealous. "Maybe it is," she admitted.

"I've got a job in a machine shop," Eddie told her. "Got my own car."

"Silver has a car, too," Teresa said. "A Chevy. Deep blue with white seats."

"Listen," Eddie said. He leaned over the tabletop and took Teresa's hand in his own. "Don't mention that motherfucker to me again, understand?"

Teresa nodded and took her hand from him. Her pulse was pounding—all she had to do was say one word to Silver. Just get up, walk home, and tell Silver that Eddie had grabbed her hand. One word and Silver would be at Eddie's front door, banging on the screen, ready to fight for her. Teresa leaned back, smiled, then took a cigarette from Eddie's pack of Marlboros. She lit a match, then blew it out while staring at Eddie.

"If I told Silver what you just called him, he'd kill you."

"Let's just say he'd try," Eddie said.

They were doing something dangerous and they knew it. They smiled at each other across the table.

"I think you're beautiful," Eddie said. "I've always thought that."

"No you haven't," Teresa said, suddenly shy.

"Well, I think it now," Eddie told her. "You are."

Teresa's face felt hot, she lowered her eyes. "I have a job, too," she told Eddie. "Babysitting. Tonight I'm at Forty-five Greene Street. There's a two-year-old, but he's in bed by eight o'clock."

"Eight o'clock," Eddie repeated.

They sat at the table and smoked cigarettes. Outside the rain was ending.

"If he knew we were sitting here together we'd be in trouble," Teresa said in a low voice.

"Oh, yeah?" Eddie said. "And what if he knew I was going to be at Forty-five Greene Street tonight?"

"You wouldn't," Teresa said, but she knew he would, and what's more, she wanted him to be.

By the time Teresa left the café she was dizzy with excitement and shame. She was relieved when Silver wasn't home for dinner; she didn't have to face him before she left the house. She had dressed with the same ease as she would have for any old date; she pretended that she wasn't nervous, that every step she took didn't feel like a betrayal. She tried to convince herself that seeing Eddie had nothing to do with getting back at Silver for avoiding her, but she was edgy as a fugitive, and when Linda and Joel Harmon left that night to go to the movies, Teresa almost begged them not to go. She regretted having told Eddie where she would be working. There was no way around it: Teresa had agreed to date Eddie because she knew that when she and Eddie kissed, Silver would be there too. Late in the evening when they went into the bedroom and pulled down the shades, when Eddie took off his jeans and folded them over an oak chair, Teresa would be thinking of Silver so intently that Silver would nearly be pulled back from the bar in Oakland where he was drinking a beer and waiting to meet one of Gregory's connections.

But it was too late to cancel, too late to lock all the doors and windows. Teresa put the two-year-old to bed, and then she waited. At eight-thirty Eddie pulled up into the driveway. Teresa ran a comb through her hair and checked her mascara; she got out the bottle of whiskey Joel Harmon hid under the kitchen sink. By ten o'clock they were on their second whiskey and water, they had smoked nearly half a pack of Eddie's cigarettes. They sat in the living room, barely speaking; they listened to the wind. Eddie sat on a rocking chair. The sleeves of his shirt were rolled up, his eyes were trained on Teresa.

"You don't look like fifteen years old to me," Eddie said. "What you look like is my type."

He took her hand and led her into the bedroom as if he had been there a hundred times before. Teresa pulled down the shades, then sat on the bed and took off her shoes. She reached around to unzip her sweater.

"I'll do that," Eddie said. He came over and slipped Teresa's sweater over her head, then he told her to lie down. He guided her onto the sheets covered with a pattern of palm trees. "Don't rush me," he told Teresa. "We've got all night, don't we. And I've been waiting for this," he whispered. "I've been waiting a long time."

All of the boys Teresa had known had rushed, they had pulled down their jeans in the back seats of cars, they had rushed as fast as they could. But now, Eddie took off all of Teresa's clothes and his own; he made her lie still on the bed, he ran his hands over her breasts so slowly that she shuddered; she felt that he was laughing at her, she could sense it in his fingertips. When the telephone rang, Teresa began to get up to answer it, but Eddie held her back.

"Let it ring," he said.

"It could be Mrs. Harmon," Teresa said. "It could be anyone."

"I don't care who it is," Eddie said. "Let it ring."

Once he was on top of her, Teresa couldn't move. He ran his tongue along the raised line in her ear, as the telephone rang, again and again. Then he whispered, "Maybe it's Silver. Maybe he knows what I'm doing right now."

Teresa shuddered; in the dark she was nervous, in the dark she knew they weren't alone. She wasn't the only one who had been thinking of Silver, and it was now clear that Eddie was there for only one reason. He was rough, as if he wanted her to cry out, because when she did gasp he seemed to want her even more, he seemed to hear Silver's voice in every cry. There was nothing he told her to do that Teresa wouldn't have done; when he told her to turn around and raise herself up on her hands and knees so that he could force his penis inside her rectum, Teresa closed her eyes and did just that. Eddie was doing the telling, Eddie was arranging acts he had thought about for a long time, and even when Teresa was certain that he had walked over to her table in the café only because she was Silver's sister, she didn't curse that meeting. It wasn't until she realized that he had probably never thought she was beautiful that she started to cry. But she was quiet about it, no sound escaped, there were just some stray tears that fell onto the sheets. Over and over again, Teresa imagined that she was being punished; in silence she begged Silver's forgiveness. When Eddie had moved away from her, heaving himself face down on the bed, Teresa curled her legs up, she held the pillow as tightly as she could.

"I knew it," Eddie said later, when he turned to her. "I knew I'd have you sooner or later. I knew it the minute he said I wasn't good enough."

Teresa leaned back against the wooden headboard, her arms were still wrapped around the feather pillow. Eddie got dressed; he reached for his boots and his denim jacket. In the room next door the two-year-old turned in his sleep; across town his parents watched a movie in the dark, and, in their bed, Teresa drew her knees up, just beginning to realize how sore she was.

Eddie lit a cigarette and sat at the foot of the bed; Teresa wished he would just go, he wanted to go, he wanted to turn around and walk out the door without another word, Teresa could see it in his eyes, in the way he played with the buttons on his jacket.

"You understand, I won't call you," Eddie said.

Teresa shrugged; when she looked at him she barely recognized him.

"I know you won't say anything to Silver," Eddie said now. "You're not that stupid."

Teresa looked at him carefully; she couldn't believe that moments ago he had touched her. He patted the quilt on the bed; now that it was over he seemed nervous. But Eddie had nothing to worry about, it was too late for Teresa to tell Silver. If she ever did, he would stare at her, nothing more, but in his eyes there would be hundreds of accusations, grim planets of betrayal.

"No," Eddie said. "Of course you won't tell him. You wouldn't dare."

Teresa didn't walk him to the door when he left; she stayed where she was, she listened to the front door close. And even when he had gone, Teresa didn't bother to get up and turn off the lights in the kitchen, she didn't care whether the front door was locked. She left her clothes in a pile on the floor, she pulled the quilt up so that it almost felt as if she were held in someone's arms rather than feathers and cotton. She thought about summer, and imagined there were crickets outside the window who sang her to sleep. And that was how the Harmons found her when they came home at one-thirty that night. Linda Harmon knelt by the bed and whispered for Teresa to get up; Joel Harmon stood in the doorway of the bedroom and stared at the pile of clothes on the floor.

That night, the Harmons slept in the living room. First they called Dina to say that Teresa was staying over, then they took the pillows off the couch, pulled out a bed, made it up with blue sheets, and checked on their son. Then they noticed the two whiskey glasses left half full, they choked on the smoke which hung in the air, and they whispered about the lecture they would give the babysitter in the morning. But in the morning Teresa would still not wake up.

Joel Harmon wanted to call the police, he wanted Teresa taken away on a stretcher, her sleeping hands bound in white cotton. But when Linda went in to the bedroom, when she bent down and listened to Teresa's slow breathing, all of the anger she had felt toward the girl last night turned to fear. She persuaded her husband it would be best to call Teresa's mother again; it would be better, she told Joel, for them not to touch the girl, better not to even look at her.

After the telephone call, the Harmons sat on the couch. They couldn't have been more nervous if a brown bear had been sleeping in their bed. A few blocks away, Dina stared at the phone for a moment after she had returned the receiver, then she went up to Silver's room and woke him. "I want you to go over to Greene Street," she told him. "You have to pick up Teresa."

Silver pulled the sheet over his head. "It's early," he said. "I didn't get home till three o'clock."

"Now," Dina said. "Teresa's sick again."

Silver got up and got dressed, he threw on rumpled jeans, a blue shirt, a black leather jacket; he didn't even bother to run a comb through his hair. He kept his foot pressed down on the accelerator when he drove to Greene Street, he hadn't had a cigarette yet, not even one cup of coffee. When he pulled up in the driveway, Joel Harmon was waiting for him at the front door.

"I don't know what the hell went on here last night," Joel Harmon said. "Drugs," he guessed. "Some sort of drug party, and now we can't wake her up."

Silver went into the bedroom; the shades were still drawn, it might have been midnight. He scooped up Teresa's clothes, then went into the living room and handed them to Linda.

"Could you put these in a shopping bag?" he asked.

Linda Harmon nodded; she went to the kitchen, pulled out a brown paper bag, then folded the clothes inside. Her heart was racing; she wanted them out of the house, both of them, the sleeping girl and the young man who wore black leather so early in the morning.

Silver had gone back into the bedroom. And once he was there, he felt hypnotized, he could have watched Teresa sleep forever. He wondered if he'd be able to move at all, and when he did, he moved quickly, as if he believed that if he stopped for an instant he would be forever transfixed. Silver pulled back the quilt; Teresa's legs were curled up, her left arm covered one breast. He tried not to look for too long, he tore off the top sheet and covered her in it, then lifted Teresa off the bed. Her long hair fell in strands, and each strand attached itself to

Silver's skin, each strand felt like electricity.

"Just where do you think you're taking that sheet?" Joel Harmon asked when Silver stopped in the living room to pick up the bag of Teresa's clothes.

Silver smiled briefly. "She's naked," he told Joel Harmon. "Do you want to take this sheet off her?"

"Take her home," Linda Harmon urged Silver. "That's all we want."

Silver went outside; he opened the passenger door of the Chevy and lifted Teresa into the front seat. While he drove home her head was leaning against his thigh, the sheet slipped a bit and showed her bare shoulders. At home, Dina had already made up Teresa's bed, she had lit a candle on the bureau and drawn the curtains. She stood watching at the bottom of the stairs as Silver carried Teresa up to her room. And while Dina closed her eyes, leaned on the banister, and wished for better fortune, Silver put Teresa down on the bed. He pulled back the blankets, unwound the borrowed sheet, then stood there for as long as he dared. When he finally covered her, he knew he would never ask what had happened the night before. He couldn't stay there a moment longer, not without thinking of the reservoir, not without remembering a day when there were hawks overhead in a sky that was blue as sapphires. Silver walked out, closed the door behind him, and went downstairs to tell Dina that everything was all right, everything was in order.

Teresa slept for almost twenty hours; by the time she woke up, the candle Dina had placed on the bureau had burned itself out and Silver had already left for the night. No matter how hard Teresa listened for him on the other side of the bedroom wall, she wouldn't hear Silver pacing the floor—for he had already delivered all his packages for Gregory, and now he was parked outside a two-story house on the other side of town. On the second floor a seventeen-year-old girl named Lee was waiting to sneak out her bedroom window; nearly every night she edged across the garage roof, then climbed down the drainpipe. When she was sure her feet dangled close to the ground, she jumped and then went running over to Silver's car. It was not really that Silver wanted a steady girlfriend, a sweetheart with big blue eyes. He saw Lee because it was easy—he had never even asked her out. Lee had come over to him one night at the Dragon. She had used her older sister's driver's license as proof of age, and when she saw Silver across the room she felt more like twenty-five than seventeen, she felt drawn to him, pulled by hot, white strings.

Lee made certain to ask for nothing—not birthday presents or telephone calls, not promises of undying love, not even faithfulness. It wasn't that she didn't want all these things, but she knew they were together on Silver's terms or not at all, and she sensed that his terms could change without a moment's notice. When she didn't see the headlights of Silver's car outside her house at midnight, she couldn't sleep all night; on the darkest edge of insomnia she imagined Silver with other girls, older women who knew more than she did about love and forgiveness. She thought about heartaches, she whispered his name, she bit her fingernails until they bled, leaving red traces on her nightgown, on her blue lambswool sweater.

But on the nights when he did appear all of the waiting seemed worth it. When they walked down the street every woman turned to stare at Silver, but it was Lee who held on to his arm, and she tossed her head so that her blond hair swung out in bands of victory. She knew that her position was shaky; any of her girlfriends would have gladly changed places with her, and she was certain that they would all betray her if given the chance, one telephone call, one wink, one invitation to a night of desire and they would be in her place. So she held on to Silver tightly, she wrote his name and her own in the toilets of every bar in town, and she circled their names with blood-red hearts. When women at the Dragon looked at Silver a little too long, Lee put her hand into Silver's jeans, she didn't care who was looking, she wanted them to look, she'd stare them down until they looked the other way.

It was so easy to be with Lee that Silver found himself spending more and more time with her; there were rumors that he was going steady, gossip that he was finally in love. And frankly, Silver didn't care what other people said—he knew the truth—he wanted a woman at all times, and he didn't really care much who she was.

On the night when Teresa was just waking up from the sleep which had begun on Greene Street, Silver had his first serious argument with Angel Gregory. Silver was edgy that night, he had been from the start. He couldn't stop wondering what had gone on at Greene Street—and wondering made him powerless and mean. When Lee had run through the darkness and gotten into the car, Silver hadn't said a word to her. He was hunched over the wheel, thinking about Teresa, and when Lee leaned over and kissed him, Silver didn't push her away, but he looked at her, confused, as if she were a stranger. She had brought the odor of lilacs in her perfume with her; when she had kissed him, her mouth had felt cold.

"Do you have to work for Gregory tonight?" Lee asked as they drove away toward the Dragon. Even though Lee had accompanied Silver on some of his late-night runs and had waited for him in the parked car, she had never asked him just what his business was. She had learned that he would tell her exactly how much he wanted her to know.

"I don't *have* to work for anyone," Silver said sullenly, and Lee could tell that he'd already been drinking.

"Did you make all your deliveries tonight?" Lee asked, as if Silver drove a car for a pharmacy or an auto parts shop instead of a drug dealer.

"Shit," Silver said. He wrinkled his nose. "What is that goddamned smell?"

Lee sank into the leather upholstery. "Perfume," she told him.

"Well, I don't like it," Silver said. "Don't wear it any more."

Later, when they got to the Dragon and Silver had ordered a shot of tequila for himself and a seven and seven for Lee, Lee went into the ladies room and scrubbed her neck and wrists with a damp paper towel. She rubbed at her skin until every bit of the perfume was gone, and even then, when she walked back to the bar she was afraid that the odor of lilacs—Desire, the perfume was called—was still with her, betraying her, forcing Silver to turn away. When she walked past the bouncer, he smiled at her and didn't ask for any proof of age, he knew she belonged to Silver and that was proof enough. At the bar, Gregory was standing next to Silver, but Silver looked straight ahead, his eyes were narrowed and dark.

"I'm not your boy," Lee heard him tell Gregory. "So don't call me that."

"As long as you're working for me, I'll call you what I like," Gregory said.

"Working for you?" Silver said. "I could run your business in no time flat. I'd give your customers more satisfaction than they ever got from you."

"Is that what you've got in mind?" Gregory said. "Because I'll tell you right now, I don't have room for a vice-president."

"What are we fighting for?" Silver said to Gregory then, and he bought the other man a drink, he even toasted to Gregory's continued success. But later, when he and Lee were parked on a dirt road near Cannon's Field, Silver couldn't get Angel Gregory out of his mind.

"He acts like a fucking dictator," Silver said. "But the news is—nobody tells me what to do."

"Forget about him," Lee said. She turned the car heater on, then climbed into the back seat. "Think about me," she whispered as she took Silver's arm and urged him to come into the back with her.

They made love in silence. All the time he was holding her, Silver was thinking of ways to take over Gregory's business, and by the time they had finished, and Lee's arms were pulling him down for one last kiss, Silver had figured out exactly what he would do.

For the next few weeks Silver didn't give Gregory any backtalk, he was the perfect employee. But every time he stopped to make a pickup, Silver led the customers around to their dissatisfaction with Gregory. When he knew that a fire was lit, he proposed that they switch their business to him. Silver offered discounts, he spoke with sincerity, when it was necessary, he lied. He insinuated that Gregory had once turned state's evidence against one of his customers, that he wasn't a man to be trusted. In no time there were dozens of connections ready to switch their allegiance to Silver. The only problem was how to get rid of Gregory, a way short of murder if possible.

Not long after his eighteenth birthday, Silver was civil to Bergen for the first time; he had a plan and he wanted the detective's opinion. And so, on a Saturday night, Silver surprised the family by being at dinner.

"What would you say," Silver asked Bergen, "if you were a cop and you got an anonymous call, a tipoff about some criminal activities."

Bergen poured gravy over his roast beef. "I never was a cop," he told Silver. "So I can't really tell you what I'd say."

Silver stopped himself from sneering. "Well, hell," he said, pushing his plate away, "use your imagination." Silver reached for a bottle of beer. "Do you act on it and go pick the guy up, or do you shrug it off as a crank call?"

"I see if there's a file on the guy," Bergen said. "If there is, I might watch him. If there's not, I forget the whole thing and go home and have dinner." Bergen turned to Teresa. "This is what experience does for you. Gives you the upper hand in playing guessing games."

"If he's got a record you go after him?" Silver pushed.

"I might." Bergen nodded. "Why are you so interested?"

"Interested?" Silver said. He finally reached for his fork and began to eat. "I'm just curious about the way your mind works, Bergen. That's all."

"His mind works just fine," Dina said. She patted Bergen on the head as she passed by, on the way to the stove for more gravy. "That's more than I can say for you," she teased Silver.

"Oh, really." Silver smiled. He was pleased, certain that Bergen had the slow mentality of a cop. The old detective had just given him the go-ahead. "We'll just see about that," Silver told his mother.

When Silver called the station house later that week, he made certain that the trunk of Gregory's car was full of dope. He offered to run so many errands that Gregory wondered if so much dedication didn't deserve a raise in salary. But in fact, whenever Silver had access to Gregory's apartment he planted evidence in the clothes closets, in the drawers where Gregory kept his sweaters, in the vegetable bin in the refrigerator. He didn't make any deliveries that week and instead filled two suitcases with drugs and left them in the hall closet at Gregory's apartment, and finally on the day before he turned Gregory in to the police, he stole the red leather address book Gregory kept on his desk, so that he finally possessed the names and phone numbers of all Gregory's most important connections. On the day that he called, Silver didn't bother to disguise his voice, he didn't waver when he gave Gregory's name and address, he was even kind enough to mention Gregory's one felony conviction—assault in

1964. When he hung up, Silver smoked a cigarette and then picked up the phone and dialed Gregory's number. He left a message on the dealer's answering machine— he wouldn't be in for work that night, perhaps not for the rest of the week, he had the flu, he was much too weak to make even one pickup.

On the night when three officers knocked at Angel Gregory's front door, Silver was in the living room of his own house, watching TV with Dina and Teresa. He sat with his boots propped up on the coffee table; every face on the TV screen was Gregory's just at the moment when the cops went straight to the hall closet, and came up with two suitcases full of dope.

"You're in a good mood," Dina said to her son.

"Is there a law against it?" Silver asked.

Teresa was sitting on the floor, her back against the couch, homework in front of her. "A girl I know at school told me that you're going steady," she said to Silver.

"Going steady?" Silver said. "Do I look like the steady type?"

"That's what she told me." Teresa shrugged.

"Give me that girl's name," Silver said. "I'll interrogate her."

"Well, are you or aren't you?" Dina asked.

"Of course I'm not," Silver said. He turned to Teresa. "Don't believe gossip," he told her.

"You're blushing," Dina said, hoping to trap him into telling the truth.

"Like hell I am," Silver said. "I don't blush—I don't believe in it."

"Well, it's all over town," Teresa said.

Silver tapped Teresa with his boot. "Don't worry," he said. "When I'm going steady, you'll be the first to know."

"I'm not worried," Teresa said. She turned the pages of her textbook without really looking at any of the words; she wanted to believe that if Silver had women, he had dozens, but no one special, no one he loved.

"Oh, no?" Silver said. "You're not worried?" He lowered his voice. "I told you the truth, there's no girl."

"Well, of course not," Dina said. "We all know that no one is good enough for you."

"That's right." Silver nodded. "Goddamn right."

Silver kept a low profile until Gregory was booked and charged without the slightest hope of bail. When he was certain that Gregory wouldn't come looking for him, Silver moved quickly. He got into his car and visited every one of Gregory's connections; before the night was over, Silver was no longer a runner—he had taken over Gregory's business, when he walked down the street he felt as though he were wearing Gregory's red snakeskin boots. But because Silver would never make the mistake Gregory had—letting some hungry kid know too much about his business—he had to work twice as hard as before. At night he was in the Dragon making local connections, and during the day he drove his old route to Oakland and San Francisco. He slept very little—from dawn till nine or ten in the morning. He lost weight, he saw double, sometimes when he reached for a drink his hand shook. He stored cartons of dope in the garage, he kept two shoeboxes of cash under his bed, and when they were full, he began to store the largest bills in the first drawer in his dresser. But he didn't have the chance to spend his money; he was far too busy, and he felt as though he couldn't get a moment's rest.

In no time, Bergen figured out that something was going on.

"He doesn't look good," Bergen said to Dina one Saturday.

"I never worry about Silver," Dina said. "I know he can look out for himself."

"He's lost at least ten pounds," Bergen said. "Maybe he's working too hard. Maybe he should cut down his hours at that restaurant."

"Leona's?" Dina said. "He hasn't worked there since the summer."

Bergen looked at her quickly, then looked away. "You never told me that," he said, a soft accusation.

"You never asked," Dina said. "And anyway, I thought you knew. Silver wasn't meant to be a dishwasher."

Bergen spent the day putting down a new linoleum floor in the kitchen. When he took a break to have some lemonade, he mentioned Silver again. "If he quit his job, then where does he get his money?"

"That corner isn't straight," Dina said as she examined the new floor.

"How does he afford the car?" Bergen asked. "Where does he get all his new clothes?"

"He's a smart boy," Dina said.

"Dina!" Bergen said. "He's not smart enough to make money appear out of thin air."

"All right," Dina said. "I don't know where he gets his money. And I don't want to know."

Bergen didn't say another word. He went outside to the garden and stood in the spot where he and Dina had turned the earth, preparing for the following year. If it had been anyone but Silver, Bergen would have figured it out a long time ago, but even now, he tried to find excuses for the boy. Each time he thought of Silver he thought about Dina as well—Dina on a bus to Vacaville prison, in summer, when the bus was much too hot and passengers stuck to their seats—Dina at a courthouse, a cemetery, Dina crying out Silver's name, Dina pale with worry, sick with age, Dina without her son, without Silver.

By the time she had walked out into the garden, wearing a sweater the detective had given her as a present, Bergen had already decided not to tell Dina any of his theories, whatever he guessed about Silver he would keep to himself.

Dina came up close behind him, he could smell her—a scent of coffee, and cologne, and fear.

"Where do *you* think he gets his money?" Dina asked now.

Bergen stared at the slate border around the vegetable patch he and Dina had laid down; miles away, the river was so high it covered the tops of some trees. "It doesn't matter," Bergen said. "I don't want to talk about Silver." He turned and held Dina. "It's you I'm worried about," he whispered. "Out here without a coat. Maybe I'd better take you out to dinner."

"Just because I don't have a coat?" Dina asked.

"Maybe I ought to buy you a new coat after I take you out to dinner," Bergen suggested.

"Somebody could love a man like you," Dina said.

Bergen searched for the signs of an admission, but Dina was staring at the ground.

"Someone like you?" Bergen asked.

Dina buried her face against him. "Take me out to dinner," she said. "I want it to be just the two of us."

If Bergen had wanted to, he could have easily found out every move Silver had made in the past few weeks, he could have followed him to Oakland in a rented car that Silver wouldn't recognize and written down every drug connection in a looseleaf notebook. Instead, he took the woman he thought the most beautiful in the world to an Italian restaurant where globes of candlelight attracted the pale yellow moths of wintertime. If Bergen had wished to, he could have found Silver right then, in only a matter of hours, but he had already decided—he would never follow Silver, he would try not to even talk to the boy, he wanted to know nothing about him.

Lee, however, would have given anything for some of the tricks of Bergen's trade; alone in her room, surrounded by white furniture and longing, she hadn't the faintest idea how to contact Silver. For weeks she had looked out her window, waiting for the headlights of his car to appear, ready to run to him. She hung around outside the high school until dark, hoping that Silver would know how much she needed to see him. When the telephone rang, she ran to answer it.

She was certain that Silver was angry, that she had said something wrong. She couldn't bear to think that he just wasn't thinking about her. But the truth was Silver was preoccupied. And although there was a woman in south San Francisco he sometimes spent the night with, there really was no one else—he was simply too busy, he no longer had time for Lee. When she hadn't heard from him for nearly a month, Lee started telephoning the house. Teresa picked up the phone the first time she called—Lee immediately hung up. And although she wanted to stop, she couldn't help herself; she called again and again, but Silver never answered the phone.

"It was for you," Teresa told Silver one day when she picked up the phone and no one was on the other end.

"How do you know?" Silver asked.

"Some girl," Teresa shrugged. "It's always for you when they call and then hang up."

Because Lee telephoned at least once a day, Teresa began to feel a connection with her. She was certain that the girl who refused to speak had been terribly hurt, perhaps she and Teresa passed each other every day on the street or in school, both thinking about Silver at the very same time. Every time she called, Teresa hoped she wouldn't hang up, and because Silver never did answer the phone, though she prayed he would each time she called, Lee finally did speak.

"Is Silver there?" she asked in a low voice.

Teresa was so surprised that the caller had finally spoken, that she didn't answer.

"Is he there?" Lee asked.

"No," Teresa told her. "He's never here after dinner. If you want to reach him, this is a terrible time to call." Teresa could hear the girl sigh. "I could give him a message," she suggested.

"No," Lee said. "He'd kill me if he knew I tried to call him at home."

"Are you his girlfriend?" Teresa asked.

Lee hesitated. "Yes," she said.

"Oh," Teresa said. Now that they had actually spoken, Teresa felt the connection between them breaking down. Talking to Lee now seemed a betrayal of Silver. "Well, don't worry," Teresa said, "he'll probably call you sooner or later."

But he never did, and Lee soon discovered that she couldn't think of anything but Silver. Each time she saw a man on the street who was his height, Lee had the urge to follow him, and there were times when she did just that. She wound up tracking men who were thirty instead of eighteen, men who revealed themselves as counterfeit the minute she got a good look at them in the light. And even then, when she found that the man she had pursued didn't resemble Silver in the least, Lee was never quite certain that it wasn't Silver in disguise, that in order to avoid her he had somehow managed to rearrange his own flesh and blood.

She began to walk past his family's house in the mornings and late in the afternoon, even though she knew how furious Silver would have been if he had ever come to the front door and discovered her out on the sidewalk. He had told her from the start that she was never to bother him. They were to see each other only when he wanted to, and when he wanted her she'd know—she'd see his car parked outside her house, she'd hear his heartbeat, she'd feel him call to her, she'd feel it in her bones. But after a month of silence, Lee couldn't wait any longer for Silver's call. One night, in late winter, she climbed out her bedroom window, jumped to the ground, and hitched a ride to the Dragon. She no longer had her sister's proof of age with her, and without Silver beside her they wouldn't let her past the door. So she waited outside, she leaned up against the brick wall and studied every man who walked by. Sometime after midnight it began to rain, and Lee tied a scarf around her hair; she intended to wait all night if she had to.

It was nearly three in the morning when she saw his car. Silver parked, turned off the windshield wipers and the headlights, then got out and slammed the door shut. His collar was turned up and he walked quickly, avoiding the puddles on the sidewalk. When Lee came out of the shadows, Silver didn't miss a step. He walked over to her as if he'd been expecting her all along. He leaned up against the brick wall, and if Lee had reached out, just a little, she could have touched him.

"It's late for you to be out all alone," Silver said.

Now that she was face to face with him, Lee discovered that she couldn't speak. It would be so easy to say something wrong, so easy to make him mad. Even when she looked down at the sidewalk she could feel him watching her, his eyes burning right through her skin.

"You're not following me, are you?" Silver's voice was harsh. "You're not checking up on me to see if I've got another girl, are you?"

"No," Lee said. "I just wanted to see you."

Silver took out a cigarette and lit it. "Well, now you've seen me," he told Lee. "Satisfied?"

Lee started to cry then, and she surprised herself—she had never dared cry in front of him before.

"Oh, shit," Silver said. "Come on. Don't cry."

Lee covered her face with her hands, but it was too late—she couldn't have stopped herself even if she wanted to.

"Look, just don't cry," Silver said. He pulled her near and whispered in her ear. "I'm sorry I haven't called you. But don't act like it's a goddamned felony. Let me buy you a drink and we can forget about it."

Lee shook her head no.

"Let's go inside," Silver urged. "I'll buy you a whiskey sour."

"I'm pregnant," Lee told him.

Silver took a step backward. He threw his cigarette onto the cement and carefully ground it out with his boot heel. "What?" he said to Lee.

Mascara had flooded Lee's eyes; beneath her silk scarf the rain had set her hair into small cold ringlets. "I'm pregnant," she said.

"It's not mine," Silver said immediately.

"It is!" Lee said. "It is too yours."

"Just calm down," Silver told her. "How do you expect me to think when you're crying?" He walked in a circle, walked to her, then away. "Goddamn it, Lee."

"It's not my fault," Lee whispered.

"This is all I need," Silver said. He narrowed his eyes and when he stared at her that way Lee looked like a ghost, and he wondered why she had ever tempted him at all. "What do you plan to do?" Silver asked her.

Lee shrugged. She reached into her purse for a Kleenex. "It's yours," she told Silver.

"All right!" Silver said. "All right, all right, it's mine!" He stared at her so cruelly that Lee had to look away. "You want to get married," he said finally. "Is that it?"

Lee looked up then; she knew that she had him. "Yes," she said, and she was calmer than she'd ever been before. "I want to get married."

Silver pulled at his collar; his knuckles were white. "I don't even love you," he said. "Do you know that? I don't even love you."

Lee raised her chin; she wasn't wearing high heels, but she still felt quite tall. "Well, that's what I want," she told Silver.

Only a few feet away, inside the Dragon, men Silver's age fed quarters into the jukebox and ordered whiskey and beer. But out on the sidewalk steam was rising, the rain fell harder, and Silver felt himself age, as if he were already a husband, and father, a family man. He could have walked away and left Lee alone on the sidewalk, he could have given her the money to leave town and driven her to the bus station right then. But Silver had been raised with a sense of duty; maybe King Connors and Reuben could run away when their lives weren't turning out as they'd planned, but not Silver. He leaned up against the brick wall calmly. "Okay," he said to Lee. "If that's what you want."

Lee swung her purse on its gold chain; she wiped the mascara out of her eyes and smiled. Silver took her arm and led her toward the Dragon; he was determined to celebrate their sudden future together.

"I'm going to buy you a drink," he told her. "Just like I promised I would."

After he had driven Lee home, Silver parked his car in the driveway of the house on Divisadero Street. As he sat smoking cigarettes the rain stopped falling, but the air itself seemed to have become liquid. This early in the morning the scent of the river was everywhere, it coated Silver's windshield with a cool green film, it got into the strands of his hair. The streets were empty, and all over the front lawn a gray mist rose up in cold waves, shock waves, billows the color of iron. When the sun had risen above the roof of the house—when the night which had seemed to last forever was finally over—Silver got out of his car and went inside. He heard Dina, already awake, downstairs in the kitchen. Before long Dina would be out in the garden; she would weed the earth where the scallions and peas were just beginning to break through the ground. When Silver walked into the kitchen, Dina had already poured herself a cup of coffee and was stirring in a spoon of sugar.

"I'm moving out of here," Silver told his mother.

"I've heard that before," Dina said calmly. "I've heard it a hundred times. I know you like living here—you like your shirts ironed the way I do them. You'd never run off like Reuben and your father."

Upstairs, Teresa was still asleep, and Silver wondered who would take care of her when he left. He tried to imagine the words that might make what he was about to do seem like anything less than desertion.

"I have to move," Silver told his mother. He leaned against the refrigerator; it was as if his legs were no longer strong enough to hold his weight. "I'm getting married," he said.

Dina dropped her coffee cup; it broke into pieces on the linoleum and coffee spilled over the floor. She shook her head as if she hadn't heard right. "What did you just say?" she asked.

"I'm getting married," Silver repeated.

Dina went to him and held him. If she had thought about Silver marrying and moving away before, she refused to accept the notion. She wanted to believe he would always come back home. He might be gone for days or weeks, she and Teresa might grow lonely looking out the window— but there would always come a night when he would return. Now he was going and Dina could tell—it would be for good. Silver closed his eyes; he was being pushed even closer to the refrigerator and there was a hum inside his head. He moved away from his mother, then went to the closet for a dustpan and broom. While her son crouched down low to the floor, Dina wished that she could kneel down beside him and check his fingers for sharp bits of pottery. Instead, she went to the cabinet over the stove, took a clean cup, then poured herself more coffee. By the time Silver had swept up the blue and white cup that had shattered into a thousand pieces, Dina was able to smile, just as if she'd been truly happy for him.

Silver took the trash out through the back door. The sun was covered by low clouds now; snails had left holes in the strawberry plants Dina had set out in narrow rows. As he stood by the side of the house, Silver held onto the trashcan so tightly he could feel every muscle in his arms. He was used to staying out all night, to only a few hours sleep, but after he covered the trashcan he was too tired to move. He inhaled deeply, and because it was still so early in the morning, and still so quiet, Silver's breathing echoed in the garden, and then hung beneath the wisteria vines that grew over the porch, vines that would turn, in only a matter of days, into a violet ceiling, a color so delicate it always seemed edged with desire.

Teresa didn't want a party for her sixteenth birthday, and if Arnie Bergen hadn't insisted on taking her out to dinner, she would have ignored the day, preferring to avoid all celebrations so that she could watch the slate-colored rain from the safety of her room.

"It always rains on my birthday," Teresa told Bergen. They had run to his car, yet had still managed to get soaking wet.

"So you think it's personal?" Bergen said. "You think it's a comment from the heavens?"

Teresa shrugged. She crossed her legs and pulled her skirt down. "You don't have to do this," she said politely. "I don't care if we go out to dinner."

"It's my pleasure," Bergen said. He started the car and drove down Divisadero Street. "It's not every day I get to take someone out to celebrate the fact that she's sweet sixteen."

"I'm not so sweet," Teresa said.

"You are in my book," Bergen said.

For the first time, Silver had forgotten her birthday. He hadn't been home for days; he was looking for an apartment in San Francisco, he was putting his business in order, moving the boxes in their garage to a warehouse he had rented in Daley City. He was too busy to leave behind a silk scarf or a box of chocolates, he hadn't even remembered to send a card.

"Chinese, French, or Mexican?" Bergen asked.

Teresa looked at him as though he'd just asked the stupidest question in the world. "I don't care," she told him.

Bergen chose Chinese; they parked in the center of

town, and then ran to the restaurant. Inside, Bergen hung up Teresa's coat and then his own. They sat in a red booth, and Bergen ordered for them. Teresa curled a strand of hair around her finger and sighed.

"I know being young isn't easy," Bergen said, after the waiter had put the dishes of food on the table.

"Are you telling me that when I'm old I'll be happy?" Teresa asked.

Bergen put food on both their plates. "I'm happy," he said.

"I'm glad someone is," Teresa told him.

"What would it take?" Bergen asked softly. "What would it take to make you happy?"

Teresa picked up the chopsticks by the side of her plate. "I can't use these," she said, close to tears.

"Use your fork," Bergen suggested. "You know," he told her once she had begun eating, "I wanted us to go out together, just you and me, because I've started to think of you as a daughter."

Teresa put down her fork. "Well, I'm not," she said. "I'm not your daughter."

"I don't care," Bergen said. "I think of you that way anyway."

After the meal, Bergen put the present he had bought her in the fortune cookie bowl. When Teresa opened the small black box she saw a pair of pearl earrings.

"They're beautiful," she said. "They're perfect."

"The other part of your present is from your mother. She'll take you to a jewelry store tomorrow where they'll pierce your ears. I don't know who would want that as a present, but that's what she said you wanted."

Teresa got up, went around to the other side of the booth, and kissed the detective's cheek. "It's just what I wanted," she said.

On the way home, Teresa turned on the car radio. "I had a pretty good time," she admitted.

Dina had stayed home so that she could surprise Teresa

with a chocolate fudge cake. But once they were back in the house, Teresa no longer felt like celebrating; she sat down at the kitchen table and rested her head on her palm.

Dina opened the box Bergen had given Teresa and looked at the earrings approvingly. "You can wear these to Silver's wedding," she told her daughter.

Teresa pushed her plate of cake away. She had met Lee once, at a dinner arranged to introduce the families. Silver had barely been able to stay in his seat; he wandered around the dining room in Lee's house, as if desperate to stretch his legs. Teresa had been careful not to look at Lee for too long, but one glance told her how happy Lee was, how much in love.

Bergen reached for Teresa's plate. "If you don't want that cake, I'll take it."

"Go ahead," Teresa told him, "I hate chocolate."

"Since when?" Dina asked her daughter. "Since Silver decided to get married?"

Teresa glared at her mother. "I don't care what he does."

"Oh sure," Dina said. "What good does it do to pretend we won't miss him?"

After Bergen had gone into the living room to switch on the TV, Dina asked where he had taken Teresa to dinner.

"A Chinese restaurant," Teresa said. "He ordered. I don't know the name of anything we had."

Dina went to the kitchen doorway and looked into the living room. "Too bad," she said to herself.

"Too bad about what?" Teresa asked.

"None of your business," Dina told her daughter. "Anyway, you're too young to know about romance."

"Too young," Teresa echoed.

"That's right," Dina said. "Otherwise you'd know exactly what I meant."

But Teresa did know; she knew that some things couldn't be forced into being, no matter how hard you tried. Arnie

Bergen couldn't be her father no matter what he did, just as certainly he couldn't be the man of Dina's dreams, that Aria who rode across the desert.

"I know you wish you were in love with him," Teresa said.

"Let me see those earrings," Dina said, ignoring Teresa. "I want to make certain he got the right ones."

They were the right ones, small pearls on fourteen-karat studs. Teresa had her ears pierced the following day. She sat in the back of a jeweler's in the shopping mall outside town, a woman dabbed at her ears with alcohol and then made tiny holes with a thin needle. Teresa was told not to remove the earrings for at least six weeks, and so she did wear them to Silver's wedding; she wore a blue ribbon in her hair, and the pearls took on a sea-colored cast, bluish, as if veins ran through them. The wedding ceremony was in Lee's parents' living room; streamers had been hung across the ceiling, a tall vase of roses stood by the doorway. Lee's older sister, Joyce, was the maid of honor, she wore purple and had flowers threaded through her hair. Lee's wedding dress had been her grandmother's—the hem had been taken up, and because her grandmother was stout, the wedding dress fitted over Lee's stomach, and no one would have guessed that she was more than four months pregnant, they would not have guessed until they noticed Silver at the far edge of the living room, unless they saw his panic, and his dark eyes which seemed to be calling out a dare, even from a great distance.

Silver had already found an apartment—a first-floor flat in the Mission District with two bedrooms and a wooden porch overlooking a yard where nothing but weeds and stray birds of paradise grew. On the day of his wedding, Silver wore a new black suit, tailored in Italy, and a shirt so white it seemed to have been made out of neon. He stood in the center of the living room, right beside Lee in front of the justice of the peace. When they took their vows, Teresa held on to the back of a wooden chair, she held on so tightly that her fingers turned pale. After the ceremony, after he had kissed Lee quickly, Silver shook hands with his new father-in-law and with Bergen. And when the relatives gathered around the dining-room table, holding plates in one hand and drinks in the other, Teresa ran up to the second floor and locked herself in the bathroom. She left the light off, but leaned over the sink and looked at herself in the mirror. She was still staring into her own eyes when Dina knocked on the bathroom door.

"Where are you?" Dina said. "What are you doing in there? Her relatives are all pigs; if you're not downstairs in two minutes all the food will be gone, it will be too late."

Teresa ran the water in the sink and washed her hands and face.

"Do you hear me?" Dina said.

In the bathroom, Teresa shivered; Dina's voice echoed off the tiles, the water in the pipes sounded like a thousand frogs.

"This is ridiculous," Dina said to her daughter through the door. "You can't spend the whole time in the bathroom. What will Silver think?"

Downstairs Silver was thinking he had never felt so sick—he couldn't eat a bit of the food spread out on the dining-room table, not the small cheese sandwiches, not the little pink cakes. When he looked around the room he saw only strangers: Lee's mother, Lee's sister Joyce, and in the corner, smoothing down her hair, Lee herself.

Silver walked over and took her by the arm. "Come on," he said. "Let's get out of here."

"I haven't had anything to eat yet," Lee said.

"I said, come on," Silver told her. He grabbed a beer from the table and got his car keys out of the pocket of his new black suit.

Even though Silver wanted to make a quiet exit, everyone followed them outside to see them off—it was a tradition, there was rice to be thrown. Silver swallowed hard and turned the key in the ignition; when he backed out of the driveway he had to drive slowly so that he didn't run anyone down.

Lee sat close to him. "Where are we going?" she whispered.

Silver looked at her as though he had never seen her before. "What are you talking about?" he asked.

"Tonight," Lee said. "Where are we spending our wedding night? We should go somewhere special."

"We're not going to any fancy hotel, so just forget it," Silver said. "We're just going to go home—we might as well, we have to go there sooner or later," he told his new wife as they pulled out of the driveway.

Upstairs, Teresa was opening the bathroom door.

"Well," Dina said. "It's about time."

"I felt sick," Teresa said.

Dina narrowed her eyes. "Listen to me," she said. "He's married now, and there's nothing you can do about it."

"I don't care about that," Teresa said. "I don't care if he's married."

"I couldn't stop him," Dina said, as if apologizing. "He never listened to me. You know that."

"I'm sick," Teresa cried. "It's not because of Silver— you're crazy if you think it is."

When they got downstairs the house was empty; there were beer bottles left open, small cakes with one or two bites taken, a stack of presents piled on the couch.

"We've missed saying goodbye," Dina said, and she rushed outside so that she would be in time to wave. "Hurry up," Dina called as the screen door slammed behind her.

But Teresa didn't hurry, she didn't even move; alone in the house, behind the screen door, she watched as Silver's car made a turn in the road and disappeared. When she closed her eyes she could still see him, she could see him more clearly than any relative who had gathered in the driveway to throw rice. He had one hand on the wheel, his collar was open, the new suit jacket had been thrown into the back seat.

When Teresa opened her eyes and stared into the mesh of the screen door it was just as if she were looking into a fortune teller's crystal ball, just as if she stared into a cup where only the tea leaves remained. She could still see Silver: he was driving west, following the sun, but he looked into his rearview mirror, and when he did he somehow managed to see beyond the glass, he could see right into the living room where Teresa stood alone, still wearing pearls in her ears. There, among the roses and the regrets, she looked back at him, she called to him and finally let him know, after all this time, that her heart was breaking, it had shattered into thin pieces that fell onto the floor. And in his car, on his way to San Francisco, Silver heard her cry, and it was then he knew that there wouldn't be a day when she wouldn't be looking to the west, watching the constellations, listening to the sound of the river, waiting for him to come back.

CHAPTER
FOUR

✝

THOSE DAYS WHEN DINA SEARCHED THROUGH MEDICAL
textbooks looking for a disease were long forgotten.
She had become another woman, everyone said so. She
polished the wooden floors all through the house until
they shone like mirrors; in the mornings, when she added
cinnamon to the coffee she brewed, the scent filled every
room; her garden was the loveliest on the block—sunflowers grew in rows, blackbirds sang in the trees. In
the place where she had always parted her hair a streak

of white had appeared, but if anything it made her look younger; she seemed surrounded by a white halo, a circle of clouds, and her dark eyes looked twice their size. Whenever she caught sight of her own reflection, in the mirror at the end of the staircase landing, or in the glass above the medicine cabinet in the bathroom, Dina smiled shyly. She never thought to question why she suddenly looked exactly as she had years before; miraculously, she didn't seem one day older than the girl who had waited by the iron gate on evenings when the air smelled like sage, and hoofs shook the ground, and evenings were long, as blue as heaven.

Because Dina was so unused to being happy, because she still feared the evil eye, she never dared admit to anyone how crazy she was about Friday nights, the time when Bergen drove up from San Francisco to see her. She never told a soul that she had fallen in love, she couldn't even tell Bergen. But during the week, with not even fifty miles between them, Dina wrote Bergen letters every night. And then, each morning, she would walk down to the corner. She stood in the sunlight opening and closing the letter slot of the mailbox carefully, with the tentative touch of a girl who was head over heels.

Alone, in his apartment, Bergen sat in an easy chair by the window each afternoon. He opened the letters Dina sent him with his fingers instead of reaching for the brass letter opener on his desk. Her letters were always written on translucent notepaper, and the paper shimmered when light from Bergen's windows fell onto them: those letters nearly blinded the detective with longing. And even though she never once wrote that she loved him, Bergen knew that she did. He knew that she had given up the notion of being rescued by an Aria even before she confided it to him in one of her last letters. And though Dina no longer looked anything like that girl whose photograph he had carried for so long, Bergen was more in love than ever before, and he unfolded each letter she sent with the passion some men save for a kiss.

When he drove up to see her Bergen never talked to Dina about the letters she sent: his emotions seemed far too clumsy, his words too coarse. Instead he brought her gifts, which he hid for her to find in the breast pocket of his sports jacket. During the week he shopped carefully, spending hours looking for the right cologne, a perfect shawl, a bottle of Portuguese wine, new work gloves to use in the garden. It amazed Bergen that he could love her even more the way she was: a woman of forty-five whose dark hair no longer shone with youth, whose flesh was ringed with thin veins the color of turquoise. It was not that he had forgotten the girl in the photograph, or that he no longer loved her, but the woman who ran out to meet him in the driveway was the woman he now dreamed about every night.

They had more time alone than ever before. Since her graduation from high school, Teresa had worked as a waitress at Max's Café on Webster Street. Whenever she was given the weekend shift, Bergen and Dina had the whole house to themselves. They played gin rummy in the kitchen, they watched the sky from beneath the wisteria vines on the back porch, they held hands in the dark. And although Bergen still checked in to the Lamplighter Motel each time he came to Santa Rosa, there were times when he stayed with Dina till morning, and on those nights they held each other tight, and each felt they had never lived before. After four years they saw each other as if for the first time, and that may have been why Bergen never noticed that Dina was losing weight, that her skin had become discolored and her hands were now so fragile that in sunlight her bones seemed to rise up through her flesh like pale fish forced to surface. Bergen overlooked everything but Dina's beautiful eyes, her smile when she saw him. He overlooked it all, and, in the end, it was too late to do anything; Dina had cancer.

There wasn't a cure in the world that could bring her back; if there had been, Bergen would have found it. He would have driven her to every clinic in Mexico, he would have sold everything he owned in order to buy a machine that could breathe life back into her, for however short a time—for one more hour, one more kiss, one last night spent beside her. When the doctors at the Haven Street Clinic told them it was too late for surgery or radiation, too late to do anything at all, Bergen moved out of his apartment in San Francisco and into the Lamplighter Motel. He put Dina's picture on the dresser next to his alarm clock, he brought all five of his sports coats with him and hung them in the closet. Every day, after he and Teresa had spent hours on the wooden chairs they had set up next to Dina's bed, Bergen drove back to the Lamplighter and at night, after the moon had risen, Bergen took long walks, but he always wound up in the same spot; no matter what direction he started off in, he ended up standing at the edge of the motel pool, surrounded by empty chaise longues, circled by a chain-link fence that had been painted the same odd green as the water in the unused pool.

"Move into the house," Teresa said finally. "You're here every day. It doesn't pay to stay in a motel."

Bergen shook his head no. "She wanted us to live in separate houses. She was independent." The detective surprised himself by talking about Dina in the past tense, as if she were already gone, instead of only asleep in the upstairs bedroom. "She's still independent," he added. "She'll always be that way."

"You can move into Silver's room," Teresa said. "She'll never even know you're here."

"She'd know," Bergen insisted. "The motel is fine. Anyway," he teased, "I get a free breakfast at the Lamplighter every morning—eggs and toast."

Bergen didn't bother to add that he never ate the eggs and toast; instead he had two cups of black coffee, one right after the other, then got into his car and drove straight

to Divisadero Street. The detective continued to live in
the motel all winter long; the women who changed the
sheets and vacuumed the carpets all knew him by name,
the waiter in the dining room left a pot of coffee on
Bergen's table every morning. At the end of March, not
long after Teresa's eighteenth birthday, Bergen noticed
that Dina could no longer raise her head from her pillow
without his help. Soon it was difficult for her to swallow
the tea he brought to her. And so, one evening after Dina
had fallen asleep, Bergen asked Teresa to walk him out
to his car.

"I think you'd better call Silver," Bergen told Teresa.
"Maybe we should try to reach Reuben and King too."
The detective found he now also had trouble swallowing;
he looked up at the clouds that hung above them in the
sky. "It's the end," Bergen said.

"You're not a doctor." Teresa was stubborn. "For all
we know she could be getting better."

"She's not getting better," Bergen said.

"She might be," Teresa insisted.

"Teresa," Bergen said. "No."

Irises had begun to grow by the side of the road; they
formed a circle around Bergen's car. Even though it was
nearly spring, Teresa buttoned the sweater she wore; it
was lambswool, a present from Silver for her last birthday. He hadn't forgotten to send a present since Teresa's
awful sixteenth birthday—that year he was married. But
he never telephoned and he hadn't been to Santa Rosa in
more than two years. Even when Lee came up to visit
her mother and sister, Silver stayed away. He said he
was too busy, he told himself he just didn't have time,
but the truth was that the thought of Santa Rosa made
him dizzy, and the one time he decided to drive up he
started to smell roses as soon as he entered the city limits,
and by the time he reached Divisadero Street the scent
was so strong it was as if Teresa was right there beside
him and Silver had to turn back. Teresa had seen him

only twice since the day of his wedding, once at his son Jackie's christening, five months after the wedding, and then, nearly a year and a half later, at a Thanksgiving dinner celebrated at Lee's family's home. Both occasions were ruined by Silver's bad temper; he fought with Lee at the christening, he refused to sit at the dining-room table Lee's mother had decorated with small pumpkins and yellow chrysanthemums. At those two meetings, Teresa and Silver avoided each other; but at the Thanksgiving dinner, Dina insisted Teresa go into the kitchen and bring Silver back to the table after he had stormed out of the room, insulted by the food, or the weather, or the sound of his mother-in-law's voice. He had been standing with his back to Teresa when she found him, and when she reached out and touched his shoulder, Silver jumped.

"Don't touch me," he had told her. "Understand?"

Teresa had felt as though they had gone back in time; instead of in an unfamiliar kitchen they were at the edge of the reservoir. Her ears were ringing and she could barely hear the voices in the dining room, the scraping of metal as Lee's mother sharpened a carving knife. In spite of herself she remembered everything that had happened between them, in spite of herself she remembered more than kisses, more than lies.

"You just better not touch me," Silver had warned her that day. "What if somebody came in here and saw you do that?" he whispered.

Teresa had left the kitchen without saying another word; at the table, surrounded by Silver's in-laws, she heard the back door slam as Silver left the house, she heard his car start in the driveway, and the scream of his tires when he stepped on the gas. Later, he had come back and tried to apologize. "Look, I'm sorry," he had said. "I didn't mean it. I didn't mean to talk to you that way."

Lee was waiting impatiently in the car, while in the kitchen Dina washed and Lee's mother dried, then put the dishes back into the cabinets. Silver waited for Teresa to forgive him, to say just one word. But even if Lee hadn't gotten out of the car and begun calling Silver's name, Teresa wouldn't have forgiven him, not then, not ever; when he told her, point blank, not to touch him, Teresa felt exactly as she had years before, when they had stood on a street corner and Silver had promised her that no one would ever know. That Thanksgiving day, when Silver finally left her and went outside to his wife, Teresa admitted to herself what she had already known for years: somebody knew, she knew, and no promise, no warning, could make her forget. And it seemed to her then that the only way to fight her memories was to avoid Silver altogether, and avoiding him became the most important thing in the world.

On that day when Bergen suggested that she call Silver, Teresa shook her head no. She called Atlas over to her and kept her palm on the dog's head. "I can't do it," she told Bergen. "I can't talk to him any more."

Bergen watched Teresa carefully. "Since when?" he asked. "I always thought he was the only one you could talk to."

"You do it," Teresa said. "You call Silver."

And so it was the detective and not Teresa who telephoned Silver to tell him that his mother was dying. But before Silver could gas up the brand-new Camaro he had owned for less than a month, it was too late; Dina was gone. She died in the bed King Connors had built out of redwood in the first year they were married, she died with a tortoise-shell comb her father had given her still in her hair. Dina called out for Bergen, but no one heard her— the detective was downstairs in the kitchen with Teresa drinking tea, making call after call in the hopes of contacting Reuben and King Connors, since he felt he owed them at least that courtesy. Dina called his name a second time, but after that it didn't seem to matter that Bergen hadn't heard her, hadn't run up the stairs two at a time. Dina didn't bother to call out again, because it suddenly seemed that Bergen was with her, he was right there by her side. And even though the old detective was downstairs reaching for a pitcher of cream, Dina was certain he was in her bedroom. When she closed her eyes she could feel him sit down next to her, and she was grateful that Teresa had made up the bed with clean white sheets just that morning. He held her hand, and Dina whispered, finally, that she loved him, and he answered that he had known it for years; and she sighed because at this, the very end, Dina was sure he was with her even though it was the pillowcase she held on to rather than his hand. And later in the morning, when Teresa came upstairs to the bedroom, the lace curtains in the window moved back and forth even though there was no breeze. A bloodstain the shape of a wild orchid was on the pillow and Dina's fingers were still reaching toward the white edge of the pillowcase, just as they had been before she let go.

Bergen didn't say a word when Teresa told him; he went out to his car and sat behind the wheel. It had begun to rain and, without the windshield wipers turned on, Bergen couldn't see anything in front of him; still he sat there, in the silent car, for nearly an hour before he could go back inside the house. He insisted that Teresa eat lunch and, because she was in shock, she walked right over to the refrigerator. After he was certain that Teresa had fixed herself a sandwich, Bergen went to the hall closet, put his sports coat on, then went into the living room. He pulled down the shades and drew all the curtains. And after that, the detective sat down on the couch, right in the center where the two pillows met unevenly, and he cried, certain that he would never recover, never be able to face a life without Dina.

Silver got to Santa Rosa late in the afternoon; when he parked his Camaro in the driveway, Dina was still upstairs, no one had moved her. But as soon as he got out of his car, Silver knew it was too late—all of the window shades in the house were drawn, the collie sat out on the porch, grief

clung to the sparse grass on the front lawn. Although it
was not yet four, the sky was dark, what had begun as a
rain shower had become a storm. When Silver looked up
he saw a line of lightning above the house, the shingles
that King Connors had put on the roof shone like rough
stars. Silver went in the front door, but he stood where he
was, on the woven doormat—the house smelled like roses
and the scent was hypnotic. He found himself unable to
move. From the hallway Silver could see into the living
room; Bergen sat on the couch, hunched over so that he
seemed part of the fabric. All the houseplants in the living
room—the begonia and the Swedish ivy, the jade plants
and the cactus—all had died. Teresa and Bergen hadn't
thought to water them throughout the months of Dina's
illness and the plants had wilted in their ceramic pots, a
thin carpet of brown leaves now covered the floor. When
Bergen looked up and saw Silver, the old detective came
out into the hallway to shake his hand.

"I've taken care of everything," Bergen told Silver.
"I've arranged the funeral, and Teresa knows that she can
stay on in this house for as long as she wants."

"Where is she?" Silver asked.

"Upstairs," Bergen said. "She's still upstairs in her
bed."

"I mean Teresa," Silver said.

"Oh," Bergen said. "Teresa. I thought you meant Dina.
Dina's still upstairs in bed."

Silver put his hands in his pockets; he was dripping
with rainwater and a pool was collecting around each
of his black leather boots. "Thanks for taking care of
everything," Silver said.

Bergen blinked, surprised that Dina's son knew how to
be polite. "You don't have to thank me," Bergen said.
"Nothing I did saved her, did it?"

Silver left Bergen in the hallway and went toward the
kitchen; he knew Teresa was in there, the odor of roses
was so strong it made him dizzy. What Silver needed

was a drink, a warm dinner, a night of pure uninter-
rupted sleep, but he went on into the kitchen. She had
her back to him; there was a cold cup of coffee in front
of her, an uneaten sandwich on a blue and white china
plate. She hadn't combed her hair, it was knotted and
thick, and fell down her back like a flock of blackbirds
in flight. Silver imagined that if he frightened her, if
she moved too quickly, dark feathers would drop onto
the floor.

"It's happened," Silver whispered, "just like I told you
it would."

Teresa had been sitting in the same place for hours;
if she closed her eyes for even a second she felt she
was surrounded by wild horses with hoofs so sharp they
were like daggers. Now that she heard Silver's voice she
could no longer control her grief; she bent her head and
cried, and her tears fell into the untouched cup of coffee. Although he tried not to go any closer, Silver was
drawn to her; he stood right behind her, then reached
down and put his hand on her neck. He could feel her
rapid pulse.

"We're orphans now," he whispered.

Beneath his touch, Teresa was melting. She had more
tears inside her than she thought possible; she was sure
that if she turned to face him, she would throw her arms
around Silver, she would never be able to let go.

Silver bent down; he was so close that when he spoke
Teresa could feel his breath on her skin.

"It's just the two of us now," Silver told her, and even
though Dina was still upstairs in her bed, and Bergen sat
in the living room staring at the photograph Dina's father
had given him so many years ago, Teresa felt her heart
leap, and being near to Silver seemed more dangerous than
ever. And in that dark kitchen on a day when lightning
moved across the sky, she couldn't pretend that she hadn't
been waiting for Silver to say exactly those words for as
long as she could remember.

* * *

It rained on the day of the funeral, it poured all that following week. The river overflowed and even the houses
built above the flood line on stilts soon had pools of
water in every room. Cows were swept away, dogs got
lost on familiar roads, pelicans nested in chimneys and
the feathers of their young became coated with ashes. In
town, anyone who didn't have to go out stayed home;
all over Santa Rosa roofs leaked and backyards became
reservoirs. On Divisadero Street, snails drowned in circles
in the vegetable patch where Dina had insisted Bergen
spread mulch only a few weeks earlier.

Silver's wife and son had come up to Santa Rosa by
bus. Days after the funeral, Lee still continued to wear
her black wool dress; although she had packed a suitcase
full of clothes for Silver and Jackie, she hadn't thought
to bring a change of clothes for herself. The house was so
quiet that she found herself walking on tiptoes, barefoot
so that her high heels wouldn't echo across the floor. It
was a house thick with sleep. Teresa had locked herself
in her room after the funeral, she refused to come out;
Bergen, torn between remaining at the Lamplighter Motel
and returning to San Francisco, wound up sleeping on the
living-room couch. Silver spent his nights at the Dragon,
searching out old connections; when he came home he
slept till noon in his old room, then spent the rest of the
day wandering through the house. The house was so damp
that Bergen had begun to wheeze, and his heavy breathing
set Silver on edge.

"Why don't you take some cough medicine?" Silver
asked Bergen a few days after the funeral. "You're driving
me crazy."

Bergen took the hint. "I know I should leave," he
said.

"Listen, I don't have the right to ask you to leave,"
Silver admitted. "This house belongs to you, so I'm not
kicking you out, understand?"

"You're not kicking me out," Bergen agreed. "I could never live here without your mother."

"If you want to go, I'm not going to stop you," Silver said, and when the detective finally got up from the couch Silver felt as though a weight had been lifted off his back; he had never understood what his mother saw in the old man, he didn't like the stare the detective often fixed him with, especially when Teresa was in the same room.

"I'm just going to wait to say goodbye to Teresa," Bergen told Silver after he had gone to the hall closet for his sports coat.

"Christ," Silver said. "That could be days." He lowered his voice. "She's been sleeping a lot."

"That's all right," Bergen said. "I've got time."

As soon as they had come home from the funeral, Teresa had gone to her room. She had slept for eighteen hours straight. In her dreams two black butterflies had attached themselves to her shoulders. Though their wings were delicate, the butterflies lifted Teresa off the ground. Even when she had wakened, Teresa had still felt those butterflies attached to her skin; when she walked across the floor she imagined her feet were inches above the wood.

She let them all think her spell went on for much longer than it did; she stayed in her room, waiting till long past midnight to come down to the kitchen, no matter how hungry she was. In the days since the funeral Teresa had managed to avoid them all, but at night in her room she looked out the window, she studied the stars; already she missed Dina, already a tide of despair rose up to the ceiling. On the day that Bergen left, Silver came to her room; he put his ear to the door and listened for a sigh, or the rustle of a sheet. When he knocked on the door, Teresa considered not answering. She could have pretended to be asleep, but the walls of her room were closing in on her, and no matter how much she wished for a long sleeping spell she was awake, and lonely, and finally she opened the door.

"Bergen's leaving," Silver told her. "At long last. He wants to say goodbye."

When they walked downstairs Teresa held on to the banister; she heard the whir of a butterfly's wings just above her head, and she nearly stumbled on the last stair. Silver put his arm around her waist to steady her, but as soon as he saw Bergen he backed away from Teresa. He reached into his pocket for a cigarette, but he didn't make a move to leave Bergen alone with his sister; he found himself afraid of what she might say.

Bergen came over to Teresa and shook her hand formally; his clothes were wrinkled, he carried a brown paper shopping bag which he opened to show Teresa.

"Tell me if you don't want me to take these things," Bergen said.

Inside the bag was some forsythia that Bergen had wrapped in a scrap of tin foil, there was the white wool blanket Dina had always kept on her bed, and a bottle of Chanel he had bought her one Christmas and Dina had thought too expensive to use.

Teresa closed the paper bag. "This is your house," she said to Bergen. "You own it, and if anyone should leave it's me."

Lee was in the kitchen, baking a lemon-flavored angel cake she would serve later that day when her mother and sister came over to visit. She balanced the mixing bowl on the counter when the phone rang, then called to Silver. And so, even though Silver hadn't planned to leave Teresa and Bergen alone, he reluctantly did just that, and went to talk to the bartender of the Dragon, who wanted to buy some cocaine. While Silver made his arrangements, Teresa walked Bergen out to his car.

"I'm going to miss you," she admitted. "I've gotten used to you."

Bergen opened the trunk of his car and put the paper bag full of Dina's belongings inside, making certain to take out the forsythia and place it inside the car, on the front seat next to him.

"What should I do now?" Teresa asked Bergen after he locked the trunk.

"I can't tell you what to do," Bergen said. It had finally stopped raining, but there were mud puddles all up and down Divisadero Street. "All right," Bergen said. "You want to know what I think you should do?"

Teresa nodded her head emphatically. "Yes."

"Anything," Bergen said. "Anything but go with him."

Silver came out of the house then; he slammed the door shut behind him, waved at Teresa, then got into the Camaro and started the engine. Bergen's mouth puckered, as if he had just eaten a lemon. He had never trusted Silver, not from the first when Silver was nothing more than a rude boy who aspired to a life of danger. Toward the end, even Dina had admitted that Silver always looked for trouble; toward the end, he was no longer her favorite child. And it wasn't because he had married and moved away, it was because she had begun to compare him to Bergen, and, compared to kindness, blind courage and recklessness seemed trivial. And a man who traveled beneath an orange moon on nights that were scented with wildflowers and thick with heat suddenly seemed much less marvelous than a man who would sit on the back porch and hold her hand for hours without having to say one word.

But Dina had never told Teresa about her disillusionment with Arias, and with Silver, and when Silver drove away Teresa stared after him, and even if Dina had warned Teresa it might not have made any difference, because even now Teresa never gave her grandmother's parting words a second thought. What she thought about was Silver.

"You asked for advice, so I'm giving it to you," Bergen said. "Start a new life. Don't think you need anyone to protect you—your mother spent twenty years doing that and look what it got her. That's why I never pressured

her to let me move in here. It's no good to need someone
more than you want them. And sometimes you just have
to start over again."

After Bergen had left, Teresa went back into the house.
For a moment, only a moment, she wondered if the detective could possibly know about her and Silver, if he had
just sensed it, if he had found some proof. But clearly,
Bergen had always disliked Silver, certainly it was nothing
more than that. Later that day, when the detective was
back in San Francisco and the sun was lower in the sky,
Teresa would sit with Lee and her mother and sister; she
would hold a plate full of lemon cake and drink a cup of
hot tea. But now, alone in the living room, listening to Lee
run the water in the kitchen as she washed the breakfast
dishes, Teresa wondered what she would do next, and she
wasn't at all certain that the best thing to do might not be
to simply disappear, leaving behind nothing more than a
thin, inky line of despair.

On the morning of the day when they were to leave Santa
Rosa, Lee woke up early. She got out of bed when the
sky was still dark; she put on her black dress and then
went to the portable crib to get Jackie, making certain to
keep her hand over his mouth so that he couldn't cry out
and wake Silver. She went downstairs in her bare feet,
and at the bottom of the stairs she paused by the oval
mirror and looked at the bruise on her cheek—the bruise
itself was yellow, but all around it, in a circle, her skin
had turned purple. At three in the morning, when all the
neighbors on Divisadero Street were fast asleep, Silver
had hit her, he had turned on her for no reason at all.
He had had too much to drink at the Dragon, then hadn't
been able to sleep, he paced across the room, he opened
the window and tilted his head, as if listening for a voice
he couldn't quite hear. It was then Lee had gone over to
him; she put her arms around him and told him to come
back to bed.

"Don't tell me what to do," Silver said, and maybe she should have known enough to keep quiet, but every day they spent in Santa Rosa seemed to be taking him farther away from her, so Lee put her hand on her hip, and she pushed him too far.

"What the hell are you listening for?" she said. "What the hell do you think you're going to hear in the middle of the night?"

That was all she said when he turned on her; he caught her by surprise and hit her hard, just as if she were his enemy. He had been sorry then, he had kissed her, called her darling, led her back to bed. And Lee was so stunned that she hadn't said another word, hadn't even cried. They fought often, that was nothing new, there were weeks when it seemed as if they did nothing else. But Silver had always cooled down before; he may have wanted to hit her, but he didn't. Now, as she studied her face in the morning light, and afterwards, when she went into the kitchen to get Jackie some breakfast, Lee was certain that it was whatever Silver had been listening for that had made him strike her; it was Santa Rosa, she thought, it was being home.

Lee sat Jackie down on the floor and got him a bowl of Frosted Flakes; she took out a Pepsi for herself and watched her son. She was worried about him, and she grew more so each day. He was so uninterested, so quiet that he sent chills down her spine. Lee was too frightened to take him to a doctor; she hoped he was a late bloomer, only a little slow. At first she had spent all day every day talking to him, hoping that sooner or later he would respond; now, when she was with her son, she was as silent as Jackie, and she watched him with an odd feeling of distrust.

Lee was halfway through her Pepsi when she heard the basement steps creak; she reached to the drainboard and picked up a knife. She tried not to breathe. When the cellar door opened and Teresa stood there, dressed in a cotton

nightgown which reached past her knees, Lee threw back
her head and laughed.

"You almost got yourself killed," she told Teresa and
she showed her the knife.

"A robber would have to be crazy to come in this
house," Teresa said. "There's nothing here except this."
She held up a jar she had found; it was blackberry jam left
over from the canning Dina had done the summer before.
"I was hungry," Teresa explained, but the truth was she
had been dreaming all night of Dina, Dina standing in the
kitchen filling Mason jars with sour tomatoes and jam.
Teresa filled the tea kettle, then ran the jam jar under
hot water. When she unscrewed the top it seemed as
if summer filled the room. She took a spoon from the
drawer, then sat at the table and began to eat the jam
straight from the jar. Lee sat across from her and sipped
her Pepsi and it was then that Teresa noticed the bruise.

"What happened?" Teresa asked. She reached over and
touched Lee's face, drawn to the violent mark.

Lee brushed at her cheek as if she were wiping away
some rouge. "It's nothing," Lee said. "I walked into a
wall."

Teresa brought her feet up and covered her knees with
her nightgown; her hair fell carelessly, like strands of
knotted black pearls. She felt herself grow jealous; around
her mouth the traces of blackberry jam were the same
color as the bruise on Lee's face.

"Did he do it?" Teresa asked. "Is he the wall you
walked into?"

Jackie had finished his breakfast and had wandered over
to a corner of linoleum that Bergen had put down years
before; the corner rose up like a knife. The moment Jackie
cut himself on its ragged edge he began to cry; in seconds
his cry had become a deep howl. Lee ran over to her
son; she got down on her hands and knees, and when her
soothing voice couldn't comfort Jackie, she put her hand
over the boy's mouth.

"Goddamn it," Lee whispered to Jackie. "You're going to wake him up."

But up in his old bedroom on the second floor, Silver was already awake. He had decided there was no way around it: Teresa would have to come and live with them. He hadn't bothered to discuss his decision with Lee, and the more he thought about it the more her living with them seemed the only possible choice, no matter how uncomfortable it would be for all of them. Silver had gotten dressed quickly; he had put on a clean pair of jeans and a white shirt and left his soiled clothes on the bed for Lee to pack. On his way out the door he tripped over Lee's high heels, and so he was already muttering to himself about his wife's stupidity as he walked down the stairs, and his mood was black when he reached the kitchen and found Lee crouched on the floor with their son. He stared at her, disgusted, then went to the table and examined the half-empty Pepsi bottle.

"What the hell is this supposed to be?" he asked Lee. He held the soda bottle in the air and walked over to his wife; he stood so close that his boot crushed the hem of her skirt. "This may come as a shock to you, but most human beings drink coffee in the morning."

Teresa tried not to look at them; she was afraid that her jealousy would reflect in the open jar of jam. She got up and poured boiling water through the coffee filter and into the pot.

"Thank God someone around here knows how to make coffee," Silver said. He reached down and pulled Lee to her feet. "If there's something you do right I wish somebody would tell me about it."

"Maybe somebody else would appreciate me," Lee said. "Another man would think I did a lot of things right."

"Oh, yeah?" Silver said. "Tell me one, just one."

"Will you stop it?" Teresa said to them. "Just stop."

Silver and Lee looked away from each other, silenced. Teresa brought two cups of coffee over to the table and sat down; she closed her eyes and leaned her head back so that her neck arched. Silver spooned sugar into both cups.

"Go on," he told Teresa, "drink this. You've been sleeping too much," he said with more concern than Lee had ever heard from him before.

Teresa did as he told her. "I can't stand to hear it," she said. "Don't fight with her."

"I can speak for myself," Lee said. "You don't have to protect me."

"After you drink your coffee, get dressed," Silver said to Teresa. "I'm taking you with us to San Francisco."

"When was this decided?" Lee asked.

Teresa shook her head. "I'm going back to work today."

"Maybe Silver's right," Lee said, hoping to please. "It's depressing here, it's dangerous. You can't go on living here alone."

The more Lee talked, the jumpier Silver became. He took his car keys out of his pocket and tossed them up so that they chimed like bells; he imagined the three of them in the same house, separated by so little: a bedroom wall, a breakfast table set with brown bowls filled with orange slices. Every night, when the lights had been turned out and the quilts were still cold on the bed, Silver would sleep beside Lee, but all the while he would be thinking about Teresa, worrying that she might someday decide to announce all that had happened between them.

"You don't want to come to San Francisco?" Silver said to Teresa. "Is that it?"

When Teresa didn't answer, Lee grew tense; she was certain that Silver would set his sister straight, but all he did was lean against the stove and say, "If you want to stay here I won't force you to go."

"I don't know what I want," Teresa said. Her voice was dangerously thin.

"Okay," Silver said softly.

Teresa stood up so quickly that her chair fell backward; one wooden leg splintered as it hit the floor. "You

think you can just come back here after all this time?"
Silver turned away; he looked out the kitchen window
and watched two blackbirds walk along the porch railing.
"You can't expect me to live in your house," Teresa
told him.

"All right," Silver said. "All right, all right, stay here
if that's what you want."

Teresa ran from the room; she went upstairs and
slammed her door shut. And while Teresa was pulling
her waitress uniform out of the closet, Silver turned away
from the window to find his wife staring at him from
across the room, her eyes so blue they seemed like bits
of glass.

"What the hell are you looking at?" Silver asked her.

Later, after Lee had packed all their clothes, and Silver was outside loading up the car, Lee went back into
the kitchen. The back door was open, and through the
mesh of the screen she could see Teresa walking across
the garden, dressed in a white uniform and the sweater Silver had sent her for her last birthday. Teresa cut
across the yard, then went out the side gate, avoiding the
driveway where Silver was now checking the oil in the
Camaro. Alone in the kitchen, Lee watched her sister-in-
law; she would have given anything to know why Teresa
felt even more abandoned by Silver than she herself did,
but by the time Lee had found the courage to ask, Teresa
was already running down Divisadero Street, she was
already gone.

Teresa continued to work at Max's Café all through the
spring and summer. Every Thursday, after the dinner shift,
she got her paycheck, and in return she wrote down orders,
polished the countertops, delivered hot plates of fried eggs
and hamburger specials. There were two waitresses at
Max's—Teresa, and Lucy, a woman who had been in the
same grade as Silver in high school and who still remembered watching Teresa's brother longingly, finally shoring

up the nerve to leave a love note in his locker, a note that Silver never bothered to read, much less answer. Lucy was the only person in town Teresa spoke to regularly all summer long; after work, Teresa was always alone. In the evenings she did her shopping. The huge aisles at the Safeway where Reuben had once worked made her dizzy, and so she went to a corner grocery on Divisadero Street, a small shop where lettuce was piled up in a wooden bin and dust coated the jars of apricots stored in syrup. Late at night, she listened to the radio; she learned old songs by heart and knew every word Roy Orbison and the Drifters had ever sung. The radio she listened to was an old Magnavox King Connors had bought; Teresa kept it on her night table so that even when she slept the dial glowed and there was a never-ending lullaby of blue chords to keep her company. She kept KCAX tuned in; she got to know each D.J.'s favorite songs. Music crept into the corners of the house, even into the rooms Teresa now avoided: Dina's bedroom, Silver's room, the living room, where the shades had been drawn for months.

Aside from the D.J.s on KCAX there was only Lucy, and conversations with her were as limited as a weather report. Lucy talked about men, always customers—a truckdriver who had left a five-dollar tip, a boy who had stared at Teresa for so long that his hamburger special had grown cold as ice and he had left Max's without eating lunch.

"You could get a date just like that," Lucy said again and again, snapping her fingers in the air. "You don't have to sit by yourself and listen to the damned radio every night."

One afternoon when the two women had a break between the breakfast and lunch rushes, Lucy decided to give Teresa some stern advice. Teresa was eating a tunafish sandwich she had fixed for herself more than an hour before, Lucy had a salad with no dressing.

"If you were a little friendlier you could get any man who walked in here," Lucy said. "Otherwise, you're going to wind up alone."

"One of our customers?" Teresa said. "Forget it."

"I don't think they're so bad," Lucy said.

"They are," Teresa said. "They're that bad."

"I'm seeing someone I met here—Sal, he owns the auto parts store down the street. The problem with you is you're stuck up. That's why you can't even get a date."

"Maybe I don't care," Teresa said. She put down her half-eaten sandwich and walked to the end of the counter.

Lucy went over and put an arm around her. "You don't have to be crazy about every guy you go out with," she said. "You don't even have to like him. There are other reasons to go out with a man."

Teresa looked over at Lucy. "What other reasons?" she asked.

"Hell," Lucy said, "I'm not an heiress and neither are you."

"Are you talking about money?" Teresa said. "Going out with men and getting money for it?"

Lucy glared at Teresa, then shot a look at the short-order cook behind the grill. "I'm talking about getting a little something back for what you put out," she whispered. "That's all."

"Well, that's disgusting," Teresa said. "That's what's called being a prostitute."

"Oh, yeah?" Lucy said. "Really? I'd like to know what's wrong with getting something back. I'm not talking about millions. Thirty dollars for a good time, twenty if I can do what they want without having to take off my clothes."

"I don't want to hear any more," Teresa said. She began to clean the countertop with Windex; she hummed a Bob Dylan song she had heard on KCAX that morning.

"I could fix you up with someone in a minute," Lucy whispered. "It's not all work, you know. Some of it's fun.

What's wrong with having a good time?"

That night, when Teresa walked home from work, she felt lonelier than ever. Nothing helped, not Atlas waiting for her at the door, not the radio or the sound of her favorite D.J.'s voice. It was nearly the end of the summer, five months had passed since Dina's funeral, and in all that time Teresa hadn't gone dancing once, she hadn't had one gin and tonic, she hadn't been kissed on the mouth. She looked through her closet—nothing was new. She studied her face in the mirror, and carefully painted her eyelids with shadow. That night Teresa listened to the radio without really hearing any lyrics; she washed her hair and then combed it until it stood away from her head, electrified, glowing; she rinsed out a lace slip she'd forgotten she owned and stayed up well past midnight polishing a pair of high-heeled shoes she hadn't worn since high school. The following day, when she went to work at Max's, Teresa felt exhausted, but she looked sharp—she wore eyeliner and the polished high heels, and Lucy could tell, in an instant, that Teresa had decided to make a change in her life. But she didn't pressure Teresa, she waited for Teresa to come to her, and in the afternoon, soon after lunch, Teresa went over to Lucy and looked her straight in the eye.

"Who're you going to introduce me to first?" Teresa asked.

"You got tired of being alone." Lucy nodded.

"I don't know about that," Teresa told the other waitress. "I think it's more that I just got tired."

On a Friday night in the last week of August, Teresa was wearing a black skirt and a red satin blouse. She had been waiting outside the Dragon for fifteen minutes—long enough to have second thoughts, but not long enough to act on them—when Lucy pulled up in her yellow Pinto.

"Don't expect too much," Lucy said as the two women stood in the dark. She ran a comb through her hair. "He's a friend of Sal's, he's married, and he wants to have a good time tonight."

"Well, so do I," Teresa said. "I want to go dancing. I want to go everywhere."

"For now, let's just try the bar," Lucy said as they walked into the Dragon. "He's not going to be a Hollywood movie star, you know."

It turned out that his name was Roger, and when he saw Teresa he wished that his wife had gone to visit her sister down on the Peninsula for more than just one night; he wished he had a couple of hundred dollars in his pocket, and more than a spoonful of hope left inside. He bought her two drinks—gin and tonics with slices of lime that burned the roof of her mouth. They left the Dragon after less than an hour, just the two of them, gone before Lucy and Sal noticed their absence. They drove to a club in Petaluma and danced until midnight, and even then Teresa didn't want to stop. On a crowded dance floor, in that last week in August, she had found an antidote for loneliness; every time she stepped onto the dance floor another arrow was removed from her flesh, leaving behind nothing more than a perfect circle, a wound so tiny it could be seen only in starlight.

"Come on," Roger said to her finally. "We've got better things to do."

They drove back to Santa Rosa; while Roger went into the office of the Lamplighter to register for a room, Teresa reached under her skirt and pulled down her panty hose; her legs were burning hot, on fire. When she saw Roger walking back to the car, the key to their room in hand, Teresa opened the glove compartment and threw the panty hose inside, then got out and followed Roger past the pool, which was surrounded by amber lanterns and laced with chlorine. The night air chilled her bare legs; she thought, briefly, about turning back, but didn't.

They made love on a bed covered by an orange bed-spread; the white sheets had been burned through the center by a cigarette carelessly dropped onto the linen. They kept the lights off, and all the time they held each other Teresa could hear the motor of the ice machine, which stood in a courtyard just beyond their room. He whispered to her: how beautiful she was, how much he wanted her, had always wanted a woman like her, a dark woman with skin that was cool beneath his fingers, someone who knew when to be quiet and when to sigh out loud. At first, Teresa felt as though every inch of her was white with desire; she hoped that the stranger she held was the man of her dreams, this night would become every night, all other memories would be forgotten. But it was no good; when she kissed Roger, when she closed her eyes, she was imagining another man's kisses, another man's heart, a man who, if he knew where she was, would have driven all night to find her, jumping out of his car before the wheels had come to a stop, breaking down the motel-room door if he had to, just to get to her, just to find her again. It was Silver she thought about that night, and her thought shocked her. Still it was Silver whose name pounded in her head and echoed off every tile, each piece of teak furniture in the motel room.

When Roger drove her home the next morning, Teresa got out of the car and didn't look back. Atlas had been left out all night and when Teresa walked around the yard to the back door, the dog didn't come to greet her; instead, he sat beneath the eucalyptus tree and stared at her mournfully.

"Well, come on," Teresa said to him.

Atlas didn't move an inch. Two sunflowers grew in the abandoned garden, they stood there like witnesses, facing east. Teresa sat down on the steps of the back porch and cried. She didn't want to think about Silver, didn't want to compare every man to him. She wiped her eyes on the cuff of her satin blouse; she pulled her skirt down to cover her bare knees. Atlas walked over to her slowly; the earth was dusty, the sky was as blue as a bird's feathers. When the collie sat next to her on the porch and coughed like an old man who had spent a sleepless night, Teresa realized that she had forgotten to ask Roger for the thirty dollars he had promised to pay for a night of dancing, a night full of red stars and seduction, a little time with a woman like her.

Although Lucy was annoyed when Teresa admitted she hadn't gotten a cent from Roger, she laughed out loud when she heard that Teresa had left her panty hose in the glove compartment of the car.

"That'll cost him more than thirty dollars when his wife gets hold of them," Lucy crowed. "But just don't forget what you want," Lucy reminded Teresa. "Otherwise you'll make it tough for me—I've got to survive, you know. I've got to put gas in my car, and pay to have my hair styled. Just remember, what you want is cash."

Still, Teresa almost never took money, although she did accept midnight suppers, gin and tonics, bottles of wine, beds in motels where the wallpaper was peeling and the sheets were less than white. Every time she met a new man, Teresa began the evening crazy with hope; each time it was possible that a stranger could make her forget the day at the reservoir, and lately she had begun to think about it all the time. Even when every stranger's promise grew dim, Teresa was determined: she would prove that there could be a man in her life who wasn't Silver, she would find him. All autumn, she looked for that proof; she bought new blouses trimmed with ribbon, she wore high leather heels that she had tinted purple at the shoemaker's, she braided blue beads into her hair and offered herself to anyone who would take her, anyone who had the nerve to sleep beside a woman who could never hide her disappointment, who never even tried. When Bergen telephoned, two or three times a month, Teresa always told him the same thing: she didn't need money or company. She lied to the detective and told him she had hundreds saved in a bank account; she described the garden to him, an imaginary list of wildflowers and winter onions in place of the coppery weeds and mud puddles. She insisted she was doing just fine.

Eight months after Dina's death Teresa still dreaded having dinner alone, the kitchen walls closed in on her and she took to leaving the back door open in the evenings. One October evening, when the air was oddly warm and blackbirds sang in the eucalyptus tree, moved by the false promise of summer, Teresa didn't have a date for the first time in months on a Friday night. She ate dinner alone, she switched on KCAX and sang along with the radio as she washed the dishes. Atlas was on the back porch; he leaned against the screen door and each time he breathed the metal molding of the door rattled. When Teresa had just about finished washing up, Atlas began to bark. Teresa ignored him; she heard the dog's claws hit against the wooden steps as he ran into the yard, but she was certain the collie was chasing the neighbor's cat under the bushes which separated the yards, where Teresa and her friend Maureen had hidden when they were children. The Raleighs no longer lived next door; they had sold their house soon after Maureen was sent away, and Teresa had never found out if her friend had kept her baby, or if the child had been a boy or a girl. Still, Teresa always thought of next door as "Maureen's," and that was where she was certain Atlas had run off to.

In fact, it wasn't a cat Atlas barked at but a stranger who walked through the yard. If the collie had been younger he might have stood on the back porch and blocked the stranger's path, but Atlas was nearly ten, he hadn't the heart to do anything more than stand beneath the eucalyptus tree and yelp until his voice gave out. When Teresa turned from the cabinet where she had stored her washed supper dishes, the stranger was already in the house. Teresa leaned against the sink; the small of her back got soaked with dishwater; she stared up at a man who had gold rings on three of his fingers.

"I'm not going to hurt you," he told Teresa after he had closed the door behind him.

"You've got a lot of nerve," Teresa said. She brushed stray strands of hair out of her eyes. "The least you could have done was call. I told Lucy not to give out my address—just my number. You really have a lot of nerve."

Teresa wasn't wearing a bit of makeup, her feet were bare, she hadn't expected company, but when she narrowed her eyes and inspected the stranger's face she began to wonder if the man in her kitchen might be the one who could drive Silver out of her thoughts. Teresa took his hand.

"Come upstairs," she said to the stranger.

"Wait a minute," he said, but he was smiling. "You don't even know my name."

"Let me guess," Teresa said as she led him out of the kitchen, and then upstairs. "Arthur," she tried. "Lloyd. Robert, but they call you Bobby."

"You haven't guessed right yet," the stranger told her as she led him into her bedroom.

If Teresa had ever asked Silver, years before, what he did all night and who he worked for, she would have known the name of the man she took to her bed. If she had ever gone with Silver to the Dragon, late at night when all the stars were in the center of the sky, she might have met the man who now watched her take off her clothes and place them on the back of a wooden chair; she would have known the man she kissed was not really a stranger at all. He was Angel Gregory and he had been planning a visit to the house on Divisadero Street for nearly four years, but he had never, ever, expected to be greeted like this.

When they made love they were both tentative—Gregory, because he had never expected to be taken up to her bedroom, and Teresa because for the first time she wasn't thinking of Silver when she held another

man. Instead she was thinking of deserts and hope—and
she found herself wondering what sort of man she had
discovered at her own back door. Each time she responded
to Gregory's touch, Teresa was shocked by the tenderness
she felt toward a stranger. And after they had made love,
she still felt the urge to hold him, as if, finally, there was a
possibility she might not be lonely forever. Gregory stroked
Teresa's neck with his fingertips, they were side by side,
there was no reason to speak, and as soon as Gregory did
speak he ruined everything, because the first thing he said
was Silver's name.

"That's why I'm here," Gregory admitted. "I'm looking
for your brother."

Teresa eyed him as if he were a cobra on her pillow.

"He doesn't live here any more, so you might as well
leave if that's all you're here for."

"Don't lie to me," Gregory warned. "I hate dishonesty.
I hate it worse than murder."

Teresa blinked. "Let's not talk about murder," she told
the man in her bed. She wished, now, that she had kept
the back door double locked.

Gregory got up and pulled on his jeans; he stood inches
away from the wall that separated them from Silver's old
room; he tossed Teresa's bathrobe to her, then nodded to
the door.

"I'm starving. I lost thirty pounds in prison, and now no
matter what I eat I never gain any weight and I'm always
hungry."

There wasn't much in the house, but Teresa cooked him
a dinner of green tomatoes and rice; when she walked over
to the table carrying the hot frying pan, Gregory shook a
finger at her.

"Don't throw that thing at me," he warned. "This is
nothing personal. I've got nothing against you. I like
you," he admitted. Teresa gazed at him coldly. "You
were pretty friendly before," Gregory said, "when you
didn't even know who I was."

Teresa leaned against the countertop and watched Gregory eat; she had spent a whole week's salary on the silk robe she wore and the man who had just gotten out of prison hadn't given it a second glance.

"Silver lives in San Francisco now," she said, when Gregory had finished eating and still hadn't made a move to leave. "You won't find him here."

"You could be lying, trying to protect him. He could walk in the door at any minute."

So Gregory stayed; soon Teresa grew braver with him— she let Atlas inside, then made a pot of coffee, and sat across from Gregory at the table.

"Am I the first woman you've been with since you got out?" she asked.

"What if you are?" Gregory teased. "Does that mean we're engaged?"

"What's prison like?" Teresa asked then.

"You don't want to know about it," Gregory said. He rolled up his sleeve. "This is the only good thing I got in Vacaville."

Teresa bent over and touched his arm; there was the tattoo of a red dog, his head thrown back as if he howled, all four paws close together, ready to leap.

"This here is nothing like your dog." Gregory nodded to the old collie, asleep on the linoleum, his nose buried between his paws. "This dog's a hunter." Gregory smiled. "Like me. I'm going to follow Silver until I find him, and once I do I'm not going to let go."

The closeness Teresa had felt before, when they were lovers, was returning, and Gregory seemed less and less like a stranger all the time. When he spoke about Silver, Teresa felt as if he were using words that were her own, and when it was nearly midnight and Gregory got up to put his dinner plate in the sink Teresa realized that she didn't want him to leave.

"I've waited so long for Silver," Gregory told Teresa, "I can wait a little longer. I could try to get you to give me his phone number and address, but I don't want to put you in the middle. I'm not going to force you to make a choice."

"What makes you think there's a choice?" Teresa said. "He's my brother."

"So what?" Gregory said. "That doesn't stop you from knowing what he's like."

When Teresa walked Angel Gregory outside there was no moon, and the air was warm; it was a night of Indian summer, and for the first time in years Teresa felt as if she had a friend.

"He sent you to prison," she guessed, and Gregory nodded his head yes.

"My mistake was to think that Silver was only a kid. He had me busted, then he set himself up in business."

Out on the front porch Teresa felt totally at ease with Gregory—there was a lovely caution in the dark; no blinding sunlight, no hawks above them in the sky. Teresa took Gregory's hand in her own and opened his fist so that she could look at his palm, but it was too dark to see his love line, too dark to see the life line in his skin.

"I always thought he was going to come back for me someday, but he hasn't," Teresa whispered, and the words came out before she could stop them.

"It's a shame you can't give him up," Gregory said, understanding that Silver was in Teresa's blood just as he was in Gregory's. "It's a shame I can't either," he admitted. "So I'm not going to ask you to be in the middle. Call him," Gregory told Teresa before he left that night. "Let him know that I'm looking for him. I understand that you have to, just like you understand that sooner or later I'll find him."

Before he was out of the yard and into the old blue Ford Falcon he had bought earlier in the week, Teresa started missing him; she missed standing in the dark with someone who also thought about Silver all the time. Together, they had managed to conjure up Silver so true to life they could hear his breathing; alone, there were suddenly a hundred other sounds echoing around her—crickets on the lawn, the screen door rattling, sunflower seeds falling onto the ground, one by one. She went back inside, then up to her room; she had decided that she wouldn't call Silver, even though Gregory had told her to. A call to Silver felt like a betrayal of a man who had left her with a desire for something she couldn't quite name, the need for company, for a friend she wasn't afraid to tell all her secrets to. But all that night Teresa couldn't sleep. She turned on the radio and called Atlas onto the bed where he dozed on the quilt by her feet. She chased sleep like a hunter, she felt as if she were burning up, she imagined that the cool October night was as hot as Egypt. Sometime near dawn, she could no longer fight her loyalties. She slipped on her bathrobe and went downstairs, and without giving herself one more moment of hesitation she called Silver. As the phone rang, Teresa imagined her brother walking down a hallway, still winding down from a night spent out in the streets, in countless bars, in Cadillacs and alleyways. When he finally did pick up the phone, Teresa was hypnotized by the sound of his voice; she couldn't speak until Silver had repeated himself several times, demanding to know who was there, ready to hang up.

"It's me," Teresa whispered, finally.

"You," Silver said. He sat down on a wooden chair near the phone and closed his eyes. One of his customers, Rudy, a regular who bought cocaine from Silver and then resold it in Oakland, had arranged a date for Silver with one of his cousins, a woman who had made love to Silver any way he asked for it. All he had to do was promise her a thimbleful of cocaine, and she fixed him with her odd-shaped eyes, set much too far apart, and called him her handsomest boyfriend. But Rudy's cousin had reminded him of Teresa—it was her long, dark hair, her white cotton dress, and Silver had left her in the middle of the night. He wasn't thinking of Lee when he left Rudy's cousin, he wasn't afraid that his wife would discover the scent of another woman's perfume, he was afraid of what had happened a long time ago in Santa Rosa, he was afraid of how often he found himself thinking about that time. When Teresa telephoned only a few hours after he had made love to Rudy's cousin, Silver wondered if Teresa was clairvoyant—it was as though she knew when he was thinking about her. Distance just couldn't separate them, or ease the guilt Silver felt whenever he heard her voice.

"Someone's been looking for you," Teresa told her brother. She could practically feel his pulse quicken; she thought she heard him light a cigarette and inhale. "Angel Gregory," Teresa said. "He's out of jail."

"Lock the door," Silver said immediately.

"He's already been and gone," Teresa said.

"Lock the door and stay right where you are," Silver said. He reached for his boots, he cursed himself for having ever left Teresa alone when he had promised her that was something he'd never do.

"Don't worry about me," Teresa said. "Gregory's looking for you, he won't come back here."

"I'm driving up to get you," Silver said. "I'm leaving right now."

Now that she had called Silver she was a little afraid of what she'd begun, she thought about Gregory's advice to give Silver up, and she wondered how long she could stay away from him if she went back with him to San Francisco.

"Please," Teresa whispered. She would have never thought she might try to stop him driving up for her. "Don't start anything. Don't come here."

Silver didn't listen to her; he reached for his jacket, he had his car keys in his left hand. "Wait for me," he told her.

When he hung up, Teresa stared at the phone receiver. She should have been happy, she always imagined that she would be on the day when he came back to Santa

Rosa for her, but instead she felt dizzy, she could barely see, everything in the house seemed trapped between layers of gauze. She began to wander through all of the rooms she had avoided since Dina's death. In the living room long strands of dust hung down from the ceilings, and in Silver's bedroom the twin beds were still pushed together from the time he and Lee had been in the house. Teresa found it was harder to go into Dina's room; she stood in the hallway, finally she pushed open the door. She had expected cobwebs, a thick film on every bit of furniture, but when Teresa went to the window and pulled up the shade the room was oddly clean. A cream-colored shawl had been left on the back of a wooden chair, the wallpaper looked like silk which had been tinted in a kettle full of chinaberries, and when Teresa went to sit on the bed she noticed that there was still the indentation of a woman's body in the mattress, the scent of dark coffee spiraled up from the feather pillows. Teresa thought she would rest, just for a moment; she had spent a sleepless night and the bed seemed so warm, heat rose up through the sheets, it embraced her, circled her ankles and her wrists with coils of exhaustion. Teresa fell into a deep sleep without wanting to, without trying to, without any dreams. Outside, in the hallway, Atlas paced back and forth; he peered into Dina's room, but wouldn't go inside. In the garden, the blackbirds kicked up dust all around the rows where asparagus had once grown, and as Teresa slept the sun came up, and the bare wisteria over the back porch shone with its own blue light, and it seemed as if everything inside that house on Divisadero Street stood absolutely still; the only evidence of life was a heartbeat, an old dog, and one white bed of dreamless consolation.

There was just one waitress working the breakfast shift at Max's the next morning; Lucy waited on customers at her own tables and Teresa's as well, and by noon she had called an old friend in Rio Nedro to offer her Teresa's job. Early that same morning, Atlas had let himself out of the house through the back door, but the screen had slammed shut behind him and he hadn't been able to get back inside. When Silver drove up, at a little after six, the dog was circling the yard; patches of the collie's fur drifted over the lawn and took root like strange flowers. Silver went inside, then upstairs; the door to Dina's room was ajar, and Silver opened it the rest of the way with his foot.

By nine that morning, Silver had packed up all of Teresa's clothes. The skirts and dresses that wouldn't fit into the suitcases were taken out to the car still on wire hangers. Silver let Teresa sleep all that day, and for a while he dozed on the living-room couch, but he woke with a start, certain he had heard the grinding sound of King Connors's engine in the driveway. In the early evening, Silver walked down to the corner grocery and bought a six-pack. He was out on the front porch, finishing his fourth beer and throwing stones for the collie to chase, when Teresa finally woke up, got dressed, and came downstairs. He felt her before he heard her; it was as if pure electricity was circling closer and closer, his oldest memories fell about him like an avalanche, his sister sat beside him. She took one of the full cans of beer and held it to her forehead to cool her skin. In all the other houses on their street, dinner was already over, dishes were being washed, television sets turned on. In their kitchen, there was no one; only the remains of Gregory's dinner from the night before—green tomatoes on a china plate, a spoon still in the sugar bowl, tap water that dripped in a slow steady rhythm.

"I'm not afraid of Gregory," Silver told Teresa as they sat out on the porch, slapping away the mosquitoes that always appeared as soon as the sky was dark. "He's all talk. But I don't want him bothering you. I don't even want him talking to you. Let's face it," Silver said quietly, "you can't live here any more."

He left her out on the porch and went inside; he turned off all the lights, rinsed off the dishes in the sink, took the trash out through the back door, then came back around to the driveway. He opened the back door of his new Camaro and let Atlas climb into the back seat, then went around to the driver's door and got in behind the wheel. In the yard the crickets' call was slow; it was the end of their season. She had wanted him to come back, but not like this, not when their destination was an apartment in the Mission District where a wife and child waited. Not on an October night when she was wearing old blue jeans and it was too early for the stars to be out. If he hadn't locked all the doors, Teresa would have run into the house, she would have hidden until the time was right, until she could see him from her open window on an evening when she was dressed in a long skirt made of linen or silk. But he was waiting for her, and the passenger door had been left open, and so she got up, and she walked to the car, and she didn't look back at the house, not once. She kept her hands folded, but each time Silver shifted gears his hand was so close to hers she could feel its heat; she kept her distance, she wouldn't talk to him, not when he suggested they stop for dinner or when he asked what radio station she wanted tuned in. In the back seat the collie nosed at the windows and shed all over the clean upholstery. And all the way to the city Teresa wished for one thing: that he had not come back for her at all or that he had waited until they could have driven to the very edge of the ocean, until there was just the two of them driving faster than any hawk could fly. She never told him how disappointed she was, but all the same Silver knew, he reached over and stroked her arm, and it was as if no time at all had passed since that day at the reservoir; she remembered it all. And when she turned to him it was just as it had always been: she saw nothing but him, just him, always him.

*   *   *

All that following winter there was a drought; city offi-
cials suggested that dishwater be used on gardens, and
bathwater be recycled to clean the floors. The hills surrounding the city remained brown, and on rooftops all
over the Mission District, pigeons fought each other for
single drops of water. In Silver and Lee's first-floor flat,
there was always dust on the floors, no matter how often
Lee swept the rooms; it seemed as if Teresa had brought
the dust with her all the way from Santa Rosa. The two
women tried to be friendly to each other: they sat in the
kitchen each morning, drinking coffee, folding laundry,
pretending there wasn't a man still asleep in the front
bedroom. But as soon as Silver woke up, his presence
came between them; his every move, whether he reached
for a cigarette or the telephone receiver, separated Lee and
Teresa, made them eye each other with cool disdain.

At the beginning, Lee had hoped they would be a real
family, she was alone so much of the time that she was
grateful for Teresa's company, even though her sister-in-
law seemed standoffish, maybe just shy. And, more than
anything, Lee had hoped that once Teresa was living with
them, Silver wouldn't seem so damned angry all the time;
she imagined it was worrying about his sister living alone
that set him off. But once Teresa had moved in, Silver got
worse. He had trouble sleeping, often he didn't manage to
fall asleep until after the sun had come up, and then he
had nightmares, he was being followed, his every move
charted through telescopes. He was so irritable that asking
him a question was hazardous, asking for a little affection,
impossible. One night in November, Silver found a pack
of Lee's cigarettes hidden between two silk slips in the top
dresser drawer. Teresa and Jackie were in the living room;
KSAN was tuned in and Teresa held Jackie in her arms
and danced with him. She was so concerned with trying
to get her silent nephew to repeat some of the lyrics she
sang along with that she didn't hear Silver drag Lee into

the bathroom. Silver locked the door and held a pack of Virginia Slims up to Lee's face.

"I told you I didn't want you smoking," he said to his wife.

"You smoke all the time," Lee countered. "You smoke more than a pack of Marlboros every day."

Silver took out one of the cigarettes and held it so close to her that it grazed Lee's lips. "We've got a kid, remember. Don't think you're going to give yourself cancer and leave him all to me."

Silver emptied the pack of cigarettes into the toilet. He flushed them away, then slammed the toilet cover down.

"I want you to quit, understand?"

"I won't," Lee said.

Silver grabbed her; with his hands around her neck he studied her, as if he were considering murder. Then he turned away from her.

"You're killing me," he told Lee.

"You hate me," Lee whispered. "I didn't even do anything and you hate me."

Silver sat down on the rim of the bathtub; he could hear the radio playing in the living room, the song was "Imagine," and Silver suddenly felt tired.

"I don't hate you," he told his wife.

Lee sat down on the toilet seat and began to cry. "You do," she said. "You hate me. It's even worse since Teresa moved in."

"Listen to me." Silver reached and took Lee's hand. "Everything's going to be okay."

"I'll do anything you want me to," Lee said. "Just tell me what to do. I want you to be in love with me."

Silver let go of her hand. "You've always got to push it. I'm here, aren't I? I'm married to you. So leave it alone."

"Just tell me," Lee whispered. "I'll do anything."

Silver reached into his shirt pocket for a cigarette of his own; he threw the match into the sink and inhaled. Lee sat

with her hands folded in her lap; her shoulders were thin,
her pale blue eyes were flecked with green, she looked
younger now than she had on the nights when she first
jumped out her bedroom window to run to Silver's car.
Even though Silver had known her for years, even though
he now sat less than a foot away from her in their own
bathroom, Lee could have been anyone: any stranger on
the street, a young girl he had picked up for the night, an
old sweetheart he'd just as soon never see again.

"Listen to me, darling," he said. His voice echoed off
the tiles in the bathroom. "What's the point in fighting?"

Lee reached over and took Silver's hand, she raised it
to her mouth, she kissed his palm and then his fingers, all
the time wishing that the man who had married her would
someday fall in love with her, or, at the very least, not look
at her from such a great distance, as if he were more than
a million miles away.

But nothing between them had changed and Lee had
continued to smoke, secretly, a tiny act of rebellion, an
invisible way to get back at him. One day in the middle
of winter, when it still had not yet rained, Lee decided
not to hide it from Teresa any more. She went over to
the cabinet where the dishes were stored and, from behind
the saucers and the cups, she pulled out a pack of Virginia
Slims.

"Do me a favor," she said to Teresa after she had struck
a match and inhaled, "if he wakes up and comes in here,
say this is yours. He wouldn't dare yell at you." Lee
smiled. "Sometimes I think he's afraid of you."

"I didn't know you smoked," Teresa said.

"No one knows," Lee said. She tapped her ashes into
an empty coffee cup. She studied her sister-in-law. It
was not just Silver's concern for his sister that made
Lee jealous, it was the way Teresa looked at him when
she thought no one saw. "I don't know if I should trust
you. Maybe you'll tell Silver, you two being so close
and all."

Teresa got up and poured herself a cup of coffee; she didn't want Lee looking at her, she was afraid of what might be read in her face.

"Silver was talking in his sleep last night. He does that lately," Lee informed Teresa. She went over to the sink, put her cigarette out under some running tap water, then carefully hid the butt in the trash. She was close to Teresa again; close enough to look right in her eyes. "Last night he was talking about you in his sleep."

"He wasn't talking about me," Teresa said immediately.

"He sure was," Lee said. "He said your name."

Jackie was outside; Teresa went to the sliding glass doors and watched him. Dust had risen up and left bracelets of earth around his wrists; he had Lee's blue eyes, her pale blond hair.

"People think I'm lucky," Lee said. "I know other women wish they were in my shoes." She lowered her voice. "I love him, you know."

Teresa opened the glass door and went outside. A gardenia Lee had made certain to water with used dishwater was still green, but the birds of paradise had withered and no grass grew in the yard. Lee came out and stood behind Teresa, she wasn't about to stop talking now; even out in the fresh air, she still smelled faintly of smoke.

"I'm not going to let him go," Lee said. "Not to anyone. Not for any reason."

Jackie was collecting stones; there were pieces of red glass among them, but they were dull, they had no edges, each one was thin as a dime.

"I'm not dumb," Lee said, and she breathed heavily, as if it took all her strength just to go on talking. "I see the way you look at him. It's the same way those women on the street look at him."

"I don't look at him," Teresa insisted.

"A lot of women wanted to get Silver away from me," Lee said. "But no one ever has. Maybe they had him for a night, but that's all. And no one's going to get him." Lee held up her hand and studied her wedding ring. "We're married," she said. "We're married," she said. "We're married for good."

Teresa turned to her sister-in-law; in a sudden bolt of cold bravery, she smiled.

"You don't have to remind me," she said to Lee. "I was there, remember? I was right there in the same room."

Silver wouldn't allow Arnie Bergen into the apartment; he was convinced the old detective brought bad luck with him. But Teresa still telephoned Bergen, sometimes as often as once a week. Bergen preferred to live on Social Security and his pension rather than take the occasional divorce case that came his way. He was finished with that sort of business. Instead he spent his days sorting through his old files; he had filled up his bedroom with crates full of old cases when he closed down his office on Market Street. But the truth was he was low on cash, and in January he rented out the house on Divisadero Street; he left most of the furniture for the new tenants, and finally, for the first time in months, he was able to pay the real-estate taxes.

"Sell it," Teresa continued to advise Bergen, but when he refused she was relieved; she couldn't imagine another family owning that house, or a time when she couldn't arrive back in Santa Rosa and feel that she was home. The apartment where she now lived certainly was not home, certainly not now that Lee had turned against her. In the same month that Bergen rented out the house in Santa Rosa, Teresa got a job at the Crescent Incense Factory, near Union Street. At last she was able to leave the apartment; she went out at eight in the morning and didn't return until after four. Finally, she could escape Lee's distrustful eyes. She was able to avoid Silver, and the longing she felt each time she passed him in the hallway, every time she sat across from him at the kitchen table.

But it didn't take long for Teresa to discover that she hated her job. She packed sticks of incense for so many hours that her hands felt permanently cramped, a dusty vanilla coated her skin, the scent of cedar and sandalwood filtered into the fiber of all her clothes.

If the owner of the factory, Carlos, hadn't bought his marijuana from Silver for years, he would have fired Teresa after her first week. He tried to ignore the fact that she fell asleep at the wooden packing table, her long hair coiled over the natural soaps and circular tubes of incense. Teresa could barely keep her eyes open, her sleeping sickness had descended with its full force; she packed patchouli in with the vanilla, she confused boxes of cinnamon-scented blocks with blocks of lavender. And, in spite of her desire to stay out of the apartment, Teresa began to miss work. She slept for long hours at a time, and her spells frightened Lee; Lee no longer let Teresa babysit for Jackie, and if Teresa cooked dinner, Lee was right there watching her, making certain one of Teresa's spells wouldn't strike after she had turned on the gas. Teresa began to fall asleep in buses; she tumbled to the floor in a Bell Market, knocking over a display of herbal tea; finally, she was fired from the Crescent Incense Factory in February.

"It's not that I don't like you," Carlos told her. "I like you fine. But it's dangerous for you to work here, you could hurt yourself. It's no disgrace to be fired from this job. Any idiot could work here; I could have monkeys filling up these boxes. Listen to me, Teresa, this isn't a skill you can acquire. It's boring, so you fall asleep—I can understand that, but I also have to fire you."

After she was fired, Teresa continued to leave the house at her usual time each morning; she bought a bottle of perfume that smelled like vanilla and doused herself with it before she came home. She didn't want to spend her afternoons with Lee and so she looked for another job, but after a while she gave up. Even if she was hired at one of the restaurants or offices she had applied to, she was sure she wouldn't last long—she'd have too many absences, she'd fall asleep on the very first day.

Late in February, when Teresa had tired of the aimless bus rides she took around the city, when she was sick of filling out job applications in shops she knew she'd never return to, she went to Bergen's apartment. She hadn't planned it; one morning she was suddenly on Dolores Street, a block away from the second-floor flat where the detective lived. She had never been to his flat before and Bergen hadn't expected company; his apartment was messy, he hadn't swept for weeks. There were no curtains in the windows, but there was southern light and he had hung a cage which held a yellow canary in the brightest window. Because the bedroom was filled with crates from his office, and with Dina's personal belongings, picked up the weekend before the new tenants had moved into the house on Divisadero Street, Bergen had taken to sleeping on the Castro Convertible in the living room. Occasionally he had visitors: an insurance investigator named Molloy, whom Bergen had known for years, came over on Thursday nights to play cards; a widow who lived on the third floor brought him a shoebox full of coffee cake once in a while. Fact was, his loneliness didn't hit him at bedtime or in the middle of the night, as it did some men, but in the mornings, when the whole day stretched out before him—his whole life seemed to stretch out, too, all of it without Dina.

When he opened the door that morning to find Teresa, Bergen was delighted. He had been worried about her, had even looked up Silver's address in the telephone book and driven by the apartment a few times.

"What do you know!" Bergen said when he opened the door. "Lucky for you I went shopping yesterday and just happen to have a chocolate cake."

Bergen went into the kitchen to boil some water for tea, and Teresa looked around his apartment. She peered into the canary's cage. "How long have you had him?" she asked when Bergen returned with two cups of tea and a package of Sara Lee brownies.

"Too long," Bergen said. He cut two brownies and set them out on paper napkins. "I bought him for company, but he's driving me crazy."

Teresa sat down and kicked off her shoes; she apologized for not having invited the detective over to Silver and Lee's for dinner.

"Don't put me and Silver in the same room if you want to have peace," Bergen said.

"I can't live with them any longer," Teresa said, suddenly realizing it was true. Living with Silver and Lee forced Teresa to be an acrobat balanced between waking and sleep, between desire and lies. The walls that separated her from Silver were growing thinner every day, turning from plaster into thin bamboo.

"Maybe when the new tenants move out, I can go back to Santa Rosa," Teresa said.

"They want to buy it," Bergen said uncomfortably. He sipped some tea. "I don't see any point in making coffee," he told Teresa. "I can never make it the way Dina did; no matter what I do, it's always too weak."

"Sell the house," Teresa said. She got up, and when she walked around the room she noticed things she had ignored at first, bits and pieces of the Santa Rosa house were everywhere: a lace tablecloth, a low oak coffee table, a photograph of Dina in a silver frame, the blue and white dishes displayed in an open glass cabinet.

Teresa turned back to the detective. "You're lonely," she said.

"I got this damn canary," Bergen said. "He happens to be driving me crazy. Want him?" the detective offered. Teresa shook her head no; Silver wasn't too happy about having Atlas in the house, he would never agree to another pet, especially one that once belonged to Bergen. "Know anybody who might?" Bergen asked.

"Maybe you should go out with another woman," Teresa said.

Bergen looked at her as if she were crazy. "I'm only lonely sometimes," he said. "Most of the time I still feel like Dina's alive. After all, how could she be dead?"

All that day they drank cold tea in the sunlight; when it was close to four, Teresa got ready to leave.

"I've missed you," Bergen said when he walked her to the door. They passed by the bedroom, and Teresa peered inside the dark room where Dina's possessions were stored.

"I could give you some of this stuff," Bergen said, nodding to the suitcases full of clothes and linens, the hairpins and brushes and combs. "Actually, you could take it all."

"I don't have room for anything," Teresa said. "You keep it."

"The dishes?" Bergen said. "She would have wanted you to have the dishes."

Teresa stood by the front door of the detective's apartment; she covered her eyes. It was then she understood why she had avoided Bergen: she knew she would cry as soon as she spent any time with him, as soon as she saw all the things that had once belonged to her mother.

"Teresa," Bergen said. "What can I do? What would make you happy?" The detective studied the crying girl; he reached for his checkbook. "If I lend you two hundred dollars you can get your own place, you won't have to live with Silver and Lee any more. How would that be?"

Teresa waved the checkbook away; she shook her head so hard that her hair whirled around and hit the walls of the hallway.

"What?" Bergen said. "What can I do?"

She wouldn't answer, or she couldn't, so Bergen was silent too. When she had stopped crying, Bergen put his arm around her and walked her downstairs, then waited with her for the bus. Teresa wanted to tell him to go away,

he didn't have to wait with her on a street corner when the
sky, at long last, seemed seconds away from a storm. But
when she tried to speak, her voice broke, words refused to
form on her tongue. The detective didn't seem to notice
her difficulty, he turned up the collar of his sports coat
and kept watch for the bus.

"You know what I keep wondering?" Bergen said, just
before the bus appeared. "What was the secret of Dina's
coffee? Why was it so wonderful?"

And although Teresa agreed to meet Bergen on Thursday of the following week just before they parted, she
didn't tell the old detective that Dina's secret was as
simple as cinnamon. She let him go on believing that the
ingredient whose name he didn't know was as intricate
as one seed pearl thrown into the pot just before the
water boiled, or a blackbird's feather tossed in with the
grounds, when it was just the beautiful difference a brew
of dedication can make.

They saw each other every week, and to Bergen it didn't
matter if Teresa even talked, he was with Dina's daughter,
the girl he now thought of as his own child, who might
have indeed been his child if he and Dina had only met
a few years earlier. They usually met on Thursdays. Lee
didn't notice when Teresa took Atlas with her in the
mornings when the weather was good, and then Bergen
and Teresa took him on long walks through the city,
stopping on street corners to let the old dog rest. When
it rained, which was now nearly all the time, they went to
the aquarium and spent hours watching the slow motions
of the manatee in a tank of still, green water. There were
times when Teresa didn't show up at his apartment, and on
those days Bergen knew that she had her sleeping sickness
again. Teresa was sleeping more and more, and Bergen
brooded over it, he wished he had lived in the house on
Divisadero Street from the start, he wondered if that would
have made a difference.

Bergen was convinced it was all those stories about the Arias that held Teresa in a web of sleep. The first time he and Dina had ever talked about them was one night when they were waiting for Teresa to go to sleep so that they could pull down the sheet on Dina's bed and make love until the time when he went back to the Lamplighter Motel. Bergen had sat downstairs in the kitchen for an hour, playing solitaire while Dina went upstairs to check on the girl, and when he was fairly certain that Dina was waiting for him in her own bedroom, he put the deck of cards away and went upstairs.

The hallway was dark, but the door to Teresa's room was open, and through it he could hear Dina. Her voice was hypnotizing, seductive as sleep. Bergen edged toward Teresa's room, drawn closer by Dina's voice, and the glow of light from a candle on Teresa's night table. It was then he first heard the story that Dina's father had told so long ago, on nights when the sky was wild and the scent of sage was in the air. Dina was slowly listing the contents of an Aria's saddlebag; she had added to the stories her father had told her until she was certain that she knew every detail about the men who wandered across the desert.

"He has a map in his saddlebag," she whispered that night to Teresa. The girl was beneath the covers; her eyes were closed, and each time Dina mentioned another one of the Aria's belongings, Teresa could see it; she could see the map and the turquoise rings, the canteen filled with icy water, the extra shirt with clean white cuffs, the necklace of rubies, the wildflowers that somehow managed to bloom days after they were plucked from the ground.

At first Bergen thought that Dina was talking about an early romance, that she was recounting the dovelike flirtations of her youth as a bedtime story for Teresa. But soon he realized that the man she called an Aria had never existed, at least he was not truly made up of flesh and blood; no Aria had ever knocked at Dina's front door, or put his arms around her waist and danced with her till dawn. And as he stood listening by the door, Bergen realized something more: the man Dina was describing looked exactly like Silver.

"He has dark hair," Dina whispered as her daughter fell asleep; in her dreams Teresa was already traveling across the mesa she had never seen. "His eyes are like ebony, his skin smells like fire, no woman can take her eyes off of him when he walks into a room, the white shirt he wears looks like cotton, but it's really the finest silk. And sometimes it seems as if you're waiting a long time for him, sometimes it seems as if it's forever, longer than a hundred years, but all the time he's circling closer and closer, it's just that he's so silent, that he's the sort of man who can't be rushed, who needs hours spent alone, time to look for water, to travel over the highest plains where the sky is always purple and shooting stars fall onto the earth."

After Teresa had fallen asleep, Dina blew out the candle and went out into the hallway. When she saw Bergen she gasped; she hadn't expected to find him right outside the door.

"Why are you hiding here?" Dina asked. "My husband used to eavesdrop all the time—it's a quality I hate."

When Dina began to walk toward her room, flustered because Bergen had overheard, the detective held her back.

"What kind of story was that?" he asked Dina.

"A bedtime story." Dina shrugged. She nodded toward her room. "We don't have all night," she whispered.

"It's a made-up story?" Bergen asked, though he had already been convinced by her tone as she whispered to her daughter that Dina believed every word she said.

"Sure," Dina said to Bergen. "It's made up."

Later, after they had made love and he held Dina in his arms, Bergen began to cry. Dina politely ignored his tears, but she stroked his forehead with her fingertips.

"You believe that story. You're still waiting for someone else," Bergen whispered once he was able to speak.
"Some man who rides out of the desert. I'm too old to
have a rival, especially one who doesn't really exist."

"But Arias do exist," Dina said with absolute confi-
dence. "If you really want to know the truth, Silver is
one of them."

"You're going to find out that I'm right," Bergen said.
He kissed her, he heard her sigh. "You're going to find
out that I love you more than a dozen Arias would."

And much later, when she had begun to write him
letters every night, she shyly admitted that she no longer
believed in Arias. Bergen wished now that he could show
her letters to Teresa. But he doubted that any of those
letters could remove the spell of years of bedtime stories,
those hours spent listening to the heartbreaking perfection
of Dina's imagined men.

Bergen was still thinking about the Arias when he
met Teresa at the aquarium to celebrate her birthday.
They were to share sandwiches in the park if it didn't
rain, but first they walked from room to room, studying
Pacific fish in huge dark tanks. It was Teresa's nineteenth
birthday, and Silver had given her a small blue sapphire
on a platinum chain. She had found it on her bureau when
she woke up, and the knowledge that Silver had been in
her room while she was sleeping made her dizzier than
the gift itself did. Silver was still asleep when Teresa left
the house to meet Bergen, so she would have to wait to
thank him. She hadn't even dared put the necklace on
in the house for fear Lee would see what an expensive
gift Silver had given her. In the double-tiered room where
they stood watching the dolphins and the sea lions, Bergen
spotted the sapphire right away.

"A boyfriend?" Bergen guessed.

Teresa shook her head and laughed. To Bergen, the gift
looked very much like something an Aria might keep in
his saddlebag.

"The only gift I have is two cheese sandwiches," Bergen said. "And this," he added as he handed her a small box wrapped in tissue paper. Inside was the tortoise-shell comb Dina had been given by her father long ago. Teresa took a handful of her hair and pinned it up, then turned so that Bergen could admire her.

"Very nice," Bergen said distantly. He was distracted, thinking of the letter of Dina's he had brought with him to show to Teresa, wondering if it was a terrible breach of faith to show Dina's letters to anyone, even her daughter.

When they ate their lunch in front of the bandshell, the sun was shining, and Dina's letter was still in Bergen's inside pocket. Later, when he drove Teresa home, careful to pull over two blocks away from the apartment so that Silver would not see his car, Bergen still wasn't certain that he would really show Teresa a letter that was intended only for him.

"I had a terrific birthday," Teresa said when Bergen stopped the car. "I can't believe it didn't rain."

The letter Bergen carried with him was one of the last Dina had written. Dina no longer believed that Arias existed; somehow the entire notion had disappeared into a layer of filmy ash, and with it her passion for Silver.

"It's not that I love him any less," she had written about her son, "maybe I love him even more than before. It's just that all of a sudden I know him, and when I think about who he is I feel like it's my fault and I can't help but cry."

"I've got another present for you," Bergen told Teresa. He reached into his pocket and then handed Teresa the letter. She examined the envelope closely, recognizing Dina's handwriting immediately. She turned to the detective, puzzled.

"She wrote to me all the time," Bergen explained. "She wrote about what she believed in, and what she used to believe in."

Teresa took the letter out of the envelope and smoothed down the paper.

"She wrote about Arias," Bergen said softly.

Teresa's face grew hot. "She told you about the Arias?" she said accusingly. She had always been sure that the stories Dina told her were family secrets, not to be given to any stranger, not even Bergen.

"She told me that she didn't believe in them any more, that Silver wasn't one of them, that a woman who waited for an Aria would wind up waiting the rest of her life."

Teresa ignored the detective and read Dina's letter; the ink grew blurry before her eyes, the words ran together in a dark desolate line.

"None of this is true," Teresa told Bergen.

She looked over the letter once more; she couldn't believe that her mother had written the words she read, that her mother would be so cruel toward Silver, that she would practically disown him with a few scratches of her pen.

Teresa handed the letter back to Bergen. "She had cancer. My mother was delirious. She didn't know what she was saying." Teresa turned to look out her window; the air was foggy and gray. She closed her eyes for a moment and when she did she saw an orange moon in the sky and a boy who wore a white shirt, a boy who carried a saddlebag loaded down with maps.

"I'm worried about you," Bergen admitted. "That's why I showed you this letter. I'm worried about your sleeping spells and your living with Silver and not having a life of your own."

"Just because you think you know about the Arias doesn't mean you understand anything," Teresa told Bergen. "You don't understand anything at all."

Teresa got out of the detective's car and slammed the door behind her. She stopped when she reached the corner near Silver and Lee's apartment, and then she turned to make certain that Bergen drove away. Reluctantly he did, the letter hidden once more in his pocket; and Teresa waited until the taillights of his car disappeared as he turned a corner. She wondered what an old man like Bergen could possibly know about dark nights, about passion so sharp it was like daggers, and men who were wilder than the untamed horses they rode. And as she watched Bergen drive away, Teresa thought about the manatee in its green watery cage at the aquarium, and all of the hours she had spent with Bergen, just waiting for that shy creature to turn toward them, and at that moment in her life all of those hours seemed suddenly wasted. As she walked the remaining block back to Silver's apartment, she decided that she would call Bergen later in the week and cancel her Thursday meeting with him, and, in fact, as she opened the door of the apartment she knew that it would be a very long time before she dared to see that old man again.

CHAPTER
FIVE

✝

ONCE A MONTH SILVER MET THE MAN CALLED VALLAIS in an apartment on Russian Hill. Vallais couldn't be telephoned. The only way to reach him and set up an appointment was through a post-office box, and his address was the most important thing Silver had stolen from Angel Gregory's apartment in those days before Gregory was sent to Vacaville Prison. At first Vallais had asked why Gregory no longer came to see him, why Silver had taken his place; after a while he no longer asked, it made very little difference to him whether he sold cocaine and marijuana to one man or to that man's enemy, and he guarded himself against betrayal: his apartment was nothing more than a front, there was no way to trace him, no possessions that belonged to him on Russian Hill other than a small oak table and three wicker chairs. Besides, Silver was a perfect client; he asked no questions, he wore his black linen suit cut so close it seemed a part of him, he never complained, he was always polite. But waiting hours for Vallais when he was late was not in Silver's nature. Each time he went to Russian Hill, Silver was more convinced than ever that someday soon he would have to find a way to bypass Vallais; he would find a route to small Mexican towns where there was never any wind, he would make his own journeys to Colombia, to villages where the earth was the color of geraniums, he would not have to depend on Vallais, he wouldn't have to smile at another man unless he chose to.

At first Silver hadn't even kept a few ounces of marijuana when he resold the drugs he bought from Vallais. He didn't care much for drugs, he liked feeling wired; when he walked down the street he had more than a thousand eyes, he was ready to strike, and nothing got by him—not a whisper, not a move. But lately there had been nights when he couldn't sleep. It was then Silver reached for the carved redwood box in which he had begun to keep some extra marijuana, rolled a joint, and sat in the dark, watching Lee sleep. It would not be until much later, when the sky had just begun to grow light, that Silver would finally put his head on the pillow. And even then he was sometimes unable to sleep; very often he would think about the summer spent in New Mexico, and by morning it always seemed that his grandmother's rosebushes were growing up the side of the house, covering the windowpanes with thorns, with petals so sweet their scent could hypnotize.

It was in the spring of that year when he first had difficulty sleeping, and Teresa came to live with them, that

Silver realized that he was being followed. He heard footsteps behind him every time he walked down the street, he
sensed another man's heartbeat. When he drove through
the city, a blue Ford Falcon slipped in and out of traffic;
sometimes the Ford was right on his tail, other times it
disappeared altogether, leaving Silver to wonder if he had
been hallucinating. Soon, there was a shadow on every
street corner, a shadow much more threatening than any
flesh-and-blood enemy; no place felt safe, no room was
quite dark enough, there wasn't one man Silver could call
his friend. Early one evening Silver spotted his enemy for
the first time. He had gone to meet Rudy at a bar called El
Calderon, less than two blocks from the apartment. It was
a place Silver thought of as his own, a place that no longer
felt safe when he noticed a stranger at the bar. When the
stranger had paid his bill and was about to leave, Silver
saw a blood-colored tattoo on the man's arm, a familiar
pair of boots, a certain slope of his shoulders.

"Do you know that guy?" Silver asked Rudy.

"What guy?" Rudy said, because when he turned to
look the stranger was already gone.

That night Silver went home early, long before midnight. Rudy accepted Silver's invitation to walk back to
the apartment with him; he was surprised that after two
years Silver had suddenly decided to be more sociable,
but he never guessed that Silver didn't want to walk home
alone and that his own block seemed dangerous to him, as
foreign as Mars. In the apartment, Rudy took out some of
the cocaine he had just bought from Silver and separated
the powder into long narrow rows on a plate. On this night
Silver didn't refuse the cocaine, on this night what Silver
wanted least in the world was a thousand eyes. When Lee
heard voices she threw on her robe and walked into the
living room, to find Silver snorting cocaine.

"I don't want any drugs in here," she told her husband.

"Come on," Rudy said to her. He introduced himself, he
told her how pleased he was to finally meet Silver's wife.

"You live with this man," he said, "there must be dope all over this house, you've got to be used to it by now."

"That's different," Lee said. "There may be drugs in this house, but nobody uses them." Lee had never cared what it was that Silver did to earn money, as long as she didn't know the details. And so, Silver had never bothered to tell her where he went at night, he never mentioned that he had removed the floorboards under the bed so that each night Lee slept just above a cache of Quaaludes and hashish. "I've got a kid in there," Lee said to Silver. She pointed to the bedroom door, she lowered her voice. "I'm not going to have him grow up in a house where drugs are used."

Silver sat on the couch and lit a cigarette; Atlas came to sit by him and he stroked the collie's head absently. "Go back to sleep," he advised Lee.

"I'm telling you I don't like it." But as she spoke Lee saw there was no point in arguing; she watched Silver tap the ashes from his cigarette into a candy dish which had been a wedding present and she felt much older than the girl who had fallen in love with Silver; at least a century had passed since the night she had told him she was pregnant, that moment when she thought she was about to get everything she had always wanted.

"She doesn't like it," Silver mimicked. "Do you think I care?" he said to Lee. "Do you think I'm going to listen to a word you say?"

Lee went back to the bedroom, and before he left, Rudy congratulated Silver on knowing how to treat his woman. But if Rudy thought Silver was about to follow Lee into the bedroom and make love to her, he was wrong. Silver had decided to spend the night on the couch. He kept his boots on, he tried to envision the stranger's face at El Calderon and couldn't. He tried to sleep, but lay awake till morning. The collie paced through the apartment, his claws hit against the wooden floor like chains, the walls in the living room seemed to breathe. Silver found he

was drawn to the window; he looked beyond the limits
of the glass, certain that someone was out there, sure that
any man who followed him had to be Angel Gregory.
He wished that Teresa would come out of her room and
assure him that Gregory had never really come to the
house on Divisadero Street, or that perhaps she would
give him a talisman—a scrap of her slip or a strand of
hair—something to protect him from an invisible enemy,
or at least give him courage.

But Teresa didn't come out of her room on that or any
other night, and Gregory never showed himself. There
were only the endless nights of footsteps and the dark
possibility of an attack, and by May Silver had become an
insomniac. He began to buy large orders of amphetamines
from Vallais, he drank more coffee than ever before, he
lost weight and his cheekbones stood out like arrows.
Silver was burning up, he couldn't rest, couldn't sit still
for a minute. In the past he had never wanted to take Lee
out, now he would agree to anything that would keep him
moving—if he spent too long in any one room he started to
pace as if bees followed him, ready to sting if he dared to
slow down. It was clear to everyone who saw him: Silver
was ready to explode. It was clear to everyone but Teresa.
To her, Silver was always the same, forever that boy who
wore clean white shirts and smelled like fire, the boy who
would never be afraid of anything, not even on the day
he led her to the reservoir and held her tight. She still
couldn't think of him as married; Lee and Jackie seemed
like blond strangers who had somehow managed to slip
into their lives. On the day of Lee and Silver's wedding
anniversary Teresa wanted to ignore all the time that had
gone by, but Silver insisted they go out and celebrate, all
three of them.

"Why does she have to go with us?" Lee whispered
to her husband as she dressed to go to the Black Turtle, a restaurant Silver had always before told her was
too expensive. Down the hall, Teresa was fastening the

sapphire necklace around her throat, she fixed Dina's
tortoise-shell comb in her hair. "It's *our* anniversary,"
Lee said.

"Sure," Silver said. "Go ahead. Ruin tonight before it's
even started."

Lee knew that Silver was moving closer to the edge
each day; one false move could leave the night shredded
into thin strips of recriminations. She wished that she
could erase Silver's dark moods, that she could cool him
with the touch of her palm to his forehead, and if being
with his wife didn't seem to be enough of a celebration,
Lee certainly didn't want his sister's company to do any
more. So it pleased her that Silver ignored both of them
in the restaurant, that he shifted back and forth in his chair
and drummed his fingers on the tabletop in a crazy rhythm
and didn't even bother to look across the table to where
Teresa and Lee sat side by side. He ordered two tequilas
and a beer before the waiter took their dinner order and
in between the time when the waiter served the salads and
brought over the steaks Silver couldn't sit still any more;
he got up and walked past the bar to the men's room.
There in the metal booth he smoked a joint, but his spirits
didn't lift. Everywhere he looked the walls seemed painted
with a hundred shades of sorrow. On the way back to the
table he felt dizzy, unsure of himself, and it was then, as
he walked past the long mahogany bar, that he saw Angel
Gregory, that too familiar stranger, the man who had been
following him through the night for so many months.

Silver was so shaken that he didn't dare stop; he went
back to the table and sat with his back to the bar. He
ordered another tequila and another beer. He tried to look
casual, but when the steaks were served he couldn't eat,
he didn't even bother to try. He looked over his shoulder; he couldn't keep his eyes off Gregory. Teresa knew
that something was wrong, and by the time the dessert
menus were brought over she had spotted Gregory. She
had allowed herself to forget Angel Gregory—she had

forced herself to forget. If she even began to think about
him, Santa Rosa seemed much too close; the scent of the
river left a trail through every yard, crickets sang beneath
a violet sky. She had not been with another man since
that night, and oddly, when she saw Gregory at the bar
she felt as if they had been together only hours before, as
if he were still her lover. She blushed and couldn't look
at Silver, she felt as if she and Gregory had secrets to
hide. That night in October, Teresa had been sure she
had never known anyone quite so well as she knew Angel
Gregory. She knew what he thought about first thing in
the morning, what he dreamed about all night long, she
knew that he couldn't move any farther than one day in
Santa Rosa when a boy betrayed him, a boy in a white
shirt who had never been afraid of anything.

"Let's go home," Teresa said to her brother. "I don't
care what they say about this restaurant—it isn't so great.
I'm tired," she whispered. "Let's leave."

"Not yet," Lee said. She held up the dessert menu.
"They have chocolate mousse here. They have rum cake
with raisins."

Teresa stared at Silver. "Please," she said, "take me
home."

Not far away there was a man who drank bourbon and
water, a man who had thought about Silver for so long he
wouldn't have been surprised if someone had slit open his
veins and found Silver's blood inside. When he caught
Silver's eye, he nodded slowly, slowly and only once.
And at the table, halfway across the room, Silver's throat
was dry.

"He's been using psychology on me," Silver said.
"That's what he's been doing all these months. Using
a little psychology on me."

"What are you talking about?" Lee said.

"Does it matter to you?" Silver said. "Does it concern
you?" He lit a cigarette and faced the bar. "He's blowing
it now. He should have kept on creeping around in the

dark, he should have waited, he could have made me crawl. Now that I see him I sure as shit am not afraid of him."

Silver put his napkin down on the table; he stubbed out his cigarette without ever having taken a drag.

"Don't go over there," Teresa said. She was frightened of Gregory; he made everything seem all wrong, he made Silver seem all wrong.

"What am I supposed to do?" Silver said. He stood up and his shadow fell over the linen tablecloth, it fell across the gold-rimmed plates. "Run? Is that what I'm supposed to do?"

"Do you know what the hell is going on here?" Lee asked as Silver walked toward the bar. She noticed Gregory signal the bartender to bring him another drink. "Do I know that guy?" she asked.

Lee had sat at the same table with Gregory at the Dragon in Santa Rosa dozens of times, she had had drinks with him, and had listened to Silver complain about him night after night. But there were dim lights in the Dragon, lights meant to make it difficult to recognize anyone, and in those days Lee hadn't seen anyone but Silver, she wouldn't have thought to look at another man.

"He's somebody from Santa Rosa," Teresa said. She knew that Silver didn't like Lee to know too much about his business, and so she called the waiter over. "Let's order brandy," Teresa suggested, hoping to distract her sister-in-law. "Let's really celebrate your anniversary."

At the bar, Silver sat down on a stool right next to Gregory and ordered a shot of tequila.

"You're ordering tequila in a fancy place like this?" Gregory said. "Shame on you."

Silver turned to the other man as if it were the most natural thing in the world for the two of them to be having a drink together. "Who let you out?" he asked.

"I served my time." Gregory shrugged. "You saw to that." He took a sip of his drink. "I see you've got Teresa with you." He turned to look at her; Teresa was staring at him, just as she had on the night when they seemed like allies, like long-lost friends, both of them counting Silver's betrayals, so many they were like stars in the sky. But now, when Gregory lifted his glass to her in a toast, Teresa quickly lowered her eyes. "She's beautiful," Gregory said. "But there's one thing she's not smart about—she's loyal to you." He looked Silver straight in the eye. He took a sip of his bourbon, and he waited, and finally he said, "She's as loyal as a wife."

Silver made certain that no part of him reacted. He finished his drink and put his glass down. When he stood up, he towered over Gregory. He kept his voice low, so that no one would hear. "If you keep looking at my sister I might have to do something to prevent it."

"Oh?" Gregory smiled.

"I know what you're doing. I know all about it. You've been using psychology. You've been following me, you've been trying to get on my nerves. Now all that's over with. You're going to quit it."

"You know I can't do that," Gregory said. "I've been thinking about you night and day. Been thinking about you ever since I went to Vacaville. Now how do you expect me to stop? How do you expect me to quit that?"

"Yeah, well if you keep on following me, somebody's going to get hurt," Silver said, and he made certain there was the suggestion of knives in each word.

"That's probably true," Gregory agreed. "It's certainly true."

Up close, Gregory looked much older than Silver had remembered him. He was a man who had spent four years behind bars and it showed. Silver should have felt that he had the advantage, and he might have if Gregory had started a real fight, if he had come after Silver with a real weapon—a knife or a gun. But Gregory wasn't making a move, he was calm as ice, he pulled out a twenty-dollar bill and paid for Silver's drink and his own. It was only the red dog on Gregory's arm that seemed ready for blood, and that dog howled at a distant moon, that dog sent shivers down Silver's spine.

"You want to pay me back?" Silver whispered. "You want to kill me? Come outside with me now. Let's go right now and we'll settle it."

Gregory smiled and ordered another drink. "It doesn't work that way. This time it's when I say. This time I'm calling the shots, and you'll never even know what hit you."

"Oh yeah?" Silver said. He wished he had not had quite so much to drink because he felt unsteady and as inexperienced as he had years before when he had told Gregory about his first robbery, bragging about the two hundred dollars he had stolen. "Maybe I'm going to start to go after you. Maybe you'd better understand that if you keep on following me you're the one who's going to get hurt."

"You try that, Silver," Gregory said. "Just try and hurt me," he whispered.

When Silver walked back to the table he felt exhausted, his legs buckled, his head was light and he blamed all the amphetamines he had been taking, and his sleepless nights.

"Let's call it a night," he said to Lee and Teresa.

Teresa pushed her coffee cup away and reached for her sweater. Gregory was watching her and she wanted to get out of the restaurant as quickly as possible; she was being torn in half, she felt as if crickets were winding their way through the strands of her hair, making her deaf with their song. Lee, however, wasn't ready to go.

"I haven't finished my brandy," she said. When she lifted her glass to take another sip, Silver reached out and took hold of her hand. He brought the brandy glass back to the table so violently that it vibrated, and for a moment they were all certain the glass would break.

"Don't embarrass me," Silver whispered. He was amazed at how relieved he was when the glass didn't break; the slightest accident could show Gregory how effective the time he had spent following Silver had been. "Get your coat," Silver told Lee. "Do it now."

"What did that man at the bar want?" Lee asked. "He sure knows how to put you in a bad mood."

"Did you hear me?" Silver said. "Did you hear a fucking word I said to you?"

While Silver went to the parking lot to get the Camaro, Lee and Teresa waited outside the front door. Lee watched Silver walk away, then she took a cigarette from her purse.

"Some anniversary," she said. She blew out smoke in short staccato breaths.

"He's just tired," Teresa said, but she had never seen Silver so rattled before. She wished that she could run back to the bar and beg Gregory to leave them alone, beg him to stop following Silver, to stop filling Teresa with doubt. But she was afraid of Gregory: afraid he would say no, afraid that once she sat down next to him at the bar he would tell her more than she wanted to know, and that Santa Rosa would appear before them—there, at the mahogany bar, the heat would become unbearable, the day would be blinding, hawks would drop their feathers beside the cold glasses of bourbon and ice.

"Don't you tell me what my husband is," Lee said to Teresa. "He's not tired. He drank too much and now he's just goddamned mean."

When the Camaro's headlights appeared, Lee threw her cigarette into the gutter; inside the car she continued to sulk. "What a terrific night. An anniversary I'll always remember."

"Don't start up with me," Silver warned her. "Don't even think about it, Lee. Not tonight."

Tonight, Silver felt ready to break; he wanted to rush back through the years and change nearly everything that had happened. He didn't want to be a man who was celebrating his wedding anniversary, a man with responsibilities, and enemies, and lately with very little hope.

"You don't care a thing about me," Lee told him. "And you don't care about Jackie, either. I'll tell you what I think," she added, glaring at Teresa, "I think Jackie's allergic to that goddamned dog." She turned back to Silver. "Another man would be concerned about his wife and son."

"Another man," Silver said. "Go on, go find another man. I'll pay for your carfare. I'll pack your bags."

He looked in the rearview mirror; Gregory's blue Ford wasn't following them, but Teresa was staring at him, and once their eyes met Silver found he couldn't look away; she was taking him back through time.

Silver nearly went through a red light, he stopped at the last minute, he didn't notice that Lee had taken a cigarette from her purse until smoke had already begun to fill up the car.

"Put that out," he said. "I've told you before—I don't want you smoking."

Lee ignored him, she inhaled furiously. "If you don't care about me you don't have the right to tell me what to do. I'm not your slave."

Silver had been driving fast; now he stomped on the brakes and pulled over to the side of the road. Teresa wondered why Lee couldn't tell that this was the worst possible night to start a fight with Silver, and sure enough he reached across and threw open the passenger door.

"Get out," he said.

"You never tell me anything," Lee said. "You never introduce me to your friends, you have your own secret life. Well, I can have my own life too, you know."

"You want your own life?" Silver said. "First you wanted to get married, so I married you. Now you want your own life? You go ahead," he told her. "You go right ahead."

As always, Lee felt herself giving in. She thought about the nights when she had climbed out of her bedroom window to meet him, thought about his first kisses, the way every girl on the street turned to look at him.

"Put it out," Silver said.

Lee reached over and killed her cigarette in the ashtray, then leaned back in her seat. This was where it usually ended—when she backed down from an argument, Silver would grimly ignore her and then she knew that the fight was over. But not this time; this time Silver didn't cool down, this time he shoved her toward the door.

"I want you out of this car," he told her.

Lee looked over at him, surprised that he hadn't put the car back into gear and begun the drive home; she had no idea that his past had been chasing him all night long, that it had been following him for years.

"All these years of being married, and now if you're so goddamned unhappy you'd better leave." He shoved her harder; she had to grab onto the Camaro's upholstery or be thrown from the car. "Get out," Silver told her.

"I won't," Lee said, frightened at what she'd begun.

Silver wrenched up the emergency brake; he got out, walked around the car, then pulled Lee out onto the sidewalk.

"You heard me," he said. "Start walking."

"Don't do this," Lee whispered.

In the back seat, Teresa had made certain to turn away from them. Still she could hear them, even when she covered her ears with her hands she could hear them tearing each other apart. She wanted to disappear, but silently, quickly and without a word, so that she would not have to see just how cruel Silver could be.

Now Silver reached into the car, took Lee's purse and threw it on the ground. It landed by her feet, a lipstick in a gold case fell out and rolled into the street.

"Stop it," Lee pleaded. "I love you," she said.

"Well, don't," Silver told her. He stared at her coldly. "It won't do you any good, so just don't."

He turned away from her, slammed the passenger door shut, then walked around and got back into the car. He put the Camaro into gear and stepped down on the gas so hard that Teresa fell back in her seat. As they drove away, Teresa turned and wiped off a circle of glass in the rear window; Lee was running after them, she followed for nearly a block, she followed until she turned her ankle and the heel came off one of her shoes.

Silver drove fast, he didn't give a damn about speed limits, he ran one red light, and finally stopped at a second. When he stopped, Teresa climbed over into the front seat. She took one of the Marlboros from a pack on the dashboard, lit it and handed it to Silver. He took the cigarette gratefully, and smiled to think that his sister would know what he needed even before he did. And he drove carefully after that; for the first time that night he felt a little like his old self, the sort of man who didn't shake with fear the minute an old enemy showed up, the sort who didn't blow up the minute his wife said one wrong word.

"She asked for it," he explained to Teresa. "She's been driving me crazy."

Teresa sat with her back against the passenger door so that she could watch him.

"I'm not worried about Lee," Silver said. "She'll find her way home sooner or later. Or she'll go up to her mother's and call me in the morning, crying and begging me to drive up and get her. That's what she'll do—she'll make me drive all the way to fucking Santa Rosa."

The words Lee and Silver had said to each other echoed in Teresa's ears. "Did you marry her just because she wanted you to?" she asked.

"What was I supposed to do?" Silver said. "Was I supposed to disappear when she got pregnant, just take off and go to Los Angeles?" He wanted to be nothing like King Connors, and he wondered now, as they drove home, if his father had ever married again, if he had left a string of wives, each time using a new excuse: a walk to the corner for a pack of cigarettes, a job in another city, a night-fishing trip from which he would never come back. "I could have done it," Silver told Teresa. "Could have done it easy. Except for one thing— it wasn't right. That was the reason." He shrugged. "I did what was right."

All the rest of the drive home Teresa was silent, but when they reached the apartment and Silver was parking the car, she turned to him again.

"It wasn't because you loved her?" she asked.

Silver turned the key in the ignition, he switched off the headlights; he knew what she was asking, and he leaned over so that he was barely an inch away.

"What do you think?" Silver said. "Do you think she's the love of my life?"

Teresa got out of the car and ran all the way to the front door. She had wanted to ask him for years, wanted him to say it out loud, and so finally she knew for sure: he didn't love Lee. That was all there was to it. When Silver came up on the porch to unlock the front door, Teresa put her arm around his waist; in the shadows of the porch he looked exactly the same as he always had, not one thing about him ever seemed to change, and the doubts Teresa had felt about her brother when she saw Angel Gregory in the restaurant all disappeared.

"You're not afraid of Gregory," Teresa said.

"Me?" Silver said mockingly. "Afraid?"

"He wouldn't hurt you," Teresa said.

"That old man? He wouldn't dare."

Silver saw himself reflected in Teresa's eyes and he felt as though he could never be afraid; when she looked at him that way he could almost forget she was his sister. Teresa went to push open the front door, but he stopped her, then lowered his voice.

"You're the only one who really knows me," he said. "The only one who understands me."

Inside the apartment there was a fifteen-year-old baby-sitter who had spent all night making long-distance phone calls, dialing random numbers in the hope of reaching her favorite star. And in Lee and Silver's bedroom, Jackie slept in a crib that was much too small and dreamed of rooms where no one spoke.

"Come over here," Silver said and he pulled Teresa close before she had time to answer. "We never get any time alone," he whispered. "And I've missed you. I've missed you a lot."

Silver lifted her hair away from her throat; he bent down and kissed her, a kiss that left behind a mark in the shape of a rose, the imprint of his tongue.

Teresa closed her eyes; she wanted him never to stop. "I wish she would never come home," she said, and she spoke in a whisper, as if there was a watchful adult inside the apartment, rather than a girl who had just learned how to put on mascara.

"You don't love her," Teresa said. "You told me you don't."

For a second Silver felt as sober as he'd ever been. "Forget it. Forget all about it." He opened the door for her. "Get inside."

"You don't," Teresa whispered before she went in. "And I know you don't."

They walked into the kitchen, Teresa following behind. Silver went to the refrigerator and took out a bottle of beer, and Teresa sat down next to Marie, the babysitter. She felt out of breath and angry; she wished that she and Silver were strangers; she was certain if they were, if they had just met, if they hadn't had the same last name, he would never have stopped with one kiss.

"Are you making those phone calls again?" Silver asked the babysitter.

"What phone calls?" Marie said.

"Come on," Silver said to Marie. He left the half-empty bottle of beer on the table. "I'll walk you home. We can discuss the calls you made to Los Angeles the last time you were here."

"I can walk myself home," Marie said, but Silver insisted.

"Nothing doing," he said. He wanted to get out of the apartment; Teresa's faith in him had given him a boy's courage, he wished that Gregory would come out and face him in the street tonight, he was certain he could win any fight, except, perhaps, the fight to stay away from Teresa. She was sitting at the table, she was watching him with those eyes, eyes that were the color of slow midnights.

"Let's go," Silver told Marie. "I told your parents you'd be home early."

"You're lucky," Teresa told the babysitter as the girl put on her jacket and reached for the stack of movie magazines she had been reading all night. "A lot of girls would give just about anything to have Silver walk them home."

"Oh, yeah?" Marie said. To her, Silver seemed much too old for romance.

"What girls are those?" Silver teased. "Give me their phone numbers. Give me their addresses." And when Marie had walked down the hallway to wait for him at the front door, he lowered his voice. "What girls are those?" he whispered.

Silver noticed now that the kitchen was a mess; Lee hadn't done that day's dishes, a coffee cup with a ring of her lipstick on it was on the counter, a gray sweater was draped over the back of one of the chairs.

"Maybe she took me seriously," Silver said. "Maybe she's not coming home tonight."

He took the cup with the lipstick and rinsed it out, then placed it carefully on the drainboard.

"So what if she doesn't?" Teresa asked, and she was surprised to find her voice taking on the tone she had used with dozens of men, each and every one of her Santa Rosa lovers, men she had known would take her to bed the minute she saw them. "What if she doesn't come home?"

"It's dangerous without her here," Silver said simply. "And I don't like it." Silver found himself thinking of roses. He imagined a bed covered with silken petals. "Maybe you'd better go to a motel tonight," he told his sister. "Or go to Bergen's. Maybe you'd better not be here when I get back."

But when Silver left to walk Marie home, Teresa didn't call a cab, she didn't make reservations at a motel or telephone Bergen, though she knew the detective could drive over and pick her up in less than fifteen minutes. Instead, she opened the door of Lee and Silver's bedroom and made certain that Jackie was asleep, she put Atlas out on the back porch, then went into the living room and pulled down all the shades. And after she had made up the bed in her room with cold, clean sheets, she noticed that her knuckles were white, the veins in her wrists were as green as aquarium water. She took off all her clothes, she shut off the light, and she knew she could have Silver that night if she wanted; as long as Lee didn't come home, he was hers. Teresa put her head down on the pillow and imagined that she was in her own bed in Santa Rosa; irises the color of the sky grew outside, and in the room right next door the sheets on Silver's empty bed were still wrinkled from when he had wakened at noon. Dina was sitting at the foot of her bed, she wore a mohair shawl with fringes, she whispered a story about the night riders who always traveled west.

"You'll hear their horses long before you see them," Dina told her. "The earth will shake and then you'll see that one horse is tied to the front porch. When this horse shakes his head his mane will be the color of snow, and you'll know it can only be an Aria who has a horse like that, only an Aria who would dare to ride up to your front door in the middle of the night."

And by the time Silver came back home it was nearly the middle of the night; he had considered not going back at all, he could have spent the night in the back seat of the Camaro, could have easily found a woman to take him home and hold him tight till morning. He had stopped at El Calderon and had two beers, he had watched a woman dressed in black velvet slacks dance alone to a song playing on the jukebox, but in the end he walked home, he couldn't help himself. The neighborhood felt deserted, his boots echoed on the cement, and he knew, as soon as he walked in the front door, that Lee hadn't come back. He didn't stop to think, he couldn't have stopped to think, he went straight to the bedroom at the back of the house. Teresa had moved close to the wall to leave room in the bed for him. He took off his shirt, but he was still half dressed when he got in beside her, he didn't dare give himself the time to reconsider. As soon as he was next to her the sheets seemed burning hot. He put his arms around her, and she wrapped her legs around his; when they kissed their loneliness surfaced like a knot, and Teresa felt every part of her shudder, every part of her sigh.

"This is crazy," Silver murmured. "Crazy."

And later, when he had already moved and was on top of her, Silver couldn't help but go on; he tried to stop himself, he whispered about his doubts.

"If anybody knew about this . . ." he said. "If Lee came home."

Teresa's eyes were closed; she touched his lips with her tongue, she whispered his name, over and over again, and the sound gave him courage, and he got out of bed and took off his boots, and folded his black linen slacks over a chair. He hurried, he knew she was waiting for him, knew she was still calling his name, and he told himself no one would ever know, he convinced himself that it was

impossible for anyone to ever find out, and he went back
to the bed and lay down on the sheets that had been cold
only a few hours before and he held her like a man who
was drowning, a man who didn't dare test his passion by
waiting any longer.

Silver had been right to guess that Lee would think about
going back to Santa Rosa, and she did go as far as the
bus station on Market Street. She sat in the bus station
for hours, she was overwhelmed by the sense that if she
didn't go back home that night it would be too late,
she might never be able to return. She thought about
Dina's funeral, about the night Silver had hit her and
then regretted it. She thought about his clothes hanging
next to her dresses and skirts in the closet in the bedroom,
she imagined him sitting in the dark on those nights when
his insomnia wouldn't leave him alone and he thought she
was sleeping, when really she was lying in bed with her
eyes open, just waiting for him to come back to bed. She
got out of that bus station, and she got out fast. Lee took a
cab home; she unlocked the front door and walked inside.
Because Jackie was asleep, she took off her shoes and
went through the house quietly, but even though Lee had
seen the Camaro outside, Silver wasn't in bed, he wasn't
in the living room watching a late-night movie on TV, or
in the kitchen, angry at her for having stayed out so late.
Lee went into the bathroom and stood by the sink, but she
didn't wash; she stared at herself in the mirror, she was
surprised to find that she looked as tired as she did, and
as scared. She walked down the hall to Teresa's bedroom,
a room that really should have been Jackie's—he was too
old to share Lee and Silver's bedroom, too old to sleep
in a crib. Lee stood outside the bedroom door for a long
time, even when she finally opened it she didn't want to,
but her hand acted on its own and she couldn't seem to
stop it, she couldn't do anything but watch as her fingers
turned the doorknob, and after she had done that it was

                                                    •

certainly too late to close the door, and go back to her own bedroom and wait for Silver to come back to bed.

Teresa had kept her eyes closed all the time they had been together; but even with her eyes closed she could see Silver, as if each one of his features had been stamped onto the insides of her eyelids. With her eyes closed she could see his dark hair, his high cheekbones, the eyes which were the same exact color as her own. Once he was inside her, once they began to move together she closed her eyes tighter, and in doing so saw him even more clearly, saw him as if there were a thousand electric lights surrounding him. He licked her skin, tasting her, making her feel as though no space separated them, as if it were impossible for their bodies to ever be separated. When the door opened, Teresa heard the wood scrape, she turned quickly and opened her eyes to see Lee standing there, watching them as if she had stumbled across the worst thing she had ever seen, as if she had discovered something worse than murder.

A stream of light had come into the room from the hallway; the light hit Silver's back and shoulders and he could feel it penetrate his skin. He turned to the door, he blinked in the glare of the hallway light but his eyes wouldn't focus. It was then Teresa really looked at him, she looked at him for the first time since he had come into the bed, and maybe it was the combination of darkness and light in the room, maybe it was that her eyes wouldn't focus, but for a minute she didn't know who he was. For a second her throat was dry, her heart absolutely still. Silver was a stranger; he wasn't the boy she thought had been making love to her, his face was wrong, all wrong. His eyes weren't as dark as they should have been, his features were much too sharp. Teresa backed away from him, she edged up against the cold plaster wall and tried to breathe, but each breath was like a knife, each breath brought a fist that reached upwards to her throat and wouldn't let in any air.

As soon as Silver's eyes adjusted to the light, and he saw Lee standing in the doorway, he jumped out of bed. He ran to the door and kicked it shut so viciously that the wood around the hinges split, and the door missed slamming into Lee's face by less than an inch. Silver stood motionless, staring at the closed door until he realized that he was shivering, the small bedroom suddenly seemed as cold as ice. He turned to Teresa; she was sitting up, her back against the wall. She couldn't catch her breath, she was wheezing now, a soft choking noise. Silver went over to the bed and held her.

"Breathe," he told her. "Just breathe."

Finally, Teresa knew who he was, finally she began to cough and then, at last, to breathe again.

"All right?" Silver whispered, and when Teresa nodded Silver picked up his clothes and began to get dressed.

They could both hear Lee now; she had gone into the kitchen, she was opening every cabinet, taking out each glass, every ceramic cup, anything that was breakable she threw against the wall. Jackie had been awakened, and his cries echoed everywhere. The whole house was shaking, the air in the bedroom was heavy, it was the air of earthquake weather, even though the sky outside the window was calm, in only a few hours the sun would be leaving thin streams of orange light all over the backyard.

"There's nothing for anyone to be upset about," Silver said softly. He buttoned each of his shirt buttons carefully; he had to, his fingers were shaking. "Nothing happened here."

Silver tucked his shirttail into his slacks, he reached for the comb on Teresa's bureau and ran it through his hair.

Teresa was still having difficulty breathing, she paused between words. "Silver, she saw us."

"Saw what?" Silver said. He sat down on the bed and pulled on his boots; he reached toward his crotch, annoyed that his erection hadn't disappeared as quickly as his memory had. "She didn't see anything," he told

Teresa. "She'll believe whatever I tell her, and I'm telling her nothing happened."

Teresa wrapped the top sheet around her. "Why would you do that?" she asked. "It's a lie."

Just when he was beginning to look right to her again he was ruining it all, running back to Lee, running away from her, acting as if nothing more than an innocent kiss had been exchanged.

"What am I supposed to tell her?" Silver asked. "The truth?"

Teresa's mouth was set in a thin line. "You're afraid," she told him.

"Shit," Silver said. "Afraid?"

Out in the kitchen, Lee had begun to throw the contents of the refrigerator all over the floor; cartons of milk, bottles of mustard, containers of relish and salads and beer.

"You listen to me," Silver said to Teresa. "It is wrong, understand me? Understand what that word means? So don't you look at me with those eyes of yours any more, don't come after me with that little tongue of yours."

"Me!" Teresa said. "Me? You're acting like it's all my fault."

"Forget about it," Silver said. "Forget about whose fault it was."

He buckled his belt, he walked to the door, he concentrated on all the possible excuses he might give to Lee.

"Where are you going?" Teresa said.

Silver opened the door a crack and looked out; he turned back to Teresa, put a finger to his lips to silence her, then nodded out to the kitchen.

Teresa raised herself up on her knees. "Don't go," she whispered. "Don't leave me here."

"Relax," Silver said. "I'm going to take care of everything."

"Don't go out there to her now," Teresa said, her voice rising, and dangerously loud.

Silver walked back to the bed and put his hand on

her throat; his fingers touched her pulse and the shock of her skin made him pull his hand away, as though he'd been burned. "Shut up," he whispered. "Keep your voice down," he urged. "Everybody's got to calm down. Everybody's got to go to sleep."

Teresa nodded and backed up toward the wall; her palms and the soles of her feet were cold.

"I mean, it's almost morning, right?" Silver whispered.

Teresa didn't say a word.

"Right?" Silver said.

"It's almost morning," Teresa whispered.

"It's time to quiet down," Silver said, gently, as if he were talking to a child. He reached for a blanket which had fallen onto the floor and put it around Teresa's shoulders. "I'm going to take care of everything," he promised.

When he left the room Teresa pulled her knees up and stared at the closed door. By tomorrow Silver would be able to persuade Lee that she had not really seen him in bed with Teresa, he would blind her with kisses, convince her with lies, settle it easily because she wanted to believe him. Right now Teresa could hear Lee yelling in the kitchen, but by tomorrow Lee would be ready to believe anything Silver told her, and Teresa couldn't blame her. Even now, alone in the bed, Teresa could still imagine his face; she fought to keep her eyes open, she couldn't risk thinking about him, forgiving him, and she certainly couldn't risk sleep. Teresa had decided that by morning, not long after Silver and Lee had finally stopped fighting and had gone to sleep in each other's arms, she would already have left the house.

Later, she packed her suitcases, she took everything she owned; she slipped out the front door, went around to let Atlas out of the yard, and then walked down the street as quickly as she could. And when Silver went to her room, later that day, he saw Teresa's outline on the sheet, and he couldn't help wondering what might have happened if he had let Lee break every glass in the house, if he had turned to Teresa instead of his wife, and had dared to stay with her all night long.

Teresa's first instinct was to head north; and because there was no way to get Atlas onto a bus, she hitched a ride to Sonoma with two women who were going all the way to Santa Rosa for a baby shower. Teresa and Atlas sat in the back, next to a bassinet trimmed with silk ribbons. There was a great deal of sunshine as they drove out of San Francisco, the sky shone like a looking glass; Teresa felt light-headed, the radio was switched on, and she and the other two women sang along with the songs they knew by heart. But the closer they came to the Santa Rosa exit, the clearer it became to Teresa that she couldn't go home. The house on Divisadero Street was surely sold by now, and she hadn't one relative or friend left in town. She surprised the two women by asking to be let off right there on the highway, and, because she still had no idea where she was going, Teresa didn't mind waiting for an hour in the hot sun for another car to stop for her. And even then, after a station wagon had pulled over, and Teresa had opened the back door so that Atlas could climb in, she couldn't imagine any destination other than home.

Harper Ryan, the woman who drove the station wagon, had just driven to Petaluma to have a new carburetor put in her car; she didn't usually stop for hitchhikers but she had the night off from Nina's Lounge, the bar where she was a cocktail waitress, and the old Mercury station wagon was driving like a dream. As soon as Teresa got in and admitted that she didn't know where she wanted to go, Harper knew that pulling over had been a mistake.

"What do you mean?" she asked Teresa. "What am I supposed to do with you?"

Teresa leaned her head against the upholstery and shrugged; the car smelled like rosemary and mint and gasoline, and Teresa realized how tired she was.

"I'm running away," she told Harper. "I didn't have time to figure out where I was going."

Harper herself had run away once; years earlier she had left the eastern shore of Maryland and a marriage she had known was all wrong from the start. Her husband's name was Tim, and he liked deep-fried chicken on Friday nights, and though they had been married for three years Harper had never managed to fry the chicken long enough—the meat near the bone was always pink, and even now she couldn't so much as eat chicken salad without feeling vaguely ill and thinking about Tim.

"You're running away from your husband," Harper said. When Teresa shook her head no, Harper guessed again, "Some boyfriend who's not treating you right?"

From where the car was pulled over on the highway Teresa could almost see the Santa Rosa exit; she thought about blackberry jam and kisses and a boy who climbed out onto the roof to smoke marijuana and look at stars.

"You can't just wander around without knowing where you're going, without a plan," Harper told Teresa. "Take my advice. Go back to him."

"He's married," Teresa said.

"Well, Christ," Harper said. "I was married once too— it doesn't necessarily mean a whole hell of a lot." Harper turned and patted Atlas's head; ten years ago she had left Salisbury, Maryland, with five hundred dollars and this same Mercury station wagon, having decided she couldn't stand one more chicken dinner. "I'll bet you don't have any money," she said to Teresa.

"Just drop me off somewhere," Teresa said.

"Oh, sure," Harper said. "Then if you get murdered in the middle of the night all I have to do is feel guilty for the rest of my life."

When they passed by Santa Rosa, Teresa closed her eyes and breathed as deeply as she could; she thought about Silver, she couldn't quite catch her breath, and Harper reached over and pounded on her back.

"Asthma?" Harper asked, when Teresa was breathing a little more easily. "If you've got asthma I've got something that can set you right—a tonic of ivy and garlic and blackthorn."

"I don't have asthma," Teresa said. They were heading toward the river now. Harper turned off at the exit that led to Guerneville, and once they were off the highway Teresa felt instantly more comfortable, she curled her feet up under her and leaned against the door. "I'm just tired," Teresa said. "That's all that's wrong with me."

"If you ever do get asthma, let me know," Harper was saying. She turned to Teresa, but Teresa had already fallen asleep, she was dreaming about Silver, but she was moving toward that labyrinth of sleep far too deep for dreams.

Harper switched on the radio, but she kept it low, and she drove on, toward Villa Lobo, a town that had grown up around a logging camp near the river and had somehow managed to continue after the logging camp had been deserted for years. All along the highway, and up in the hills, the grass had been burned, but when Harper turned the Mercury onto the River Road it was like another season—the temperature dropped ten degrees, sunflowers and ferns grew beneath the tallest trees, redwoods grew so high that in some gardens the sun was always blocked out, and even the nighttime snails were fooled into leaving their traces along the lettuce leaves till noon. The riverbed was nearly dry; in the center of the bed was a stream only a few feet wide that ran to the west; occasional pools had collected, sienna-colored pools that tempted children into trying dangerous dives: jack knives and twists. Harper's house was only a few yards away from the river; but the riverbeds in Villa Lobo were notoriously dry in summer, guest houses that rented rooms to fishermen were never full, water frogs gathered in the sand as if they were already waiting for the winter rains and the green tides of November.

Harper didn't really decide to take Teresa home with her; she simply didn't know what else to do, she would have done the same with a stray cat, a swan with a broken wing. Once she had parked the car, Harper let Atlas out, but she didn't wake Teresa; for all she knew, the other woman might have already hitchhiked for hundreds of miles. And later, when it had begun to grow dark and there was a sliver of a moon in the sky, Harper went back out to the station wagon to call Teresa inside. She opened the passenger door, she told Teresa it was late, and when Teresa still didn't open her eyes, Harper snapped her fingers right next to Teresa's ear.

"Good lord," Harper said finally to Teresa, "you're not going to wake up, are you?"

Someone else might have panicked, someone else might have telephoned the local police or sent for an ambulance. But Harper simply helped Teresa stretch out in the front seat so that her legs wouldn't be all cramped when she woke up. If anyone was used to mysterious diseases it was Harper, she had had a lifetime of them. She had grown up in her grandmother's house in Maryland and had lived for years with an old woman who believed in love potions and in lunacy caused by too bright nights, an old woman who could brew teas that chased away fevers and melancholy and headaches.

At night, when there was a full moon in the eastern sky, Harper's grandmother had taken her for walks that ranged far beyond the magnolias and the gardens and the places where lambs were tied to wooden posts so they wouldn't wander away. Beside a stream not more than a mile away from their house, Harper's grandmother had searched for mushrooms and yarrow, for milkwood and antelope sage and lavender, and Harper's job was to keep all the herbs separate from each other. At the ages of ten and eleven and twelve she followed her grandmother and was careful not to slip in the mud and there, under the stars, she put the herbs into tin boxes.

Days later there would be something boiling on the
stove—wood avens or juniper berries—and some women
from town would always stop by. They would say they
had come just for a visit, for a slice of poppyseed cake
or a cup of lemonade on a hot day, but when they left
they always left a dollar on the kitchen table, and they
always took something back to town—a cure for fever,
an aphrodisiac, fig juice in a paper cup to cure a sore
throat. In spite of herself, Harper had learned her grandmother's remedies; although when she was a teen-ager
she suddenly refused to accompany the old woman to
the stream, she refused to drink peppermint tea, choosing to drink gallons of black coffee instead. She was
embarrassed that her grandmother believed in cures. At
high school she whispered to her friends that she was
forced to live with an insane woman, she began to stay
out late every night, choosing her boyfriends because of
their cars, spending those nights when there were full
moons at drive-in movies instead of at the stream where
wild lavender grew.

It wasn't until Harper was eighteen, already married and
out of her grandmother's house for nearly a year, that she
went back home and asked her grandmother for one of
her remedies. In less than a year Harper had discovered
that the last thing she wanted was to stay married, and
that included having a child. Harper's grandmother was
a very old woman by then, in less than six months she
would die in her sleep and Harper would be amazed at
how many people from town attended the funeral. But on
that night when Harper went home for a cure, there were
only the two of them in the house, only their shadows on
the walls.

"I know what you're here for," her grandmother had
said right away. "Your period's late. Don't even think to
try and tell me I'm wrong, 'cause I'm right."

Harper waited in her grandmother's kitchen while the
old woman went out; she didn't have far to go, just over

to the neighboring fields, where she dug out a cotton plant, saving only the root. Later that night, she gave Harper the extract of the bark to drink and made up a packet of pennyroyal tea. For three nights Harper drank pennyroyal tea mixed with brewer's yeast; she boiled the water while her husband watched a baseball game on TV, she sipped the tea when he was already fast asleep in their bed. One week later Harper had a miscarriage, and it was then she decided that whenever she got the hell out of Salisbury, and out of her husband's house, she'd set aside a place in her garden for herbs, she'd make certain to try to write down all of her grandmother's remedies she hadn't already forgotten.

And so on the night when Teresa wouldn't wake up, Harper knew enough to mix juniper berries, camomile, and birch leaves. She took the mixture out to the car and spooned some of the liquid in between Teresa's lips, but it did no good at all and Harper had no choice but to let Teresa spend the night in the Mercury. And while Teresa slept, curled up on the upholstery that was still streaked red with Maryland dust, Harper wondered if her grandmother had known about a sleep so strong it couldn't be broken by home remedies, a sleep stronger than any herbs gathered under the stars. And late that night Harper found herself wishing that she hadn't left her grandmother's house as soon as she had; she boiled water for peppermint tea, poured herself some, and then tried to see the future in the murky leaves that settled to the bottom of her cup, managing only to see the past, a recurring pattern of a flock of birds in flight.

The path to Harper's house was marked by broken stones. Out in the backyard there were lawn chairs that had been painted blue and raspberry bushes that grew wild. A low fence surrounded the herb garden; a scarecrow made of a mop handle and a wide-brimmed hat scared the jays away from the dill and mint and sweet marjoram and kept their beaks from picking through the heather and bloodroot and sweet wild onions. After her first night of sleeping in the car, Teresa began to sleep on the living-room couch, and she liked to look through the window into the garden as she drank tea in the morning. In the afternoons Teresa walked through town, and because Villa Lobo was made up of nothing more than a post office, a laundromat, and a general store that also sold bait, she was back at Harper's in time to clean the house.

Teresa imagined that the way she could earn her room and board at Harper's was to scrub the floors, wash all of the dishes in the sink, and take Harper's clothes to the laundromat where she washed, dried, and folded each blouse and pair of jeans carefully.

"Don't clean up my house," Harper told her when she woke late in the afternoon. Harper worked nights at Nina's, and often wasn't home until four in the morning; she slept all day and in the afternoons had time to climb over the fence in the backyard and pick dill and mint before she painted her eyes with kohl and put on her black and white uniform and returned to Nina's by six. "This is ridiculous," Harper said when Teresa had been at her house for nearly two weeks. "The fact is you're either going to have to get yourself a job and get your own place, or go back to him."

"I'll get a job," Teresa assured Harper.

Teresa had begun to borrow Harper's clothes, she had begun to know where every pot and pan was stored in the kitchen. Having someone else live in her house was not as awful as Harper would have imagined, but what worried her were the days when Teresa didn't wake up.

"Plus, you're sick," Harper went on. "You're sick and you don't have any money, and if I were you I'd think twice about going back to that man you left behind."

There was another reason why Harper wanted Teresa to move out, to take her dog who shed all over the living-room rug and disappear down the River Road: she had a lover, one she didn't want Teresa to meet. Harper had called Joey the day after Teresa came to stay with her, had told him that she was tired from working a six-day shift at Nina's, and had advised him not to stop by her house; when she could make time she would come by the trailer park where he was the caretaker. Her call wasn't unexpected, they had been seeing less of each other, arguing each time they spent the night together. Joey didn't like her working as a cocktail waitress, he didn't like the hours she kept, the herbs growing in the yard made him nervous, the fact that she insisted that she didn't believe in marriage just because she'd been burned once drove him up a wall. Even though they had been spending more time fighting than making love, Harper didn't quite want to give Joey up; after all the energy she had put into trying to make him understand who she was she didn't want to lose him to a stranger who just happened to pass by, and she was certain that if Joey met Teresa that was exactly what would happen.

Eventually it did happen, on a Tuesday night in late July when Harper was at work, taking an order for two whiskey sours and a tequila sunrise. Joey had had it with Harper—she was avoiding him, ignoring him, and what did they really have in common anyway? He had decided to go to her house and wait for her to come home from Nina's. By the time Harper opened the front door Joey would be sitting on the couch, his long legs stretched out in front of him, he'd be ready for a fight. When Joey got to Harper's house that night, all the lights were on; when he looked in the front window it made sense for him to assume that the woman dressed in Harper's clothes who played solitaire was Harper, that she had taken a night off and not even bothered to tell him. He watched through the window as a woman set out diamonds and hearts in a neat row on the tabletop. The night was clear, and the Milky Way seemed only inches above the roof of the house.

When Joey went to the front door and opened it, he

knew something was different right away; an old dog stood on the threshold and blocked his way. The collie barked and bared his teeth, and Joey stopped in his tracks, even though he could have easily booted the dog out of his way with one kick. Teresa got up from the table and ran to the door; she grabbed Atlas by his collar and pulled him away.

"I'm not who you think I am," Teresa explained, right away. "Harper's still at work."

As soon as he saw her Joey wondered how he could have ever mistaken Teresa for Harper, as soon as he saw her he imagined Teresa in his trailer, in his bed, behind a window where passionflowers grew on a trellis of dark leaves.

"You're exactly who I think you are," Joey told Teresa that night. "You're somebody I've been looking for all my goddamned life," he said to her, and as if in gratitude Teresa gave him back a silent smile, and Joey immediately believed that her smile was a perfect gift, the gift of a woman who had been waiting to be rescued for such a long time that it might be years before her tongue could form words, and even longer before she could conjure up the strength to say a word like no.

They were lovers weeks before she moved into his trailer. While Harper worked at Nina's Lounge, Joey and Teresa made love in her bed, careful to smooth the sheets when they were done. Each time they made love Teresa silently counted to a thousand, in her head she recited the capitals of every state, the alphabet, the days of the week, anything to stop herself from imagining that another man held her, and when Joey told her he loved her the words were like stones.

"Please don't say that," she told him. "Don't love me," she said, but every time she told him not to fall in love with her his passion was renewed. He was certain that if given enough time she would love him in return, she would thank him for finding her in Harper's living room that first night, she would vow never to look at another man.

There were times when Joey left Teresa at two in the morning only to return to the house in the afternoon, after Harper had awakened, careful to act as distant to Teresa as he had that first time Harper had introduced them, days after Teresa and Joey had first become lovers. Harper knew something had happened, but she didn't flinch when she noticed that Joey was staring at Teresa, his eyes blurry with a vision of pearls and black feathers; she didn't even consider dusting the skin near her heart with basil so that Joey would remain true to her. And when Harper finally asked Teresa to move out, she wasn't the least bit surprised to find out that Joey had asked her to move into his trailer.

"It's just temporary," Teresa told Harper on the day that she left.

"Sure," Harper said. "Admit it. He's crazy about you."

"I didn't go after him," Teresa said. "He wants me to be in love with him, but I'm not."

"Are you stupid?" Harper had said then. "You're telling *me* your troubles? You're complaining about Joey to *me*?" She shook her head. "Jesus Christ, don't cry to me because Joey's not sweet enough to you in bed, or because you don't love him. Good lord, Teresa. Grow up."

"You're mad at me," Teresa had said. "You hate me."

"Oh, God," Harper sighed. "Look," she told Teresa, "Joey and I would never have made it through another year—you just speeded it up. And now he's yours. That's all there is to it—he's yours."

And so Teresa moved into Joey's trailer, and they lived on his monthly caretaker's salary. It was late in the summer, and the trailer park was quieter than it had been in June and July, most of the summer vacationers had already gone back home and on some nights, when the moon was orange, already becoming an October light, Teresa felt as though she were living in a ghost town. As the weather grew colder and the trailer camp emptied of all but a few fishermen and Joey had to nail boards over his trailer's windows to keep the river wind out, Teresa discovered that she was learning how to spend all night by someone's side and stay awake till dawn without ever letting on that she hadn't been able to sleep. She was learning to cook the dinners Joey liked, learning to tune the radio in to the country-and-western station he listened to, in a little while she discovered that she knew the words to some of the songs. Pine needles covered the earth in the trailer camp, and it was possible for Atlas to walk so softly that the black-tailed squirrels didn't hear him, and he caught one once and brought it to the trailer's front door.

By October, when they had lived together for nearly two months and the moon was orange nearly every night, the last fisherman left the trailer park. They were alone, and that was exactly the way Joey wanted it. He didn't trust Teresa out of his sight, he had begun to suspect Harper of trying to get back at him and he wanted to make certain that Teresa didn't run into her by accident. So he kept an eye on Teresa, he didn't even want her taking the laundry into town, and he watched from the window as she hung towels and sheets on the rope clothesline that stretched from the trailer's porch to the nearest pine tree. They were together nearly all the time, they ate breakfast together and dinner, they were in bed by nine. But there were some hours every day when Joey had to leave her alone, hours when he had to board up the windows of all the trailers and sweep away the piles of pine needles and replace the paths that had been worn away. Teresa looked out the door after him as he walked across the trailer park. He was tall, nearly as tall as King Connors, he wore his hair long, and he always had on the same denim jacket no matter what the temperature outside. He was handsome, Teresa thought when she watched him from a distance, but he seemed more and more like a stranger, and she was thankful for those times when she could close the front door and be all alone in the trailer.

Now that the weather had begun to turn bad, Atlas no longer spent his days outside; instead he slept in the kitchen, his jaws snapped in his sleep as he dreamed of cats and butterflies. Because it was autumn, because there were pines surrounding the trailer, the afternoons now seemed darker than ever, and Teresa spent all of her time alone looking through the cracks of the boards Joey had put up to protect the windows. And although she tried not to think about the future or the past, though she tried to remember that she was now living with a man who promised always to love her, Teresa found herself thinking about summer, about a sky clearer than topaz, and a man who carried pearls and desire in his hand as carelessly as another man might carry an apple or a pear. And she couldn't help but wonder what Silver had thought when he opened the door to her room and found an empty bed, and she couldn't help but wish he was missing her still.

It wasn't until November that Lee realized she had become so accustomed to silence that the sound of the telephone or the front doorbell ringing could startle her. It had gotten so she couldn't stand the hum of the television or the roar of a jet overhead. Fortunately, Silver respected her need for quiet; he left her notes when he was going to be out especially late, and whenever they were in the same room they circled each other wordlessly, as if caught in separate dreams. And it wasn't until November that Lee realized how afraid she was of the time when they finally spoke to each other, a time when she would ask Silver what Teresa meant to him, when she finally asked how long he thought they could go on this way.

Jackie was in school for half the day now, but he was still quieter than any child Lee had ever known. He had never said Atlas's name while the dog was living with them, but now he occasionally called the name out loud, although he knew the dog had gone away, and with him

Jackie's aunt, a woman with long hair who danced to songs on the radio. Not that Jackie really missed her, or the dog either, he didn't mind being alone most of the time, he liked it. What he didn't like was the time when his father came home. Then the air in the house would change; when Silver stepped through the front door there seemed to be a fire burning its way down the hallway, a fire devoured the oak floors, the posters on the wall, the desire for silence Jackie shared with his mother.

Something had happened to Silver—maybe it was Teresa disappearing, or Lee walking in on them, maybe it was because he was certain Gregory was still following him. He didn't care if his blue jeans were ironed, he spent too much money, and he went out in the street only when he had to, no longer enjoying nights without moons, midnights, the sound of his boots on cold cement. He felt as if his own bones were betraying him, making him feel old. He considered hiring a private investigator to find Teresa, but he wasn't quite sure what he would do once he found her—he wasn't ready to forget that she was his sister, but he was slowly edging toward a time when it no longer mattered. He was lonely, lonelier than he'd ever been, and at the same time he felt as if he were never alone, as though someone was watching him night and day. One night Lee awoke near dawn to find Silver staring at her in the dark bedroom, and even in the darkness she could see his desperation as clearly as if she studied him through a magnifying glass.

"Tell me what's wrong," she asked, and her voice sounded terribly loud in the quiet room.

Silver shook his head; he went to the window and looked out. He didn't shout at her, didn't tell her to mind her own business; he ran his thumb over the glass and studied the street. Lee reached for a cigarette and lit it; she didn't hide her smoking from him any more, he never even mentioned it now. She went to the window and stood behind him.

"We could start over," she told him.

"Pretend we've just met?" Silver said.

"Sure," Lee whispered.

"You'd go to a bar," Silver smiled, "and I'd follow you there. I'd sit right down next to you and tell you what beautiful blue eyes you had."

"Did you ever think so?" Lee asked.

"I picked you, didn't I?" Silver took the cigarette from Lee's hand, inhaled, then put it out in the ashtray on the bureau.

Lee shook her head. "I was the one who picked you. And I'd do it again. I'd invite you up to my place, I'd sit so close to you you couldn't help but know how much I wanted to kiss you. And then, later, if you told me I was beautiful while we were making love I wouldn't even care if you were lying."

"You don't mean that," Silver said.

"Sure I do," Lee told him. "Tell me lies. Tell me dozens of them."

"You can't still want to be married to me," Silver said then.

"I do want to be," Lee said, and for a few seconds, because Silver hadn't laughed at her or turned away, she thought her fear of talking things out had been crazy, she thought they might have a chance.

"You can't want it," Silver said finally. "No woman wants to be married to someone who doesn't love her."

"Oh," Lee said. She got back into bed and pulled the covers up. Outside, in the sky, a jet was moving eastward and the sound of its engines made Lee shudder. Silver came over and sat on the edge of the bed.

"It's not that I don't care about you," he told her. "I think of you as part of my family."

"Like a sister?" Lee said bitterly. "Is that how you think of me?"

When he didn't answer he hurt her more than ever before. Lee's blood turned cold, desire left her that night, it left for good. They stopped talking to each other after that, weeks went by without one word exchanged. Lee didn't bother to get dressed in the morning any more, why should she bother, she wasn't going anywhere. After Jackie went to school she would call the grocery and order what she wanted delivered, and then she would sit in the kitchen, she'd watch the garden, stare at clouds, and before she knew it Silver would be waking up. She would hear him, every day, hear the shower running in the bathroom, hear the closet door in their bedroom open and then close, but he never came into the kitchen to talk to her, and when he was finally gone, when she heard the front door slam, and the Camaro's engine start out on the street, Lee cried. Every day she cried, and every day she was shocked to discover that she still had more tears left inside.

Even if he had been talking to her, Silver wouldn't have told Lee all that had been going on. He wouldn't have mentioned that for four days in a row the Camaro's tires had been slashed, so that he had begun to carry not only a spare in the trunk but one in the back seat as well. He wouldn't have told her that he had found a pigeon with its throat cut wrapped in a blue towel and left on their front stairs one evening, or that envelopes addressed to him, but having no letter inside, had been placed in the mailbox every day. Silver believed he could handle these threats alone, he was handling them, he tried to convince himself they were the threats of a man who lacked courage. And in the end it was a little thing that set him off, something that might have been an accident. Silver went to the Cadillac Cleaners late one afternoon to pick up his black suit. The clerk apologized, but what could he do, there was no point in looking through the back, through the containers of lost clothing, because somebody had already picked up Silver's suit, a stranger in a navy-blue coat had insisted that Silver had sent him.

The clerk offered to pay for a new suit, but Silver
shook his head, it wasn't another suit he wanted. That
evening Silver couldn't bring himself to go to work, he
missed two meetings in south San Francisco with dealers
certain to buy thousands of dollars' worth of cocaine; he
was sure that somewhere in the city Gregory was dressing
in black linen, he was buttoning each button of the tailored
jacket with long, calm fingers. When Silver went home he
went straight to the hall closet where belongings that were
never used but couldn't be thrown away were stored. In a
cardboard box, beside a tray of Dina's silverware Lee had
taken after the funeral but never used because the forks
tarnished so easily, was the gun Silver had bought from
the dishwasher in Santa Rosa years before. He took out
the gun and oiled it; he found bullets in a smaller box that
also held photographs and keys which no longer fit any of
the locks he used. Somewhere, Gregory had thrown away
his navy-blue coat and had dressed all in black; he had put
his wallet, his car keys, his gold cigarette lighter into the
inside pocket of the jacket. Somewhere, he was waiting
for Silver.

Silver rushed into the bedroom and unlocked the top
bureau drawer. Lee hadn't even known he was home, she
had assumed he was out just as he was every night, she
hadn't heard him rooting around in the hall closet. When
he ran into the room Lee was in bed reading a magazine,
she had just begun to read a column about new sorts of
permanents that wouldn't damage hair when she saw him.
As he threw open the door and ran to the bureau, Lee
could see that he was carrying a gun. She was certain he
was going to kill her. She pulled up her knees, the straps
of the slip she wore fell down on her shoulders and the
skin beneath the lace flushed.

"Don't hurt me!" she said.

Silver closed the drawer and turned from the bureau. He
had the gun in his left hand, and in his right hand he had an
envelope. He sat down on the bed next to Lee; she had her

hands covering her eyes, there were goose pimples all over her skin. Silver put the gun down on the bed and reached into the envelope.

"Look at this," he told her.

"Don't do it," Lee whispered. "Don't shoot me."

"Will you cut it out," Silver said. "Take a goddamned look at what I'm showing you."

Lee uncovered one eye. Silver had taken more than ten thousand dollars in cash out of the envelope. Lee uncovered her other eye.

"I thought we only had seven hundred dollars in our savings account."

"Shows how much you know," Silver said. He put the cash back into the envelope, then handed it to Lee. "Take it," he told her.

"Why?" Lee asked. She narrowed her eyes; she still wasn't certain that he didn't mean to kill her.

"Take it," Silver insisted. Lee finally reached over, got her pocketbook, and dropped the envelope inside. "What I do is dangerous," Silver explained then, "so this is insurance in case you wind up a widow." He sprawled out on the bed and he leaned his head against the wooden headboard. "Christ, if anything happened to me you wouldn't know what to do," Silver said.

Lee suddenly felt light-headed: she wasn't going to be murdered by her husband, there was ten thousand dollars in her purse, and the truth was she immediately knew what she would do if Silver were to die.

"I'd go home," she told Silver. "I'd move in with my mother and Jackie could go to school in Santa Rosa."

"You'd go crazy living with your mother," Silver said, surprised that Lee could think that far ahead. He got up, took off his clothes, then got under the covers with her. "Yackety yak," he whispered. "She'd drive you insane."

Now that she had begun to think about Santa Rosa, Lee found she couldn't stop. She had never wanted to come to San Francisco, never wanted to have a fenced-in yard that couldn't keep out the pigeons and the sound of firecrackers in the summer. She wanted someplace where there were front porches and stars, a bed where the man right next to her didn't think of her as a sister. She kept on thinking about that: he thought of her as a sister, he could lie right next to her and not even want to touch her, he didn't ask her to take off her slip, didn't even hold her hand.

"I'd get a job in an office that was air-conditioned," Lee said now. After work she would walk home barefoot, then sit out on the front porch in summer and drink gin and tonics; she'd meet a man who would beg her to let him take her dancing until she finally agreed. And even then, she'd insist on paying for her own drinks, she'd let him know from the start that she had been in love once and didn't plan to do it again soon.

"You've got it all worked out," Silver said accusingly. "I'm not even dead yet and you're already deciding what dress you're going to wear for your job interview."

"It's not like that," Lee said. "It has nothing to do with your dying. You're not dying," she told Silver. "But I don't see why I should wait till I'm a widow."

A long time ago, Lee had been certain that there was a recipe for love, all she had to do was learn it and she could win Silver's heart. But now, after knowing each other for nearly five years, whenever she imagined the future with Silver she imagined herself in a cold bed, forever waiting for his heart to begin a slow orbit of affection. She knew that she was a widow whether she stood in black beside a grave or stood right next to Silver at the kitchen sink, and when she thought about her son sleeping in the rear bedroom she felt like weeping out loud. Jackie had the same blue eyes as she did, the same fears: silence, speech, a father whose heart was as distant and dark as onyx. It would be easy to stay with Silver until the day one of them died; they were roped together with marriage vows, lashed together with disappointment. But when she tried to imagine Jackie grown up and living in the same house as his father, she couldn't do it. Now Jackie retreated when Silver came home, he went into his room and closed the door; sooner or later he'd grow up, he'd have to speak, have to argue and face his father. Sooner or later Lee would lose one of them, and on that night when Silver handed her ten thousand dollars the future that called to Lee sounded like the click of a suitcase, it was the hollow sound of high heels on the sidewalk, the slow rustling of sage surrounding a patio where a woman sat alone, while upstairs, in a bedroom painted yellow, a boy practiced chords on a guitar, and no one told him to be quiet.

"I know you tried to do the right thing," Lee told Silver, "but it turned out all wrong."

She got out of bed and began to dress. She pulled on a skirt and a pale green sweater, she slipped into her high heels without bothering to put on stockings or socks.

"Get serious," Silver said. He reached for a cigarette, and when he lit a match his hand looked strange, as if it wasn't his own. "You can't take care of yourself. You can't take care of Jackie. I've always done everything. Everything," he told her. "You've always had food, and a roof over your head. I may come home late but I'm home every night."

"So what?" Lee said.

"So what?" Silver repeated. "So we're married, that's what."

"You don't love me," Lee said quietly.

"What the hell has that got to do with anything?" Silver said.

"I'll tell you what I think," Lee said. She had finished packing, she put her suitcase by the door: she went and sat down on the bed and took one last cigarette. "I think if you love anybody at all it's Teresa."

"That's crazy," Silver said. He reached over and grabbed Lee by her shoulder, he could feel the straps of her slip beneath her sweater. "Don't ever say anything like that about me and Teresa again."

"All right," Lee said.

"And don't think after all I went through you're going to be the one who decides to leave. Maybe I'll take that money back right now. Then what would happen to all your plans?"

He tightened his grip on her shoulder, he knew he was hurting her, but Lee didn't flinch. "Stop it," she told him, and he did; he felt foolish, he had been acting as if he wanted her to stay with him when all along he had spent each year of their marriage wishing he had never met her. When he let go of her, Lee put out her cigarette and got off the bed. The closer it came to morning, the more Silver wished Lee would just shut up and come to bed, but instead she stood in front of the bureau mirror and brushed her hair. "If you want to know the truth," she said, "it's you who left me." The sky outside was growing light now; Lee put small ruby earrings in her ears. "I might just get myself a divorce," she told Silver.

"Sure you will," Silver said. "You leave me and you'll be back here in a week."

"And when I get a divorce I'm going to tell everyone in that courthouse the truth," Lee said, just before she picked up her suitcase and her purse. Later, when the sky was light, she would pack another suitcase full of Jackie's clothes and telephone a taxi. But right now the clouds in the Mission District were Prussian blue, and down the hall, in the rear bedroom, Jackie dreamed in the bed where Teresa had once slept, and Silver had begun to believe that his wife might really be leaving him.

"I'm going to tell everyone I see," Lee whispered before she walked out the door. "You were the one who left me."

When winter came to Villa Lobo it came slowly, but it came with the steadiness of a huge, dark wolf. Each day

the hills and the ridgetops were greener, soon they were
the color of clear jade. The rains that had begun in autumn
now fell continuously; morning and noon were untouched
by any source of light. In town, the shop owners put
wooden slats over the muddy pools that formed in the
main street; wild jays stood on porch railings like a band
of robbers; old women, whose husbands had brought them
to Villa Lobo when the logging camp was still working
only to desert them by early death, wore high rubber boots
and covered their heads with thick, embroidered scarves
whenever they left their houses.

In Joey's trailer, in a bed Harper had always thought
too lumpy for a good night's sleep, Teresa slept for so
many hours that Joey couldn't help but worry. He boiled
cans of soups, he offered to get her amphetamines, to take
her to the hospital in Santa Rosa, to bring her black cups
of coffee till dawn.

"Will you please stop worrying?" Teresa told him. "I've
always had a problem with my sleeping. But I'll be better
in a few days. I always am," she promised.

But, if anything, her spells grew worse; she slept more
often than she had that summer in New Mexico or up
in her second-floor bedroom in Santa Rosa. And after
a while, Joey realized that he was no longer worried,
he began to enjoy the shared silence in the trailer when
she slept, he was surrounded by the sound of her steady
breathing, the odor of roses which seemed to rise up from
the bed, as if Teresa were dreaming of the loveliest garden
on earth. He began to think of her waking hours as another
man might think of a rival—when she was asleep in his
bed she was his alone, and there were times when his
passion for her was uncontrollable, times when he made
love to her while she slept. It didn't seem like a violation
to Joey; he was certain that she responded to him, her
arms held him tight, she whispered what Joey was sure
was his name. But then he made the mistake of wanting
their special sort of lovemaking discussed. And so, one

night, when Teresa awoke to find Joey in bed with her, holding her tight, he asked her what she had dreamed about. Teresa was covered with a thin film of perspiration, her hair was tangled, her eyes couldn't yet focus.

"I didn't have any dreams," she told him. "I slept like a rock."

He never made love to her that way again; instead he only watched her, he breathed in the scent of roses, he noticed that while Teresa slept the trailer filled with plum-colored light, and he felt so peaceful that each breath he took was like a thick narcotic.

At Christmas that year Joey and Teresa exchanged thin golden rings. The rains were so heavy that the river was near the flood line. It was then, before the New Year, that Teresa began to have nightmares, dreams that left her terrified of both waking and sleeping. Her visions were filled with natural disasters: earthquakes that shook the house, tornadoes that lifted up horses and cars, bolts of lightning with the energy of a thousand angels. She dreamed that Dina was dressed in black and surrounded by a field of white lilies, that her brother Reuben was lost in a desert, dying of thirst. She dreamed that every lover she had ever had chased her through a landscape where the earth was salmon colored and the sky a too bright blue. Most of all, she dreamed of Silver—he walked through her dreams in a cloak of despair, he rode through a tundra bordered by rocks so strange they might have dropped to earth from Saturn. In her dreams Silver called her name, he was circled by a ring of fire, consumed by flames, and sometimes when she woke from dreaming about him Teresa felt as if her flesh had been singed, she searched in the mirror for burns, for spots of fire left behind.

Teresa grew terrified that she might get trapped in a sixteen-hour sleep, she would be stuck in nightmares, forever prowling through dreams. She couldn't ask Joey for help, she couldn't even talk to him about it; he would laugh at the series of earthquakes and storms, he would be shocked that she dreamed so often of her brother and never of him. She decided to visit Harper, and she hoped that the herb garden that grew in back of the house contained something for her dreams.

"Don't tell me," Harper said when she opened the door and discovered Teresa on the porch steps, dripping with rain. "Now that you've got Joey you've decided to come back for my car."

"I just want to talk to you," Teresa said. From where she stood she could see inside to the living room and kitchen: a copper kettle was on the stove, a rabbit's-foot fern hung in the front window, a blue jacket had been thrown over the back of a rocking chair that still moved back and forth.

Harper opened the door wider and motioned for Teresa to come in; she noticed that Teresa was wearing Joey's yellow rain slicker. She was fairly certain that Teresa wanted more than just talk, but she waited until she had made some camomile tea before she asked what Teresa wanted.

"If you've decided that you don't want Joey any more and you want me to take him back, forget it," Harper said. "I know what he's looking for—he wants to find a chapel in the pines, he wants a wife—one who's never even looked at another man."

"It's not Joey," Teresa said. "I'm having nightmares."

"You move in with a guy and you start having nightmares." Harper nodded. "I'd put two and two together if I were you."

"You must have something for bad dreams."

"My grandmother used a valerian mixture," Harper admitted.

"All right," Teresa said. "Fine. I'll take it."

"Wait a minute," Harper said. "I get paid, you know. I'm not a charitable organization."

Teresa reached into the pocket of her rain slicker for the grocery money Joey had given her the day before. She put two dollars on the table, hoping that Joey wouldn't ask for his change back.

"Gee, can you spare it?" Harper asked, but before Teresa left the house Harper had given her a mixture of anise and valerian root, and a packet of rosemary to keep under her pillow. Each night Teresa took a teaspoon of the mixture she had bought from Harper, and she tucked the rosemary into her pillowcase so that Joey would not find it. She knew that Joey didn't believe in what he called Harper's "potions," that he didn't even want Teresa to talk to Harper if they met in town, much less go to her house. But in less than a week Teresa's nightmares had disappeared, her dreams began to fill with common things: patios and parsnips, oranges and wildflowers. When she combed her hair the scent of rosemary spiraled from every strand, when she woke up, she felt rested, no one had been chasing her, Silver wasn't in one of her dreams. She was thrilled with the cure's success, and she wondered now if Harper might also be able to cure her sleeping spells. Even when Harper shook her head and said that she didn't think she could diagnose what Teresa had, much less cure it, Teresa insisted.

"I've been to doctors," Teresa said. "They couldn't figure out what I had. I'm just asking you to try, and I'll pay you really well."

"Oh, yeah?" Harper said. It had been raining for weeks, and Teresa had finally persuaded Joey to let her take the laundry into town. She had arranged to meet Harper there and now they sat on a wooden bench near the row of washing machines, and the odor of detergent made Harper wrinkle her nose. "How are you going to pay me? I know you don't have any money of your own."

Teresa reached into the neckline of her heavy sweater for the platinum chain she wore around her neck; she held up the sapphire Silver had once given her. In the light of the laundromat the stone was ice blue, it shimmered like water. Harper felt herself wanting the necklace in spite of herself; she had never had any jewelry other than a wedding band she no longer wore, and a few pairs of earrings made of beads.

"I'd be robbing you," Harper said to Teresa. "Even if I could find a cure that would work it wouldn't be worth that much."

"It would be to me," Teresa said.

Her spells were growing worse each day, and for the first time since she was a child and the spells were mysterious and new, Teresa was afraid of them. They were no longer comforting, they were no longer a relief, they lasted too long; and each time she slept, Teresa felt as if she were surrounded by hopelessness. And so, when Harper gave her a gallon jar of rosemary tea the following week, Teresa was delighted. For several nights Teresa slept with a new packet of rosemary under her pillow and in the morning and afternoon she drank rosemary tea, poured out of the jar she kept hidden in the cabinet beneath the sink in the trailer, alongside the containers of Comet and Ivory Snow. But Teresa continued to sleep, once for more than fourteen hours; the only difference now was that her dreams were filled with blue globes of light. When she went back to Harper's house, on a night when Joey had gone to Santa Rosa to play poker, Teresa got a second mixture, one made with mistletoe.

"Be careful with this," Harper advised. "My grandmother used to use this. It speeds up your pulse rate and your heart. No way you're going to fall asleep after you drink this."

But when Teresa telephoned two weeks later, Harper could tell from the tone of her voice that the mistletoe had failed. She decided to get into her Mercury and drive to Cotati to see Harriet Vance, a woman nearly as old as Harper's grandmother had been when she died. Harriet had ingredients that couldn't be bought in health-food stores or grown in anyone's yard, plants that couldn't be found anywhere else in the county. When Harper got to her house an old orange cat was sitting in the sun beyond the window, a lemon tree grew so close to the front door that Harper had to crouch in order to reach the doorbell. They shared a pot of jasmine tea, and then Harper told Harriet that this time she was looking for a special cure.

"You're telling me that this woman's been to doctors and they couldn't find anything wrong with her nervous system and they couldn't find a virus?" When Harper nodded, Harriet went to the cabinet where she stored her herbs and took out a brown bag full of leaves. "She might have a metabolism problem—doctors overlook that all the time. But she could have something nobody can cure; even your grandmother might not have been able to."

"You're talking about a hysterical reaction," Harper said.

"I don't believe in hysterical illnesses. This woman's got something all right, we just have to figure out what it is."

Harper was given some Mexican damiana and told to make it into a tea with palmetto berries and mint. And later, when Harriet walked Harper outside to her car, the old woman stopped to pluck a lemon from the tree that grew near her front door. "Frankly I've always thought that the best cure for most things is hot lemon juice and a little time," she told Harper.

Before she got into her car, Harper took out a five-dollar bill and tried to pay for the damiana, but Harriet refused to take it. "Come on," Harper insisted. "I'm getting a goddamned sapphire for this sleeping cure, the least I can do is pay you five bucks."

"A sapphire?" Harriet said. "A real one?" She took the five dollars from Harper and then asked, "Is this friend of yours rich?"

"She doesn't have a cent," Harper admitted.

"Then this woman wants something more than a cure for her sleeping, whether she knows it or not. She wants to get rid of this sapphire. It has some connection to her sleeping, and she wants you to take it away."

Harper felt her face grow hot. "I feel like I'm being used," she said.

"So what if you are?" Harriet said. She handed Harper the lemon from her tree. "The biggest favor you can do for her is to take the sapphire. If you decide to sell it you can take me out to Nina's for dinner and I'll order one of everything on the menu."

Harper got into her car and turned on the engine, but before she drove away she called out the window. "What if it's catching?" she asked Harriet.

"It's not catching," the old woman assured her. "It's something that belongs to this woman alone."

When Teresa finally came back to Harper's she apologized for her long absence—she'd been sleeping more than ever, and it was harder and harder to get out of the trailer without Joey's knowing.

"You're crazy to be so dependent on him," Harper said as she poured the damiana mixture into a jar. "You might as well be married to him if you're going to let him boss you around the way he does. My ex-husband once posted a list of all the things he didn't want me cooking for dinner: macaroni and cheese, hamburgers, tunafish casserole. I made him tofu and spinach just once, and he took that fucking sign down fast."

"As soon as I get rid of these sleeping spells I'm going to go out and get a job," Teresa said. She took the remedy and went to the door, carrying the jar under Joey's yellow rain slicker so that he wouldn't see what she had if he had gotten back to the trailer before her.

Standing at the open door, in a rain slicker that was sizes too big for her, Teresa looked no more than twelve years old, and Harper felt her heart go out to her.

"This cure's not going to work, is it?" Harper said.

"It might," Teresa answered, but then she shook her head. "The only time these sleeping spells ever go away is when he's around."

"Who?" Harper said. "Joey? Don't give me that—you've been worse ever since you moved in with him."

"Not Joey," Teresa said.

Harper followed Teresa out to the porch where Atlas was waiting. "It's that other man," Harper said. "The one you ran away from. And he's the one who gave you the necklace too, right? Well just forget it if you think you can pawn that necklace off on me."

"I'm sorry I involved you," Teresa said as she walked down the porch steps. "I shouldn't have asked you to help—it won't do any good anyway."

Harper leaned against the porch railing. She could hear the river rising over tree trunks, reaching toward the flood line only steps away from her house. "I want to help you," she called. "But I can't do anything if you keep on believing you can't be cured."

Teresa didn't hear her, or she didn't listen; she kept right on walking, the collie following behind, and after a while Harper went back inside. She felt sadder than she would have ever expected; she knew this third remedy wouldn't do any more than leave Teresa's dreams as empty as glass. And when she found the sapphire necklace in her mailbox later in the week, sealed inside a plain white envelope, Harper still found herself somewhat afraid of the necklace, she imagined that in taking it she was also challenging whatever it was that kept Teresa under a deep, dreamless spell.

It took a day or two, but after that Harper began to laugh at her own superstitions; she began to wear the necklace. On a Friday night, when she was off from work, she stood in front of her bathroom mirror and fastened the chain around her throat, and she stared at the ice-blue stone before she made up her eyes. Then she went out dancing; in a club in Forestville she spent all night in the arms of a stranger, a man with blue eyes, who bent down and kissed her just after midnight. She found herself thinking of Teresa and for a giddy moment she ran from the dance floor, to tear the necklace off and get rid of the blue stone that had been a part of Teresa's illness. But once she was in the ladies' room and she had combed her hair and doused her face with cold water, Harper felt herself grow calm; what Teresa had wasn't catching, Harper wasn't even certain it was real. And before she went back to the man who waited for her on the dance floor, Harper looked in the spotted mirror above the sink and for a moment it seemed that the stone she wore now looked green, the exact color of her eyes.

When Joey found the rosemary under Teresa's pillow he had the sense that he had been betrayed. And by the time Teresa returned from the grocery store in town she found Atlas shut out of the trailer and her packed suitcase outside the front door. When she went inside Joey was sitting in the easy chair, three empty beer cans in front of him.

"It's too cold for Atlas to be out there," Teresa said.

Joey held up the packet of rosemary. "What the hell is this supposed to be?" he asked her.

Teresa put the bag of groceries down and began to place the cans of soup and beans in the cabinets. She tried to think of a place to go if Joey kicked her out, but she couldn't come up with one answer, she couldn't think of one step farther than the trailer's front door. Joey came over to her and grabbed her arm.

"I asked you what this is," he said, and he pushed the rosemary toward her.

"All right," Teresa said. "I got it from Harper."

"Oh, great," Joey said. He walked away from her. "I told you I didn't want you seeing Harper."

"I just wanted to try some of her cures," Teresa explained.

"Her cures!" Joey cried. "She's a waitress from Maryland who thinks she knows the secrets of the universe, and you're going to her for cures?"

It had begun to rain again and Teresa could hear Atlas whining softly at the door. "I had nightmares," she said in a small voice.

Joey went over to her then and put his arms around her. "Baby, you're supposed to come to me when something's wrong."

"Okay," Teresa whispered.

"Come to me," Joey told her. "Otherwise I don't see any point in us living together."

"All right," Teresa agreed. Beneath the sink were the three glass bottles which had held three remedies, and on a shelf, behind the coffee and the tea, was a tin containing the last of the valerian root.

"You can go," Joey said. "I won't make you stay with me. You can still walk out the door."

Outside, Atlas clawed at the door, and the wind was rising off the river, leaving its watery scent everywhere: in the pine needles, all along the wire fence that surrounded the trailer camp, on each one of the saffron-colored weeds that grew around the trailer.

"I don't want to walk out the door," Teresa said. And at that moment she believed there was no point in waiting for Silver any more, there hadn't been since the night he had chosen to leave her alone in the small bedroom at the rear of the house and go back to Lee.

"We don't need anybody else," Joey told her. "Least of all Harper and her goddamn cures." He walked over to Teresa, he held her, he unzipped the yellow rain slicker and unbuttoned her blouse; he held her breasts so tightly that she nearly lost her breath, he bent and licked her nipples, and even though his tongue was hot Teresa felt a chill moving along her skin.

"I want us to get married," Joey told her, and his voice sounded urgent and thick.

Teresa looked away from him; if the window of the trailer hadn't been boarded over she could have seen her suitcase, out there in the rain; she could have seen past

the wire fence around the camp to the road which snaked
through the hills, one way leading to Santa Rosa, the other
to the Pacific.

"Married?" Teresa said.

"I want to be with you forever," Joey said. "I want to
take you into Santa Rosa to buy the most beautiful dress
you ever saw."

"I wouldn't have to go to Santa Rosa," Teresa said,
not wanting to get within ten miles of Divisadero Street.
"There's a dress shop in Guerneville."

Joey smiled and kissed her on the mouth. "You're saying yes," he crowed.

Teresa went to the door and opened it; Atlas came in
and shook himself dry. A little farther west there were
pelicans and gulls with dark wings, but before that, on
a street in Guerneville was a store where there were
dresses trimmed with blue ribbon, shawls made of ivory
lace. From where Teresa stood that evening, by the open
front door, she couldn't see any farther than the edge of
the road; there was no traffic, no headlights cut through
the rain, no wolves stood on the ridgetop and threw back
their heads to howl, frightened by the sound of hoofbeats
on the damp earth. Teresa closed the door then, and turned
back to Joey.

"I'll marry you," she told him. "I'll do it whenever
you say."

That night Teresa made dinner, she washed all the
dishes, and she made love with the man she had just
agreed to marry. And later, when Joey held her in his
arms, Teresa didn't answer when he whispered her name.
He was sure she was dreaming—of the dress she would
buy, of shoes with gold buckles, and the day of their
wedding. But all that night, Teresa thought about loneliness and the disappointment that follows a lifetime of
waiting, and long after Joey had fallen asleep Teresa
was still awake, and in spite of herself she found herself wishing that Silver would find her. Now, before she

went to Guerneville to buy her wedding dress, right now, because if he didn't take the road outside the trailer park soon Teresa was certain he would never be able to find his way, not even on a night when there was a full moon, he wouldn't be able to see past the wooden boards that shuttered the trailer's windows, and even if he changed his mind and finally drove up to find her, he'd never see that she was stranded deep inside.

CHAPTER
SIX

✝

LATE IN THE EVENING, ON THE LAST DAY OF FEBRUARY, a man wearing a black linen suit stood on a street corner and thought about revenge. He had decided that revenge was not particularly sweet; instead it was cold, it was like a wave that took him far beneath the water line. He could hear it whisper to him, a foggy voice, words spoken from the mouth of a perfect seashell. Nothing fast, it told him, and this he already knew; he had spent four years in a jail cell where a footstep outside his locked door often seemed a more terrible fate than a cleanly broken neck. Nothing obvious, it told him, and he knew this, too; he had been following Silver for nearly eight months and he could still count the times he had let Silver see his face. Something soon, it urged him, and he had just begun to realize that if he did not make a final move in the next few days he might wind up following Silver for the rest of his life, always one step behind, always waiting for the perfect moment—a moment centuries long, a time when the sidewalk and the skies came together in a flash of blinding white light.

Silver began to see him everywhere. If he went to a neighborhood restaurant for dinner, Angel Gregory was at the next table; in the morning, when he boiled water for coffee, he could look out the kitchen window and see Gregory behind the wheel of the parked blue Falcon; at night Gregory was stationed right across the street, he stood beneath a street lamp, not bothering to hide any longer, and when he reached out to light a cigarette the red dog on his arm showed long blood-colored claws. It did no good to stand out in the middle of the street and yell at him to get the hell off the block, there was no point in pulling the kitchen curtains closed or walking from one restaurant to another. Silver had tried all these things and Gregory continued to follow him, and at night Silver found himself dreaming about the red dog, he was tracked through marshland where there were no flowers and no trees, he could hear the dog following behind him, his jaws inches away from Silver's ankles.

Silver no longer went to Vallais's apartment on Russian Hill, he no longer drove across the city to sell cocaine and hashish; he stayed home, he paced through every room, the sound of a pigeon flapping its wings on the windowsill was enough to send chills down his spine. Without Lee the apartment seemed huge; the closets were half empty, there was no food in the kitchen cabinets, no toys littering the floor, no clean sheets. Silver had realized that Lee wasn't

coming back after only a few days, and it seemed right
to him that she should stay away, the air in the apartment
seemed cleaner, less cluttered by perfume and smoke.
Even the walls seemed whiter, and the bare hangers in
the closet looked somehow just right. He didn't bother to
telephone Lee at her mother's house in Santa Rosa; he
assumed they were settled in, they weren't missing him
one bit. Lee had already unpacked, she slept in the same
room she had climbed out of to meet him so long ago,
her gold watch had been tossed onto a white lacquered
dresser. Silver was sure that Jackie had his own room in
the attic, high in the eaves; he would have begun to know
the names of the streets in Santa Rosa by now, he probably
watched the fog cover the grass on the lawn each evening
at dusk.

Before long, Silver had stopped thinking about Jackie
and Lee altogether; it was as if they had never existed.
Everything was much simpler now. Silver no longer bothered to use anything in the kitchen except for one spoon
and one cup, each of which he washed every time he used
them. It was as if he had forgotten that there were cup-
boards full of dishes, drawers full of knives and spoons,
just as he'd forgotten that there had once been a time when
an enemy wasn't waiting right outside his door. It seemed
years since Silver had left the house, but it was only two
weeks; two weeks without going as far as the back porch
to breathe in some fresh air, two weeks of being afraid to
walk out the front door. He felt as if his apartment were
under siege; he sat by the window and watched Gregory
by the hour, he stared until Gregory appeared in front of
him each time he closed his eyes. He ran out of food, he
ran out of cigarettes, when the telephone rang he didn't
answer, he began to imagine that he could hear blood
moving through his own body, it pounded in his ears and
left a soft humming in his head.

And then something happened; one day, after those two
weeks of hiding, a wild kind of daring came over him. All

at once he was able to imagine his own death; he could see
the sort of knife Gregory would use and the exact hour
of the day, he could see a thousand and one scenes of his
last minutes on earth. And now he became unafraid of
what would happen—he wanted to meet Gregory face to
face and get it over with. What had been exhaustion now
turned into blind courage; suddenly he was even more
reckless than he had been as a boy. He unlocked all of
the doors in the apartment, and he dared Gregory in a
hundred ways to come after him: he began to leave the
apartment again, he wore white shirts that glowed under
the moon, he opened all the windows and let fog come
in and coat ceilings and the floors with a mist so thick he
could barely find the walls, let alone discover an enemy
in his own front hallway. He kept the gun with him at all
times, in his jacket pocket or in the glove compartment of
the Camaro. Everywhere Silver went he seemed to leave
a trail of cinders behind, his eyes were huge, black as
saucers, and he knew that the time was coming when he
would have to face up to everything in his past, because
the past seemed to swallow him a little more each day.

It was then he started to think about Teresa, and he
was reckless even in his thoughts. He no longer tried to
convince himself that nothing would have ever happened
between Teresa and him if he hadn't been drunk—now he
believed it was simply meant to be. He allowed himself
to imagine making love to her in rooms that were filled
with sunlight; he thought about buying her diamonds, red
high-heeled shoes, bouquets of orchids. There would be a
bedroom with thin curtains where Teresa would sit by the
window and comb her hair, wearing nothing but a white
slip, a violet ribbon around her throat. He imagined tying
her to their bed with strips of lace, making love to her over
and over again until he was too tired to do anything but
look at her, and even then he thought he wouldn't have
had enough of her. He began to care very little about the
way things looked, the way they seemed—to himself or

anyone else, and he had begun to believe that he had to see Teresa right away, as soon as possible. The nearness of his own death drove him nearer and nearer to desire, and so one night when Gregory was outside the front door, less than a hundred yards away, Silver called information and got Arnie Bergen's phone number. He took a deep breath before he dialed the detective's number, and he knew that this call was only the first step, that he had begun something he could never stop; he was going to find Teresa.

Bergen had gotten himself a dog. It was an accident, he had never wanted a pet; when the canary had died in its cage he hadn't mourned for a minute, he had always believed that birds were never meant to be pets in the first place. The dog was a puli, a Hungarian sheepdog; it had belonged to the third-floor tenant who had skipped out without paying the rent, leaving behind no forwarding address, no furniture, nothing but the puli. Bergen had tried to ignore the whining and the clickety clack of nails on the ceiling above him. But finally he had gone up and opened the door, and although the detective had placed an ad in the *Examiner* trying to contact the old owner, in less than a month Bergen had given the dog a new name— Bobby—and had bought him a collar and a leash.

The odd thing was that having Bobby made Bergen miss Dina more than ever. When he combed the dog's long tangled hair and pinned it out of his eyes with a clip, he did so because he knew Dina would have hated the tangles. He spent hours in the bedroom where Dina's belongings were stored; even when he played poker he thought of her, even in his dreams he saw that beautiful girl who had run away on a summer night, that woman who wrote him nightly letters in purple ink. He wished that Teresa hadn't stopped calling him; then they could have walked with Bobby and Atlas down to the bay on warm days, the dogs could have had matching leashes, he and Teresa could have talked about Dina's preference for tomatoes and sunflowers rather than asters and beans. He expected that one day Teresa would call him again; he was careful to keep Dina's set of china boxed and ready for Teresa to take with her as soon as she had the space and the time. But it was Silver who called, not Teresa, and Bergen was most surprised at how different Silver's voice sounded, how dangerous, how soft.

"You know why I'm calling you," Silver whispered.

Bergen was sure that Dina's son wanted the money from the sale of the house in Santa Rosa. The detective had sold the house more than a year before, but he still hadn't touched a cent; he was keeping it for Teresa, and now he had to admit that it wasn't fair to give so much to one of Dina's children and so little to the other.

"I'll give you half the money from the house," Bergen told him.

"The house?" Silver said. "I don't care about the house. It's Teresa. I want to know where she is."

"I thought she was living with you and Lee," Bergen said, and he began to worry, he began to wonder if he shouldn't have tried to contact Teresa even after she had told him she didn't have time to see him any more.

"Has she called you?" Silver asked. "And don't bother to lie to me."

"Listen, I've got Dina's dishes waiting for her, I've got boxes of stuff, if I knew where she was I wouldn't be using my bedroom for storage."

After that first call, Silver continued to phone the detective once a week. Silver was sure that it was only a matter of days before Teresa contacted Bergen, and each time, after he had hung up the phone, Bergen grew more certain that he wouldn't have told Silver where Teresa was even if he knew. Bergen liked to imagine that Teresa wasn't really missing, he liked to think she had taken their last talk to heart and had moved away from her brother; she might even still be in San Francisco, living in an apartment near the marina, spending each morning watering the asparagus ferns that grew around a redwood deck. But there were other times when Bergen had an uneasy feeling that something awful had happened; he grew afraid that Teresa might be missing for years, just as Dina had been. But because Silver was so sure that if Teresa contacted anyone it would be the detective, Bergen soon believed that, too. He bought an answering machine to hook up to his phone so that he wouldn't miss her call if it came while he was out walking Bobby or in the shower. When she finally did call, in early March, Bergen wasn't expecting her. The phone rang when Bergen had already put on Bobby's leash; the detective was wearing his raincoat, the dog was scratching at the door, and Bergen was in a hurry when he reached for the phone—he was certain it was the gas company bothering him again, insisting they still hadn't received last month's check. When he realized that it was Teresa's voice at the other end of the line, Bergen couldn't answer right away; he sat down and unbuttoned his raincoat, he forgot all of Silver's urgent phone calls, the only thing he felt was pleased.

Teresa was standing in the phone booth outside the general store in Villa Lobo. On the way home from shopping she had stopped to call Bergen impulsively, and when she heard how delighted he sounded she wished she hadn't waited quite so long to call.

"I've been thinking about you," she told him. "I've been wondering how you've been."

"I've got a dog now," Bergen told her. His voice was raspy, his throat was dry, and he discovered that he suddenly felt like crying. "Bobby," he said. "The truth is— he's not like other dogs."

"Good for you," Teresa said. "It's just what you needed. You should see Atlas—he's like an old man—he limps. When I take him for a walk I've got to wait for him to catch up."

"Are you all right?" Bergen asked tentatively.

"Of course I'm all right," Teresa told him.

Bergen reached for a throat lozenge from the box in his coat pocket; Teresa could hear him cough and then swallow.

"Silver's been calling here at least once a week looking for you," the detective now told her.

There was no door to the telephone booth outside the general store, and the wind rising off the river made it difficult to hear, but Teresa had heard Bergen—she just didn't answer.

"Don't hang up," Bergen said.

"I won't," Teresa said. "I'm still here."

"He acts like it's a goddamn emergency," Bergen went on. "He acts like he's going to drop dead if he doesn't talk to you pronto. I figured you didn't want to see him—I thought maybe you finally took my advice." Teresa didn't answer, but Bergen could still hear the hum of their connection. "You're not living in an apartment down by the marina, are you?" he asked her.

"No," Teresa said. "Why would you think that?"

"I thought you might have an apartment down there," Bergen said wistfully. "One of those places with a redwood deck."

"I'm getting married," Teresa said suddenly.

"Wonderful!" Bergen said. "Will I get to kiss the bride?"

It was getting dark in Villa Lobo and less than half a mile away Joey was waiting for her in the trailer; all at once Teresa found herself growing afraid of the walk home alone.

"Why does he want to see me?" Teresa asked. Some of the hope she had given up when she decided to marry Joey was resurfacing.

"I couldn't tell you," Bergen said. "I haven't quite figured out how the mind of a lunatic works."

"Have you missed me?" Teresa asked now.

"What do you think?" Bergen said. "Of course I have."

"What about Silver," Teresa said nonchalantly. "Has he missed me, too?"

"I couldn't tell you," Bergen said. "That you'll have to ask him yourself."

But the thought of reaching out toward Silver and then facing another disappointment was more than Teresa could stand, though when she hung up the phone she could think of nothing but Silver, and already she found herself forgiving him for that last night in San Francisco.

When Silver phoned, the following day, Bergen was glad that Teresa hadn't told him where she was.

"You mean to tell me you talked to her and you didn't get her address?" Silver fumed.

"That's right," Bergen said happily. "But don't worry about her. She's just fine."

"The next time she calls you'd better get an address," Silver warned.

"Are you threatening me?" Bergen asked. "Maybe I'd better remind you that you don't scare me."

"Don't make me come over there and teach you a lesson," Silver said.

"Come right over," Bergen said, "but I think you should know that I've got an attack dog here." He looked over at the couch where Bobby was sleeping. "He'll rip you to pieces on a voice command."

"Don't fool around with me, old man," Silver told Bergen before he hung up the phone. "Just do what I tell you. Find out where she is."

Silver didn't have time to argue with the old man; he had a plan now, and although it was simple, a plan he had used before, all of his energy now went into making certain that Gregory was sent back to Vacaville Prison. It was on a cold March night that Silver began the first steps of his plan—he went to Vallais and bought several ounces of heroin and cocaine. Gregory's Ford Falcon followed him to Russian Hill and then back to the Mission, and

once he was back home Silver made certain that the
Ford was still parked outside, and then he turned off
all the lights in the apartment, just as if he was going
to sleep. But he didn't sleep that night; he sat peering
through the windows of the dark living room, certain that
sooner or later Gregory had to leave his post outside the
apartment, he had to go somewhere and sleep. And when
he did, Silver followed him; he sneaked out the front door
sometime near dawn, as soon as he saw the Falcon pulled
away from the curb. He followed on foot, running as fast
as he could, staying at least a block behind Gregory.

Gregory parked and went into an apartment building
not more than four blocks away from Silver's own. Silver
stood in the shadows and watched; upstairs on the second
floor a light was turned on, and then Silver smiled and
breathed in cold morning air, and he knew it was time
for him to get Gregory, he was sure that a plan that had
worked once could work a second time, and that in only
a few days he would be free again, he would find Teresa
and he would be free.

The following evening Silver waited again by the window, but this time he put all the lights on, he turned on
the radio to top volume, he made certain that Gregory was
stationed outside the front door. Then he dressed in jeans
and a black T-shirt; he jumped out the bathroom window,
then edged across the backyard. He climbed over the tall
wooden fence that separated the yard from the street and
dropped to the cement in silence. He had to run the
long way around to get to Gregory's apartment without
passing the Falcon; still, he reached the place in less than
fifteen minutes. He climbed up the fire escape and went
in through the window of Gregory's kitchen, stepping
carefully into the sink before he eased down to the floor.
The apartment was dark, but a flash of red neon from a
bar across the street ricocheted off the far wall every few
seconds with bands of light. In the living room Silver
carefully arranged the heroin and cocaine out in plain

sight. He was ahead of schedule, he was grinning from
ear to ear; but when he turned, ready to leave, his pulse
quickened, and for a moment he almost lost his nerve:
there, in Gregory's living room, Silver had stumbled over
a pair of his own boots, boots he had thrown out in the
trash months ago.

In spite of himself, he reached for the light cord that
dangled from the ceiling; once the electricity was turned
on he was shocked to see an old dresser of Jackie's he had
thrown out, and on the dresser was a row of photographs.
There was one of Silver getting into the Camaro, one of
Teresa sitting on the back porch, dressed all in white, a
third of Lee and Jackie walking in the front door with
bundles of groceries, several of Silver standing in front
of his own living-room window, staring out at the street.
In a panic, Silver reached up and switched off the light. He
blinked as if he'd seen a ghost. After his eyes had read-
justed to the intervals of darkness and neon, Silver quickly
gathered the photographs together. He tucked them into
the waistband of his jeans and then reached for the old
pair of boots. Later, when he called the police to inform
on Gregory, he didn't want his belongings in the place: a
boot could easily be a clue, one photograph could point the
blame straight at him. And so when he left the apartment
he carried the boots in his left hand. He felt more like a
victim than a thief as he closed the window tightly behind
him, and as he climbed back down the fire escape he had
the oddest sense that he had just been robbed.

He ran all the way home, returning the same secret way
he had come. Once he was back in his own living room
he went to the window to make certain that Gregory was
still outside. As soon as he saw his enemy behind the
wheel of the parked Falcon, Silver went to the telephone
and called the police. He gave Gregory's address and
name; he identified himself as a concerned citizen who
was beginning his own neighborhood campaign against
drugs. After that Silver wrapped the old pair of boots

in newspaper and threw them into a garbage can in the kitchen, then he combed his hair, changed into a clean white shirt, and picked up his car keys. He was ready to lead Gregory on a chase through the city to make certain he wouldn't return to his apartment before the police had made their search. When he walked out to the Camaro and the air was pleasantly fresh, he got in and looked in his rearview mirror and saw Gregory's Ford, then turned the key in the ignition. He thought he might lead Gregory over the Bay Bridge, to Oakland and back; he would turn the radio on and open all the windows in the Camaro and look back at the city in the moonlight.

When Silver put the Camaro into gear and stepped on the gas he was sure that Gregory was doing the same; he had been followed for so long that he thought he knew exactly what to expect from Gregory. But on this night the moon was a chameleon moving in and out of the clouds, and Silver couldn't really see far enough; even if he had been more careful he might not have realized that there was no driver behind the wheel of the Ford Falcon, he might not have realized that he wasn't the only man who had plans, who had staked his claim on what would happen next. When he pulled out onto the street, Silver couldn't have known that he was driving into the moment that Gregory had thought about all these years; a moment when time was thick enough, a second long enough, for Gregory to jump right in front of the Camaro.

Once Silver looked into Gregory's eyes he couldn't look away, he was blinded by another man's eyes, and his foot on the accelerator and the car itself seemed to be moving at different speeds. The car moved ridiculously fast, because Silver was sure that they were staring at each other for hours, hours with Silver behind the wheel and Gregory stepping right in front of the Camaro's tires. Gregory was dressed in Silver's black suit; his face was as calm as a swimmer's and when the Camaro hit him the sound was more like a sigh than it was like thunder. It was

then that time began to move more normally, Silver
jammed down so hard on the brakes that his head hit
against the rearview mirror. The glass shattered and cut
through the flesh on his cheek. Silver ignored the blood
on his face, he jumped out and ran to Gregory, but by then
Gregory was lying in the street, and when Silver lifted his
head up his eyes were as dull as stones. Silver crouched
down next to him; the night was dark, the street empty,
and Silver's mouth was dry. Blood dripped down his
cheek and fell in drops on Angel Gregory's forehead.

"Get up," Silver whispered to Gregory. He put his
mouth close to Gregory's ear. "Get up, goddamn it," he
told him. "If I wanted to kill you, I'd do it. And it wouldn't
be any kind of hit-and-run, I'd do it right. So come on,"
Silver urged the other man. "Let's get out of here." Silver
lifted Gregory's head and shoulders off the ground, but he
was talking to a dead man and as soon as Silver realized
this he carefully lowered Gregory's head so that it rested
along the curb where some girl had written the name of the
boy she loved next to her own in blue chalk, surrounded
by a heart pierced by arrows.

Silver got out of there as fast as he could, but it took
him an hour to stop shaking, and even then the cut on his
face still continued to bleed, no matter how many times
he wiped his face with the cuff of his white shirt. Even
then he saw Gregory's eyes in every stoplight, every inch
of asphalt and cement seemed snaky with life. So Silver
stayed in his car, he kept driving; he was afraid that when
the Camaro stopped his heart would stop as well. He
panicked at the thought that some evidence would point
to him, and he knew, right away, that what had happened hadn't been an accident; Gregory had been terribly
careful, he had made sure that Silver would be followed
forever—if not by the police, at least by the silence of a
dead man's eyes.

Silver didn't dare go back to his apartment; he imagined
that an ambulance and several patrol cars had already

parked right outside his house. He didn't dare go to an emergency room or doctor's office and have his face stitched up; a warrant might be out for his arrest, someone might have written down his license number, a nurse might see the panic that traveled up and down his skin. So he drove. He circled the city, he tried to be calm and plan what he would do next. Late that night he pawned the watch he wore, and he ripped the stereo out of the Camaro and sold that, too, and then he drove to a diner on the outskirts of the city where no one knew his face or his name. At dawn he sat at the counter and ordered coffee and didn't bother to answer the waitress when she asked him where he'd been all her life. He went into the men's room and washed his face, and he tried to clean the bits of glass out of the cut on his cheek with a paper towel. And when the sun had risen, and Gregory had been carted off the street, Silver paid for his coffee without bothering to leave a tip, and he got back into his car and then he headed for Bergen's apartment on Dolores Street.

Teresa and Joey went out to have hamburgers after they bought the wedding dress and the new shirt and tie. They sat in a red leatherette booth at a place called Judy's Cottage, and in front of them were huge platters of food.

"I don't think I can eat," Teresa admitted. "I'm nervous."

"There's nothing to be nervous about," Joey told her. "Hundreds of people get married every day of the week. Do you think they would all do it if it was so terrible?"

Teresa signaled Judy over and ordered black coffee.

"That stuff will rot your guts," Joey warned her. "It'll give you cancer of the pancreas."

Teresa sat back in the booth as if she'd been stung. "You sound like my father," she said, and from where she sat she could see out the Cottage's window to the street where King Connors had once parked while she ran across the street to buy a Coke.

"Then he must have been one smart guy." Joey winked, and while he took his new tie out of the shopping bag to study it in the light, Teresa found herself thinking of King, wondering if she would have liked the sort of wedding where he walked her down the aisle. They would be arm in arm, and King Connors would be the tallest man in the room. He'd wear cowboy boots and a new blue suit, and after the ceremony he'd make certain champagne was served alongside a fruit salad filled with orange slices and the best strawberries. More likely, Teresa thought, he'd arrive in a worn gray suit, hours late, after the ceremony had already begun, and then he'd leave before sandwiches were served; his pickup truck would be idling right outside the door, a woman would be waiting in the passenger seat and checking her makeup in the rearview mirror. But the truth was, if she could find him to send him an invitation, he simply wouldn't come at all.

Teresa and Joey had gotten their marriage license, and Joey had made an appointment at the courthouse in Santa Rosa. Now he folded his new tie away and poured ketchup over his french fries. "We should think about a honeymoon," he told Teresa. "We could drive up to Eureka and stay in a motel if there's not a whole lot of flooding on the roads."

"I think I'd like somebody to be there," Teresa said.

"Not on our honeymoon." Joey smiled. "It's just going to be me and you."

"I want somebody to give me away," Teresa insisted.

"If you don't know how to reach your father, how about one of your brothers?" Joey asked. He'd been feeling generous ever since Teresa had agreed to marry him; if she wanted family around on their wedding day Joey would agree to it, even if he didn't like sharing her, not even for a few hours.

"I don't know where they are either," Teresa said, and her eyes filled with tears, right there in the booth at Judy's.

Joey reached across the table and took her hand in his. "Isn't there anybody?" he asked.

Teresa shook her head no; Joey reached for a french fry and chewed it thoughtfully.

"Not a soul?" he asked.

"Just Bergen," Teresa shrugged.

"Well, hell," Joey said enthusiastically. "Call Bergen. Call whoever you want."

"He was my mother's friend," Teresa said.

"Your mother's friend?" Joey said. "That's almost a relative. Go on. Let him give you away."

By the time Teresa called Bergen, Silver had been holed up in the detective's apartment for more than a week. Bergen had tried everything he could think of to get rid of Silver: he had gone to the bank, withdrawn eight thousand dollars from the sale of the house on Divisadero Street and given it to him. He offered to go to the airport to pay for a ticket to South America or Canada, if whatever trouble Silver was in was serious enough for him to want to leave the country. Or a lawyer—Bergen offered him the names of a dozen lawyers, experienced in drug cases, willing to pay off an occasional witness or a judge. But all Silver wanted was iodine and bandages for the scar on his face, he wanted hamburgers and coffee, and someone to bring him the daily paper so that he could see if Gregory's death had made the news, and most of all he wanted Teresa. He stared at the phone, he slept right next to it on the couch, covered by a wool blanket that had once belonged to Dina.

"She's going to call any day," he told Bergen. "Then I'll be out of here so fast you won't even remember me."

"What if she doesn't call for a month?" Bergen said. "What then?"

Silver grinned and called Bobby up on the couch with him. "I could be comfortable here for a month," he told Bergen, simply because he knew it would make the old man tear out his hair.

"We're not even related," Bergen said. "Don't you have anyplace else you can go?"

"Do it for my mother's sake," Silver said. He reached for the six-pack Bergen had bought at the supermarket that morning, took a can of beer, then raised it in the air in a toast. "She would have loved it if you thought of me as a son."

Bergen winced when Silver mentioned Dina; if not for Dina, the detective would have phoned the police the minute Silver was out of earshot. Whenever Silver watched TV or slept sprawled out on the couch, Bergen studied him, searching for some resemblance to Dina, unable to find the slightest feature that showed he was her son.

That night when the phone finally rang, Bergen was in the kitchen, boiling eggs for dinner, and Silver was asleep on the couch. The detective tried to get to the phone first; he still wasn't quite sure why he wanted to keep them apart, he was certain only that Silver was dangerous, that he had a talent for making any woman whose heart wasn't ice believe that he didn't know the meaning of selfishness, or of lies. But Silver reached for the phone first; his hands were sweating when he picked up the receiver—he had been dreaming about the desert all night, there had been a sun as hot as fire, and a posse on horseback followed him without mercy. When he heard Teresa's voice he instantly felt as though he were swimming in cool water.

"Don't hang up," he urged as soon as she had said hello. "Please. Please, just don't hang up."

"What are you doing there?" Teresa said to him. "I don't want to talk to you."

"Don't talk then," Silver said. "Just listen—that's all you have to do. Listen."

In the phone booth in Villa Lobo, a dragonfly whose wings were midnight blue was stuck to the glass. Half a mile away, in bed, in the trailer without windows, Joey slept, not knowing that Teresa had left the house to call Bergen, not knowing that chills now ran down her spine.

"I'm getting married," Teresa said. "I'm calling to ask Bergen to come to the wedding." Silver turned to glare at Bergen, who stood in the doorway between the kitchen and the living room.

"Give me some goddamned privacy," Silver whispered to the detective.

"I always thought that was my phone," Bergen said, but he backed into the kitchen, away from Silver's dirty looks.

"I have a new life," Teresa went on.

"Oh, you do?" Silver said. "Are you telling me that you're in love with this guy you're all set to marry?"

When she didn't answer, Silver knew he hadn't lost her yet. He relaxed a bit; he reached for a cigarette, lit it, and breathed in the smoke. More than fifty miles away, Teresa could hear a match lit, she could hear Silver inhale, she could imagine a room thick with blue smoke.

"I know you don't love him," Silver said, and, even though he spoke softly, Bergen could hear him. From where Bergen stood, inches away from the kitchen doorway, Silver sounded like somebody's lover, every word he said was edged with midnight, and feather pillows, kisses given in secret in the dark.

"What difference does it make to you?" Teresa said.

"Now, just listen to me," Silver told her. "Lee's gone. Do you hear me—I got rid of her."

In the phone booth, Teresa felt dizzy; she was surrounded by glass on three sides, a sheet of heavy rain on the fourth. She wished that she could hang up the phone, but Silver's voice filled her with some sort of hope, every word he said brought her closer to floating through destiny with her eyes closed.

"Now it's really just you and me," he told her.

"Don't act like you care about me," Teresa said. "Remember that night you left me to go out to Lee in the kitchen? Remember all those times you told me not to touch you? Not to let anyone know?"

"Okay," Silver said. "I made some mistakes. Forget about them."

"I'm trying to," Teresa told him. "I'm trying to forget you completely. That's why I'm getting married. So don't make any promises."

Teresa was fighting for distance; but she was lying, and nothing she said could make the lie convincing, not to Silver, not to herself. She still thought about him every night, every kiss she had ever received had been his, it was still impossible to think of living without him. As she held the phone close to her ear, as she listened to his breathing, a hundred miles away but still the one sound that could pierce her straight through the heart, Teresa tried to think of ashes instead of seduction. She thought of blue moons and midnights instead of the noonday heat of the reservoir, the impossible temperature of desire on that day when she first held him tight, when wildflowers and milkweed were pressed up against her bare spine and two hawk's feathers dropped down from the sky, brushing against her bare toes before they settled in the grass.

"Put Bergen on the phone," Teresa told her brother. "I want him to come to my wedding and give me away."

Silver refused to call Bergen to the phone. Since the moment when Gregory had fallen into the gutter, with the tails of the black linen suit spread out behind him like wings, Silver had decided that he would find Teresa and take her to Mexico. There was no such thing as scandal any more, no need to think any further than a hotel room in Mexico where a woman with long dark hair waited upstairs for him.

"No one's giving you away," Silver told Teresa. "You're getting married to spite me. I'm asking you not to do that to me. Not now."

In the kitchen Bergen wondered if he might be dreaming, or if years spent listening at keyholes while tracking down corespondents in divorce cases had left him deaf to anything but strange, imagined conversations. He shook his head, but Silver's words still echoed like black stones, like a lover's promise.

"We're going to Mexico," Silver whispered to his sister. "We have to. It's too late not to. Gregory's dead."

For a minute Teresa's heart seemed to stop; she imagined Gregory circling around Silver until he had ignited, so transfixed by Silver that he had caught fire, every bit of him burning, from the red tattoo on his arms to the dark eyes that reflected nothing but waiting, all gone in an instant.

"He can't be dead," Teresa said.

"Well, he is," Silver said. "He's dead as anybody ever is, and if I don't get out of here they might just come looking for me."

"You killed him," Teresa said. She was amazed by the sorrow that she felt: a man had managed to die in a city miles away, and Teresa held on to the phone receiver so tightly that her hands turned white, just as if she hadn't a drop of blood beneath her skin.

"I didn't kill him," Silver assured her; he imagined that it was the mention of death that forced accusations into her voice, rather than the man himself. "He's just dead, that's all. And they'll say that I did it—they'll come after me."

In the phone booth in Villa Lobo, Teresa felt weak, she was all at once horribly lonely, as if Gregory, a convict she barely knew, had been her one true friend.

"Maybe you're wrong," Teresa said. "Maybe he's still alive."

Silver's voice was soft, he didn't want the detective in the other room to overhear, but nothing could hide his urgency.

"Forget about Gregory. Just forget about everything but me."

Silver didn't need to whisper—Bergen was no longer eavesdropping, he didn't have the heart to hear any more. Bobby came over, dragging his leash in his mouth, but Bergen ignored the dog; he was thinking about Teresa, remembering a girl with long braids and sneakers, a girl with eyes as dark as planets, bottomless as a well. Bergen didn't hear Silver ask for Teresa's address, he didn't hear a drawer in the bureau open and close as Silver searched for a pad of white paper. He was wondering if there was something he could have done, years ago, if he should have insisted that he move into the house on Divisadero Street rather than stay in the Lamplighter Motel, insisted that Dina take back all of the stories she had told Teresa, carefully unknotting the imagined men she called Arias from the boy who sat at the kitchen table with a scowl on his face. He wondered what sort of detective he might be if he had never seen the deception that was going on right in front of him; and he felt old, there in the kitchen, too old to do any more than wish that Teresa had learned a little bit about deception by this time. He wished that Teresa felt as certain as he did that an Aria couldn't help but evaporate in bright sunlight, an Aria was nothing more than a bundle of twigs tied together with hope and thrown on top of a riderless horse. In spite of himself, Bergen heard the scratch of a pen on paper as Silver wrote down Teresa's address in Villa Lobo, he could sense Silver's desire and the certainty of his own fate just as surely as if an ancient secret had finally been let loose, as if a cloud of roses had begun to fill up the apartment on Dolores Street, and there was nothing the old detective could do but breathe in the scent and shudder beneath the bare lightbulb that hung from the ceiling by a wire.

It didn't take long for Joey to realize that something had gone wrong. He was used to Teresa's silences, her long sleeping spells, her nightmares, an occasional fear of the dark. But now Teresa was so restless that she paced back and forth along the length of the trailer, she chewed her fingernails, she refused to eat, she complained that all of their wedding plans were made in haste, she doubted his love, and slowly it became clear to Joey that nothing he did could possibly be right.

One morning she stood on the mattress of their bed and opened the window above it; beyond the glass were the wooden boards Joey had nailed up in the late fall.

"We need some light in here," Teresa said. "I can't stand how dark it is all the time."

Joey went over to the window, edged Teresa aside, then slammed it shut once more. "Without these boards up, any storm we get is going to tear this place apart."

Teresa sat down on the bed and sulked. "I don't care," she said.

"I thought you liked this trailer," Joey said.

"I hate it," Teresa told him fiercely. She looked around at the cheap furniture, at the lumpy mattress and the unwashed dishes in the sink, and she grew dizzy. "I can't live here," Teresa said. She jumped from the bed and continued to pace, as if her feet were on fire.

"We don't have to live here forever," Joey said. He had never really thought of living anywhere else, but it seemed wise to try to pacify her. "We can move to a house. To a cottage near the river. I know about one for rent."

"You don't know anything," Teresa told him. "My brother's coming up here, did you know that?"

"I thought both your brothers were missing," Joey said. "I thought some old man was coming up here to give you away."

"Reuben's the one who's missing," Teresa said impatiently. "Silver's the one who's coming here."

"That's fine with me." Joey shrugged. "I don't give a damn who comes to the ceremony with us." He went to the closet, took out a pair of jeans and a sweater and dressed. "It's freezing," he said. "How could you even think about opening the window?"

Teresa was standing in the middle of the trailer. "I hope you understand that he's not driving all the way to give me away or anything like that."

"Ah," Joey drawled. "He doesn't approve."

"This is serious," Teresa said. "He just killed somebody."

"What did he do?"

"Oh, I don't know," Teresa said, afraid that anything she said would somehow betray both Silver and herself.

Joey went to her and turned Teresa toward him so that they stood face to face.

"What did he do?"

"He killed somebody," Teresa whispered. "And now he doesn't want me to marry you."

"I don't care what he wants," Joey said. "I don't care who he killed. He's not going to stop us from getting married."

Teresa shook her head; all along the walls of the trailer she saw Angel Gregory, and his eyes were even sadder than those of the red dog he wore on his skin.

"You don't know Silver," she told Joey.

"How can he stop us?" Joey asked. "We're in love."

Teresa went to the door and grabbed the rain slicker that hung on a wooden hook, then opened the door and ran outside. The rain was light, but it had fallen for days and the yard of the trailer camp was thick with mud.

"Are you crazy?" Joey called after Teresa, but by the time he had pulled on his boots and grabbed his denim jacket, Teresa had already taken a hammer from the toolshed. She had brought a milk box over to the window and was standing on it as she wrenched the nails out of the wooden boards over the window.

"Cut it out," Joey told her.

Teresa had managed to get the first board off; it fell with a thud onto the wet ground and sank in a pool of rainwater.

"Stop it," Joey said. "You're going to hurt yourself," he warned, but Teresa didn't listen, she pulled at the nails in the second board with all her might. When Joey reached up and pulled her off the milk box Teresa's hammer was embedded in the wood and the second board was dragged down with her with so much force that the half-uncovered window behind it shattered. Glass fell inward and covered the bed, slivers fell over the mattress, a jagged edge lined the windowpane, and some of the largest shards of glass fell outward, toward them, and scattered in the mud like the seeds of dangerous flowers.

"What's wrong with you?" Joey demanded.

"Don't you understand?" Teresa told him. "I'm worried!"

Joey pulled her close and rested his chin on the top of her head; beads of rainwater had caught between the strands of her hair, they were enormous and clear, like a halo of diamonds.

"You don't have to worry about me," Joey said, and it took him only a few seconds to realize that her silence and the way her arms were limp at her sides rather than holding him, meant that it was not his welfare she was concerned with. Joey moved away from her then. "Or are you worried about your brother?" he asked. "Are you worried that he won't think I'm good enough?"

Teresa looked down at the ground; it seemed the ground wouldn't stay still, the mud seemed to be moving, as if Teresa stood upon a dark ocean.

"Talk to me!" Joey shouted. "If you don't want to marry me, tell me."

Beneath the yellow rain slicker Teresa was shivering. Even Joey could see it; her hands shook, she looked much too frail to be standing out there in the rain, soaked to the skin, ankle deep in mud when it was only a few days before her wedding. Joey couldn't help himself; he went back to her, he put his arms around her, he kissed her and apologized.

"I'm crazy," he said. "It's me—it's my fault." He picked her up and carried her into the house, and when he felt her arms tighten around his neck he was sure he'd been forgiven for being so cruel. "We don't have to talk about your brother," he told her once they were back inside and he had closed the door behind them. "We're getting married and that's all there is to it, and if he thinks he's going to stop it he'll find a lock on the gate out front and it'll be too late, because we're getting married whether he likes it or not."

And later that night, after Joey had swept up all the glass and reboarded the window, after he had undressed and gotten into bed, Teresa waited up in the armchair until his breathing was even and she knew he had begun to dream. She was certain now that she couldn't marry him, that the only reason she had ever agreed to his proposal was that she had believed that Silver would never dare run away with her. But now, after all these years, now that Silver was finally driving up to take her away, Teresa didn't know what to do. When she got the backpack from the closet she was clumsy, her fingers were unreliable, her heart had a panicky rhythm. She filled the backpack with cans of food, put on a pair of hiking boots, and slipped on the yellow rain slicker. If she stayed, if she was forced to stand out in the yard of the trailer camp in between Joey and Silver, she might not have the courage to tell Joey how sure she was that she couldn't marry him; she might not have the courage to walk across that yard arm in arm with Silver as Joey stared after them, as Silver opened the door and Teresa got into the front seat. But when she left the trailer at midnight, careful to open the door not more than a crack so that the wind and the scent of the river wouldn't drift over to the bed and wake Joey, Teresa felt that Silver would find her anyway. She was not escaping from Silver that night, she only wanted to get out of the dark trailer, out under the moon, under the rain that had begun to fall harder and harder.

Teresa waited on the porch while Atlas struggled to fit through the door; once the dog was outside, and he saw the sheet of rain in front of him, he turned to go back inside, but Teresa closed the front door, walked down the porch steps, and signaled for the collie to follow her. And so he followed her across the yard of the camp, past the gate and then a mile down the River Road. And then, because Teresa thought she might have heard a car, she bolted like a deer, past a clearing and into the wood, and Atlas had no choice but to follow her when, beneath a starless sky, Teresa began to walk toward the river.

That night there was a storm that was one of the worst the county had ever seen; more drownings took place in a few hours than had been reported in more than five years. It was a night when fish gulped for air, and frogs drifted out to the open sea, and huge tree trunks floated downstream with the swiftness of Chinese sailboats. Wild strawberries were covered by four feet of water, jays perched on the very top branches of eucalyptus trees, spiders wove webs out of water and air. By morning the rowboats had once again been pulled out of sheds to search for missing persons and collect cats and dogs stranded on ridgetops. Road crews prepared for more flooding with heavy sandbags, the bridges and roads that were washed away were slowly repaired.

Silver had been forced off the highway by the storm; he had spent the night alone in a motel in San Rafael, and when he set out in the morning for Villa Lobo the sky was clear, the sun was as bright as it would be in the courtyard of a Mexican hotel where the walls were painted white, and waiters served wine and pineapple that had been cut into chunks and dipped in honey. Silver took his time driving; there was no need to risk speed traps and encounters with the state police, there was no need to hurry, he was certain that Teresa was waiting for him— she might already have packed her bags, might have said goodbye to a man she had never loved, might already be waiting at her front door.

When Silver reached the bridge that crossed over the river and led to Villa Lobo he was flagged down, and for a moment he nearly turned around, he almost floored the Camaro and roared off back to the highway. As soon as he saw the red flag he imagined that he had left fingerprints behind, in Gregory's apartment, in the folds of the black linen suit, or that Gregory had not really been quite dead when Silver had left him in the street, and had managed to cough out Silver's name and license plate number before he was taken to the morgue. But there weren't any patrol cars waiting for Silver, and the flagman was only part of the road crew repairing the bridge, and instead of turning around Silver pulled over, the last in a line of cars waiting to cross over to the other side. The river had risen so high that even there, on the high River Road, muddy water splashed around the Camaro's tires. Silver turned off the engine and he watched the river, and he couldn't help but smile when he thought about Teresa, when he imagined her sitting out on the front porch of the trailer, waiting and watching the road for a sign of his car.

But Teresa wasn't waiting on the porch, she was already more than fifteen miles west of Villa Lobo. She had walked most of the night, following the river until she was exhausted and soaking wet. She had kept to the higher ground and had managed to avoid the worst of the flooding, although she continued to slip as she walked, and her clothes were coated with mud. Before dawn, when it was still raining hard, Teresa stopped and huddled under her rain slicker with Atlas curled up by her feet. She fell asleep, but that night she didn't have any dreams, and the rain continued to fall so that Teresa was surrounded by a circle of water, and the floodline that was only a few yards away continued to rise. For the first time in months Teresa welcomed a sleeping spell rather than feared it; now that Silver was on his way she was sure he would find her. She had been sleeping for nearly ten hours when Joey finally decided to go to the sheriff's office and report her missing.

He filled out all the correct forms, and then he drove up and down the River Road and through Villa Lobo looking for clues, hoping that he might discover where it was she had gone in the middle of the night. After several hours spent searching without any success, Joey went to a roadhouse on the River Road and ordered a beer, and he began to wonder if she had planned to leave him all along, if she had bought her wedding dress just to placate him, if she had planned to disappear on a night when the air was cold and rain was certain to wash away her footprints; perhaps she had never really loved him at all. Joey spent all afternoon in the roadhouse, ordering one beer after another, and so when Silver arrived at the trailer camp it was deserted. Silver knocked on every trailer door, and then he sat up on the hood of the Camaro and he feared that he had stumbled onto a ghost town, or that Teresa had given him the wrong address by mistake. By the time Joey got back to the camp, Silver was pacing back and forth in the yard; as soon as Joey got out of his car Silver ran over to him, and then he stood much too close. If Joey hadn't been drunk he might have taken a swing at Silver, but instead he reached out, as if to shake hands.

Silver didn't bother to act polite. "I just want to know one thing," he said to Joey. "Where's my sister?"

The more beer Joey had had the more he chose to believe that Teresa hadn't really decided to leave him, she would have come back to him if she could. And if she didn't return to him it was because she had been trapped in the flood; Joey imagined that she had been caught in a thicket of brambles, unable to move as the water rose higher and higher, until she was submerged in a deep green pool where water lilies surrounded her and frogs perched on her shoulders before diving into the water.

"She's gone," Joey told Silver.

He knew right away that he was facing Teresa's brother, the one who didn't want them to marry; but that no longer mattered to Joey, there was no longer anything to argue about. Joey walked toward the trailer, stopped only when Silver put a hand on his shoulder.

"What do you mean gone?" Silver asked. "She was expecting me. She wouldn't have left."

From where he stood in the trailer camp, Joey couldn't tell if he could really hear the river rising or if he was only imagining the sound of a fast current. He breathed deeply; the river was everywhere, it filled up his chest.

"She took off last night," he told Silver, but even as he spoke Joey had the oddest sense that Teresa was with him, he could feel her presence in the air, in the earth beneath his feet.

"You're trying to put something over on me," Silver said. "I know she's here. You've got her hidden somewhere."

When Joey opened the trailer door, Silver rushed inside, but Teresa wasn't there—the trailer was empty. Silver stood and stared at the unmade bed, at the white dress hanging in the open closet, at the unwashed dishes in the sink. And in that dark trailer two men who didn't know each other stood less than five feet apart, and each was convinced that if he closed his eyes he would be able to see Teresa, would feel her palm on his forehead, her touch light as air, her heart his alone.

Teresa woke up after nearly twenty hours of sleep; it was late afternoon, dragonflies skimmed over the surface of the river, water lilies that had closed against the rain now opened, and their petals were white and pale green. There wasn't a cloud in the sky, and, aside from the dangerously high level of the river and the dampness of the earth, last night's storm might have never happened. The sky was so calm that the rain might have taken place only in someone's dreams. Teresa was miles away from Villa Lobo, and when she walked to the river to wash her hands and face it was so quiet that she couldn't even hear her own footsteps. When she bent down and put her hands in the muddy edge of the river, Teresa noticed that in the center, far beyond the banks, there was a pool the color of blue china, a pool that looked as deep as an ocean. It was so silent by the river that she couldn't hear anything more than the slow hum of the dragonflies' wings; at last she whistled for Atlas. The old dog appeared from the north, his coat thick with mud. Teresa patted the collie's head, then reached into her backpack for a tin of sardines and shared them with Atlas. After they had eaten, Teresa walked the few yards to the river and threw clear stones into the water just to hear a sound. Each time a stone fell the sound was like a bell, and each time fish jumped, biting at the movement, hoping for mosquitoes or bread.

When Teresa had left the trailer she hadn't given one thought to where she was going, and as long as there was daylight she could persuade herself that she wasn't lost; she imagined that she was at a wild picnic at which Silver would show up sooner or later. But as the hours passed, and the sun began to disappear, slowly swallowed up by the foothills to the west, Teresa grew panicky. There were shadows everywhere. There was too much sound now— tentative deer edged toward the water, the trees moved and seemed to have a life of their own. Teresa was afraid to stay where she was, but when she thought of leaving and trying to find her way back to the River Road she grew even more frightened. Her clothes might stick to brambles, flocks of wild birds might attack her and carry her off to the treetops holding strands of her hair in their beaks.

To calm herself, she thought of the ways Silver might find her. She wished that she had left a trail behind her: the stones of a necklace, shreds of material from her blouse, hard crusts of bread. And if he found her, Teresa wondered if she would go away to Mexico with him. In Mexico no one would know them: they could use different names and rent a house far up in the hills, they would never have to see any strangers, never have to speak to anyone but each other. Maybe then she could forget all those times Silver had turned away from her, maybe then she could forget that she had given up hope, that she was sure she would have to wait forever for him. She would no longer remember Angel Gregory; she would finally be able to stop thinking about the night when she had felt closer to him than to anyone else in the world, a night when their combined memory of Silver had seemed more real than Silver did himself.

As it grew darker still, as the moon rose in the sky, Teresa doubted that Silver would ever be able to find her here in the woods, even if he had a map and water in a canteen and a satchel full of fruit, even if he carried fistfuls of diamonds that shone bands of light in front of him like a thousand lanterns, he might miss her, he might walk right on by. But all of those years she had spent waiting for him now left her without the will to move. And so Teresa stayed right where she was. Atlas watched her, puzzled, not understanding why they stayed in a place where everything had the scent of the river, a place where the frogs were as loud as trumpets and the moon seemed much too far away, and animals and birds moved above them, climbing from one branch to another, so used to the silence that they didn't even notice that a woman sat alone, her knees pulled up, her skin still damp, as if permanently coated with raindrops. And later that night Atlas couldn't restrain himself any longer, he went off in search of the animals he heard moving through the woods. And as he followed raccoons and bats and the frogs who moved from log to log near the river, Teresa fell asleep. She slept in spite of herself, and in spite of herself she dreamed. In her dream she heard the grass beside her rustle, and when she turned to look, it was not Atlas who had returned, it was not an Aria who had found his way to her in the woods, it was only a small dark horse who stood beneath the nearest pine tree.

The horse was so close to her that its hoofs grazed the yellow rain slicker on which she rested her head. He was so close that Teresa could see his breath, she could see that his mane was red, the color of a heart or of certain roses. In her dream she pretended to be asleep, but she was watching as he passed by her, watching as orange birds of paradise were leveled beneath his hoofs. If she had reached out her hand then, she could have touched him, but instead she let the horse walk past her, toward the river.

There was a splashing sound and Teresa got up and went to the riverbank just in time to see the horse diving. He was graceful, an expert swimmer, the water rolled off his dark back and shone in the moonlight. Water weeds and flowers attached themselves to his mane as he grazed on the wild iris which grew along the farthest banks. Teresa could now see that, although the horse's mane was red, his coat was the same color as the river— Egyptian brown, juniper-bark brown, brown as sand along a foreign beach. Teresa could see the bits of purple iris caught between his teeth, the petals were the color of amethysts or of rain that falls at night. Finally he floated downstream, he floated west in silence, without a struggle, without even seeming to move. And before Teresa knew it, the horse was out of sight and the river didn't have one ripple, there wasn't one sign that he had ever been there, nothing but logs and tadpoles and smooth clear water.

Teresa might have gone on sleeping for hours if that splashing sound wasn't louder than ever, even though the horse had long disappeared downstream. When she opened her eyes she was instantly awake, instantly surrounded by the night and by the sound of something drowning nearby. Teresa got up and ran toward the river, following the sound; she ran right past the banks where the horse in her dream had slowly chewed on new irises. She could barely see; the water was past her ankles before she knew that she had reached the river. She stumbled over a half-submerged log and then was suddenly knee-deep; her hands were covered by invisible mosquitoes, her skin itself seemed to sing. Teresa heard Atlas before she saw him; it took a while for her eyes to adjust to the darkness and to being awake. In her dream the horse had seemed to carry its own strange light with it; now everything was black, and the air itself was thick as soup. So when Teresa dove into the water she was simply following a sound: the sound of a heartbeat in water, the whisper of lungs too tired to breathe. She swam away from the bank, and when she reached the center of the pool that was as deep and as blue as china she finally saw Atlas; he was drowning, he had gone down for the third time, his long hair rose to the surface in clumps that were thicker than rope. Atlas had followed the frogs along the slippery tree trunks submerged in the water, and after he fell the water seemed to draw him to the center, right into the middle of the deepest pool.

As she swam toward the dog, Teresa noticed that the water hitting against her skin was as loud as thunder. She grabbed Atlas and lifted his head above the water, she held him around his middle and steered through the pool with her elbows and her toes. After she had managed to swim out of the deep pool, she breathed easier, and when she reached the riverbank she pulled Atlas out behind her. She put her ear to his chest to listen for breathing and found there was none. She knelt down beside him and pushed on his back, and slowly water seeped out of the collie, but he still looked broken to Teresa, and much smaller than ever before. She pushed on his back for what seemed like forever, and then when she put her ear to his chest again she heard the thick unsteady intake of air, the promise of breath.

It was then Teresa began to shiver, then she felt the cold air reach through her water-soaked skin and turn her fingers and her toes blue. She stood, then bent down to pick up the dog. He was ten times as heavy as he had been in the center of the pool, but she heaved him so that he rested on her shoulder. She could smell the river on his fur and on her own skin. She could no longer see the moon, but there were thousands of stars and Mars was in the easternmost part of the sky. Teresa stood up with the dog balanced on her shoulders; the hiking boots cut into her ankles and Atlas was heavier than a sack of stones, heavier than saddlebags filled with gold. All the same, she managed to carry him as she walked in the opposite direction from the one planet she could see in the sky. She walked away from the river, in the direction of the foothills. She walked for what seemed like hours, through thorny wild blackberries that blocked their way. And when the sky began to grow lighter, when it was nearly dawn, Teresa walked out of the woods.

Above her, in the foothills, she saw the shadows of a farmhouse; she started up the dirt path which led to the house, she climbed slowly, exhausted by the weight of the dog and her own soaking clothing. What began as a rocky stretch soon became a field of artichokes; large purple flowers had been left to wither and go to seed, the earth had been smoothed by the hoofs of cattle and sheep. She tightened her grip on Atlas; burs dug into her fingertips, the hiking boots now left a ring of blood around her ankles. Above her, clouds moved faster and faster all the time; above her, seagulls cried. Teresa continued to follow the rutted path right to the door of the farmhouse; from the ridgetop where the house had been built she could now see the mouth of the river far below. Black rocks formed the gate that opened to the Pacific, and as Teresa watched, the river rushed forward, turning to salt water in the blink of an eye, in those very last hours of starlight, just beneath a ridgetop at the farthest edge of the west.

Teresa slept in a brass bed, covered by a quilt that had been handed down through three generations. She slept for only a few hours, waking before noon. For the first time in years she didn't think of Silver in those first moments of being awake, instead she felt the cold thrill of having come to this place alone, and she thought of long evenings, cities she had never been to, the possibility of falling in love rather than being fated to it. When she went downstairs, barefoot and wearing borrowed blue jeans and a sweater, her eyes touched upon everything in the house, as if she had just arrived in a foreign land. In the kitchen, next to the gas stove, Catherine, the woman who owned the house, was boiling brown eggs over a low blue flame. Atlas slept on a flannel blanket that cushioned the hard pine floor. Teresa crouched down next to the dog, the mane of hair around his neck still damp.

"That dog's going to be fine," Catherine promised. She turned off the flame under the pot of eggs. "All the water's out of him, and now he just needs to rest."

"He looks so tired," Teresa said.

"I've got something he won't be able to resist," Catherine said. She went to the refrigerator, got a bottle of milk, and poured some into a frying pan. Then she put the pan down on the floor, right in front of the collie's nose; Atlas lifted his head, and when he began to drink, the two women smiled at each other in triumph. Later, when Catherine's husband Dan came home with their ten-year-old son Mark, they all rigged up a box so that they could take Atlas outside to lie in the sun.

"You're lucky you both didn't drown," Dan told Teresa. "We went down to the river this morning and it's risen more than fifteen feet. The beach down by Goat's Rock is nearly washed away."

And even then Teresa didn't feel that she had done anything impossible by escaping the flood and carrying the collie for so many miles. What seemed impossible now was waiting all those years for Silver, waiting all that time for a night when the moon was orange and full, so close to the ground that it brushed against the highest branches of the eucalyptus trees. What seemed impossible was never feeling the strange sort of daring she now felt. And later, when it was nearly time for Teresa to leave, and Catherine pointed out that her long hair was thick with brambles and that knots the size of sparrows were woven through the strands, Teresa reached into a kitchen drawer and pulled out a pair of scissors.

"Let's cut it," Teresa suggested.

Catherine touched her own hair. "Oh, no," she said. "You don't want to do that."

At night, when she was a child, when she spent hours listening to crickets, Teresa would often lean so far out her window that her braids would reach halfway down the wall of the house. Now she insisted that Catherine cut her hair; there seemed no point in brushing out the tangles. They compromised, and when Catherine was through, Teresa's hair was still long, it nearly reached her shoulders, but it was lighter, it circled her face, the strands surprising her by curling around her forehead. And when Teresa telephoned Bergen, calling collect from the phone in the living room, her haircut was the first thing she told him about.

"Wait till you see it," Teresa said. "I look brand-new."

"I'm not as interested in haircuts as I am in Silver," Bergen told Teresa. "He left here four days ago and he said he was driving straight to Villa Lobo to see you."

"I'm not there," Teresa admitted. "I ran away. I'm not getting married."

"No?" Bergen said. His throat felt dry; he looked over at Dina's blue and white dishes. "Are you not getting married because of Silver?" he forced himself to ask.

"No," Teresa said truthfully.

"You can be honest with me," the detective said. "I know everything. I heard him talking to you on the phone. He sounded just like he was your lover."

Alone in Dan and Catherine's living room, Teresa wished she could erase every word the detective had heard; she thought of his apartment on Dolores Street— the window where the canary's cage had been, the room full of Dina's possessions, so carefully packed.

"You don't really know anything," Teresa said, wishing that she could lie to him and passionately cry that none of what he imagined was true.

"I can guess," Bergen said. "I can guess well enough to be pretty damn certain. For Christ's sake, Teresa, I'm not judging you—I'm not even talking about what people will think, what's legal or illegal—I don't care about any of that. It's the fact that it's Silver, that you keep on thinking that he's something he's not. Teresa, you don't know him."

"Maybe I don't now," Teresa said. "But I used to," she whispered.

In the detective's apartment in San Francisco there was a photograph of Dina and all three of her children taken years before by King Connors with a borrowed camera. It had been taken on a day when the sky was so bright that Teresa blinked as King clicked down on the shutter, a day when Teresa was not more than eight years old and anything seemed possible: men on white horses could ride blindfolded across the desert, drawn by the heartbeat of the woman they loved; sand had a voice of its own, and could sing; no one ever changed, or got old, or disappeared without any warning.

"You used to," Bergen agreed.

Outside Catherine and Dan's house, Atlas rested in a brown cardboard box lined with flannel; through the living-room window Teresa could see him stretch out in the sun—slowly his bones were turning warm once more, a ten-year-old boy carefully removed the burs from around his neck.

"He used to have darker eyes than anybody else," Teresa told Bergen. "He used to wear white shirts that were ironed perfectly, and he never wore the same shirt more than once—it was always clean. I knew him better than anyone; I could tell if he walked up behind me just by the sound of his footsteps."

"An Aria," Bergen said, and he knew that sixty miles away Teresa was nodding her head yes.

There were times when Teresa would stretch out on the grass next to Atlas and the old dog Reggie; she would lie down somewhere just beyond the sunflowers and stare up into Silver's bedroom window. She could hear King trying to start his old pickup in the driveway, and the screen door slam as Reuben left the house to walk down to the Safeway. Sometimes she would wait for hours, out there in the backyard while Silver continued to sleep. Sometimes Dina would come out and sit next to her, and then both of them would stare up into Silver's window, as silent as two lovesick girls.

"I'm worried about you," Bergen said now. "I shouldn't be—we're not really related. But I still worry about you."

In only a few hours it would be dinnertime in the house where Teresa had spent the night. Catherine would give her son a ceramic bowl full of carrots to cut up in slices, the table would be set with earthenware plates. If Teresa decided to let Atlas stay here he would sleep only a few feet away from the table, his nose buried in flannel, not moving until Catherine scraped the leftovers into his plate.

"I'm glad that you came to our house that day," Teresa told Bergen.

"Are you sure you're not sorry it wasn't King who came back instead?" Bergen asked her.

"Only sometimes," Teresa admitted. "Most of the time I'm glad it was you. Do you want to know a secret?" she asked suddenly. In a little while she would clean off her muddy hiking boots with a damp cloth and walk over to Dan's station wagon so that he could give her a ride back to Villa Lobo. The air would be salty, and below the ridgetop the ocean would look as clear as glass, pelicans would be perched on the huge black rocks, Atlas would be dozing a few feet away from the field of artichokes. "It was cinnamon," Teresa whispered, wanting to give honesty to Bergen, the way someone else might have given him a gift of fragile pottery. "That's what my mother put in her coffee."

"That can't be," Bergen said.

"That's all it was," Teresa said. "I know you always thought it was something more." She wondered if perhaps she had given the detective the wrong gift. "Are you sorry I told you?"

"Cinnamon," Bergen said, and beneath his tongue the word was like a spice, and he felt his disappointment melting. "No," he told Teresa. "It's always much better to know the truth."

In the three days that Teresa had been gone, Joey started to leave the trailer early in the morning, and he took a fishing pole with him, but if anyone had asked him what fish he expected to catch, he couldn't have answered. He didn't give a damn about catching fish, and often he left the fishing pole behind once he reached the river, forgotten in the tall grass. Long before dawn Joey would crouch by the riverbank, and he stared down, just as if he were looking for the signs of trout, but in fact he was searching for very different signs of life.

Unlike Silver, Joey didn't believe that Teresa would return to the trailer camp, yet he had managed to find her. When he sat by the river he truly expected Teresa to rise from the depths, a string of orchids woven through her fingers and her toes. Joey began to recognize the calls of certain birds, though he didn't know their names any more than he knew what sort of fish swam toward the sea. He no longer checked the local papers for the names of those who had drowned in the storm, he no longer telephoned the sheriff's office for the latest reports. He forgot all the arguments he and Teresa had had, he forgot his suspicions that Teresa had promised to marry him simply because she didn't know what else to do. He felt closer to her than ever before, and much more in love than ever. He believed that if he sat at the riverbank long enough she would appear, she would float toward him, her skin would be perfect, pale and cool. And when she rose up from the bottom of the river he would be right there, ready to hold her in his arms.

Silver had spent three nights sleeping on the bare floor of a deserted trailer; his back ached, and because Joey was gone so much of the time Silver no longer feared that when Teresa came back she would run into Joey first. He decided to drive to Santa Rosa, check into the Lamplighter, and get a good night's sleep. But once he had decided to get out of the trailer camp, Silver found that he couldn't leave. The wheels of the Camaro were stuck in the mud. Silver started the engine and floored the gas, but the car only dove deeper and deeper into the mud.

He went to Joey's unlocked trailer then, having decided that anything he found inside he would consider his. He shaved with Joey's razor and a new razor blade, he drank a quart of orange juice, ate some crackers he found stored in a cabinet, then took a nap in the unmade bed. When he woke up his back no longer ached, and he searched through all the drawers in the trailer, just to see what he would find, but nothing interested him until he opened the closet and found some of Teresa's clothes. He packed all of them in a brown paper bag, he took them out to the Camaro and threw the bag into the back seat. And then, because there was no one to help him and no one to hire, he went around to the toolshed behind Joey's trailer and got a shovel and he slowly began to dig the Camaro out of the mud.

He took off the one white shirt he had with him, but he still couldn't avoid getting mud all over his jeans and his polished leather boots. And that was the way he was when Teresa first saw him—out in the center of the trailer camp, straining to lift up huge shovelfuls of heavy earth. Dan had dropped her off a quarter of a mile down the River Road, and because Silver didn't hear a car pull up, Teresa had the chance to watch him from where she stood by the metal gate. He had dug out the rear tires and was working on the front; his hair was darker than a crow's feathers, his arms were knotted with muscles, he could have been anyone, any man laboring beneath the sun of a rare March day when the sky was as clear as a diamond.

Silver had gotten a rhythm to his work; the mud flew away from his car as if it had sprouted wings. When he happened to look up for a moment and saw a woman standing at the gate his rhythm was instantly thrown off; he dropped the shovel and stared. He had expected her to come back late in the evening, after he had taken a shower and ironed his shirt with the iron he had found beneath the sink in Joey's trailer. He had imagined that she would wear a white dress, the sapphire he had once given her would be fastened around her throat; and now, when she walked across the yard to him in the blinding sunlight of the last days of winter, dressed in faded jeans and a borrowed sweater that was a size too large, Silver shaded his eyes and for a moment he didn't feel half as sure of the future as he had felt only seconds before. But he recovered quickly and by the time she walked over to him he was leaning against the Camaro, grinning.

"Have you commandeered Joey's trailer?" Teresa asked him.

"Your boyfriend seems to have flown the coop," Silver said. "Lucky for you I'm here."

He noticed the change in Teresa and he reached over and took a handful of her hair in his fist.

"What did you do?" he asked.

"I like it this way." Teresa shrugged.

Silver shook his head with mock solemnity. "Whenever you're away from me you make these sorts of mistakes." He dropped his hand to her cheek and stroked her skin. "You'd better make certain that you're with me all the time."

Teresa moved his hand away.

"You're not going to be shy with me, are you?" Silver teased.

Teresa stared at the white scar on Silver's face. A long time ago, when a summer lasted forever and the sky was the color of hyacinths, Teresa could have traced Silver's face in the sand blindfolded—she knew him that well. She knew that his breathing came through the bedroom wall, past the plaster and the wallpaper, straight into her heart. She knew that the veins in his arms turned to indigo when he reached up to close a window in the living room, that he always whistled under his breath when he ran down the stairs to the front door. Now, nothing but the brand-new scar seemed familiar; it was the unmistakable mark of sorrow surfacing through his skin.

Teresa turned away and then walked to the trailer, stepping carefully around the pools of mud.

"Wait a minute," Silver called after her. And when she didn't slow down, he ran after her. She was already inside the trailer, staring at the open closet, when Silver caught up with her. There were empty hangers all in a row.

"I took the opportunity to pack your clothes," Silver told her.

Teresa took a pad and a pen and wrote Joey a brief note of apology, in which she promised to repay all the money she owed him, including the seventy dollars he had spent for the wedding dress and the fifty dollars she was about to take from the jam jar of savings he kept beneath the bed.

"So that's where he keeps it." Silver smiled when Teresa knelt down and took out Joey's savings.

"Where did you put my clothes?" Teresa asked now.

"In the back of the Camaro," Silver told her. "All ready to go."

Teresa walked out, toward the car, and before he followed her Silver pocketed the rest of Joey's savings, and then he tore Teresa's note in quarters and dropped the scraps of paper in the kitchen wastebasket. Out in the yard, Teresa was taking the bag of clothes out of the Camaro.

"We've got to get out of here," Silver told her. "You can go through those clothes later, after we're on our way."

Teresa's throat was dry, drier than it would have been had the temperature been over a hundred degrees. "I'm not going," she said.

"Who do you think you're talking to?" Silver smiled. "This is me. Silver. I know what you're going to do." He lowered his voice. "I know exactly what you want."

"It's what I used to want," Teresa admitted.

"What the hell are you saying?" Silver said. "Are you telling me you haven't been waiting for me all this time?"

Teresa couldn't help but wonder if Gregory had left that scar on Silver's face; if he had wanted to cut through the skin so that he could once more face that boy who had first sent him to Vacaville Prison.

"Let me tell you about where we're going," Silver told her now. "It's so warm there you can go swimming every day, even in winter. They've got parrots down there—I'll bet you didn't know that. And I'll bet you didn't know that the moon's twice as big in Mexico, it's so bright no one needs electric lights."

In that sort of moonlight it would probably be impossible to see anything but that white scar, every other feature would be unrecognizable. If it had been that boy from so many years ago who now stood across from her in the trailer camp, Teresa would have run to him, she would have followed him to Mexico in the middle of the night. But it wasn't that boy who now promised her a place where there were wild parrots streaked with red, a place where no one knew their names.

"We're meant to be together," Silver told her. "It's as simple as that."

"I can't go with you," Teresa said finally. "You're not the one I love."

Silver's face grew hot. "Of course you do." He went to her and held her around the waist. "I know you do."

He held her as if for the last time; he breathed in the scent of roses on her skin. "Please," he said. "I know you love me."

When he let her go, she picked up the bag of her clothes, and even then Silver couldn't believe that they weren't going to Mexico together, he couldn't believe that there wasn't a hotel room waiting for them, the sheets on the bed already turned down, or that Teresa now walked toward the gate of the trailer camp beneath a sky that was slowly turning a deep purple color. He was still certain that if he dug the Camaro out of the mud and came after her she wouldn't have any choice but to ride next to him in the front seat. She would be so close to him that he would be able to feel the heat rise from her skin, all he would have to do would be to reach out his hand and she would be right there. Silver grabbed the shovel, he dug furiously, and before long he was covered with mud and he didn't even notice that Teresa had begun to walk east on the River Road, without once looking back.

In time the secretary at the sheriff's office finally took Teresa's name off the missing-persons list, and then neatly retyped it at the bottom of a long column of those who were permanently missing and presumed drowned. In time Joey was able to reach into the shallow waters on the river and have fish swim right into the center of his palm, and Harper began to notice that the sapphire Teresa had given her no longer changed from blue to green, but now remained the pure jade color of a cricket's wing. In time winter was nearly forgotten, and the temperature rose higher than ever before, and the flooding of the season that had passed left behind only occasional pools in the river, and a slow trickle of water that moved west, and nothing but a few hawk's feathers that had dropped from the sky collected in the shallows.

But on that night when Teresa left Villa Lobo the
asphalt shimmered like ice, the sky was black and starry
and cold. She had already walked several miles when
Silver's Camaro passed her, taking the curve in the River
Road so quickly that Teresa barely had time to move
out of its path. And when the shimmer of metal and
chrome had disappeared, Teresa knew that because Silver
had never bothered with strangers he had not stopped;
he simply didn't recognize her on a dark road where
lines of sandbags held back the tide. Teresa had seen
his reflection in the Camaro's rearview mirror before the
headlights disappeared; and even if he returned, back-
tracking, still searching for her along the road, Teresa
was certain that it was now too dark for him to find her,
and much too late.

When the moon had risen, Teresa hitched a ride into
town with a man who had been working overtime on
the road crew. She slept for a few restless hours in the
back of his pickup, parked on an unfamiliar street on the
outskirts of Santa Rosa in the driveway of one of the new
tract houses. Early the next morning, when the man from
the road crew was still in bed, his arms around his wife,
Teresa walked to Webster Street. At the counter of Max's
Café she ordered coffee, and she drank as leisurely as if
she were at her own table. She used some of the money
she had borrowed from Joey to buy breakfast, and then
she walked across the street to the five-and-ten-cent store
where Dina had always bought the scarfs she insisted they
wear when they worked out in the garden planting rows of
tomatoes.

Teresa walked up and down the aisles of the dime store
until at last she found a table piled high with shoes at
the rear of the store. She looked through the high heels, the
leather shoes with laces and straps, the sneakers and the
running shoes, and finally, on a rack just behind the table
of shoes, Teresa found a wall full of moccasins made of
strong leather. She reached for a pair that had beads sewn

into the pattern of a star, then leaned against the table and
unlaced her hiking boots. When she slipped them on, she
knew that the moccasins were exactly what she had been
looking for, and she left the boots where they stood, in a
quiet aisle at the rear of the store.

When Teresa walked up to pay the cashier, she couldn't
hear her own footsteps, and out on the street the cement
felt cool through the leather soles. She walked down
Webster Street, carrying her bag of clothes, and she was
as quiet as a spy when she turned the corner at Divisadero
Street. It was still the time of year when the fog from the
river traveled through town each morning and every night,
when a mist wrapped itself around every lamppost like a
school of silvery fish. When Teresa got to the house she
saw that it had been repainted, a pale yellow trimmed
with dark green. Someone was living there now; a radio
had been turned on in the kitchen where Dina's blue and
white dishes had once lined the cabinets, a light was on in
the living room where King Connors had stretched his legs
out to rest them on a leather ottoman. There was a Ford
Mustang in the driveway, and in the backyard laundry was
still hung out from the day before; fog circled around the
sheets and the pillowcases, it ran along the clothesline as
if a second rope had also been drawn across the yard, a
twine made up of water and air and sleep, the sort of rope
found only in recurring dreams.

Teresa had stood in this exact same place in front of
the house on Divisadero Street hundreds of times. She had
felt the concrete beneath her bare feet, she had worked in
the yard where the new owners had planted lettuce and
yellow summer squash. It was still early, and no one in
the house noticed that Teresa was standing outside, but
it was clear they were now waking up; slowly the lights
were switched on in every room. The wind was moving
off the river, it reached out for miles and brought with it
the promise of cool water. And if Teresa half closed her
eyes she could see through the windows into the rooms

beyond the glass. She could see Dina walking along the upstairs hallway, carrying a pad of violet notepaper with her so that she could go into her bedroom and write a long letter to Bergen. She could see King Connors and Reuben, each of them dreaming about southern California, a place where there were lemon trees and the past was no farther away than the day before. And then she saw Silver. Not the man who had passed her only a few hours before on the River Road, but the boy he used to be. He was at the window, up on the second floor, trapped behind the glass.

And for a moment the air was thick with all of those nights Teresa had waited, nights when she believed that she and Silver were tied together with string, forced to ride on the back of a white horse forever, fated to wander through the desert at midnight, searching for oranges and water and a few pale hours of peace. He was still up there; there on the second floor he was forever the same, just as Teresa had always imagined him, caught in a house that now belonged to someone else, trapped behind a pane of glass that always trembled at this time of year when the wind rose off the river, and the nights were filled with a thousand stars, and the wisteria Dina had planted outside the door so long ago had just begun to bloom.

On that morning, when the sky was the color of pearls and the scent of the river traveled from one house to another all over town, Teresa listened carefully for the sound of crickets, but the only sound she heard was the one made by the boy running his fingernails along the pane of glass. Teresa stared upward, and she let them go, one by one— Dina and Reuben and King Connors, and finally, Silver. They slowly unraveled right before her eyes, until no one was left. Up in those rooms where they had slept for so long, nothing moved behind the glass; the windows were open, but it was only the thin curtains that waved back and forth, and by the time Teresa had turned away from the house, all of the windows were dark.

NEW YORK TIMES BESTSELLING AUTHOR

Alice Hoffman

"Alice Hoffman takes seemingly ordinary lives and lets us see and feel extraordinary things. . .wise and magical."–AMY TAN

__TURTLE MOON   0-425-13699-X/$5.99

Welcome to Verity, Florida. Where Lucy Rosen has moved to get away from her ex. Where Officer Julian Cash watches over the town with a fierce German shepherd. Where Lucy's son Keith can't wait to get away. And he does, when a woman is murdered and her baby is left behind. Keith takes off with the baby hoping to protect it. And *Turtle Moon* takes off on a funny, touching, and exhilarating journey...

__PROPERTY OF   0-425-13903-4/$5.99

They are the girls she envies, tough and sultry in mascara and black leather. And they're the property of the Orphans, the gang on the Avenue led by McKay. No one knows how much she wants to catch the eye of McKay, a brooding loner on the lookout for honor, not love. How far she goes to be with him shocks everyone, including herself.

__ANGEL LANDING   0-425-13952-2/$5.99

Natalie, a talented therapist, is great at helping others solve their problems. When it comes to her own life, though, it's a different story. Then new client Michael Finn walks into her life with an incredible story to tell–and in the process teaches Natalie what love is all about...

__AT RISK   0-425-11738-3/$5.99

A small town. An ordinary American home. The abiding power of love. All come into play in this novel of a family challenged by a tragedy–until a charming, courageous girl shows them how to embrace life...on any term. When it comes to love, we are all AT RISK.

For Visa, MasterCard and American Express ($15 minimum) orders call: 1-800-631-8571

FOR MAIL ORDERS: CHECK BOOK(S). FILL OUT COUPON. SEND TO:

BERKLEY PUBLISHING GROUP
390 Murray Hill Pkwy., Dept. B
East Rutherford, NJ 07073

NAME————————————————

ADDRESS—————————————

CITY————————————————

STATE——————— ZIP————

PLEASE ALLOW 6 WEEKS FOR DELIVERY.
PRICES ARE SUBJECT TO CHANGE WITHOUT NOTICE.

POSTAGE AND HANDLING:
$1.75 for one book, 75¢ for each additional. Do not exceed $5.50.

BOOK TOTAL	$ ____
POSTAGE & HANDLING	$ ____
APPLICABLE SALES TAX (CA, NJ, NY, PA)	$ ____
TOTAL AMOUNT DUE	$ ____

PAYABLE IN US FUNDS.
(No cash orders accepted.)

446